PRAISE FROM THE UK FOR
Sweet Sorrow

"A bravura performance from someone with a track record in fashioning books that are both eminently readable and emotionally subtle. *Sweet Sorrow* manages to be interesting, moving, hilarious, and sad at the same time." —*Scotland on Sunday*

"If ever there was an author perfect to take with you on holiday (so to speak), it's David Nicholls. Make space in your case." —*Telegraph*

"Nicholls avoids sentimentality or mawkishness to capture perfectly the angst, the pain and the awkwardness of falling in love for the first time." —*The Bookseller*

"Adrian Mole meets *The Swish of the Curtain* in this lovely coming-of-age romcom about acting and the class divide." —*Daily Mail*

"[Nicholls] remains one of the most acute chroniclers of England as it is now . . . and few can rival his grasp of the period's minor-key class signifiers . . . And of course the novel skips along merrily; the repartee frequently sparkles, the jokes are genuinely funny, walk-on characters are brilliantly sketched into life, and his genuine affection for the main players is evident throughout." —*Financial Times*

"Poignant and insightful." —*Belfast Telegraph*

"A beautiful paean to young love . . . *Sweet Sorrow* is a book that does what Nicholls does best, sinking the reader deep into a nostalgic memory-scape, pinning the narrative to a love story that manages to be moving without ever tipping over into sentimentality, all of it composed with deftness, intelligence and, most importantly, humour. We may think of Nicholls as a writer of heartbreakers—*One Day* prompted many poolside tears—but he has always been a comic novelist, and *Sweet Sorrow* is full of passages of laugh-out-loud *Inbetweeners*-ish humour . . . Here he proves that he can still pull off that most rare and coveted of literary feats: a popular novel of serious merit, a bestseller that will also endure."
—*Guardian*

"The author of *Us* and of course *One Day* has never written with more tenderness and insight than in this bittersweet story . . . [that] perfectly captures the dizzying highs and lows of first love."
—*Daily Express*

"Full of the joy and pain of first love, fans who fell for bestseller *One Day* ten years ago won't be disappointed."
—*Sunday Mirror*

Sweet Sorrow

Sweet Sorrow

DAVID NICHOLLS

MARINER BOOKS

HOUGHTON MIFFLIN HARCOURT

Boston   New York

2020

To Hannah, Max and Romy

For information about permission to reproduce selections from this book,
write to trade.permissions@hmhco.com or to Permissions,
Houghton Mifflin Harcourt Publishing Company,
3 Park Avenue, 19th Floor, New York, New York 10016.

hmhbooks.com

Library of Congress Cataloging-in-Publication Data
Names: Nicholls, David, 1966– author.
Title: Sweet sorrow / David Nicholls.
Description: Boston : Mariner Books/Houghton Mifflin Harcourt, 2020.
Identifiers: LCCN 2019039883 (print) | LCCN 2019039884 (ebook) | ISBN 9780358248361
(trade paperback) | ISBN 9780358274278 (hardcover) | ISBN 9780358248316 (ebook) |
ISBN 9780358311812 | ISBN 9780358308966
Subjects: GSAFD: Bildungsromans. | Humorous fiction.
Classification: LCC PR6114.I27 S94 2020 (print) | LCC PR6114.I27 (ebook) |
DDC 823/.92—dc23
LC record available at https://lccn.loc.gov/2019039883
LC ebook record available at https://lccn.loc.gov/2019039884

Printed in the United States of America
DOC 10 9 8 7 6 5 4 3 2 1

What we, or at any rate what I, refer to confidently as memory—meaning a moment, a scene, a fact that has been subject to a fixative and thereby rescued from oblivion—is really a form of storytelling that goes on continually in the mind and often changes with the telling. Too many conflicting emotional interests are involved for life ever to be wholly acceptable, and possibly it is the work of the storyteller to rearrange things so that they conform to this end. In any case, in talking about the past we lie with every breath we draw.

—William Maxwell, *So Long, See You Tomorrow*

PART ONE

June

This was the summer when for a long time she had not been a member. She belonged to no club and was a member of nothing in the world. Frankie had become an unjoined person who hung around in doorways, and she was afraid.

—Carson McCullers, *The Member of the Wedding*

The End of the World

THE WORLD WOULD END at five to four, just after the disco.

Our final day at Merton Grange Secondary School had arrived, brilliant and bright and commencing with skirmishes at the gates; school ties worn as bandanas and tourniquets, in knots as compact as a walnut or fat as a fist, with enough lipstick and jewelry and dyed blue hair to resemble some futuristic nightclub scene. What were the teachers going to do on our last day, send us home? They sighed and waved us through. The last week of formal lessons had been spent in desultory, dispiriting classes about something called "adult life," which would, it seemed, consist largely of filling in forms and compiling a CV ("Hobbies and Interests: Socializing, watching television"). We learned how to balance a checkbook. We stared out of the window at the lovely day and thought, *not long now. Four, three, two . . .*

Back in our form room at break we began to graffiti our white school shirts with felt-tips and Magic Markers, kids hunched over each other's backs like tattooists in a Russian jail, marking all available space with sentimental abuse. *Take care of yourself, you dick,* wrote Paul Fox. *This shirt stinks,* wrote Chris Lloyd. In a lyrical mood, my best friend Martin Harper wrote *mates4ever* beneath a finely detailed cock and balls.

Harper and Fox and Lloyd. These were my best friends at the time, not just boys but *the* boys—the group was self-sufficient and impenetrable. Though none of us played an instrument, we'd imagined ourselves as a band. Harper, we all knew, was lead guitar and vocals. Fox was bass, a low and basic *thump-thump-thump*. Lloyd, because he proclaimed himself "mad," was the drummer, which left me as . . .

"Maracas," Lloyd had said, and we'd laughed, and "maracas" was added to the long list of nicknames. Fox drew them on my school shirt now, maracas crossed beneath a skull, like military insignia. Mr. Ambrose, feet up on the desk, kept his eyes fixed on the video of *Free Willy 2* that played in the background, a special treat ignored by everyone.

In our final assembly, Mr. Pascoe made the speech that we'd all expected, encouraging us to look to the future but remember the past, to aim high but weather the lows, to believe in ourselves but think of others. The important thing was not only what we'd learned — and he hoped we'd learned a great deal! — but also the kind of young adults we'd become, and we listened, young adults, stuck between cynicism and sentimentality, boisterous on the surface but secretly daunted and sad. We sneered and rolled our eyes but elsewhere in the hall hands gripped other hands and snuffles were heard as we were urged to cherish the friendships we'd made, the friendships that would last a lifetime.

"A lifetime? Christ, I hope not," said Fox, locking my head beneath his arm, fondly rubbing his knuckles there. It was prize-giving time, and we sank low in our chairs. Prizes were awarded to the kids who always got the prizes, applause fading long before they'd left the stage to stand in front of the photographer from the local press, book tokens held beneath the chin as if in an ID parade. We sank lower in our chairs until horizontal, then, when it was over, we shuffled out to have our photo taken.

But I realize how absent I am from the above. I remember the day well enough even across twenty years, but when I try to describe my role,

I find myself reaching for what I saw and heard, rather than anything I said or did. "What were you like?" my future wife would later ask, "before we met?" and I'd struggle to reply. As a student, my distinctive feature was a lack of distinction. "Charlie works hard to meet basic standards and for the most part achieves them"; this was as good as it got, and even that slight reputation had been dimmed by events of the exam season. Not admired but not despised, not adored but not feared; I was not a bully, though I knew a fair few, but did not intervene or place myself between the pack and the victim, because I wasn't brave either. I neither conformed nor rebelled, collaborated nor resisted; I stayed out of trouble without getting into anything else. Comedy was our great currency, and while I was not a class clown, neither was I witless. I might occasionally get a surprised laugh from the crowd, but my best jokes were either drowned out by someone with a louder voice or came far too late, so that even now, more than twenty years later, I think of things I should have said in '96 or '97. I knew that I was not ugly—someone would have told me—and was vaguely aware of whispers and giggles from huddles of girls, but what use was this to someone with no idea what to say? I'd inherited height, and only height, from my father, my eyes, nose, teeth and mouth from Mum—the right way round, said Dad—but I'd also inherited his tendency to stoop and round my shoulders in order to take up less space in the world. Some lucky quirk of glands and hormones meant that I'd been spared the pulsing spots and boils that literally scarred so many adolescences, and I was neither skinny with anxiety nor plump with the chips and canned drinks that fueled us, but I wasn't confident about my appearance. I wasn't confident about anything at all.

Soon it would be time for my friends and me to settle into some role we might plausibly fit, but when I tried to see myself as others saw me (sometimes literally, late at night, staring profoundly into my father's shaving mirror, hair slicked back), I saw . . . nothing special.

In photos of myself from that time, I'm reminded of those early incar-
nations of a cartoon character, the prototypes that resemble the later
version but are in some way out of proportion, not quite right.

None of which is much help. Imagine, then, another photograph,
the school group shot that everybody owns, faces too small to make
out without peering closely. Whether it's five or fifty years old, there's
always a vaguely familiar figure in the middle row, someone with no
anecdotes or associations, no scandals or triumphs, to their name.
You wonder: who *was* that?

That's Charlie Lewis.

Sawdust

THE END-OF-YEAR DISCO HAD a reputation for Roman levels of depravity, second only to the Biology field trip. Our arena was the sports hall, a space large enough to comfortably contain a passenger jet. To create an illusion of intimacy, ancient bunting had been strung between the wall bars and a mirror-ball dangled from a chain like a medieval flail, but still the space seemed exposed and barren, and for the first three songs we lined up on benches, eyeing each other across the scuffed, dusty parquet like warriors across the field of battle, passing and sipping smuggled bottles of alcohol miniatures in the chocolate box flavors that we preferred, coffee and orange, coconut and mint. Perhaps they'd give us courage. Mr. Hepburn, Geography, on the wheels of steel, veered desperately from "I Will Survive" to "Baggy Trousers" and even "Relax" until Mr. Pascoe told him to fade it out. An hour and fifteen minutes to go.

But now came Blur's "Girls & Boys," and as if some signal had been given, there was a great surge onto the dance floor, everyone dancing wildly, then staying on to bellow along to the pop-house anthems that followed. Mr. Hepburn had hired a strobe light and now he jammed his thumb down with a total disregard for health and safety. The dancing became frenzied, more aggressive, and when "Jump Around" played a new crazy started, the boys climbing on backs and crashing full speed into each other, jousting. Even above the music you could hear the slap of spines against the parquet. Seeking some escape, I climbed the monkey bars that lined one wall of the gymnasium, folding myself in between the rungs. By now a real fight had broken out. I glimpsed keys bunched in someone's hand, and in the spirit of public order Mr. Hepburn played the Spice Girls, a kind of musical water cannon for the boys, who scattered to the edges, the girls taking their place, skipping and wagging their fingers at each other. Miss Butcher, too, replaced Mr. Hepburn on the decks. I saw him raise his hand to me and dart across the dance floor, looking left and right as if crossing a busy road.

"What d'you think, Charlie?"

"You missed your vocation, sir."

"Clubbing's loss was geography's gain," he said, folding himself into the bars beside me. "You can call me Adam now. We're both civilians, or will be in, what, thirty minutes? In thirty minutes you can call me anything you like!"

I liked Mr. Hepburn and admired his perseverance in the face of vocal indifference. *No offense, sir, but what's the point of this?* Of all the teachers who'd aspired to it, he'd best pulled off the trick of seeming decent without being ingratiating, dropping tantalizing hints of "big weekends" and staff room intrigue, displaying just enough small signs of rebellion—loose tie, stubble, shaggy hair—to suggest comradeship. Occasionally he'd even swear, the bad language like sweets thrown into a crowd.

Still, there was no world in which I'd call him Adam.

"So—are you excited about college?"

I recognized the beginning of a pep talk. "Don't think I'll be going, sir."

"You don't know that. You've applied, haven't you?"

I nodded. "Art, Computer Science, Graphic Design."

"Lovely."

"But I didn't get the grades."

"Well, you don't know that yet."

"I'm pretty sure, sir. I didn't turn up half the time."

He tapped me on the knee with his fist once, then thought better of it. "Well, even if you haven't, there are things you can do. Retake, do something less conventional. Boy like you, boy with talents . . ." I still treasured the praise he'd lavished on my volcano project: the last word, the ultimate in volcano cross-sections, as if I'd uncovered some fundamental truth that had evaded volcanologists for centuries. But this was a small hook from which to hang the word "talent."

"Nah, I'm going to get a full-time job, sir. I've given myself till September, then—"

"I still remember those volcanoes. The crosshatching was superb."

"Long time since those volcanoes." I shrugged and, unexpectedly, mortifyingly, realized that some switch had been flicked and that I might cry. I wondered, should I scamper further up the monkey bars?

"But maybe you can do something with it."

"With volcanoes?"

"The drawing, the graphic design. If you wanted to talk to me about it, once the results are through . . ."

Or perhaps not climb the monkey bars, perhaps just push him off. It wasn't far to fall.

"Really, I'll be fine."

"All right, Chaz, all right, but let me tell you a secret—" He swung in, and I could smell lager on his breath. "Here it is. It doesn't matter. Stuff that happens now, it doesn't matter. I mean it does *matter,* but not as much as you'd think, and you're young, sixteen, *so* young. You could go to college, or go back when you're ready, but you have so. Much. Time. Oh, man . . ." He pressed his cheek winsomely against the wooden frame. "If I woke up and I was sixteen again, oh, man—"

And blessedly, just as I prepared to leap, Miss Butcher found the strobe light and jammed it down for a long, long burst and now there was a scream and a sudden surge of movement in the crowd, a panicked circle forming as, in the flickering light and to the sound of

"MMMBop," Debbie Warwick coughed and threw up in a series of rapid snapshots like some hellish stop-motion film, until she was left hunched and alone in the center of a circle of kids who were laughing and screaming at the same time. Only then did Miss Butcher switch off the strobe and tiptoe into the circle to rub Debbie's back with the very tips of the fingers of an outstretched arm.

"Studio 54," said Mr. Hepburn, clambering down from the bars. "Too much strobe, you see?" The music was paused as Parky, building maintenance, went to fetch the sawdust and disinfectant that were kept close at hand for parties. "Twenty minutes to go, ladies and gentlemen," said Mr. Hepburn, restored to the decks. "Twenty minutes, which means it's time to slow things down a little."

Slow songs provided a school-sanctioned opportunity to lie on top of each other while still standing up. The first chords of "2 Become 1" had cleared the floor, but now a series of panicked negotiations was under way at its edges as, courtesy of the lab technicians, a small amount of dry ice belched out, a cloaking device, settling at waist height. Sally Taylor and Tim Morris were the first to kick through the fog, then Sharon Findlay and Patrick Rogers, the school's sexual pioneers, hands permanently plunged deep in the other's waistband as if pulling tickets for a raffle, then Lisa "the Body" Boden and Mark Solomon, Stephen "Shanksy" Shanks and "Queen" Alison Quinn, hopping blithely over the sawdust.

But these were old married couples in our eyes. The crowd demanded novelty. From the far corner, there were whoops and cheers as Little Colin Smart took Patricia Gibson's hand, a corridor opening up as she was half pushed, half tugged into the light, her spare hand covering as much of her face as possible, like the accused arriving for trial.

"I hate this bit, don't you?"

I'd been joined on the bars by Helen Beavis, an art-block girl and champion hockey player, tall and strong and sometimes known as the

Bricky, though never to her face. "Look," she said, "Lisa's trying to fit her entire head into Mark Solomon's mouth."

"And I bet he's still got his chewing gum in there —"

"Just knocking it back and forth. Little game of badminton going on. *Pok-pok-pok*."

We'd made a few self-conscious attempts at friendship, Helen and I, though nothing had ever taken. In the art block, she was one of the cool kids who painted big abstract canvases with titles like *Division,* who always had something drying in the pottery kiln. If art was about emotion and self-expression, then I was merely a "good drawer": detailed, heavily crosshatched sketches of zombies and space pirates and skulls, always with one living eye still in the socket, imagery ripped off from computer games and comics, sci-fi and horror, the kind of intricately violent images that catch the attention of an educational psychologist. "I'll say one thing for you, Lewis," Helen had drawled, holding some intergalactic mercenary at arm's length, "you can really draw a male torso. Capes, too. Imagine what you could do if you drew something *real*."

I'd not replied. Helen Beavis was too smart for me, in an unshowy private way that didn't require the validation of book tokens. She was funny, too, with all the best jokes muttered in a low voice for her own satisfaction. Her sentences contained more words than necessary, every other word given a twist of irony so that I never knew if she meant one thing or its opposite. Words were hard enough when they had one meaning, and if our friendship foundered on anything, it was my inability to keep up.

"You know what this gym needs? Ashtrays. Fitted flush at the end of the parallel bars. Hey, are we allowed to smoke yet?"

"Not for . . . twenty minutes."

Like the best of our athletes, Helen Beavis was a dedicated smoker, lighting up more or less at the gates, her Marlboro Menthol waggling up and down like Popeye's pipe as she laughed, and I'd once watched her place a finger over one nostril and snot a good twelve feet over a privet hedge. She had, I think, the worst haircut I'd ever seen, spiked at the top, long and lank at the back with two pointed sideburns, like something scribbled on a photograph in biro. In the mysterious algebra of the fifth-year common room, bad hair plus artiness plus hockey plus unshaved legs equaled lesbian, a potent word for boys at that time, able to make a girl of great interest or of no interest at all. There were two—and only two—types of lesbian, and Helen was not the kind found in the pages of Martin Harper's magazines, and so the boys paid little attention to her, which I'm sure suited her fine. But I liked her and wanted to impress her, even if my attempts usually left her slowly shaking her head.

Finally the mirror-ball was deployed, revolving on its chain. "Ah. That's magical," said Helen, nodding at the slowly spinning dancers. "Always clockwise, have you noticed?"

"In Australia, they go the other way."

"On the equator, they just stand there. Very self-conscious." We turned back to the dance floor. "Trish looks happy," and we watched as Patricia Gibson, hand still clamped over her eyes, contrived to simultaneously dance and back away. "Colin Smart's trousers have arranged themselves in an interesting way. Weird place to keep your geometry set. *Boing!*" Helen twanged the air. "I had that once. Christmas Methodist Disco with someone whose name I'm not at liberty to repeat. It's not nice. Like being jabbed in the hip with the corner of a shoebox."

"I think boys get more out of it than the girls."

"So go rub it against a tree or something. It's very rude, by which I mean impolite. Leave it out of your arsenal, Charles." Elsewhere, hands were seeking out buttocks and either lying there, limp and frightened, or kneading at the flesh like pizza dough. "It really is a most disgusting spectacle. And not just because of my much-vaunted *les*bianism." I shifted on the bar. We were not used to frank and open discussion. Best to ignore it, and after a moment—

"So, do you want to dance?" she said.

I frowned. "Nah. M'all right."

"Yeah, me too," she said. A little time passed. "If you want to go ask someone else—"

"Really. I'm all right."

"No big crush, Charlie Lewis? Nothing to get off your chest in these dying moments?"

"I don't really do that . . . stuff. You?"

"Me? Nah, I'm pretty much dead inside. Love's a bourgeois construct anyway. All this—" She nodded to the dance floor. "It's not dry ice, it's a haze of low-lying pheromones. Smell it. Love is . . ." We sniffed the air. "Old gym kit and disinfectant."

Feedback, and Mr. Hepburn's voice boomed out, too close to the mike. "Last song, ladies and gentlemen, your very last song! I want to see every single one of you on the floor, every last one of you! Are you ready? I can't hear you! Remember, dance around the sawdust, please. Here we go!"

Obediently, we clambered down. The song was "Heart of Glass" by Blondie, scarcely less remote to us in time than "In the Mood," but clearly a great thing because now everyone was on the dance floor: the theatre kids, the moody pottery kiln kids, even Debbie Warwick, wiped down, pale and unsteady on her feet. The lab technicians poured out the last of the dry ice, Mr. Hepburn turned the volume up and, to whoops and cheers, Patrick Rogers pulled his shirt off over his head and whipped it through the air in the hope of starting a craze —then, when this didn't catch on, put it back on again. Now the new sensation was Lloyd clamping his hand over Fox's mouth and pretending to snog him. Little Colin Smart, sole male member of the Drama Club, had organized a trust game where you took it in turns to fall back into each other's arms in time with the music, and Gordon Gilbert was on Tony Stevens's shoulders, embracing the glitter-ball like a drowning man clinging to a buoy, and now Tony Stevens stepped away and left him dangling while Parky, building maintenance, poked at him with the handle of his mop. "Watch this! Watch this!" shouted someone else as Tim Morris began to break-dance, hurling himself onto the floor, spinning wildly into the sawdust and disinfectant, then leaping to his feet and wiping madly at his trousers. I felt hands on my hips and it was Harper, shouting something that might have been "Love you, mate," then kissing me noisily, smack, smack, on each ear, and now someone else had jumped onto my shoulders and we were all down in a scrum, the boys, Fox and Lloyd, Harper and me, and then some other kids I'd barely spoken to, laughing at a joke that no one could hear. The notion that these had been the best years of our lives suddenly seemed both plausible and tragic, and I wished that school had always been like this, our arms around each other, filled with a kind of hooligan love, and that I'd talked to these people more and in a different voice. Why had we left it until now? Too late, the song was nearly over: *oohooh woahoh, oohooh woahoh*. Sweat plastered clothes to skin, stung our eyes and dripped from our noses, and when I stood up from the scrum, I saw for just one moment Helen Beavis dancing by herself, hunched like a boxer, eyes squeezed tight, singing *oohooh woahoh,* and then, behind her, movement and the hauling open of the fire-exit doors. The atomic brightness poured in like the light from the spaceship at the end of *Close Encounters*. Dazzled, Gordon Gilbert tumbled from the mirror-ball. The music snapped off and it was over.

The time was three fifty-five in the afternoon.

We had missed the countdown and now we stood, silhouetted against the light, dazed and blinking as the staff shepherded us towards the doors, their arms outstretched. Voices hoarse, sweat chilling our skin, we gathered our possessions into our arms—

hockey sticks and coil pots, rancid lunch boxes and crushed dioramas and rags of sports kit—and stumbled into the courtyard.

The freedom we'd been celebrating suddenly seemed like exile, paralyzing and incomprehensible, and we loitered and hesitated on the threshold, animals released too soon into the frightening wild, looking back towards the cage. I saw my sister, Billie, on the other side of the road. We barely spoke to each other now, but I raised my hand. She smiled back and walked away.

The four of us began our last walk home, turning the day into anecdote even before it was over. Down by the railway line, in amongst the silver birches, we could see a haze of smoke, an orange glow from the ceremonial pyre that Gordon Gilbert and Tony Stevens had built from old folders and uniforms, plastic and nylon. They whooped and hollered like wild things, but we walked on to the junction where we had always parted. We hesitated. Perhaps we should mark the occasion, say a few words. Hug? But we balked at sentimental gestures. It was a small town, and it would require far more effort to lose touch than to see each other constantly.

"See ya, then."

"I'll call you later."

"Friday, yeah?"

"See ya."

"Bye."

And I walked back to the house where I now lived alone with my father.

Infinity

I USED TO HAVE a recurring dream, inspired, I think, by a too-early viewing of *2001: A Space Odyssey,* of drifting untethered through infinite space. The dream terrified me then and now, not because of the suffocation or starvation, but because of that sense of powerlessness —nothing to hold on to or push against, just the void and the panic.

Summer felt like that. How could I hope to fill the infinite days, each day infinitely long? In our final term, we'd made plans: raids on London to prowl Oxford Street (and only Oxford Street) and some Tom Sawyer–ish expeditions to the New Forest or the Isle of Wight, rucksacks packed with lager. Binge camping, we called it, but Harper and Fox had found themselves full-time jobs, working cash in hand for Harper's dad, a builder, and the plans had faded. Without Harper around, Lloyd and I just bickered. Besides, I had my own part-time work, also cash in hand, behind the till at a local petrol station.

But this only burned through twelve hours of the week. The rest of my time was my own to—what? The luxury of the midweek lie-in soon wore thin, leaving just the fidgety sadness of sunlight through curtains, the long, lazy, torpid day stretching ahead, then another and another. I knew from science fiction, rather than from Science lessons, that time behaves differently depending on your location, and from a sixteen-year-old's lower bunk at the end of June in 1997, it moved more slowly than anywhere else in the cosmos.

The house we occupied was new. We'd moved out of the "big

house," the family house, shortly after Christmas, and I missed it very much: semidetached, all squares and triangles like a children's drawing, with a banister to slide down and a bedroom each, off-road parking and swings in the garden. My father had bought the big house in a misplaced fit of optimism, and I remembered him showing us round for the first time, rapping the walls to confirm the quality of the bricks, spreading his hands flat on the radiators to experience the glory of central heating. There was a bay window in which I could sit and watch the traffic like a young lord and, most impressively of all, a small square of stained glass over the front door: a sunrise in yellow, gold and red.

But the big house was gone. Now Dad and I lived on an eighties estate, The Library, each street named after a great author in a culturally fortifying way, Woolf Road leading into Tennyson Square, Mary Shelley Avenue crossing Coleridge Lane. We were in Thackeray Crescent, and though I'd not read Thackeray, I knew his influence would be hard to spot. The houses were modern, pale-brick, flat-roofed units with the distinctive feature of curved walls inside and out, so that, seen from the planes circling the airport, the rows would look like fat yellow caterpillars. "Shitty Tatooine," Lloyd had called it. When we'd first moved in—there were four of us then—Dad claimed to love the curves, a more free-form, jazzy expression of our family values than the boxy rooms in our old semidetached. It'll be like living in a lighthouse! If The Library estate no longer felt like the future, if the table-size gardens were not as neat as they used to be, if the occasional shopping trolley drifted across the wide, silent avenues, this would still be a new chapter in our family's story, with the added peace of mind that would come from living within our means. Yes, my sister and I would be sharing a room, but bunk beds were fun and it wouldn't be forever.

Six months later, boxes still remained unpacked, jutting out against the curved walls or piled on my sister's empty bunk. My friends rarely came to visit, preferring to hang out at Harper's house, which resembled the palace of a Romanian dictator, a two-jukebox household with rowing machines and quad bikes and immense TVs, a samurai sword and enough air rifles and pistols and flick knives to repel a zombie invasion. My house had my mad dad and a lot of rare jazz on vinyl. Even I didn't want to go there.

Or stay there. The great project of that summer would be to avoid Dad. I'd learned to gauge his mental state by the noises he made, tracking him like a hunter. Most days, I'd hear him stir at around nine and shuffle to the bathroom, positioned on the other side of my bunk. No alarm clock was as effective as the sound of my father weeing near my head, and I'd leap up, quickly pull on the previous day's clothes and slip downstairs with ninja stealth to see if he'd left his cigarettes. As long as there were ten or more, it was safe to take one and quickly zip it into a pouch in my rucksack. I'd eat toast standing at the breakfast bar—another feature of the house that had lost its novelty, eating on stools—and leave before he made it downstairs.

But if I failed, then he'd appear, sticky-eyed and with the creases of the pillowcase still visible on his face, and we'd jostle awkwardly between kettle and toaster, slipping into our act.

"So is this breakfast or lunch?"

"I think of it as brunch."

"Sophisticated. It's nearly ten—"

"You can talk!"

"I didn't get to sleep till—could you use a plate?"

"I've got a plate."

"So why are there crumbs every—?"

"Because I've not had time to—"

"Just use a plate!"

"Here's a plate, here it is, in my hand, a plate, my plate—"

"And put the stuff away."

"I will when I've finished."

"Don't leave it in the sink."

"I wasn't going to leave it in the sink."

"Good. Don't."

And on and on, banal, witlessly sarcastic and provoking, less a conversation, more the flicking of an ear. I hated the way we spoke to each other, yet change required voices that neither of us possessed, so we lapsed into silence and Dad turned on the TV. There might once have been a delinquent pleasure in this, but truancy requires that there's somewhere else you ought to be, and neither of us had that. All I knew was that Dad didn't like to be alone, and so I'd leave.

Most days I'd ride my bike, though not in the slick, modern style. I wore jeans, not Lycra, on an old racer with drop handlebars, a clattering rusted chain and a frame as heavy and unforgiving as welded scaffolding. Low on those handlebars, I'd patrol The Library and lazily circle the cul-de-sacs, Tennyson and Mary Shelley, Forster then Kipling, up Woolf and round Hardy. I'd check the swings and slides in the recreation ground for anyone I might know. I'd cycle down pedestrian alleyways, swoop from side to side on the wide, empty roads on the way to the shops.

What was I looking for? Though I couldn't name it, I was looking for some great change—a quest, perhaps, an adventure with trials undergone and lessons learned. But it's awkward to embark on an adventure on your own, hard to find that kind of quest on the high street. Ours was a small town in the southeast, too far away from London to be a suburb, too large to be a village, too developed to count as countryside. We lacked the train station that might have turned it into a commuter hub. Instead, the economy relied on the airport and the light-industrial business parks: photocopiers, double-glazing, computer components, aggregates—whatever they were. The high street —called High Street—had a few buildings that might have passed as quaint: a timber-framed tea room called the Cottage Loaf, a Georgian newsagent's, a Tudor chemist's, a medieval market cross for the cider drinkers, but they were blighted by the dust and fumes of the busy road that ran alongside narrow pavements, leaving shoppers pressed flat against the leaded windows. The cinema was now a carpet ware-house, trapped in the time loop of an endless closing-down sale. Areas of outstanding natural beauty were a twenty-minute drive away, the Sussex coast a further thirty, the whole town contained within a ring road that encircled us like a perimeter fence.

I didn't hate our town, but it was hard to feel lyrical or sentimental about the reservoir, the precinct, the scrappy woods where porn yel-lowed beneath the brambles. Our recreation ground was universally known as Dog Shit Park, the pine plantation Murder Wood; for all I knew those were their names on the Ordnance Survey map, and no one was ever going to write a sonnet about that.

And so I'd walk the high street, looking in windows, hoping to see someone I knew. I'd buy chewing gum in the newsagent's and read the computer magazines until the newsagent's glare drove me back onto my bike. I must have looked lonely, though I would have hated anyone to think this. Boredom was our natural state but loneliness was taboo, and so I strained for the air of a loner, a maverick, unknowable and self-contained, riding with no hands. But a great effort is required not to appear lonely when you are alone, happy when you're not. It's like holding out a chair at arm's length, and when I could no longer main-tain the illusion of ease, I'd cycle out of town.

To reach anything that might pass as countryside it was necessary to cross the flyover, the motorway thundering alarmingly beneath like some mighty waterfall, then cycle across great prairies of yellow wheat and rape, past the corrugated plains of plastic greenhouses that sheltered the supermarket strawberry crops, then crest the hills that encircled us. I was no great nature lover, not a bird watcher or angler or poet, but solitude was less shaming out here, almost pleasurable, and each day I dared myself to travel further from home, expanding the circumference of places that I knew.

The first week, the second, then the third passed in this way, until one Thursday morning when I found myself in the long grass of a wild meadow that overlooked our town.

The Meadow

I'D NOT BEEN HERE BEFORE. Bored of the ascent, I'd dismounted and noticed a footpath to my right, shady and blessedly flat. I'd wheeled my bike through woodland that soon opened up onto a sloping pasture, overgrown to waist height, the brown and green spattered with the red of poppies and the blue of . . . something else. Willow herb? Cornflowers? I'd no idea, but the meadow was irresistible, and I heaved my bike over the wooden stile and plowed on through the tall grass. A grand timbered mansion came into view above me, one that I'd noticed from the ring road, a formal garden bordering the meadow at its lower edge. I had a sudden sense of trespass and dropped my bike, then walked on until I found a natural hollow in which to sunbathe, smoke and read something violent.

The great expanse of empty hours meant that, for the first time in my life, I'd resorted to reading. I'd begun with thrillers and horror novels from Dad's collection, dog-eared pages waffled from bath or beach, in which sex alternated with violence at an accelerating pace. Initially, books had felt like second best — reading about sex and violence was like listening to football on the radio — but soon I was tearing through a novel every day, forgetting them almost instantly, except for *The Silence of the Lambs* and Stephen King. Before too long, I'd graduated to Dad's smaller, slightly intimidating sci-fi section: scuffed copies of Asimov, Ballard and Philip K. Dick. Though I couldn't say how it was achieved, I could tell that these books were written in a different register to the ones about giant rats, and the novel that I carried daily in my bag began to feel like protection against boredom, an alibi for loneliness. There was still something furtive about it—reading in front of my mates would have been like taking up the flute or country dancing—but no one would see me here, and so on this day I took out my copy of Kurt Vonnegut's *Slaughterhouse-Five,* chosen because it had "slaughter" in the title.

If I rolled a little from side to side, I could make a sort of military dugout, invisible from the house above or the town below. Straining for soulfulness, I took in the view, a model-railway kind of landscape with everything too close together: plantations rather than woodland, reservoirs not lakes, stables and catteries and dog kennels rather than dairy farms and roaming sheep. Birdsong competed with the grumble of the motorway and the tinnitus buzzing of the pylons above me, but from this distance, it didn't seem such a bad place. From this distance.

I took off my top and lay back, practiced my smoking with the day's cigarette, then, using the book to shield my eyes, I began to read, pausing now and then to brush ash from my chest. High above, holiday jets from Spain and Italy, Turkey and Greece, circled in a holding pattern, impatient for a runway. I closed my eyes and watched the fibers drifting against the screen of my eyelids, trying to follow them to the edge of my vision as they darted away like fish in a stream.

When I awoke, the sun was at its height and I felt thick-headed and momentarily panicked by the sound of whoops and shouts and hunting cries from the hill above: a posse. Were they out to get me? No, I heard the swish of grass and the panicked gasps of their quarry, running down the hill in my direction. I peered through the high grass. The girl wore a yellow T-shirt and a short blue denim skirt that hindered her running, and I saw her hoist it higher with both hands, then look behind her and crouch down to catch her breath, forehead pressed to her scuffed knees. I couldn't see her expression, but had a sudden, excited notion that the house was some sinister institution, an asylum or a secret lab, and that I might help her escape. More shouts and jeers, and she glanced back, then straightened, twisted her skirt further up her pale legs and began to run directly at me. I crouched again, but not before I saw her look back one more time and suddenly pitch forward and crash face-first into the ground.

I'm ashamed to say that I laughed, clapping my hand to my mouth. A moment's silence, and then I heard her groaning and giggling at the same time. "Ow! Ow-ow-ow, you *idiot!* Owwwwwww!" She was perhaps three or four meters away now, her panting broken by her own pained laughter, and I was aware of my skinny bare chest as pink as tinned salmon, and the syrupy sweat and cigarette ash that had pooled in my sternum. I began the contortions required to get dressed while remaining flat on the ground.

From the house on the hill, a jeering voice — "Hey! We give up! You win! Come back and join us!" — and I thought, *it's a trap, don't believe them.*

The girl groaned to herself. "Hold on!"

Another voice, female. "You did very well! Lunchtime! Come back!"

"I can't!" she said, sitting now. "Ow! Bloody hell!" I pressed myself further into the ground as she attempted to stand, testing her ankle and yelping at the pain. I would have to reveal myself, but there seemed no casual way to leap out on someone in a meadow. I licked my lips, and in a stranger's voice called, "Helloo!"

She gasped, pivoted on her good leg and fell backwards all at once, disappearing into the grass.

"Listen, don't freak out but—"

"Who said that?!"

"Just so you know I'm here—"

"Who? Where?"

"Over here. In the long grass."

"But who the fuck *are* you? *Where* are you?"

I pulled my T-shirt down quickly, stood and, in a low crouch as if under fire, crossed to where she lay. "I was trying not to scare you."

"Well, you *failed*, you *weirdo!*"

"Hey, I was here first!"

"What are you doing here anyway?"

"Nothing! Reading! Why are they after you?"

She looked at me sideways. "Who?"

"Those people, why are they chasing you?"

"You're not in the company?"

"What company?"

"*The* Company. You're not part of it?"

The Company sounded sinister, and I wondered if I might help her after all. *Come with me if you want to live.* "No, I—"

"Then what are you doing here?"

"Nothing, I was just, I went for a bike ride and—"

"Where's your bike?"

"Over there. I was reading and I fell asleep and I wanted to let you know I was here without frightening you."

She'd returned to examining her ankle. "Well, that worked out."

"Actually, it is a public footpath. I've got as much right to be here—"

"Fine, but I have an actual *reason*."

"So why were they chasing you?"

"What? Oh. Stupid game. Don't ask." She tested the bones of her ankle with her thumbs. "Ow!"

"Does it hurt?"

"Yes, it *fucking* hurts! Running through meadows, it's a fucking deathtrap. I put my foot right in a rabbit hole and fell on my face."

"Yeah, I saw that."

"Did you? Well, thank you for not laughing."

"I did laugh."

She narrowed her eyes at me.

"So—can I help?" I said, to make amends.

She looked me up and down, literally up then down again, an appraisal, so that I found myself trying to jam my fingertips into my pockets. "Tell me again, why are you here, perving about?"

"I'm just . . . Look, I'm reading. Look!" And I scrambled back to my foxhole to retrieve the paperback and hold it out. She examined the cover, checking it against my face as if it were a passport. Satisfied, she tried to get to her feet, winced and collapsed back down, and I wondered if I ought to offer my hand, like a handshake, but the gesture seemed absurd and instead I knelt at her feet and, scarcely less absurd, took her foot as if trying on a glass slipper: Adidas shell-tops with blue stripes, no socks, a pale, mottled shin. I felt the slight prickle of new stubble, black like iron filings.

"You all right down there?" she said, eyes fixed on the sky.

"Yes, just wondering if—" I'd assumed a surgeon's air, probing with skilled thumbs.

"Ow!"

'Sorry!'

"Tell me, Doctor, what exactly are you looking for?"

"I'm looking for the bit that hurts, then I'm prodding it. Basically, I'm seeing if there's bone sticking out through flesh."

"Is there?"

"No, you're fine. It's a sprain."

"And will I ever dance again?"

"You will," I said, "but only if you really *want* it."

She laughed up at the sky and I felt so debonair and pleased with myself that I laughed too. "Serves me right for wearing this," she said, tugging the denim skirt down towards her knees. "Vanity. What an idiot. I'd better get back. You can let go of my foot now." Too abruptly, I dropped it and stood by stupidly while she attempted to haul herself into an upright position.

"Any chance that you could . . . ?"

I hauled her to her feet and held her hand as she tested the ground with her pointed toe, winced again, tested again, and I tried to take her in while looking the other way. She was a little shorter than me but not much, her skin pale, her hair black and short but with a longer fringe that she now stowed away behind her ear, and which was carefully shaved at the nape of her neck in a way that exaggerated the curve of her skull, so that it was somehow austere and glamorous at the same time, Joan of Arc just leaving the salon. I don't think I'd ever noticed the back of someone's head before. Tiny black studs in each ear, with two extra holes for special occasions. Because I was sixteen, I let my eyes slip out of focus to disguise the fact that I was looking at her breasts, confident that no girl had spotted this trick. Adidas, they said, on a bright yellow T-shirt with very short sleeves so that, in the soft flesh at the top of her arm, I could make out her vaccine scar, dimpled like the markings on a Roman coin.

"Hello? I'm going to need your help."

"Can you walk?"

"I can hop, but that's not going to work."

"D'you want a piggyback?" I said, regretting "piggyback." There had to be a tougher term. "Or a, you know, fireman's lift?" She looked at me and I stood a little straighter.

"*Are* you a fireman?"

"I'm taller than you!"

"But I'm"—she tugged her skirt down—"denser. Can you lift your own weight?"

"Sure!" I said, and turned and offered up my sweaty back with a hitchhiker's flick of the thumb.

"No. No, that would be really weird. But if you don't mind me leaning on you . . ."

In a further gesture that I've never made before or since, I cocked my elbow to the side and sort of nodded towards it, hand on hip like a country dancer.

"Why, thank 'ee," she said, and we began to walk.

The swish of the long grass seemed unreasonably loud, and searching for a clear path meant there were few opportunities to turn and look at her, though it now felt like a compulsion. She walked with her fringe obscuring her face, her eyes fixed on the ground, but in flashes I could see they were blue, a ridiculous blue—had I noticed the color of anyone's eyes quite so acutely before?—and the skin around them had a bluish tinge too, like the remnants of last night's makeup, creased with laughter lines, or a wince as—

"Ow! Ow, ow, ow."

"Are you sure I can't carry you?"

"You are *really* keen to carry someone."

There were a few spots on her forehead and one on her chin, picked or worried at, and her mouth seemed very wide and red against the pale skin, with a small raised seam in her lower lip, a fold, as if there'd been some repair, the mouth held in tension as if she was about to laugh, or swear, or both, as she did now, her ankle folding sideways like a hinge.

"I really could carry you."

"I believe you."

Soon the gate to the formal garden was in sight, the absurd house now grander and more intimidating, and I wondered: "Do you live here?"

"Here?" She laughed with her whole face, unselfconsciously. One of my smaller prejudices was a suspicion and resentment of people with very good teeth; all that health and vigor seemed like a kind of showing off. This girl's teeth, I noticed, were saved from perfection by a chip on her left front tooth, like the folded corner of a page. "No, I don't *live* here."

"I thought maybe they were your family, the people chasing you."

"Yeah, they do that a lot, me and Mum and Dad, whenever we see a field—"

"Well, I don't know . . ."

"It was a silly game. It's a long story." Changing the subject: "What were you doing here again?"

"Reading. Just a nice spot to read." She nodded, skeptical. "Nature boy."

I shrugged. "Makes a change."

"And how's *Slaughterhouse-Five*?"

"S'okay. Not enough slaughter."

She laughed, though I was only half joking. "I've heard of it but not read it. I don't want to generalize, but I always thought it was a boys' book. Is it?"

I shrugged again . . .

"I mean, compared to Atwood or Le Guin."

. . . because if she was going to talk about literature, then I might as well push her into a bush and run.

"So. What's it about?"

Charlie, can you tell the class something about the author's intentions in this passage? Your own words, please.

"It's about this man, this war veteran, who has been kidnapped by aliens and he's in an alien zoo, but he keeps flashing back to scenes in the war, where he's a prisoner . . ."

Yes, that's what happens, but what's it about? Keep going, Charlie, please.

"But it's also about war, and the bombing of Dresden, and a sort of fatality—not fatality, um, fatalism?—about whether life matters or free will is a delusion, illusion, delusion, so it's sort of horrible, about death and war, but it's funny too."

"O-kay. Does sound a *bit* like a boys' book."

Use better words. "Surreal! That's what it is. And really good." *Thank you, Charlie, sit down, please.*

"O-kay," she said. "Okay. Usually when people say "alien zoo" I switch off, but maybe I'll read it. Have you read—?"

"No, but I've seen the film." She looked at me sideways. "I'm joking. I just mean that I've not read much. I'm not much of a reader."

"Well," she said, "that's all right." Then, as if there were some connection, "What school d'you go to?"

It was a dull question but decreed by law, and I thought it best to spit it out:

"Just finished at Merton Grange," I said and watched, expecting the usual emotions, the face you might reserve for someone who tells you that they've just left prison. Though I couldn't honestly spot a trace of this, I still felt a twist of irritation. "You're Chatsborne, yeah?"

She tucked her fringe behind her ear and laughed. "How did you guess?"

Because Chatsborne kids were posh, were arty stoners, were hippies. Chatsborne kids wore their own clothes to school, which meant vintage floral dresses and ironic T-shirts that they'd screen-printed themselves at home. Chatsborne kids were clever, were wimps, were wimps because they were clever, a school composed entirely of head boys and head girls, eating vegetarian tagine from self-carved bowls on furniture they'd made from reclaimed wood. Estate agents boasted of inclusion in its catchment area before they even mentioned the number of bedrooms, the circles of affluence and confidence and cool marked on the map like a radiation zone. Walk those streets on a summer's evening and you'd hear the violin, cello and classical guitar calling to each other at grade-eight level. Of all our tribal instincts, above team or label or political party, loyalty to school was the strongest, and even if we hated the place, the bond remained, indelible as a tattoo. Even so, I already missed the brief moments before we'd fallen into our roles of Merton Grange boy, Chatsborne girl.

We walked a little further in silence.

"Don't worry, I'm not going to steal your dinner money," I said, and she smiled, but frowned too.

"I didn't say anything like that, did I?"

"No." I'd sounded bitter. I tried again. "I've not seen you around," I said, as if I roamed the streets looking for girls.

"Oh, I live . . ." and she waved vaguely towards the trees.

We walked a little further.

"Your school used to have those fights with our school," she said.

"Up the precinct, outside the Chinese. I know. I used to go."

"To fight?"

"No, just to watch. Was never much of a *fight*. Everyone used to talk about *blades,* there's going to be *blades,* but that was only if you counted a protractor. Mainly it was just kids chucking water and chips."

"Never bring a protractor to a water fight."

"Merton Grange did always win, though."

"Yeah," she said, "but does anyone ever really *win?*"

"War is hell."

"Fights up the precinct; it's all a bit Sharks and Jets, isn't it? I hate all that stuff. Thank God it's over, I won't miss that. Besides, look at us two now, completely at ease . . ."

"Just talking . . ."

"Getting along, breaking down boundaries . . ."

"It's very moving."

"So how d'you think you did in your exams?"

Thankfully, we'd reached the grounds of the big house, a rusted metal gate giving onto a patchy lawn, the great timbered mansion behind, imposing enough to provide a distraction.

"Am I allowed in here?"

"On t'mistress's land? Aye, course thou art, lad." I held the gate open for her, then hesitated. "I can't climb that hill without you," she said. "You are *literally* my crutch."

We walked on, clambering over the sunken earthworks, called a ha-ha, both the source of and the response to weak jokes since the

1700s. Close up, the ornamental gardens seemed scrappy and sun-blasted; dried-out rose beds, a brittle, brown-tipped slab of privet. "See that? It's the famous maze."

"Why didn't you hide in there?"

"I'm not an *amateur!*"

"What kind of house has a maze?"

"Posh one. Come on, I'll introduce you to the owners."

"I should get back, my bike's still down—"

"No one's going to nick your bike. Come on, they're really nice. Besides, there's people here from your school, you can say hello."

We were crossing the lawn towards a courtyard. I could hear voices. "I really should get home."

"Just say hello, it won't take a minute." I'd noticed now that she had looped her arm in mine, for support or perhaps to stop me running away, and in a moment we were in a central courtyard, with two trestle tables laden with food and a crowd of ten or so strangers, their backs to us; the sinister private rituals of The Company.

"Here she is!" bellowed a florid young man in an untucked collar-less shirt, flicking a great wing of hair out of his eyes. "The champion returns!" He seemed familiar from somewhere, but now the rest of the coven had turned, cheering and applauding as the girl hobbled towards them. "My God, what's up?" said the young man, taking her arm, and an older woman with cropped white hair frowned and tutted as if the injury was my fault.

"I fell over," she said. "This guy helped me back. I'm sorry, I don't know your name."

"It's Charlie Lewis," said Lucy Tran, the Vietnamese girl from Merton Grange, her mouth tight in frank dislike.

"Bloody hell, it's Lewis!" shouted another voice. Helen Beavis cackled and gathered salad leaves into her mouth with the back of her hand. "Get out of here, you freak!"

"I was just on my bike, in the field, and—"

"Hello, Charlie, welcome aboard!" said Little Colin Smart, sole male member of the school Drama Club, and now the young man with the fringe marched towards me, dark sweat marks in his armpits, hands outstretched, with such determined force that I took a step backwards into the wall.

"Hello, Charlie, are you a new recruit? I do hope so! We *need* you, Charlie!" and he enclosed my hand entirely in his and pumped it up and down. "Grab some salad and we'll see how we can slot you in," he said, and I knew where I had seen this man before and what he represented, and that I should run away.

Full Fathom Five Theatre Cooperative

IN THE FINAL WEEKS of our final term, we'd all been ushered into the hall for a very important assembly with very special guests. Usually this meant something lurid, perhaps a lecture on road safety with gory illustrations. Last term, a policeman had smashed a cauliflower with a mallet to illustrate the effect of ecstasy on the brain, and soon after, a nice, nervous lady had come to talk to us about sex within the context of a healthy, loving relationship. The doors had been solemnly closed and the lights dimmed. "Could you please be quiet, please?" she'd pleaded, clicking through the vivid pink and purple slides to laughter and screams and appalled cries. I'd been thinking a lot about work and wondered what strange, twisted career path had brought this woman here, traveling anxiously from school to school with a box of slides showing some varieties of penis. "Worst holiday photos ever," said Harper, and we laughed as if none of this concerned us. Click, click went the slides. "Like snowflakes," said the nice lady, "no two penises are exactly alike," and I wondered—how do they *know*?

"How *do* they know?"

"They use a microscope," said Lloyd and punched me between the legs.

So there was a palpable sense of disappointment as we took our seats in front of a florid, grinning young man with a great wing of hair across his eyes and an angular woman of the same age, her black hair pulled back tightly. In front of them, a beat-box cassette player sat like a dark threat.

Mr. Pascoe clapped his hands twice. "Settle down, everyone. Lloyd, does the term 'everyone' include you, or are you possessed of unique qualities hitherto undisclosed? No? Then settle down. Now. I'd like to introduce you to our special guests today; special in their achievements, special in their ambitions—"

"Special in their needs," said Harper, and I laughed.

"Lewis! Charles Lewis, what is wrong with you?"

"Sorry, sir!" I said, looked to the floor, then looked up again and noticed that the young man onstage was directing his grin towards me. He winked collaboratively. I hated that wink.

"Our guests here are graduates of the University of *Oxford!* They're here to tell you about a very exciting project, so please give a big Merton Grange welcome to . . . bear with me . . ." He consulted his notes. "Ivor and Alina from . . ." Another consultation. "The Full Fathom Five Theatre Cooperative!"

Ivor and Alina bounded forward with such force that their chairs skittered back across the parquet. "How are you doing, kids, all right?" shouted Ivor, plump and wide-eyed like a spoiled King Charles spaniel. Fine, we mumbled, but Ivor had the bumptious, cajoling demeanor we knew from kids' TV. He cupped his ear. "I can't hear you!"

"Course he can fucking hear us," said Fox. "It's a trick."

"A ruse," said Lloyd, "a wily ruse."

"Let's try it once again! How ya doing?" We stayed quiet.

"Oh, you sound so sad!" said Alina, pulling down the corners of her mouth, tilting her head to one side.

"Christ, there's two of them," said Lloyd, but Alina had a European accent, Czech or Hungarian perhaps, which made her vampish and intriguing to us.

"We're here to tell you about a fantastic opportunity," said Ivor, "coming your way this summer, a great project we're very excited about. Tell me, who here has heard of a Mr. William Shakespeare? Is that all? Wow, you're shy. Okay, let's try this: who here has never heard of a Mr. William Shakespeare? The Swan of Avon! The Bard! The Upstart Crow! You see—you've all heard of him!"

"And who here can quote some Shakespeare for us?" said Alina.

One hand rocketed. Suki Jewell, the deputy head girl.

"To be or not to be," whispered Harper.

"To be or not to be!" shouted Suki.

"That is the question! Very good! *Hamlet*! Anyone else?" From the front rows of the hall, the book-token kids were calling out:

"Alas, poor Yorick!"

"Is this a dagger!"

"Now is the winter of our discontent!"

"It is better to have loved and lost," shouted Suki Jewell, "than never to have loved at all."

Ivor frowned consolingly. "Actually, that's Tennyson."

"Yeah, that's Tennyson, you slag," said Lloyd.

Now Alina took over. "Here's the thing—did you know that we all use Shakespeare's language, even when we don't realize it!" Dark-eyed, sharp-featured, hair scraped back harshly, Alina seemed less comfortable in her hoodie and tracksuit, a ballet dancer absconding from an open prison. "Are you listening to me? Because I simply won't speak if you are not listening. Very well, tell me—has anyone here heard the phrase 'brave new world'? A few of you. Okay, how about 'break the ice,' as in, 'Hey, let's break the ice at this party'?"

"How about 'fainthearted'?" said Ivor. "Or 'foregone conclusion'?"

"Did you know—" said Alina.

"No," said Fox.

"—that when you use the phrase 'method in my madness,' you're quoting Will?"

"Who the fuck says 'method in my madness'?" said Lloyd.

"And when you tell a knock-knock joke, you're quoting . . . the Scottish play!"

Ivor winked and whispered from behind his hand, "She means *Macbeth*!" and Little Colin Smart from Drama Club laughed.

"Oi! Smart," Lloyd hissed down the line, "don't laugh at that, you dick."

"Play fast and loose!" said Alina.

"In the mind's eye!" said Ivor.

"Laughingstock!"

"Love is blind!"

"The milk of human kindness!"

"F'fuck's sake," said Harper, "you made your point."

But they were not done yet, because now Ivor crossed his arms and struck a pose while Alina pressed play on the tape deck. They crouched, hands on knees, faces close. A pause, uncomfortably long, and a thin hip-hop beat began. As we feared, it was another attempt to convince us that Shakespeare was the first rapper.

"You're dead as a doornail!"

"To the crack of doom!"

"You've eaten me out of house and home!"

"It was a dish fit for the gods!"

"We don't even like rap," sighed Lloyd. "What makes them think we like rap?"

"You play fast and loose!"

"Had that one already," said Harper.

"You set my teeth on edge!"

"No, you set my teeth on edge," said Lloyd.

"You've seen better days!"

"I'll kill you with kindness!"

"Kill me with something," said Fox. "Please!"

"You're the devil incarnate!"

"Ha! Jealousy's the green-eyed monster!"

"These are literally the worst people in the world . . ."

And now suddenly Mr. Pascoe was on his feet. "Harper! Fox! Lloyd! What the hell are you doing?"

"Quoting Shakespeare, sir," said Fox.

"There's method in our madness, sir," said Lloyd.

"Outside. Now!"

"Foregone conclusion," murmured Harper.

"We're a laughingstock," said Lloyd.

"In one fell swoop," said Fox as the three of them squeezed past me, scraping chairs. Once the swing door had closed, Alina pressed stop and Ivor stepped forward once again.

"So. Here's the deal—"

"There's this play—"

"It's about *gangs*, it's about *violence*, it's about belonging and prejudice and love and"—Ivor paused before delivering the punch line —"it's about sex!" He waited, head tilted, for the murmur to pass through the hall. "It's a play by William Shakespeare. And it's called—"

"*Romeo. And. Juliet*. If you think you know all about it, trust me, you do not. The FFFTC will be putting it on here, this summer, in an exciting new venue."

"And you"—Ivor stretched out both arms, two fingers of each hand pointed sideways, gangland-style—"are going to be the stars! Five weeks' rehearsal, four shows. We're going to learn to *dance*, we're going to learn to *fight*—"

"We are going to learn how to *be*," said Alina, scanning the rows with her dark eyes, and for the first time we were entirely silent and still. "How to *be*, both onstage and off. We are all going to learn a little about how to move through this world, both present and alive."

"Remember," said Ivor. "Full Fathom Five is not us, it's *you*." He pressed his palms together, interlaced his fingers and rang his hands like a school bell. "We *need* you. We simply can't do this without you."

"Please," said Alina. "Come. Join us."

"I haven't come to join," I said now. I may even have shouted.

"Okay," said Ivor. "But you don't know what—"

"Whatever this is, I'm not part of it, I was just helping her." I looked for the girl, who was standing at the table, spooning food onto a paper plate. "I've got to go now."

"Okay. You're sure? Because we badly need young men."

"Yeah, not me. I've got to go. Sorry. Bye, Lucy, Colin. Bye, Helen," and before they could reply I was walking briskly from the courtyard, across the lawn and past the maze—

"Hold on!"

. . . leaping down behind the ha-ha for cover, storming onwards . . .

"Excuse me! Can you wait a moment! Oh, for crying out loud . . ."

. . . and I turned in time to see her hobbling towards me, a buckled paper plate sowing a trail of food. I waited at the gate. "Look," she said, laughing, "you've made me drop my couscous." She shook the last of the sandy stuff onto the grass. "Couscous on the ha-ha. Fucking hell, that's just about the most bourgeois—anyway, I just wanted to say thank you. For helping me out."

"That's fine."

"You're sure you don't want to stay?"

"I'm not an actor."

"Trust me, I've been here all week, and no one here is an actor, me included. It's just . . . fun, you know? To start with, it's just Theatre Sports and improv. I realize that's not selling it necessarily—"

"I can't really—"

"I mean, 'theatre' and 'sports,' there's two words you don't want to see coupled together."

"Sorry, I've got to—"

"But we start on the play next week. It's *Romeo and Juliet*."

"It's not for me."

"Because it's Shakespeare?"

"This whole thing, it's not my . . ."

Don't say "thing" again.

. . .

. . .

"Thing."

"Okay. Well. Shame. Nice to meet you."

"You too. Maybe I'll see you around?"

"You will if you come tomorrow! No? Okay." She began brushing at her bare leg. "Bloody couscous. I don't even like couscous. Nine thirty if you change your mind. You won't regret it. Or you might. What I mean is, you probably will regret it, but at least—"

"Well, I'd better be—"

"I didn't get your name."

"Charlie. Lewis. Charlie Lewis."

"Nice to meet you, Charlie Lewis."

"You too. So."

. . .

. . .

"Aren't you going to ask my name?"

"Sorry, you're . . . ?"

"Fran. As in Frances, with an 'e,' so Fran Fisher. What can I do, my parents are idiots. Well, they're not, but—anyway. Well, like I said. Thank you. Bye."

She turned and walked away, and I watched her folding the paper plate into a wedge and tucking it into the pocket of her denim skirt. Then she turned back, confirming what she must have known, that I would be watching her.

"Bye, Charlie Lewis!"

I raised my hand and she did too, but I never did go back, and that was the last time I ever saw Fran Fisher.

I wonder where she is now.

First Sight

I KNOW WHERE SHE is now. I did go back, because it was inconceivable that I would not see that face again, and if doing so meant half a day of Theatre Sports, then that was the price I'd pay.

But perhaps that's not quite true either. Perhaps I'd have forgotten her soon enough. When these stories—love stories—are told, it's hard not to ascribe meaning and inevitability to entirely innocuous chance events. We literally romanticize; one glance and something changed, a flame was ignited, cogs interlocking in some great celestial device. But the "love" in "love at first sight" is, I suspect, only applied in retrospect, laid on like an orchestral score when the outcome of the story is known and the looks and smiles and hands brushing against each other can be allocated a significance that they rarely carry in the moment.

It's true that I thought she was lovely, but I thought this about someone five to ten times on any given day, and even alone, I thought it while watching TV. It's true that during our first encounter a clear, insistent voice in my head had told me *concentrate, this will matter, concentrate,* and true, too, that part of this was probably just sex, the noise of which underscored almost any conversation I had with a girl at that time, like a car alarm that no one can turn off. Part of it was a less torrid, more conventionally romantic vision, a momentary flash-forward to a montage—holding hands, browsing in WHSmith or laughing on the swings in Dog Shit Park—

and I wondered what that would look like and feel like, all that *company.*

I had never in my life, before or since, been more primed to fall in love. Catching that fever, I felt sure, would inoculate me against all other worries and fears. I longed for change, for something to *happen,* some adventure, and falling in love seemed more accessible than, say, solving a murder. But even though I thought she was lovely, I was not touched by some wand, there was no flourish on the harp and no change in the lighting. If I'd been busier that summer, or happier at home, then I might not have thought about her so much, but I was neither busy nor happy, and so I fell.

Later, when I met the woman who became my wife, we spent the first few months distilling more than thirty years of lived experience into a series of anecdotes and lists, the most important people, the best and the worst of times, inventing fake epiphanies and turning points—*it was then that I realized*—and boiling off the messy, the everyday, the great long stretches in which nothing much happened. We simplified things by turning them into stories, about school, about friends and parents and past relationships and, when it was safe to do so, the story of our first loves.

"Her name was Fran Fisher."

"When was this?"

"'Ninety-seven. The summer I left school. We did a play together, so—"

"Whoa, hang on. You were in a play."

"Oh, yeah. *Romeo and Juliet.* I was Benvolio."

"I don't believe you."

"*Here were the servants of your adversary, and yours—*"

"Don't do that—"

"*—close fighting ere I did approach—*"

"Stop, please. I don't like it—"

"*—I drew to part them. In the instant came the fiery Tybalt—*"

"I hope that wasn't how you did it."

"More or less. And yet I never acted again."

"Theatre's loss."

"I know. That's the *real* tragedy."

"What happened to her?"

"Fran Fisher? No idea," I said, which was true at that time.

"And when you met her, was it like in the play? Was it love at first sight?"

"Nah. At most it was fancy at first sight."

"Fancy at first sight. Is that from Shakespeare too?"

"I just mean love's a big word for it. You're a different person then, aren't you? At that age. It's . . . something else. They should have a different word for it."

"Luff —"

"Luve —"

"And did you, did she — ?"

"What?"

She laughed. "Steal the flower of your innocence?"

"Well, now you ask, yes, she did."

"Oh, God. Was it *amazing?*"

"What d'you think? A sixteen-year-old boy —"

"Still, at least you lost it to someone you actually liked."

"I did like her. I mean, really. Fran Fisher. She was great."

"That's nice. So when you met me?"

"Pretty jaded by then."

"Big shrug?"

"'You'll do.'"

"'You *partially* complete me.'"

"Exactly."

"But first sight, when you met her, whatshername —"

"Fran Fisher."

"What did you think?"

I remember worrying that I wouldn't be able to remember her face. Freewheeling at great speed through the strobing light of that wooded lane, straight in the saddle, wind whipping at my chest, I tried to pair what I could recall with someone familiar, someone off the telly whose face I might use as a template. But no one quite fitted, and before I'd reached the junction and turned towards town, her face had begun to fade like an unfixed photograph — shape of nose, shade of blue, chipped tooth, the great curve of her skull, the precise constellation of spots and freckles; how would I remember? I had a corny idea that I might draw her as soon as I got home — a few lines, a gesture, the way she tugged at the back of her denim skirt or stored her fringe behind her ear. Until then I'd focused mainly on zombies and alien insects. Perhaps Fran Fisher was my first worthy subject, the "something *real*" that Helen had told me to draw, and I continued to summon up her features in turn in the same way that you might try to memorize a phone number — *shape of nose, shade of blue, chipped tooth, the curve of, constellation of* —

Phone number. Why hadn't I just asked for her phone number? That was what I needed. I'd get it the next time I saw her.

Next time.

I remember feeling a great surge of jealousy towards her boyfriend, without knowing who he was or if he existed. Surely she must have one, because all Chatsborne girls came with a boyfriend of equal beauty and status, constantly doing it in their parents' pools or at drug-fueled sleepless sleepovers. There were kids at Merton Grange who had "relationships," but they'd quickly settled into a sort of parody of domesticity, tea on laps in front of the TV, walking around the shops, as if trapped in a particularly committed game of Mums and Dads. Chatsborne kids, on the other hand, were decadent, wild and free like the gilded youth of *Logan's Run* or foreign exchange students. Of all the markers on the road to adulthood — voting, driving a car, legal drinking — the most elusive for a Merton Grange boy was to see a bra strap without pinging it. To not be a dick: this was the great rite of passage that we had yet to pass through. Even if she were single, why would Fran Fisher be interested in a boy like that, like me? Finally, there was the realization that I was experiencing an entirely new emotion, and if it was still too early to call it love, then I was prepared to call it hope. Of course, none of this could be said out loud —who would I tell?—and neither did I have much time to dwell on it, because as I turned back into Thackeray Crescent I saw the red of the brand-new Mini, with my sister Billie's face in the back window, looking up from her book.

Mum had come to visit.

Mum

WHEN I WAS SMALL —when the story still seemed credible—my parents used to tell me how they'd fallen in love. They were students, my mother training to be a nurse, my father halfway through an accountancy course that he had more or less abandoned in order to play saxophone in college bands of variable quality, in this case Goiter, a punk-funk, or funk-punk, five-piece, playing their first and last-ever gig at the student union of Portsmouth Polytechnic. Punk and funk, it seemed, were proving incompatible, but in the moments when she'd not been looking at the floor, my mother had spotted the one band member who'd had the sense to be embarrassed: the saxophonist. She laughed at the satirical faces he pulled behind the lead singer's back and noted, too, that he was capable of playing his instrument, so made a point of digging in next to him at the bar where he stood hunched, wiping madly at his eyeliner with the corner of a beer towel like someone hurriedly removing a disguise. She held him by the arm. "That," she said, "was just . . . *awful*," and he looked at her closely for a moment and laughed. "And that was it," my father used to tell me, "love at first sight," and my mum would groan and roll her eyes and throw a cushion, but still, I loved the story: Mum stood next to Dad at the bar and so I came to be.

There's a photograph of them, taken shortly after that first meeting, with matching cigarettes and leather jackets on a fire escape in the only part of Gosport to resemble the East Village. Short, her black eyes peering through a black fringe, my mother looks ferocious and unstoppable, and Dad stands behind her, cigarette held high as if writing her name in the air above her head, laughing with his ragged teeth; *my God, look at this amazing woman*. All couples should have a photo like this, the sleeve of their imaginary album. They seem invincible, full of fire and hope for their shared future.

Mum left Dad in the spring of 1997, though I suspect that she'd been planning her departure for some time. My father's business — a small chain of record shops — had finally succumbed, and in the miserable winter that had followed the final closure, we'd found ourselves increasingly reliant on her determination and resilience and powers of persuasion. How would we manage without her? Thinking about leaving must have felt like choosing the moment to leap from a runaway train: no sense in staying on board, no way of jumping without pain.

And so she hung on. I remember the brisk, unsentimental energy she brought to clearing out the salvageable remnants of Dad's last shop, boxing up the remaining stock, pulling up the carpet, like the footage of families inspecting the damage after a disastrous flood. I remember, too, the smile she'd summoned up in the carefully phrased presentation, telling us that we would be moving out of the family home. Selling would release some equity, whatever that was, to pay off some debts. The new house, smaller, different but perfectly nice, would give us all a chance to start again. Catch our breath, get back on our feet: it was the language of the boxing ring, and Mum was the coach, dedicated and unshakable as Dad slumped, bruised and beaten, on the stool in the corner.

Late that night, unable to sleep, I came down and found her in the kitchen, going through paperwork. Longing for reassurance, I forced myself to say the word.

"So are we . . . bankrupt?"

I saw her shoulders stiffen. "Where did you hear that?"

"You and Dad talking."

"I wish you wouldn't eavesdrop."

"You were shouting, so . . ."

She'd reached out with her hand over the back of the chair and beckoned me over. "Well, yes, technically. Not us, certainly not you, but Dad, because the business was in his name, but actually—it's not a disaster!" I let her reassurances wash over me. "Bankruptcy's just a legal term, it's a way of settling debts when something fails, not *fails*, ceases to trade. It's a clean slate; it means we don't have people knocking on our door. We just . . . liquidate everything and give everyone their share."

"Their share of what?"

"The assets, whatever we've got left to sell."

I thought of the ripped-up carpet, the shelves, the box of CDs labeled "World Music." I did not hold out much hope for the debtors and yet I knew my father was pathologically honorable about money. He had borrowed heavily to save the business, and as each shop had closed in turn, the necessity of paying back the debt had required further debt on secret credit cards, personal savings transferred to business accounts until there was nowhere left to hide. As a kid, I used to sneak unwanted vegetables off my plate and simply drop them on the floor, and my father's strategy was scarcely more sophisticated. He was the architect of a pyramid scheme in which he was both the scammer and the scammed, and when the whole thing inevitably collapsed he was left standing, stunned by unpaid bills, unpaid rent, unpaid wages. To fail to buy his round of drinks in the pub was a kind of agony to him, and so to not pay his staff . . . Irrespective of the clean slate offered by bankruptcy, the failure had turned him into a criminal, a thief.

Still Mum hung on. "Really, it's an opportunity in disguise. All things considered, it's actually a good thing," which made me wonder, how might we manage if something bad were to happen?

So Thackeray Crescent was a kind of penance, and that's how it felt. With the first heavy rain, great gray rosettes of damp appeared on our bedroom ceilings. The cost-effective storage heaters left us writhing and sweaty at three in the morning, shivering and blue-nosed at four in the afternoon. When we'd been shown the house for the first time, Dad had explained how submariners, crammed together on long tours of duty, overcame claustrophobia by taking just a few possessions, stored away immediately after use and always in the right place. But instead of living a life of efficient minimalism, we were perpetually struggling to find places to put stuff. We'd viewed the house unfurnished, and now the curved walls meant that the furniture, the washing machine and the TV all intruded into the rooms as if advancing on us. Nothing was flush and nothing looked right. One hundred little irritations — cupboard doors that didn't close, a sink too shallow to fill the kettle, a bath too small for Mum to straighten even her short legs. "I just want a flat wall to put a picture on! A corner, a corner I can put a chair in!" She had always possessed the ability to laugh at adversity, huddling in a tent on windswept Exmoor or waiting for a car mechanic on the hard shoulder of a motorway, but now that gift was failing her, and she was slamming doors, kicking walls, throwing shoes: "Why are these here? This is not where we put shoes!" *Das Boot,* Mum called it. No wonder submariners went insane. It wasn't the fault of the house, but even so, I wonder how many otherwise stable families fracture because of the faulty double-glazing, the trauma of underpinning, the little twist of rage that starts each day.

Our parents became strangers to us, abducted and reprogrammed as adversaries. From the ages of, say, twenty-one to sixty-five, when they officially became old, I had always assumed that adults stayed pretty much the same, and parents in particular. Wasn't this the definition of adulthood, an end to change? Wasn't it their job to remain constant? Now my father, known for his amused, baffled mildness, became increasingly angry, an emotion that we'd barely witnessed before now. With too much time on his hands, he became obsessed with "home improvements," struggling to replace the fogged bathroom mirror, the leaky skylights, the collapsing shower rail. He'd screw shelves into the plasterboard walls with the end of a teaspoon, fix the resulting cracks with filler mixed in a cereal bowl, applied with the butter knife, then block the sink with leftover filler, and there'd be more doors slammed, more screaming through the fragile walls.

Mum's response to all this constriction was to straighten up and burst the confines. Seemingly without effort she got a job at the local golf club, helping to coordinate events, weddings, anniversaries, seventieth birthday parties. This was the kind of institution she'd once have dismissed as provincial and square, but she had always been efficient, persuasive and capable of great charm, and the money was far better than anything she could have hoped to earn back on the wards. If you've run the night shift on an overcrowded geriatric unit, she'd told them, then a big Rotary Club dinner could hold no fear. In fact, they were pretty much the same thing! This was her pitch, and it worked, and we got used to her pulling on a pair of heels early on a Saturday morning and hearing the car return in the early hours of Sunday. She began to paint her nails and to iron her blouses in front of the TV. A blouse! The idea of my mum owning such a thing as a blouse or a slip, a pencil skirt, a Filofax, her own email address—the first time I'd heard of such a thing—was bizarre, but something we could live with if it meant less anxiety about the electricity bill. Perhaps we might even get used to Dad's alarming presence at home now, the forced and manic jollity he brought to serving up breakfast, checking our homework, doing the big shop. We were catching our breath, we were getting back on our feet.

But still a deep disquiet lingered, and Billie and I would lie in our bunks, twisting with anxiety as we listened to the voices, alternately snapping, shouting, soothing. "I think Dad's going mad," said Billie

one night. "Mad Dad." And that became our secret code for those
moments when we'd catch him, standing and staring and staring.

Mum hung on. She made new friends, worked longer hours. She
got the praise and the overtime, changed her clothes and her hair, and
Dad would see this and be uncharacteristically mean and sarcastic.
She had always been staunchly and unsentimentally left wing. Now
she wondered, was it possible to get the bride's helicopter to land on
the eighteenth fairway? Now they avoided each other's gaze, except
for the times when my mother answered her mobile phone—a mobile phone!—outside of work hours, at which time they would glare
at each other with barely suppressed fury while she spoke in a voice
he no longer recognized. It wasn't just love fading away. Respect and
understanding were going too, with nothing we could do to stem the
flow, and fear for where this might end began to wrap around and
smother my every waking thought. Just before the Easter of my final
year, I returned from another undistinguished day to a silent home.
I'd presumed the house was empty and so was startled and shouted
out loud when I went to the sofa and found Dad lying there, his face
scoured red, his hands pulled into the sleeves of his jumper.

"Mum's gone, Charlie," he said.

"What, to work?"

"She's met someone else. I'm sorry."

"What are you talking about, Dad?"

"Please, my love, don't make me say it. She's gone. She's gone with
someone else."

"But she'll be back, right? She's coming back?" I had seen my father cry a few times but only at a party or a wedding, a sentimental
reddening of the eye and never this awful grimace. It happened, I'm
sure, but behind closed doors. Now here he was, curled up in a ball as
if protecting himself from blows, and I wish I could say that I instinctively embraced him or tried to offer some comfort. Instead I stood

some distance away, a bystander unqualified to take action and unwilling to get involved, too panicked to do anything but run outside,
scramble back onto my bike and race away.

Billie was turning into the close, returning from school. "What's
wrong, Charlie?"

"Go and see Dad."

Her eyes opened wide. "Why, what's happened? What's happened!"

"Go!" I shouted, glancing back to see that she had broken into a
run. My sister, twelve years old, would know what to do. I pounded
on, out of the estate, around the ring road, to find out if she'd finally
let go.

Best Behavior

THE GOLF CLUB WAS an absurd building, as puffed up and pomp-ous as its members. Whitewashed and crenelated, it would have made a fine location for some Agatha Christie whodunit if it weren't for the 1980s conservatory glued to one side, and on visits with my mother I'd grown to hate the place, the odor of aftershave and gin and tonic, the guffawing from the bar, the piped classics, a loop of "The Blue Danube" that followed you even into the loos, where incomprehensi-ble golf cartoons hung at eye level. I hated how Mum behaved when on the premises, the voice she put on, the ridiculous waistcoat. "Best behavior," she'd say. I was not prone to bad behavior, but those words made me want to snatch a heavy-headed club from one of the bastards in the lobby and set about the bowls of potpourri, the little packets of shortbread, the wing mirrors of the BMWs and Range Rovers in the car park, which I sprayed with gravel now, jumping from my bike and leaving it, wheels spinning, as I hurtled into the lobby.

Excuse me, can I help you? Are you looking for someone? Excuse me, young man! Young man, stop! The receptionist slapped at the bell, *ding-ding-ding,* as I looked left and right and saw Mum ap-proaching from the bar, *clack-clack-clack,* that brisk little pencil-skirt walk, smiling—smiling!—as if I'd arrived to discuss the rates for the firm's Christmas dinner-dance.

"Thank you, Janet, I'll deal with this. Hello, Charlie—"

"Dad says you've left home."

"Shall we go through here?" She had taken me by the elbow and was marching me across the lobby—

"Is it true?"

—like a security guard, as if I'd been caught shoplifting, and now opening doors to conference rooms and offices, looking for somewhere to hide me—

"I left you a letter, Charlie. Did you read the letter, Charlie?"

"No, I came straight here."

"Well, I did ask him to give it to you."

—and finding each room occupied, she smiled her professional smile and crisply closed each door.

"Mum, is it true?" I wrenched my elbow from her grip. "Tell me!"

Her smile faltered. She took my hand and, holding it tightly, touched her forehead against mine for a moment, then looked sharply to left and right then to a door behind us, barging at it with her shoulder and spinning me into a hot muffled cage of a storage cupboard, soundproofed with toilet rolls and hand towels. We stood amidst the mops and buckets.

"Charlie, you can't come here—"

"Is it true, though, are you moving out?"

"For the moment, yes."

"Where to? I don't understand."

"It was all in the letter." She tutted. "I told him to give it to—"

"Just tell me! Please!"

She sighed and, as if deflating, allowed herself to slide down the door, folding her legs beneath her.

"Your dad's not been easy to live with these last years—"

"Really? 'Cause I'd not noticed that—"

"—not easy for any of us. I've done my best, I think, to hold things together, and I do still love him, I love all of you. But . . ." She paused, frowned, licked her lips and then selected the words one by one. "I've made another friend. Here. At work."

"Who?"

"I put this in the letter, I don't know why he didn't give you the letter—"

"Fine. I'll go and get this famous letter . . ." and I began to clamber over her, kicking at buckets, knocking mops to the ground.

"Don't do that, Charlie. Sit down. Sit down! I'll tell you! Here!" She grabbed my hand and pulled me to the floor so that our legs were tangled, jammed up against the bales of toilet roll. "His name is Jonathan."

"He works here?"

"Yes, he runs corporate events."

"Have I met him?"

"No. Billie has, when she's come in to work with me. And no, he's not here today, so don't get any ideas."

"And how long—?"

"Couple of months."

"You've only been here since January!"

"Yes, and since then we've become really good friends."

I gave my best bitter laugh.

"You're not being very mature about this, Charlie."

"*Really good friends.* You sound like you're nine—"

"Okay, *lovers,* then. Is that better?"

"For Christ's sake, Mum—"

"Because I can treat you like a child if you want, if you'd prefer that?"

"No, I just want—"

"—me to explain what's been going on, and that's what I'm trying to do. I don't mind you being angry, I expect you to be angry but I also expect you to be respectful and listen. Okay?" She kicked out at a bucket with her toe. "Christ, I wish I had a cigarette!"

I patted at my pockets.

"And that's not funny either. *Do* you smoke?"

"No!"

"Because if you smoke, I will kill you—"

"I don't. Just tell me."

"I met Jonathan here. He's a widower, two girls, twins. He's a nice man, very nice, and we used to talk a bit. I'd tell him about Dad and he was very understanding, because he'd been a bit down himself, so he knew what that was like, and we were friends and then we were . . . more than friends. Don't look like that. These things happen, Charlie, you'll know one day. Being married—it's not as simple as loving one person all your life—"

"But that's exactly what it is! That's what marriage is meant to be. Look—" I grabbed at her hand, peeling her finger back to show the ring was still there, and she grabbed my hands and squeezed them tight.

"Yes, yes, meant to be, yes, but it's fuzzy, Charlie, it's messy and painful and you can have strong feelings for different people, absolutely sincere and strong. You'll understand when you're older—"

As the phrase left her mouth I could see her try to suck it back, but too late. It enraged me even more than "best behavior," and I kicked out at the door, and she pressed her hand on my knee, placating. "Stop that! Stop! Charlie? Listen, I have no doubt that your dad's the love of my life, and you shouldn't doubt that either. But I'm his nurse now, not his wife or partner, his nurse, and sometimes—sometimes you can really get to hate the people that you're meant to care for, hate them *because* you're meant to care for them—"

"You hate him?"

"No! I don't *hate* him, I love him—didn't you hear me? I put this all so much better in the letter—"

"Just tell me!"

"Oh, Christ! I'm—"

But her voice snagged on something. An oily glint came to her eyes, and she closed them and pressed her fingertips hard into the sockets.

"I'm tired, Charlie. I'm just very, very tired. It doesn't do him any good, my being there, and I can't spend my life looking after him. To you, I know, I'm ancient, but I feel too young to spend my days just . . . stuck."

"So you're leaving."

"For a while, yes, I'm moving out."

"You're running away."

"He doesn't want me there either! He knows about Jonathan, things have been said, it's impossible—" She groaned, exasperated. "I've done everything I can do! Everything, you know that, unless you want more of me and your dad, years and years of us shouting and screaming and hissing at each other in the middle of the night—"

"When I got home, he was curled up in a ball—"

"Oh, Christ—I've not done this lightly, Charlie, it's not for giggles. I'm doing it because I think it's for the best!"

"Best for you, maybe."

"No, for everyone!"

"Cruel to be kind?"

"There's an element of—"

"'Cos it's certainly fucking cruel—"

"And that's enough of that!" she said sharply, then growled and dug her fingers into her hair and pulled as if trying to hoist herself up. "Christ, Charlie, you're not making this easy."

"Did you want me to make it easy?"

"Well, yes, to be honest, yes, I wouldn't mind," she snarled, then exhaled, taking a moment to correct herself. "No. You say exactly what you want to say." She put her hands across her eyes, like a visor. "What do you want to know?"

"You're moving in with—"

"Jonathan. For the time being, yes."

"For how long?"

"Don't know. We'll see."

"And me and Billie are staying with Dad."

"Well . . ." She chewed her lip and looked to the wall and, with some precision and care, spoke. "The current thinking is that Billie will come and live with me and you will stay with Dad."

A moment passed, a held breath, before I could speak again. "Can I come?"

"What?"

"Can I come with you?"

"I don't—"

"With you and Billie."

"Oh, Charlie—"

"I'm serious! Take me."

"I can't!"

"Because I'll go nuts if I stay there."

"Jonathan's got a family, he's got twin girls."

"I don't mind."

"There's no bedroom."

"I'm all right on the sofa."

"Charlie, I need you to stay with your dad!"

"Why me?"

"Because . . . you're the oldest—"

"No, *you're* the oldest!"

"You've always been close to your dad—"

"No, we're not close, you like to think we're close because it's easier for you."

"When you were little, you were close—"

"I'm not little!"

"No, but you can get that back, get close again."

"I'm closer to you. I want to come with you and Billie!" I had tried hard not to panic, to keep fear from my voice, but to my embarrassment, I now found that I was crying—

"Charlie, I'm not emigrating, I'm only going up the road. I'll be around! You'll see Billie at school every day!"

—crying like I was four or five, jagged and breathless. "You won't be there when we wake up, you won't be there nights—"

"You'll be fine, the two of you. Your dad loves being with you—"

"It'll be horrible! I want to be with you!"

She was crying too now, trying to hold me as I tried to push her away. "But what can I do, Charlie? I love you but I'm so unhappy, you have no idea, you think because we're grown-ups—I know I'm being selfish and I know you'll hate me for it now but I've got to try *something*. I've got to do this and see what happens—"

Suddenly she lurched towards me, propelled by someone shoving at the store cupboard door. "Who's in there?" shouted a male voice.

"Greg, go away!" said Mum, struggling to hold the door closed. "Amy? I need a roll of towels for the dispenser!"

"Go. Away!"

"You got someone in there with you? Saucy wench—"

She slapped the door hard with the flat of her hand and said, "Greg, I beg you, please, just . . . fuck off!" then mouthed to me, "Sorry!"

We waited for a moment, tangled on the floor as if the small room were a lift that had plunged to the basement. I couldn't quite tell which limb was mine, which my mother's, but somewhere in the mess she found my hand, squeezed the fingertips and tried to smile. We stumbled to our feet. Rolls of fluff like fat caterpillars clung to her pencil skirt and she began swatting at them with the back of her hand. "Christ, look at me. How's my—?" She indicated her eyes.

"Panda," I said, and she grabbed a whole toilet roll from the catering pack and blotted at one eye, then the other.

"I'll get money to you, and you can phone anytime, and I'll call in once a week or so, check that you're surviving. Not just surviving, I mean check that you're happy, you're eating." She tossed the roll like a netball onto the top of the metal shelving. "I really don't think it'll be that different. It might even be better for you. Boys together! You can do your schoolwork, revise in peace. Or I'll help you! The timing's horrible, I know, but at least you won't be living on a battlefield."

"I'll be living in a mental hospi—"

"Stop that!" she snapped. "Stop it now!" and, turning quickly from me, she reached high for a cylinder of toweling and, brisk now, as if I'd failed the interview, she tucked the drum under her arm.

"You're old enough for all this now, Charlie." She held the door open. "And if you're not—well. Time to grow up."

Corners

IN THE DAYS IMMEDIATELY after their departure, I had a vision, clear and inevitable, of our domestic future: the house as cave, animal bones scattered on the floor like the opening of *2001*, my father and me communicating in grunts and howls. It would require effort on my part if we were to avoid this descent into total degradation, and an unexpected desire for order kicked in. Quickly, I learned what an airing cupboard did, how a thermostat worked, how to restart the pilot light on a boiler. The first batch of pale pink school shirts taught me the importance of separating the colors from the whites; the growing pile of unopened post, still largely in my mother's name, taught me how to forge her signature.

I wish I could say that I learned how to cook. Rather, I learned how to order food. A varied and balanced diet meant ensuring the strict rotation of Indian, Chinese and Italian, meaning pizza, which we ordered on a three-day cycle, the fourth day given over to "leftover day," a sort of reheated global buffet. I knew the phone numbers by heart, but even the pleasures of cheap, bad food were soon beyond our means, and so the great world cuisines were supplemented with something called Dad's Pasta Bol, a great saucepan of undercooked spaghetti, stuck together in sections like the mighty cables on a suspension bridge, stirred in the saucepan with an Oxo cube and half a tube of tomato puree or sometimes, very late at night, a teaspoon of curry paste, which transformed it into Dad's Pasta Madras. There were, I'm sure, Elizabethan sailors who ate healthier, more balanced diets, and though we were never hungry—we forced food into our mouths even before our plates hit our laps, as if it were a competition —we soon developed the coated tongue and greasy, sallow complexion of those who pass off pesto as a vegetable. We were slipping into a life that was unhealthy in every respect, but I won't deny there was a squalid pleasure in it too. "Use a plate," Dad would say if he found me eating cold curry from the foil container, "we're not cavemen." Not yet, but we weren't far off.

Occasionally we would rebel against this life, walk the extra mile to the superstore and throw lentils, apples, onions, celery, in amongst the white sliced loaf and economy meat. We'd stride home, full of plans for hearty soups, stews with barley, food we'd seen made on TV: tagines, paellas, risottos. Dad would put on some mad helter-skelter blast by Gene Krupa or Buddy Rich. "Let's get this place shipshape," he'd say, just as he used to when I was small and Mum was due home, and there'd be the same sense of collaboration and defiance as we wiped out the fruit bowl and loaded it up with pears, peaches, kiwis and pineapples. The last few cigarettes would go in the bin—I'd fish them out later—and the ashtrays were rinsed and stashed on the top shelf.

"We do all right, don't we?" Dad would say. "Boys together. We manage," and he'd put another record on. Music was as clear and reliable an indication of Dad's mood as the temperature on a thermometer. I'd be obliged to listen—no, *really* listen, sitting up straight, no newspaper, no distraction—to *A Love Supreme* or *The Amazing Bud Powell,* both sides, because "you wouldn't watch half a great film." He'd stand at the stereo, bopping his head, raising a finger—"Listen to this, here it comes!"—and watching my face to see if I'd heard it too. And sometimes, very occasionally, as if feeling the tug of a tidal current, I'd almost, almost be carried along. Mostly, though, it was an exercise in indulgence, straining to love something that he loved too. "It's really good!" I'd say, but I couldn't tell good from bad, could only hear the generic cymbal-wash that I thought of, secretly, as Pink Panther music.

But Dad's optimism was a precarious state, and I soon learned that such highs were temporary and paid for with an equivalent low. Gloom rolled back in like a fog, the music replaced by great slabs of TV, watched without engagement or enjoyment. The pears would remain as hard as stones while the peaches turned to pulp. Kiwis would fizz and burst, the pineapples shrivel, an unnamable sticky black liquid pooling in the bottom of the bowl. My father would empty it into the bin, ashamed once more of another failed initiative to restore some decency to how we lived, how we moved through the world. Then he'd go out for cigarettes.

As for Mum, I still hated her for leaving us, but there was something theoretical about the hatred now, as if it was something that, like a marriage, had to be worked on and maintained. More instinctive was the stab of betrayal that felt sharper every time I saw her, the humiliation of not being picked for her team.

But I also felt, I think, a certain pride in being her representative in the house. I'd never been a prefect, but perhaps I might fulfill the role at home, which was why I liked to know that she was coming, so that I could create the impression of wholesome orderliness, plump the cushions, empty the fridge of foil containers, make sure Dad was either presentable and fully dressed or, if that was not achievable on that day, then fully absent. Given notice, her visits had the quality of an inspection. I'd watch her eyes take it all in. No plates in the sink, good; clean tea towels, clean washing snapping on the line, nice to see. Her guilt was essential to me; I wanted to stoke it like a furnace because I wanted her back. But I did not want her back because we were incapable. Even while I strained to hate her, it seemed important that she should be proud of me.

On the day I met Fran Fisher, Mum was already in the kitchen, load-
ing the shelves with groceries. I watched her, standing in the open
doorway, as she used her fingernails to lift a moldy crust from the
bread bin and drop it into a bin bag. Somewhere in the house a fat
bluebottle patted its head against a window in the afternoon light,
and she muttered to herself as she unpacked, a private commentary
of minor criticisms and complaints.

"Hello," I said.

She glanced over her shoulder. "Where have you been?"

None of your business. Our conversation carried a commentary
as easily read as the subtitles on a foreign film. "Just out. Went for a
bike ride."

"Dad's out too?"

"Looks like it." *Thank God he's not here.*

"Any idea where?"

"Don't know." *Some mad walk.*

"Is he sleeping much?"

"I think so." *Not at night. The sofa, in the afternoons. Your fault.*

"Seeing people?"

"Only me." *Also your fault.*

"Looking after himself?"

"Same as always." *He doesn't shave and drinks too much; he wears
the same clothes for days. Your fault.*

"Has he mentioned the possibility of looking for work?"

"He has, yeah."

This was only partly true. On days when our joint presence in the
house became unbearable, Dad would grab pens and paper and turn
the TV over to the Situations Vacant pages of Ceefax. Could either of
us be a gas fitter? Insurance salesman? Diver on an oil rig? We contemplated new professions in the same way that children do: train driver,
cowboy, astronaut, could we fit our faces to the role? The answer was
invariably no and the exercise was both dispiriting and deeply uncom-

fortable. Looking for work was not something father and son should do together, the discomfort greater even than when watching sex scenes, and soon we'd snap back to the program, change the subject, mention it no more. I changed the subject now.

"How's *Jonathan?*" Jonathan is a perfectly nice name, hard to say with derision.

"All good, thank you for asking," said Mum levelly, slamming the cupboard door closed with the flat of her hand, then doing so again and again until it finally remained shut. *Bangbangbang.* She rested for a moment, both hands on the counter. "You know the best thing about living there? No jazz and all those lovely *corners!*"

"Well, as long as you're happy, Mum," I said, but I knew that if she'd given the word, I'd have run upstairs and packed a bag in a heartbeat. Perhaps she knew this too, because now she changed the subject.

"What are you doing with the summer? In general, I mean."

"Riding my bike. Reading."

"Reading? You were never much of a reader."

"Well. I am now."

"All those years we went on at you to read . . ."

"Well, maybe that was the problem, you going on at me."

"Hm. Yes, I see now that it was my fault. At least you're outdoors. Are you spending time with other people?"

I've just met this amazing girl; could I ever have said that? I had heard tell that there were people who could talk openly and honestly with their parents, in conversations that were not simply long volleys of sarcasm and self-righteousness. But honestly, who were these freaks? Even if I'd found the words, it was impossible now. We could hear my father's voice outside, artificially bright and loud. "Hey, Billie! What are you doing here?!"

Bracing herself, my mother turned back to the cupboards. "Don't fight," I whispered, but Dad was leaning in the doorway, his face set into a look of proud defiance that he couldn't quite pull off.

"Still here, are you?" said Dad.

"No, Brian, I left fifteen minutes ago."

"I only came back because I thought you'd be gone."

"Did you not see my car in front of the house? It's not a big car, but still, I thought you'd notice it."

"What are you taking this time?"

"Actually, I was *bringing* stuff — food, something not served in a foil tray. I can always take it back."

"Please, do."

"It's for Charlie, mainly —"

"Charlie's fine. We both are, thank you."

Without looking away from the cupboard, she held above her head an open jar of raspberry jam, tufts of white mold like candy floss sprouting from its neck. She tossed the jar into the sink with a clatter. I already knew how this one ended, the volume increasing then snapping off with the slam of the door, and so I left and walked out to Mum's car, where Billie sat, head down, reading with her hand pressed to her mouth like a gag. The day was still hot but the window was up, so I had to rap twice with my knuckle, and this alone saddened me more than anything else that had happened that day. Were we close? When we lived together we'd nipped and provoked each other in the expected ways, but in the dark days of our parents' transformation the bickering had been exchanged for a weary solidarity, whispering between bunks like squaddies under the command of drunk and incompetent officers. Now the alliance had been broken, and even the most inane domestic conversation seemed loaded. Happiness in her new home would be a betrayal, unhappiness just one more thing to be angry about.

Billie waited for the window to go all the way down. "All right?"

"Yep."

"They arguing?"

"Just starting now," I said and looked at my watch as if the event was scheduled.

"How's it here?"

"Same as before. How is it over there?"

"Bizarre."

"How are '*the twins*'?" Casting Billie in the role of Cinderella was the sole small amusement that we could find in her new situation.

"The twins? They're very *sporty*. You open a cupboard and there's this rain of footballs and hockey sticks and badminton nets. They keep trying to get me *involved,* like I'm this sickly orphan and they're trying to make me feel at home, so we can be *pals* or something, bond over lacrosse. They're all 'Billie, come out and play *lacrosse* with us!' And I'm all 'What is this, *school?* I don't do games unless it's on the timetable.' Every time I look up, they're in their *sports* bras, warming up or down or whatever. Their dad's the same, can't stop chucking stuff. 'Billie! Catch!' 'No—just *pass it to me.*' When he's not chucking stuff at people, they sit and watch cricket, days and days of it."

"What, Mum too?"

"Yeah, though you can tell she's glazing over after three minutes. She calls it *making an effort,* I call it *collaboration.* She even played *golf.* Talk about crossing to the dark side. 'While we're guests here, it's important that we *make an effort.*' I mean, fuckin' hell—golf!" Billie's swearing was an innovation, self-conscious and furtive. Like a toddler pretending to smoke, it seemed wrong to me and, awkwardly, we both looked towards the house.

"Want to come in?"

"Nah. Leave them to it. Dad still Mad Dad?"

Opening the car door, I slipped into the back seat furtively, like an informer. "He's all right mostly, then he goes a bit manic, stays up late and drinks, which he's not meant to do on his pills. Some days I don't see him at all." From inside the house, we heard Mum's raised voice, the clatter of cupboards. "I hate it here. I mean I hated it before, but I *really* hate it now."

Billie reached back and patted my hand. "Be *strong*, my brother," she said in a portentous, *Star Wars* voice. We both laughed, and I tried something for the first time. "Miss you."

"Oh, puh-lease," she said, and then, "You too."

But now my mother was out of the house, slamming the door, my father opening it immediately so that he might slam it himself later. For now, he would stand in the doorway, arms crossed, a rancher protecting his land. I jumped from the car, slammed that door too — would we ever close a door gently again? — and now Mum was in stunt-driver mode, spinning the wheels, over-revving as she reversed the car and then drove away.

I glimpsed Billie, sticking out her chin and screwing her index finger into her temple, and I raised my hand and went back inside, back to my own team.

The Name Game

FOR THE FIRST TIME in weeks, I set my alarm.

But for some reason sleep escaped me (*shape of nose, shade of blue, great curve of, precise constellation*), and in the restless hours I made a plan: I would turn up at nine thirty, join in with whatever the hell they did up there, approach Fran casually at tea break, lunchtime at the latest, ask for her number, then, once I had it in my hand, run like Indiana Jones runs from that boulder.

I practiced what I might say — *great to talk to you yesterday, how's the ankle, listen, hey, I wondered* . . . I may even have muttered the words out loud, experimenting with *can we get coffee?*, trying to shed the American drawl. *Get coffee? Go for coffee? Have coffee? Cup of coffee?* If "coffee" was going to cause this much angst, perhaps I should just ask her for tea, but *come for tea* was something people in bonnets said. Tea was insipid and sexless, and coffee was the darker, more intoxicating beverage. They did cafetières at the Cottage Loaf Tea Rooms, and I imagined Fran, chin in hand, toying with a sugar cube as I told some story, then tossing her head with sudden laughter while I pushed down the plunger like a detonator. *Hey, shall we go on somewhere else, get a proper drink?*

But where would we go? We certainly couldn't come here, with the children's bunk beds and the resident nervous breakdown on our sofa, and Fran Fisher was not the kind of girl you took to the swings in Dog Shit Park, with or without cider. Was it ungentlemanly to offer her cider? An imported lager perhaps, something posh, not a can? Should I put some vodka into a screw-top bottle? Tea or coffee, lager or vodka, bottle or can? I fell asleep at six and woke to the alarm at eight, got out of bed and showered, straining not to wake Dad, willing the water to fall quietly, then shaved with the care of a surgeon. I reached for the Lynx, the variety called Aztec ("So this is what wiped them out," Dad would say, sniffing the air), and sprayed the best part of a can, enough to give each armpit a coat as thick as the icing on a wedding cake. It crackled as I lowered my arm.

Wedging my feet beneath the edge of the bunk bed prison-style, I resolved to do fifty sit-ups in the hope of instant results, and managed twenty, scuffing my head on the skirting board with each one. I folded two slices of toast into my mouth and wrote a hasty note, saying that I'd be gone all day but with no further explanation—how could I explain?—then mounted my bike and retraced my journey out of Thackeray Crescent, Forster then Kipling Road, down Woolf then Gaskell, Brontë and then Thomas Hardy Avenue, around the ring road and over the roar of the rush-hour motorway. On the outskirts, a municipal white sign marked the town's limits, along with its frank motto, "A Good Town" (in Latin, *Bonum Oppidum*), which was about as much as they could plausibly get away with.

I cycled on silent roads, past the PVC greenhouses and through the wheat fields, the direction less certain now. I turned too early, retraced my route, paused opposite a concrete bus shelter, a lane shaded with low branches. I crossed the road and began to climb. The day was already hot, the sun slicing through the canopy of trees. Ascending the lane, panting and gasping, I saw the footpath but wanted to make a more official entrance and so continued to climb until I saw a small mock-Tudor gatehouse. Beyond two five-bar gates, a driveway curved through woodland, screening the house from the lane. "Fawley Manor," read the plaque. I stood on the pedals but the gravel shifted beneath the wheels and I gave up and walked. The driveway followed the edge of a wood, then widened, opening out onto a lawn between ancient yews.

It was a typical home-counties mansion, a greatest-hits medley from the last thousand years of architecture — columns and porticoes, diamond-leaded double-glazing, 1930s pebble-dash between stick-on Tudor beams, a satellite dish sprouting from the ivy. If I'd been more knowledgeable, I might have felt less impressed, but I only saw its size, its isolation and apparent age. I'd never felt more like a trespasser, fully expecting the crunch of the gravel to alert the hounds. Looking for somewhere to leave my bike, I took in the ornamental goldfish pond, abandoned croquet mallets, a dovecote, all this grandeur marred only by a decrepit Transit van with two masks above a flourished ribbon painted on its flank, both masks laughing above the words "Full Fathom Five Theatre Cooperative." Out of the rear doors tumbled a figure dragging two large netted sacks. I froze, but Ivor saw me and immediately bounded over, a sack on each shoulder.

"Hulloooo. It's our mystery man from yesterday! I knew it, I knew you'd be *compelled* to return. Just dump your bike there, it's perfectly safe, and take one of these, will you?" The string sack was packed with foam footballs, beanbags, juggling pins and, alarmingly, assorted hats. "Hate to be a wanker, but I've forgotten your name."

"Charlie."

"Knew it was something like that. Charlie or Charles? Not a Chuck, are you? You don't seem the Chuck type."

"Charlie."

"Okay, Charlie, let's go!" He showed the way with a flap of his hair. "Have you done a lot of theatre?"

"No, this is . . . I'm just . . . It's a new thing for me. I'm just trying it out."

"Fresh meat! Well, you'll *love* it, I know you will. Come, join us!"

We headed towards a sound, a slow, rhythmic slapping and clapping, crossing the courtyard and coming out onto the wide, green expanse, bracketed by what I suppose must have been the east and west wings.

"The Great Lawn, where we're creating our fair Verona. Hard to believe, I know, but you wait and see—and here they are!"

The company sat in a large circle, their legs crossed, slapping their thighs and clapping their hands in a solid 4/4, the rhythm stumbling as I approached. In quick succession I saw Lucy Tran scowl and whisper to Colin Smart, linchpin of Merton Grange's shadowy Drama Club, who sat open-mouthed with surprise. I saw Helen Beavis grinning and shaking her head, and there in profile, laughing with some boy, was Frances Fisher. She smiled brightly, mouthed, "You came!" or maybe "Hooray!," but I looked away. This would be my policy: aloof, blasé, just a guy who feels like some Theatre Sports, that's all.

"Okay, quiet everyone, quiet down. Eyes on me! Eyes! I want to see all those eyes, people!" Fingers in a V, Ivor pointed to his eyes. "Okay, I'm pleased to say we have a late addition to the company. "Everyone say hellooo to Charlie, Charlie . . ."

"Lewis."

"Hello, Charlie Lewis!" they chorused, and, head down, I raised one hand and squeezed between strangers in the circle.

"We don't know who Charlie's going to be playing as yet; we're going to talk about that later. For now, we're going to do some exercises, yes? Yes?"

"Yes!"

"Then this afternoon, Alina is going to talk to us about movement!"

Alina planted her hands on her knees and set her elbows at ninety degrees. "We're going to talk about how we carry ourselves, about how we hold ourselves, independently and in relation to each other, how we breathe, how we move through this world, present and alive, responding naturally and spontaneously to others. Because we don't just talk to each other with words, do we? We can say something without opening our mouths. We communicate with our bodies, our faces, and even when we don't move—" She froze, and in a whisper, "We. Still. Move."

Under normal circumstances, I'd have found someone to scoff with, but scanning the circle I saw earnest, spellbound faces. Only Lucy Tran met my eye, glaring at me with telekinetic force, talking without words. You do not belong here, she seemed to say, you are behind enemy lines in a stolen uniform, and you will be found out. If I sprinted back to my bike, I could be away in thirty, perhaps twenty seconds, but turning back, I caught a look from Fran. She smiled and for a moment I thought I saw her cross her eyes. I laughed and the next thing I knew we were all on our feet, shaking all the tension from our hands—shake, shake, shake, shake it out—and then the beanbags really began to fly.

We played Catchy-Come-Catch and the Parrot Game. We played Follow My Nose and Scuttlefish and Fruit Bowl. We played Anyone Who? and Orange Orang-utan and Zip, Zap, Zop and Keeper of the Keys, then Chase the Chain and Panic Attack, That's Not My Hat and Hello Little Doggy, and while the others laughed and joked and threw themselves around, I strived for an air of detachment, like the older brother at a children's birthday party. A phone number was all I wanted. I even had a pen in my pocket, and every now and then it poked me in the groin to remind me. A phone number, and I'd trouble these people no more.

But it's hard to remain cool through a game of Yes, No, Banana, and all too soon we were shaking it out again, shake, shake, shake, and then getting into pairs and pretending to be mirrors. I glanced over to see Fran pairing up with Colin Smart, the palms of their hands pressed together, while in my own mirror I found a middle-aged man, large, red-nosed and rosy-cheeked like the life-size jolly butcher outside the local shop. "Hello, I'm Keith. You're the mirror." He hoisted and shook his tracksuit bottoms to settle the contents as the exercise began. "I'm playing Friar Laurence," he whispered from the side of his mouth, placing one finger, then another on his nose. I did the same. "Because of this, probably . . ." He placed one hand on his head, which was bald but with a fringe of hair, the tonsure of a movie monk. I copied. "Been drafted in from the Lakeside Players. You seen any Lakeside shows? *Fiddler on the Roof? Witness for the Prosecution*?" He let his jaw hang slack and tapped a rhythm on his cheeks, and I did the same. "Not sure what I think of all this touchy-feely stuff. At Lakeside, we'd have blocked the first three acts by now. But you've got to go with it." Our noses were touching now and I could smell the coffee on his breath. "Got to keep an open mind, haven't you?"

"No talking, please! If you talk, your mirror has to talk!"

Keith slapped his cheeks, tugged his ears, put his fingers up his nose, and I thought, *why can't my reflection just stand still? What if she sees me?*

"Okay, get into different pairs, please!"

But she didn't see me, or even glance my way, and instead I was thrown into the next act of enforced intimacy, this time with a boy called Alex: black, very tall, skinny, with the world-weary sophistication and maturity of the sixth-former. This exercise was sculptor and model. Alex looked me up and down.

"I think, Charlie," he said, "we're going to get the best results here if I pose you."

"Okay."

"Don't resist me."

"Sorry."

"You're resisting, you've got to bend and stay there."

"I'm trying!"

"You're pushing back."

"Not on purpose. I'm trying not to —"

"My God, the tension in your neck . . ."

"Sorry."

". . . like knotted rope." He probed with his thumbs.

"Ow!"

"Am I making you tense?"

"No."

"Then relax!"

"I've just not done a lot of this kind of thing."

"No, I got that," he said, pinching my calves.

"Maybe I could be one of those mannequins that just . . . lies on the floor."

"And where's the fun in that? Besides, I'm the sculptor here. Let it go! Do as I say!"

"Okay," said Ivor, clapping his hands. "Sculptors, let's see your work! Alex and Charlie first."

They gathered round. I was Eros, tottering on one leg, bow and arrow in hand and able, from the corner of my eye, to see Fran and Helen Beavis both holding their chins, nodding, judging.

"Ten minutes, everyone! Ten minutes, please!"

In the courtyard, the company gathered round the tea urn, laughing and joking. In my imagined version of the day, I might have strolled across, said hello and folded into the group, but self-confidence was not a switch that could be thrown, and in reality the journey seemed too treacherous and fraught, the distance immense. Perhaps I'd be admitted, perhaps I'd find myself ricocheting off the edge, spinning out into the void. Best to stand here, eyes fixed on the plastic cup of water in my hand.

Standing still brought danger too, and so I began to stroll around the edge of the courtyard with my cup, taking in the architecture like a tourist circling a cathedral. In my peripheral vision, I saw someone break off from the group and approach at speed, the older woman who had tutted at me the day before. Now her hand was on my forearm as she grinned widely and alarmingly with neat, white teeth that looked younger than the mouth they occupied, bright, wide eyes and lines like the cracks in an oil painting, the ravages of deep tans and yacht excursions. "Hello, mystery man," she whispered, her voice low and smoky. She must have been seventy, quite tiny, her white hair cropped and brushed forward, a white, long-sleeved leotard visible under some sort of airy white muslin smock, like the ghost of a yoga instructor. "When it comes to the morning biscuits, it's dog eat dog, I'm afraid. You have to be quick."

"I'm all right, thank you."

"Well, you look terribly moody and charismatic, standing all alone, like someone from Chekhov. I'm sure that's your intention, but wouldn't you rather join in?"

"No, I was just looking at the—" I indicated a window, a drain-pipe.

"The house. Yes, it's a bit of a Frankenstein's monster. The main part's Jacobean, but there's all this other stuff just . . . glued on."

"I've seen it from town. I always thought it was a mental home or something."

She laughed. "Well, I suppose it is, in a way. You see, we live here."

"Oh. I'm sorry."

"It's quite all right, you're not to know. I'm Polly, that's my husband over there, Bernard." A tall man, military in his bearing, was pouring water into the tea urn from a plastic bucket. "Would you like the tour?" No one had ever declined the tour, and so she looped her arm through mine. "We've lived here all our lives, though it's just the two of us now. Without the children, it started to feel rather *big*, which is why it's *so* lovely to see all you young people here. Ivor's our nephew. This is our second year. We did the *Dream* last year, did you see it? When we heard that he was setting up his little company, we thought—why not! There's only one condition, I said, I demand a role! I used to act when I was younger, you see. Ivor went quite pale,

I think he thought I might ask for Titania, but no, I was Hippolyta —very dreary—but this year I'm the Nurse. It's the part I was *born* to play. I'm doing her east London: '*Even aw odd, ov awl days in da year, com Lammas Eve shall shee bee foureen.*' I toyed with doing it Glaswegian, but that's a terribly hard accent—even some Glaswegians can't quite pull it off—so for the moment at least am doin it loik vis. Of course Ivor and Alina have got some *very* esoteric plans for the production. 'Concepts'—is that the word? I'm sure it's going to be set in deep space or a Venezuelan bus depot or something and I do worry that there's going to be an excess of *movement*. Not just normal walking, the other kind. I have a particular distrust of mime, because why mime a jug when you've got a cupboard full of the things? My main hope is that we won't cut the text, because what is Shakespeare if he's not *the language?*"

We agreed, Shakespeare *was* the language. She was, she said, "a Shakespeare nut." Apart from suggesting that he was the first rapper, there was little I could add, and no need because Polly barely paused for breath as we toured the orangery, the rose garden, the rockery and something called the grotto, a hollow concrete sandcastle the size of a family car, embedded patchily with seashells. In her low, cracked voice, she asked: Do you have a dream Shakespearean role? Where did you go to school? None of the answers were in my favor, but I did notice that my own voice had become that of a nice young man, polite and well spoken, with no hint of irritation as my chances of getting the phone number slipped away. By the time the tour was completed, Fran was in conversation with a handsome, shaggy-haired boy, their heads too close together, his hand on her shoulder . . .

"Romeo and Juliet," sighed Polly. "Don't they look a picture? D'you think they'll fall deeply in love in real life? I believe that's the tradition, at least for the length of the production. Method and all that."

"Right, everyone!" shouted Ivor, juggling. "Back to work!"

Games with balls, games with bamboo sticks, games with blind-

folds and handkerchiefs and hats. We climbed a cliff face on the floor
and curled like dried leaves on a bonfire, clambered on each other's sweaty backs and molded our partners' faces like clay with our
grubby fingers, and all the time I wrestled with the paradox of how to
do these things and not do them at the same time. Then games with
language, stories built one word at a time:

Once—
Upon—
The—
Ocean—
There—
Tangoed—
Twelve—
Kumquats!

And it was maddening, the way each time we were approaching
something sensible and coherent, someone would throw in something
mad and nonsensical and send it off into idiocy:

I—
Tickle—
Everybody—
Who—
Smells—
Soporifically—
Of—
Wombats!

And they'd be off in hysterics again. Artichoke—Telephone—
Shampoo! Dromedary—Ladder—Bin! God, these people loved this
stuff, and it confirmed something that I'd long suspected: that within
a theatrical environment, people really will laugh at any old crap.

"Okay, everyone, shake it out! Shake, shake, shake! Lunchtime!"
This time I would not fail. I timed my walk with care, hand on the

pen in my pocket. In the courtyard, Fran stood by herself at the table, but—

"Charles Lewis, why *are* you here?" Helen Beavis held me by the elbow. "As if I didn't know. Christ, you're predictable."

"I don't know what you're talking about."

"Sniffing around that perfectly nice girl."

"Actually, it's nothing to do with her, Helen."

"Ha! Yeah, you're here because of your interest in *Theatre Sports!*"

"So what are *you* doing here?"

"I'm doing the set! Production *design*. I did it last year, it was fun. I'm not ashamed, I'm interested, I'm nurturing my skills. What I'm *not* doing, Lewis, is wasting everyone's time."

"Well, maybe you've got me wrong."

"I don't get people wrong."

"Why can't I be interested?"

"In Shakespeare? Ha!"

"Why not? It's better than sitting at home all day. Let's . . . let's see what happens."

"Fine," she said and placed both hands on my shoulders. "But if you're going to do it, Lewis, you've got to do it properly. It's no good sitting out and sneering, you're not with the boys now. You've got to *commit!*"

Romeo

SOMEWHERE BETWEEN THE COURTYARD and the Great Lawn, Fran had disappeared. Short of hiding in the woods, I had no option but to join the cast, lolling in the sun while Romeo held forth on the demands of playing the eponymous role, his handsome head resting on his meaty arm. The eponymous role, he noted, wasn't always the *best* role, and yet it was the eponymous role that always came his way, and this was his curse, always to be eponymous, using the word so frequently and with such emphasis that I began to wonder if there was someone in the play called Eponymous. *Behold, here comes the Duke Eponymous . . .*

"I mean, look at *Othello!*" he said.

Alex, the skinny black kid who'd sculpted me, laughed. "Miles, I would *love* to see your Othello."

"Hey, it's a great part. As a white actor, I would refuse to play it—"

"That's very gracious of you—"

"—but Iago's a better role. Like in this play, it's my name in the title, but I wonder if I'm naturally more of a Mercutio."

And Alex laughed again. "Oh, you mean *my* role? The role in which *I* have been cast?"

"And Alex, mate, you'll be amazing. But with the eponymous role, there's such a weight of expectation, like it's all about *me*."

I watched him resentfully. He was handsome, I suppose, with the kind of hearty, old-fashioned good looks you might find in an old

B-movie, fighting a stop-motion dinosaur. "Handsome and he knows it" is the phrase my mum would use, and, as if hearing this, the boy turned to me, pointing in lieu of my name. "What's the better part, Romeo or Mercutio?"

I meant to shrug, but twitched. "Who are you playing?" he said.

"Me? Don't know yet."

"What school d'you go to?"

"Merton Grange," I said, and Romeo nodded, as if this somehow provided an answer.

"Same school as us," said Colin Smart, who had been hugging his knees and gazing at the boy throughout.

"Bit of a first for Charlie," said Lucy Tran, nastily. "Not really famous for his *acting* at Merton Grange."

"I'm Miles," said Romeo. "I'm at Hadley Heath, like our George over there."

Miles indicated a hunched boy sitting a little way off, eating a banana and reading an old Penguin copy of *Madame Bovary* in the merciful shade of a wall.

"Hm?" The boy looked up through aviator frames, the lenses as thick as aquarium glass. He wore what looked like a white school shirt underneath an unnecessary jumper, his hair a cap of glossy black like a Beatles wig, his skin inflamed, the color of raspberry juice around his mouth and nose.

"George's part of my crew, aren't you, Georgie?" barked Miles.

The pimpled boy shook his head. "No, Miles, I'm not part of your *crew*," then, returning to his novel, "you absolute simpleton."

Miles gave a hearty Sir Lancelot laugh then lunged at him, holding George's chest down with one hand, mashing the banana in George's fist with the other. Five miles from town, in its own high-walled compound, Hadley Heath was the kind of private school whose name is prefixed with the word "minor." With good reason, the students tended to avoid the town center, and like snow leopards, it was almost unheard of to observe their behavior close up. We sat and watched in awkward silence until—

"Hey, Miles," said Alex, speaking up. "Miles, maybe stop that?"

Miles rolled away, wiping his hand on the grass. "We've got a really strong drama department at Hadley Heath."

"Why are you such an arsehole, Parish?" muttered George.

"Amazing studio space, really versatile, we do a lot of stuff in the round, you're practically in the audience's *lap*. I've played Pal Joey in *Pal Joey* there, Arturo Ui in *Arturo Ui*, Cyrano in *Cyrano*—"

"Headline in the student paper: 'Cyrano Ham.'"

"Don't provoke me, George! We just did *Murder in the Cathedral*—"

"Miles played the Cathedral," said George.

"*Actually*, I was Thomas à Becket, which is quite a marathon. Okay, it's not the Dane, which is the role I really want to play, but it's pretty substantial."

"Which Dane's that, Parish?" said George, still pulling banana from his hair. "The *eponymous* Dane?"

"Don't make me come back there, George, you little squit."

"You know you don't have to keep saying 'eponymous.' You could say 'titular.' 'I was the *titular* role.'"

"It's just such a fucking responsibility, you know, carrying the show?"

"Except there is this other character called Juliet," said Alex. "She's quite important too."

"Hm," said Miles, skeptically.

"What's your favorite Shakespeare soliloquy, Miles?" said Lucy, reverently, and I saw Helen and Alex roll their eyes.

"You know a funny thing?" said Miles, rubbing his chin, actually rubbing it. "You won't find any of my favorite Shakespeare in a play. Because"—the punch line—"it's actually a sonnet!"

"Fuck me," murmured Helen.

"Lucy," mumbled George, "do you have any *idea* of the monster you've unleashed?"

"My mistress' eyes," said Miles, turning his face to the sky, "are nothing like the sun!" and I lay back on the lawn and pinched my own eyes shut, my lips already gummed together from silence and ignorance. If this creativity business was meant to make us more free and confident, then why had I never felt so constricted and self-conscious? Alina had said something about learning how to move through this world, responding naturally to others, and I'd snapped to attention; to a boy who could not walk across a crowded space or share a sofa with a parent or stand next to a girl he liked without losing the power of speech, this was a talent worth possessing. But I wouldn't acquire it by molding a stranger's face or pretending that my bones were disappearing one by one or by listening to Shakespeare burble out of some confident, arty bastard who knew poetry off by heart. I just wanted to know what to do with my hands, that's all. Where do I put my hands?

If my mission was doomed, there now seemed something dishonest and dishonorable about it too. I was taking part in an initiation rite for an organization that I had no wish to join, and which did not need me as a member. Helen was right: it wasn't fair to waste their time. I would wait until the end of the day out of politeness, then leave without the telephone number. The picture of Fran would fade, the feeling too, like recovering from a mild cold. Or perhaps I'd go insane; I'd find out soon enough.

Cross-legged on the ground, Miles was now telling sad stories of the death of kings, and I listened with the sun on my face. If I couldn't quote Shakespeare, at least I could tan.

I felt the coolness of a shadow on my face. "Charlie, could we have a word?" I'd fallen asleep. The others had long gone, and now Alina and Ivor crouched over me like detectives over a body on the beach.

"Sure," I said and, dizzy, stood between them, sweat chilling on my back as they escorted me to the house. They'd seen my papers and knew that they were false, and now I would be taken out to the rockery and shot.

"Hey, great work today," said Ivor, and I wondered what part had been great. Being a leaf, drying in the sun? Making myself as small as can be?

"We wanted you to take a look at this," said Alina, holding out a ring-bound document. "It's the text that we're using. You know the play of course."

I shook my head and nodded at the same time.

"Well, Monday's our read-through. Nothing to worry about, we're not looking for a polished performance—"

"—but we'd love you to take a look at a guy called Sampson," said Ivor. "He's one of the Capulet gang."

"He is a bit of a jack-the-lad," said Alina. "Great fun, though."

"Lots of *bawdy* jokes."

"And he practically opens the play."

"Just give it a go."

"No pressure."

Here was my chance: *thank you, but I'm not coming back, it's not for me.* But Ivor looked so hopeful and Alina looked at me so intently that, not for the last time, I missed my cue. I nodded—sure, okay— and the rest of the afternoon was spent pretending to be a steam-powered machine.

By the end of the day I was exhausted, full of unexpected aches, dusty from all that scuttling and crawling, and still no nearer to the magic phone number, or even the briefest of exchanges. Fran must have been avoiding me, and while the rest of the cast stood around and hugged each other, I gathered my possessions and the last of my pride.

"Have a great weekend, people!" shouted Ivor. "But remember, Monday is Shakespeare day. We're going to dig into the text, and we're going to dig deep. Nine sharp in the orangery. But remember—no acting allowed! We're reading through, just reading through . . ."

My bicycle was where I'd left it, abandoned under one of the old yews that lined the driveway. I hid the play script on the other side of the tree, my letter of resignation, and mounted my bike to ride away, but the gravel slipped beneath me and I fell to the ground in one final act of degradation. From behind me, I heard laughter and applause. "Arty wankers," I murmured to myself and then turned to see Fran walking briskly next to me.

"Hey."

"Oh, hi there."

"You forgot this." The abandoned script.

"Yeah, right. Thank you."

"I'm hoping it was by accident." She held it out as if it were a contract to sign.

"Yes, I must have . . ." I looked left and right, unwilling to take it.

"My dad picks me up at the bottom of the lane every night. I mean, if that's all right. If you're not in a rush . . ."

I was not in a rush.

Walking Home

WE WALKED THE LENGTH of the driveway in silence, and it was a long driveway. Then out into the canopied lane that led down to the main road, and still the only voice was the one in my head, the voice that ordered me: *concentrate, this will matter, concentrate.*

"I'm sorry we didn't get to talk today," she said.

"Yeah, it was quite full on."

We walked further.

"I thought maybe you were avoiding me," I said.

"Not at all! I tried, but every time I looked up you were pretending to be a cat, so . . ." and here she laughed, too much I thought, and stowed her hair behind her ear.

"Yes, sorry about that."

"If anything, I thought you were avoiding *me*."

"God, no!" It had never occurred to me that being aloof might be interpreted as aloofness. "It's just I'm not used to that kind of stuff."

"I don't think anyone ever gets used to it."

We walked on. The heat of the day still lingered under the canopy; the still air blurred here and there with clouds of midges like thumbprints on a photo. Some way off we could hear the low hum of the motorway, and I was aware, too, of the chatter of the company members behind us, keeping their distance, stalking.

"So—be honest," she said, "*did* you hate every second of it?"

"Is that how it looked?"

"Sometimes. When you were being a statue, I thought you were suddenly going to, like, lash out."

"I'm no good at that stuff."

"You were! I thought your human steam engine was amazing, and I don't say that kind of thing lightly. Even then, you did look . . . furious!" And she laughed again, putting her hand to her mouth.

"Well, like I said, it's not my thing . . ."

"So why did you come?"

I kept my eyes ahead. "Try something new. Keeps me busy."

"Off the streets."

"Out of trouble."

"*Are* you in trouble?"

"Not really. Just bored at home."

"And were you bored today?"

"Not *bored* . . ."

"Well, there you are, then."

"Embarrassed."

"Yeah, well everyone gets that to begin with. It's like when you join the Foreign Legion or the SAS and you have to carry a fridge on your back and drink your own wee or whatever. Here, you have to play the hat game. It's so we're all *bonded* and *uninhibited*. Do you feel bonded?"

"Not massively bonded."

"Uninhibited?"

"Inhibited."

"Well, maybe once we start working on the play . . . What's your part?"

"I don't know, Sam-something."

"Sampson. Well, there you go. Lots of insults, lots of bawdy jokes. He's a reeeeeal saucy little lad."

"Oh, God."

"Just don't do that thing where you thrust your hips. Leave that to Juliet."

"Which is you?"

"It is." She pulled a face. "It is."

"The eponymous role."

She laughed. "Though the eponymous role is not always the *best* role."

"Ideally, you'd rather be playing Sampson."

"That's my *dream*." We smiled at each other and walked on through the soft green marine light, dappled and shimmering like the water in a rock pool. Observations like this would come to me occasionally, things that might pass as poetry, and I thought about pointing it out, the rock-pool thing, unsure if this would make me seem poetical or a bit of a knob. There was some overlap between the two, so I decided to keep my observations to myself. Fran spoke instead.

"This summer's a bastard, isn't it? Sun comes out, sky's blue if you're lucky and suddenly there are all these preconceived ideas of what you *should* be doing, lying on a beach or jumping off a rope swing into the river or having a picnic with all your *amazing* mates, sitting on a blanket in a meadow and eating strawberries and laughing in that mad way, like in the adverts. It's *never* like that, it's just six weeks of feeling like you're in the wrong place with the wrong people and you're missing out. That's why summer's so sad—because you're meant to be so happy. Personally, I can't wait to get my tights back on, turn the central heating up. At least in winter you're *allowed* to be miserable, you're not meant to be wafting about in a field of sunflowers. And it just goes on and on and on, doesn't it? Infinite, and never how you want it to be."

"I think that's exactly right," I said and suddenly she grabbed my arm.

"Which is why you should do this play! New experiences, new people . . ." She glanced behind her, lowered her voice. "I know they seem a bit"—she pulled a face—"but they're all right, really, once they calm down."

"I can't."

"Why not?"

"I've got a job."

"That's exciting. Where?"

"Petrol station attendant."

"Ah, and what first drew you to that world?"

"The smell on the forecourt. I like the way it gets into your clothes and hair."

"That and the confectionery."

"Exactly: the crisps, the sweets, the pornography . . ."

"D'you get to help yourself? Not the porn, the sweets."

"Well, the porn they keep wrapped up in cellophane—"

"Like some beautiful gift."

"—but the sweets, no. Occasional Twix, but no."

"Well, you're a professional. Good money?"

I glanced at my fingernails. "Three-twenty an hour."

She whistled. "And how many hours?"

"Ten, twelve."

"Well, there you are, we can work round *that*. It's not an excuse after all. In fact, there *are* no excuses."

We had reached the bottom of the hill now, the junction with the main road, the concrete bus shelter to our side. "This is where Dad picks me up. We live that way," she said, and mentioned a village, a hamlet of twenty or so houses, thatched and whitewashed and enviable. *Yes,* I thought, *that makes sense, that fits.* "Do you want to wait here with me? He'll be a while yet."

But I was aware of the rest of the company passing us now, nodding and grinning, and I felt furtive, awkward and keen to be gone. "No, I'd better head off. I'm working tonight." I climbed on my bike, snagging my inside leg on the saddle, suddenly inept.

"You all right there? Having difficulties?"

"Nope, fine, fine."

"Well. I'm pleased we spoke."

"Me too."

"And here—" She held out the play script in both hands. "You can't say I don't try."

I glanced towards the bus shelter where the company grinned and giggled, then turned back to Fran and spoke in a low, urgent voice, like a spy.

"Look, I'll be honest, I'm not coming back on Monday."

"Why not?"

I shrugged and peered the length of the road. "I'm just not much of a joiner."

"Yeah, everyone likes to think that. No one ever says, the thing about me, I'm a real *joiner*, I'll join in with any old shit, me."

"No, but in my case—"

"This not-joining thing, is it because you're a maverick or a loner?"

"Bit of both, I like to think."

"I bet you do. Well, it's no good," she said and held the script out again. "There's nothing wrong with joining if you join the right thing."

"And this isn't right! The only reason I came today ... well, can I ... I don't know, take you for coffee or tea or something? Either, really, I don't mind. Or we could try and get into a pub, I know somewhere, they'll serve practically *anyone*—I don't mean, I just—just as long as we keep our heads down and sit in the beer garden, whatever you want, really, but I just can't do this Shakespeare thing. I'll make a tit of myself. Even more than I'm doing now."

During this, I'd watched as she raised her eyebrows, knitted them, squinted, pulled her hair into her mouth and bit it then tucked it away, each expression derailing me, compelling me on into some other half-finished phrase, with some words barely more than sounds, until they ran out like the last drips from a hose.

"So. Anyway. What d'you think?"

And when they'd finally run dry, she said, quite clearly, "No."

"No?"

"No."

"Right. Well, fair enough."

She shrugged. "Sorry."

"Is it a boyfriend?"

"Nope."

"Is it Miles?"

"What? *What?* No!"

"Okay."

"I just thought—"

"Why would it be *Miles?*"

"I don't know, I just—maybe you don't like the idea, that's fine."

"It's not that either."

"Well, tell me, 'cause it's embarrassing to keep guessing."

"I haven't got time! I'm doing this, I've got lines to learn . . ." She wafted the pages of the script.

"Well, it *is* the eponymous role."

"Exactly! I want to do it properly."

"But surely weekends . . ."

"No, that's when I see my friends. The only way you're going to see me . . ."

"Go on."

"Come back Monday."

I looked left and right, saw the faces watching from the bus shelter. "Just Monday?"

"No, let's say the whole week. You have to make it to Friday."

She held out the script at arm's length and, like the poet, I said, "Fuck. Fuck, fuck, fuck."

She laughed. "Sorry, that's the deal."

"But on Friday we can go out?"

"No, on Friday I will give it some serious thought."

"And make a decision?"

"Yes."

"Depending on what?"

"The usual. How we get on . . ."

"Whether I'm any good?"

"No, course not. It's not an audition."

"Well, not in *that* sense, maybe."

"Not that kind of audition."

"But it's not definite? The coffee?"

"At this stage of negotiations, that's all I'm prepared to offer."

"You realize this is blackmail."

"It's only blackmail if you do something you're ashamed of."

"What, like Theatre Sports?"

"It's more of a bribe, really. Or an incentive." Once again, she held out the pages, and I took them and bundled them quickly into my rucksack.

"I'll think about it," I said and placed my foot on the highest pedal to push off. "Bye."

"Bye then!" she said, and she quickly put her hand on my shoulder, and as I turned, she leaned in, pressed her cheek against mine so that I could feel sweat on skin—hers or mine, I wasn't sure—and whispered in my ear.

"Sweet sorrow and all that."

Then she was walking towards her friends, stopping to turn. "Monday!" she said.

I cycled off to work, thinking, *sweet sorrow, that's exactly right.* Sweet sorrow. It wasn't until Monday morning that I discovered she'd taken it from the play.

PART TWO

July

I've seen *plays* that were more exciting than this. Honest to God—plays!

—Homer Simpson, *The Simpsons*

Wedding

WE'D DECIDED ON A winter wedding, and to make a virtue of the fact. "Small and exclusive, but not because no one likes us." Niamh was my fiancée, though I'd learned not to use the word. "It sounds so *fancy*," she'd said, "with that little accent and all those 'e's."

"It's very you."

"Oh, you think?"

"Even when we're married, I'm still going to call you my fiancée."

"Yes, try that."

In the ten years that we'd been together, we'd been to many weddings: an Italian olive grove at sunset, a picture-postcard English country church, on the roof of a New York skyscraper. Niamh was from Dublin, and we'd stood on an immense windblown Irish beach, the bride arriving on a white stallion from a vast distance away, like Omar Sharif in *Lawrence of Arabia*, too far by far, so that Niamh had to retreat into the dunes to hide her laughter. I found it impossible to imagine the two of us in any of these scenarios, and Niamh felt the same. "When I look in your eyes and think of what you mean to me," she said, "I just think 'registry office.'"

"Maybe not even that. Can we do it online?"

"Or we could elope, just the two of us. Though we'd have to bring my parents. The four of us."

"Is it still eloping if you bring your parents?"

We'd met in a briefly fashionable east London restaurant during the messy and unwholesome years of my late twenties. I bartended, Niamh was the manager, and before too long she had joined the list of two, perhaps three people who I can plausibly claim have saved my life. Our existence at that time was practically nocturnal and steeped in vodka, and the rate of attrition amongst our friends was high, but a few had gone on to run successful restaurants, and this was how we'd found the venue for our wedding, our very small wedding, in the top room of a pub. The scale would be a sign of our security and confidence. Only the insecure rode white horses, and we'd just mumble "I do" out of the side of our mouths, then see our friends. We would invite just ten people, later twenty, then thirty. If we set the tables in a square, we could make it forty, and surely this would be enough.

We looked at the list that night in bed. The number stood at thirty-eight.

"But these are all my friends," said Niamh.

"They're my friends too."

"But aren't there old school friends you want to invite?"

"No, I'm okay."

"Or old girlfriends?"

"Why would I want to do that? Why would you even want me to?"

"I want to see whatshername."

"Who?"

"You know . . ."

"No."

"Shakespeare girl."

"Her name was Fran Fisher."

"Yes! Invite her!"

"I'm not going to invite Fran Fisher to our wedding."

"Why not? If she was *so* great."

"I don't know where she is!" I said, which at that time was true. "I've not spoken to her for . . . twenty years!"

"But I want to see her!"

"Aren't you scared that I might just walk off during the vows?"

"That's exactly why I want her there. Get a bit of a *Four Weddings* vibe going on, bit of tension, bit of an edge."

"She's probably married by now. Probably got kids."

"So? Look her up online, it can't be hard."

"Like I said, I'm fine. I don't ever think of her."

And I didn't ever think of her, except from time to time.

Over the years I'd watched a cult of nostalgia grow, facilitated by technology, and noticed, too, how the very notion of "the past" had been subject to a kind of crazed inflation, so that friends went misty-eyed when recalling the events of the last bank holiday. I tried not to dwell on my own history, not because I thought of it as more than averagely unhappy or traumatic, but because I no longer felt the need. At other, less happy times of my life, I'd made a religion of the past, resorting to it like alcohol—no wonder they go together —and I can still cause my shoulders to touch my ears when I remember the drunken phone call I made to Fran's mother on the millennial New Year's Eve. How was she? Could I maybe have her number? "I'll tell you what, Charlie," she'd said, kind and calm, "phone me in the morning, and if you still want it, I'll happily give it to you."

I'd not called back, not spoken to Claire Fisher since, and what reason could I possibly have to go back now, now that life was finally taking on some shape, some permanence? I had no photo albums, no diaries, no old address books; I resisted social media. No need to draw on the past to fill gaps in the present. Thirty-eight guests would be plenty.

And then a month before the wedding, an email arrived, a screen grab of a Facebook page announcing a London reunion for the Full Fathom Five Theatre Cooperative, 1996–2001. Above it, a note from my best man: *Got to be done, don't you think? See you there.*

Heron

IT WAS ALSO THE summer that I began my life of crime.

The petrol station was at the edge of town, the last stop before the motorway on a long, straight road that ran through the pine plantation. I'd got the job through Mike, a barrel-chested local businessman who flirted with Mum at the golf club's reception desk. Mike owned a franchise—he loved this word—of three small petrol stations. "The thing about the franchise," he'd told me at our first meeting in his scrappy office cubicle, "is that it's like a family. Big business but with a human face." Mike's own human face was dominated by a drooping mustache, the weight of which seemed to drag his features down, and as he spoke he would stroke it with the back of his forefinger as if trying to lull it to sleep. The job, I knew, was part of his flirtation with Mum, and because I was not yet seventeen, I was encouraged to treat it as "an apprenticeship." I would get paid cash in hand, and there'd be none of that fuss with national insurance, holiday or sick pay. I could even sign on if I wanted to, soon as school was over. It was, said Mike, a win-win, and so I'd started work on the day of my last exam, twelve hours a week, three pounds twenty an hour.

But just as every job brought duties, responsibilities and a uniform, so every job came with its own scam, and it didn't take long to find a way to subsidize the scandalous wages. As part of his franchise, Mike took part in a popular scratch-card game, with instant cash prizes or, more commonly, the consolation of cheap crystal-effect glasses.

As cashier, I'd hand over a card with every qualifying purchase, wait while they scrubbed away with the edge of a coin, then, with a certain ceremony, present the driver with six gorgeous champagne flutes. One in every twenty cards brought a cash prize too, but I needn't imagine I could sit there and scratch away. All prizes would be accounted for, and the security camera over my shoulder would make sure of that. But on my first solo shift, dazed and overwhelmed with the sudden rush of commuter trade, I'd neglected to hand one or two of the cards to impatient customers, then three or four or five. If I kept a tally and used my body as a shield, it was possible for me to palm these extra scratch cards and slip them into my pocket.

Back at home, bedroom door locked, heart pounding, I scraped away the thin foil. Soon a set of four cut-glass brandy snifters was mine, then four lager glasses, then nothing and then—ten pounds, more than three hours' wages. It would be reckless to take the cash myself, but I could plausibly forget to hand out, say, one in four cards. As long as I kept a careful tally of those I'd missed, as long as I slipped the cards away with my back to the camera, there was nothing to stop me passing them on to an accomplice. As my best friend, Martin Harper was the obvious choice.

After a few weeks, I was only handing out scratch cards if specifically reminded by the customer, at which point I would slap my forehead in a pantomime of forgetfulness. The unclaimed cards I'd palm stiffly into my pocket like an amateur conjurer, and then, in an extra flourish of squalid paranoia, into my underpants while holding my breath in the fetid customer toilet. Once a week, I'd take the stack of cards to Martin Harper's house, where we'd close the door to the den, put on loud music and scratch away like old gangsters counting our haul, which, in our most audacious week, came to seventy pounds, thirty-six champagne flutes and twenty-four highball tumblers.

There was, of course, no justification for any of this, beyond a vague, unexamined sense that someone needed to teach petrol a lesson. Yes, I was being paid off the books, but Mike was always per-fectly affable and decent to me. On the other hand, Mike wouldn't be losing a penny or a single customer, the vast majority of whom left the station none the wiser. Who was the victim? This was a game of chance, and who was to say that they had any more right to good fortune or glassware than I did? Philosophically speaking, the money didn't even *exist* until the foil was scraped away, so the customers were losing nothing but the *possibility* of gain, rather than the gain itself. Like the falling tree in the forest or the cat in its closed box, these mental gymnastics made my head spin but were necessary if I was to convince myself the crime was victimless, and this was how I passed many of the guilty hours between three and four and five in the morning.

Perhaps I'd have felt better if I'd been using the cash to help sustain the family, a dutiful and noble son, but this was only partly the case. Dad had been on the dole since bankruptcy, and the arrival of a bill or a request for a new pair of shoes could easily send him spinning into panic and gloom. I sometimes pictured myself handing him a roll of banknotes—*there you go, Dad, just chipping in*—but was unable to finish the scene without indignity or embarrassment on both our parts. My contribution had to be secret. If Dad gave me cash to buy groceries or takeaway, I would pay and return the money to his wallet, and this gave me a terrific, self-congratulatory sense of piety, like a sort of sneaky Jesus.

But the pleasure was fleeting, and for the most part I spent the money on booze, computer games, trainers; protection from the humiliation of "I can't afford it." Stealing stopped me feeling poor, and for all my guilt and worry there was a swagger to it too. I could buy my round and any excess cash was rolled tightly and stashed in the hollow tubing of the bunk bed, like tools for an escape hidden in a cell.

On that particular Friday night, I left Fran and looped round the ring road, changed into my green nylon uniform, chatted to my coworker Marjorie and took her place at the till. Six until seven thirty were the busiest hours, then a lull, broken only by the gang of kids from the estate down the road bundling through the doors to grab confectionery from the shelves: not shoplifting, more a brazen smash-and-grab. I went into my speech—*please don't do that. Put it back, please. You have to pay for that*—and they bundled out and stood at the forecourt window, cramming chocolate and crisps into their mouths and laughing while I pretended to call the police.

Then another lull. I took the play script from my bag and stared for some time at the cover. Turning the page felt like opening an exam paper for a language I didn't speak, a meaty, strange language with weird grammar. I looked at the cast list, found Sampson some way down, then turned to act 1, scene 1. *Two households, both alike in dignity.*

I closed the script, went to the confectionery rack, stood in the camera's blind spot and quickly ate a Twix.

I read *Maxim*.

At ten minutes before nine, a battered VW pulled up. Harper stepped out of his brother's car, checked left and right. I hid the play beneath the counter and slipped into character. The following performance was carried out with deadpan sobriety, as if in the shadow of the Brandenburg Gate.

"Hello."

"Hello."

"How are you?"

"I am good."

"My brother has won some money on the scratch cards. Can I please cash them in here please?"

"Certainly! May I see the cards?"

"Yes. Here are the cards."

I inspected them with professional care and took the cash from the till. A smirk played around Harper's lips and with a wink he folded the money, walked back to his brother's car and drove away. A queasy, anxious period of time followed as I sat listening for the sound of sirens, imagining a squad of police cars sweeping onto the forecourt, the click of the cuffs, a large hand protecting my head as I was folded into the back seat.

But nothing happened, and I sometimes wondered—was this the perfect crime? As far as I could tell, the scam had only one flaw: each ten-pound cash prize could generate enough glassware to stock a small bar. To begin with, I'd been smuggling the surplus home in my rucksack, until all available cupboard space was crammed with more garage glasses than we could ever hope to use. They were not something to hand down through the generations; molded like a pineapple hand grenade, the "crystal" was of such low quality that it would shatter with an alarming pop if used for anything as unconventional as, say, a cold drink, turning the enjoyment of a chilled beer on a warm day into a kind of Russian roulette. Still I brought them home until the day I found my father on his hands and knees, sweeping up the shrapnel with a dustpan and brush. "I swear, next time it'll take my face off. Don't bring any more home now, Charlie, please?"

Another plan was needed. Turning off the pumps and forecourt lights at nine, I patted the stack of cards in my underpants and, in the darkness of the stock room, loaded a small chandelier's worth next to the pages of *Romeo and Juliet*, then climbed gingerly on my bike and cycled away, avoiding any bumps or vibrations for fear that one exploding glass would start a chain reaction. I pictured my corpse, shards of highball tumblers and champagne flutes embedded down my spine like the plates on a stegosaurus. I imagined the stack of bloodied evidence handed over to my parents, who would be torn between grief and embarrassment. "We found these scratch cards in his underpants."

I cycled on, and after a mile of plantation the road passed through a small, scrappy copse, Murder Wood, and here I turned off, wobbled along a woodchip path, stashed my bike and, crouching low like a commando, followed another path down to the shore of Fallow Pond, a semi-industrial reservoir, fetid and stagnant, its surface silver-black like pewter and more likely to be broken by a lifeless human hand than the leaping of a trout. Last summer, as an end-of-school dare we'd watched as Harper's older brother tried to swim through the viscous water, staggering out almost immediately, eyes red and weeping, skin as glossy as an otter's and coated with a tar-like substance that no amount of soap could remove. Now, in the summer-evening light, a single heron stood guard, shoulders hunched like a cartoon gangster, one leg embedded in the muck. I crouched on the bank in a swarm of gnats, listening out for human noise, then stood and opened my bag. As the first glass hit the water, the heron sucked its leg from the swamp and flapped away. Another followed, and another. My aim was consistent, and I imagined a pyramid forming of flutes and tumblers and goblets and snifters, slowly blanketed by the black pulp of rotting wood and, below that, the skeletons of mammoths and saber-toothed tigers. I imagined far-future archaeologists wondering at the find—so many identical glasses, how did they get here?—and failing to hypothesize a worried teenage boy standing alone with a stack of scratch cards tucked into his underwear.

Four lager glasses remained. I'd give them as a gift. Harper was having mates round to the den, and we were going to get absolutely slaughtered.

Cinnamon

ROUND THE RING ROAD, through the retail park to the north side, where the Harpers' house stood in the center of a plot of churned land, scattered with building materials and vehicles. I laid my bike on the forecourt in amongst the 4x4s, the quad bikes, the timber and bricks and Transit vans and Mrs. Harper's little Mazda runabout.

"Oi-oi," said Martin, opening the door, beer in hand, "the master criminal." He pulled me into an embrace, then held me at arm's length. "You're sure you weren't followed? Here—" Banknotes, rolled into a tight tube, were tucked into my hand. "I gave you fifty because I love you," and he held my head between his hands like a squeezebox and, squeezing, kissed the top. "Petrol. You need to wash your hair. Come on, the boys are in the den."

Tubs of white emulsion and sacks of plaster lined the hallway, and in the vast living room on our left, a TV, miraculously flat, hung like an Old Master next to the wall-length tropical fish tank. Jaded, chic Mrs. Harper lounged in an archipelago of modular white leather like Michelle Pfeiffer in *Scarface*. In our regular polls of sexiest mum, Mrs. Harper was the undisputed winner, a source of complicated pride for her son. "Evening, Mrs. Harper," I said in my nice-young-man voice.

"I've told you, Charlie, call me Alison!"

"Don't call her Alison," said Harper, "it's weird."

"Got these for you, Alison!" I said, producing the four lager glasses that I'd spared from the swamp, and Harper groaned and rolled his eyes.

"Thank you, Charlie, they're exquisite."

"It's just shit from the garage," said Harper. "They explode if you put ice in them."

"I'm sure that's not true," said Alison.

"It is true," I said, "but it is quite rare. Just don't hold the glass near your face longer than you have to." Alison laughed, and I felt sophisticated and worldly-wise.

"Put them on the side there, charming boy," said Alison.

"Yeah, we'll chuck 'em out later," said Harper, jabbing me in the ribs to propel me down the hallway. "Pack it in, you pervert."

"But she really likes me."

"She gave birth to me, you freak."

"I love you, Alison!" I whispered back down the hall, and we clambered over breeze blocks for the extension to the extension that was currently under way. Mr. Harper had built the house with his own hands, or the hands of his workers, altering and expanding the floor plan as casually as if it were made of Legos, and we pushed through hanging plastic sheets, through the new double garage and down into an earthly paradise.

The concept of Harper's "den" had been lifted from American movies, and kitted out to that blueprint: a large, low space with a pool table, a drum kit, electric guitars, weights and a rowing machine, another huge flat-screen TV, a dizzying entertainment library of videocassettes and DVDs, PlayStation games, vinyl and CDs, a complete run of *Maxim* and a fridge, the famous self-stocking fridge with its limitless Pot Noodles and Mars bars. No natural light or air penetrated the den. Instead testosterone was pumped through vents, or so it sometimes seemed, because here was Lloyd, laughing hysterically as he smothered Fox with a beanbag while a can of lager glugged onto the old underlay that carpeted the concrete.

"Oi, leave it out!" Harper was by some way the most prosperous middle-class person we knew, his father the Conservatory King, which made Harper the Conservatory Prince, yet he maintained a cockney accent with the discipline of the most committed Method actor. We all did, dialing it up or down depending on the circumstances. In the den, we went full barrow-boy. "Oi-oi! Stop trying to suck each other off and say hello. Nobody's here."

Nobody was another nickname. Surnames were acceptable, but nicknames were far more prevalent, a system as complex, ritualized and intricate as anything from the court of the Sun King. Harper had it lucky: because of his noble lineage, demeanor and good looks, he was The Prince, and the lustrous, feathery black hair that he flicked perpetually from his eyes made him Head and Shoulders or Tim, short for Timotei shampoo. He sometimes wore a necklace made of dusty white, pink and orange coral, and this made him Candy or Beach Boy. Fox, inevitably, was Fucks, but he'd once drunkenly confessed to breaking into the golf course and lowering his penis into one of the holes "to see what it felt like," and this confession had turned him into Tiger Woods, or Hole in One or Royal Troon or Lawnshagger or Groundskeeper Willie. A famous lunchtime incident of bad breath had turned Lloyd into Bin Breath or just Bins, his prominent nose made him Can Opener or Monkey Wrench or Monkey, his short curly hair made him Bubbles, but all of these were just the starting point for great spiraling flights of abuse that could last for many hours.

"Pack it in, Monkey!" said Harper.

"He started it!" said Lloyd. "Eyeing me up like I was one of his fancy golf courses . . ."

"What's that smell?" shouted Fox from under the beanbag.

"Like I was Royal St. Andrews . . ." said Lloyd.

"Is it bin day? Has someone put the bins out?"

"I'm not your caddy, Fox," said Lloyd, pressing down with his knee.

"Pack it in!" said The Prince.

"Your hair looks gorgeous tonight," said Lloyd. "Who does your hair, Prince-y?"

"Same girl who does your perm, Bubbles, now get off him!"

"Leave him alone!" I said.

"Who said that?" said Lloyd. "Is there someone there? I hear voices."

"I hear maracas," said Fox. "Who's playing the maracas?"

"Nobody's playing the maracas," said The Prince.

Nobody, Mr. No One, Invisible Man, and there were others. I'd mentioned once that I was named after one of my father's favorite jazz musicians, Charles Mingus, and this had been corrupted to Charlie Minge, then Curly Minge, then just Minge. Council was another, because I lived on The Library estate, and Bunkie or The Convict, because I still slept in a bunk bed, though this was not to be deployed in the early stage of battle. Council, too, was something to be earned.

"Council's here," said Lloyd. "He's really excited to see a house with an upstairs."

"My house has got an upstairs, Lloyd."

"Top bunk doesn't count as an upstairs," said Lloyd, and this brought a sharp inhalation from the others. Lloyd had a tendency to take things too far. I had a photo of us on Bonfire Night, taken with a long exposure during my photography phase, and while Harper is using his sparkler to draw a love heart, and while Fox is writing his name, Lloyd is scrawling "fuck you" in the night air. That's how I always thought of him, as the kind of kid who uses a firework to write "fuck you," who hides the stone in the snowball.

Now I had no choice but to pile on top, taking care to grind the point of my elbow into Lloyd's shoulder, and then The Prince jumped on top of me, using the pool table to maximize impact, and we groaned and dug fingers deep into each other's armpits and screamed and laughed until we couldn't breathe. We were all aware of the theory that boys matured more slowly than girls, and contested it loudly, yet here we were, exhibit A.

It always started with lager, which we drank through a straw because "the oxygen makes it stronger." If spirits were available, the can might then be topped up with vodka or gin and aspirin, which was rumored to make it more potent and prevent the hangover. Some years earlier, an ambitious young food technician had managed to combine the buzz of alcohol with the mouth-puckering sweetness of the soft drink, in mouthwash blue, stoplight red or tree-frog green, but these were for special occasions. Drugs were a source of debate—Lloyd and Fox were keen, but I thought only of the mallet and the cauliflower. God knows, wasn't the chemistry of the Lewis brain precarious enough? The Prince, like his father, was puritanical about drugs, thinking them hippie-ish and soft. Drunkenness, on the other hand, was larky and boys-y, and anything up to the point of hospitalization was sanctioned.

But we also put great effort into pushing at the limits of what alcohol could achieve, and sometimes Harper's den took on the earnest air of a research laboratory. We snorted booze or slammed it, mixed it or chugged it down at maximum speed to get the highs associated with drugs, and when that didn't work, we raided the kitchen cupboards in search of drugs that weren't drugs. Nutmeg, the gateway spice, if crumbled and smoked in industrial enough quantities, supposedly had a shamanic effect. Or was that cinnamon, or oregano? The dried pith of an unripe banana? We forced down a bunch of them, dense and waxy, draped the skins on radiators overnight, then gathered the next evening to smoke it silently and earnestly through *The Matrix* in a sweet, low-hanging fog. Perhaps the bananas were too ripe or not ripe enough, because nothing ever happened, and I now wonder why we didn't just do drugs. It would have been so much easier and cheaper than acquiring all that pith and cinnamon.

Instead we stuck with lager and straws, and played on the PlayStation, laughing and turning on each other like dogs in the park, and it was fun, I suppose. But I sometimes found myself trying to imagine a world in which friendship was expressed in some other way than belching in each other's faces. I had no doubt that we were fond of each other, even loved each other, and I had my own personal reasons to feel loyal and grateful to Harper, who, during some of the recent disasters, had gone out of his way to look after me without appearing to do so.

But we always succumbed to the tyranny of banter, and a further tension came from what I suppose might be called "group dynamics." Since the third year I'd considered Harper to be my best friend, and privately thought of the other two as our sidekicks, just as the other two thought of Harper as their best friend, the other two as sidekicks, and this jostling for favor gave a steel edge to every scuffle, particularly with Lloyd, mates despite not liking each other. Could I tell them about Fran? The Shakespeare thing made it tricky, and I'd either have to lie or present it as a joke, a scam on my part. I might feasibly be able to tell Harper, if I got him alone, but perhaps the harder question was could I imagine Fran in this room with my friends? It seemed unlikely, especially now that Harper was standing in the doorway with a bottle of vodka, a carton of juice and a strange, wheel-shaped object: twenty-four glass spice jars, Schwartz brand, hung by their necks from a notched wooden turntable. Harper gave the wheel a spin.

"Gentlemen — it's time."

Time to play Spice Roulette, the Herb Hunter. Solemnly, we took our places in the circle, each with a teaspoon in hand, Fox the first to spin the rack, closing his eyes and muttering a prayer as the wheel slowed and slowed and came to a halt and he took the bottle nearest to hand and read the label.

"Marjoram!"

One of the Italians, nice easy one to start; only parsley was more bland. He filled his spoon with the ancient, dusty flakes and we slapped the floor and cheered as he clamped the whole thing in his mouth, grimacing and chewing and then rinsing his mouth with the vodka and orange. "Just like pizza," he said. My turn next, and I watched the wheel click past tarragon, past basil, coriander, thyme, dill, chives, before coming to a stop at . . .

"White peppercorns!"

"Noooooo!"

And there was no escape as Harper tapped the little pellets out, taking care to pile them high in the spoon. The slapping on the floor began, the cheering, and then they were in my mouth, gritty but not unpleasant, and I began to crunch and say, "No big deal," until 1, 2, 3, each crunched seed released an acrid vapor that scalded the insides of my nostrils and made my eyes stream with hot, viscous tears that temporarily blinded me, my mouth puckered so tight that I could barely gulp down the vodka and orange, which had no taste now, my mouth anesthetized, blood pumping in my ears, and the music louder . . .

. . . and now I'm laughing and choking at the same time, throat burning as the gritty slurry makes its way down, some of it finding a home in the folds of my esophagus. I cannot swallow or breathe or feel my tongue, and Lloyd's pointing and laughing harder than the rest, and I make a note that I'll get back at Lloyd later.

Another spin and now The Prince. "Chives, chives, chives," he mutters, "make it chives," and perhaps it's the vodka, but the word "chives" seems hysterically funny to me now, "chives, chives, chives," but instead he gets . . . nutmeg, a mellow, regal spice, which he taps from the bottle into his hand, tosses into the air and catches like a peanut, crunching away, all smiles until he grimaces suddenly, sticks out his tongue, which is covered in mashed cork, and so he also gulps and gulps at the vodka until it's gone.

And now it's Lloyd's turn. "Come on, come on, come on," he mutters, hoping for parsley, praying for mint . . .

"Saffron! Yesss."

We boo and jeer, because there's something so insipid about saffron. "Saffron's gay," says Fox, as Lloyd places two or three red strands on his tongue and shrugs.

We play another round, drinking all the time. Fox gets another easy one, cumin. "Smells like armpits," he says and swallows it down. I get mint, which tastes of a greasy Sunday lunch and sucks all the moisture from my mouth, and I drain another glass of vodka and orange, mostly vodka thanks to Harper, who in turn gets cardamom, weird one, not unpleasant, the taste of the curry house. Could kill a curry now. Lloyd's turn. Am pretty drunk, so even watching the spinning rack makes me dizzy. It slows, the tension builds, we slap the floor, "Oooooooooh," and then hysteria, we're all on our backs laughing because . . .

"Cinnamon. Bastard *cinnamon*."

Cinnamon is the monster, the killer, the anthrax of the spice rack, and so Harper is careful to fill the spoon to overflowing and hand it solemnly to Lloyd, who looks at it with the concentration of a martial artist about to punch through a breeze block. He centers himself, breathes in through his nose, breathes out in a series of short puffs. The spoon is in his hand . . .

. . . then in his mouth, and he turns the spoon over and withdraws it without breaking the seal, eyes wide, both hands on the top of his head, lips pouting. The seconds stretch and for a moment it seems that he might make it. But then his mouth explodes open as if blasted from the inside and a great cloud of red dust billows forth and we laugh more than we have ever laughed before, holding our stomachs, rolling on the floor and pointing as the brick dust fills the room, and he's coughing and choking and spluttering for water, at which point we grab all the glasses and bottles, dodging out of the way as he doubles over, spluttering. I've a bottle of water in my hand and he gasps, "Give me that!"

I hold the water high above my head.

"Give it here!" and Lloyd throws himself at me, grabbing me around the waist, pushing me back onto the pool table so that I can feel the balls grinding into my spine, and it's harder to laugh now because I'm coughing too, but I continue laughing even as the powder coats my face and stings my eyes, and I manage to keep the bottle upright, holding it out of reach, and now Lloyd, red-faced, billowing smoke from both nostrils like a cartoon bull, is jabbing at my ribs with quick short punches and I try to push his hands away. "Ow! All right, here you go!" and I offer the bottle so he can clear his throat.

But the moment for peace offerings has gone. I drop the bottle and use that hand to push at Lloyd's face but he keeps jabbing away, and I'm alarmed by his expression, like my dad's when he gets angry, and suddenly a pool ball is in my hand, heavy and smooth and satisfying, my knee is somehow up in Lloyd's chest and I heave and push him right across the room and in the same moment sit, pull back my arm and arch my wrist and hurl the pool ball at his head.

Too many evenings ended like this. It seemed that we could only stop by going too far.

In this instance, the ball hit plasterboard with a great hollow thud and, just for a moment, stayed nestling in its new indentation before dropping quietly to the floor. Cinnamon dust hung in the air like the smoke from a revolver. I looked round, grinning, to see my three best friends crouched, covering their heads, silent until Lloyd spoke.

"Fucking hell, Lewis, you psycho—"

"I wasn't aiming at you!"

"Yes, you were! You could have killed me!"

"Whoa!" Fox stood at the wall, testing the depth of the hole with his finger. "Look at that! Jesus, Lewis!"

"It's fine," said Harper. "It's just plasterboard. You all right?" His hand was on my shoulder, consoling and sincere, and I loved The Prince at that moment, and wondered if I should say so.

"Yeah, yeah. Just lost it for a second."

"Too right you lost it," said Lloyd. "Good job you're such a shitty shot."

"Lloyd . . ."

"If you could actually *throw* I'd be fucking dead."

"LLOYD!"

"I'll pay for the wall," I said, "obviously."

"Forget about it."

"You can't pay for a *wall,* you stupid prick."

"Lloyd, leave it."

"You *lunatic,* Lewis!"

"I'm going to go home," said Fox.

"Yeah, I should go home too," I said, as if none of this had anything to do with me, but when I got to my feet I found that I needed to sit, then lie down on the sofa, head back, and it was then I noticed that the den had started to twist and pitch, the walls elastic. Closing my eyes transported me to one of those machines they use to test g-force on astronauts, and when I opened them to say goodbye to Fox, time had also taken on an abstract quality because Fox had vanished, and so I closed my eyes again. I could hear voices, but the blood roared in my ears so loudly that I couldn't make out words, and when I opened my eyes once more and tried to stand, the sofa cushions seemed like quicksand, sucking me down so that Harper had to pull me out.

"God, Lewis, you're really pissed."

"Going to go home."

"Yeah, you should."

I raised one hand to Lloyd. "Bye, mate."

But Lloyd did not look at me. "Yeah, bye."

The house was quiet, the lights dimmed, as Harper led me back along the corridor.

"Hey. Hey! Now it's just us, I want to tell you—"

"Shhhh!"

"I meant to tell you, I met this girl . . ."

"What? Not now, eh?"

"Okay. I'll phone you. Good night, Mr. and Mrs. Har—" I shouted up into the darkness, then stumbled over a stepladder, dragging it some way down the hall, entangled with my foot.

"Sh! They're asleep!" hissed Harper.

"I want to say goodbye to your mum . . ."

"Shhhh."

And then in another of those tricks of time, I had been teleported to the doorstep, Harper's hand on my shoulder once again, propping me up.

"Are you all right, Charlie?"

"What? *What?* Yeah."

"You're sure you can get home?"

I told him I'd be fine, was just a bit pissed.

"Bit what?"

"Bit pissed."

"You said 'lost.' 'Bit lost.'"

"What? No, bit pissed."

"All right. All right. Here's your bag."

"Love you, mate," I said, mumbling the offending word so that he might hear it and not hear it at the same time, and then I was alone.

My bike lay on the drive, but someone had adjusted the seat so that I could no longer lift my leg high enough, and I cursed and fell, and swore again, then found that if I stood astride the bike then hoisted it up to meet me, I could start to pedal. Home was ten minutes away and I longed for bed, for an antidote to the poison in my veins, or a transfusion, to be sucked dry, emptied out and refilled with something better, something pure. If I went home now, even if I managed to line up the key in the lock, I would not sleep, I'd close my eyes and find myself back on that centrifuge, and what if Dad was awake or slumbering on the sofa, what if I had to speak? I dreaded the thought and swore to myself, never again, I would no longer live like this, I would start afresh tomorrow and I would be clean and honest and kind and new and better, better, better, like Alina said, I would *find a way to move through this world, present and alive, find a way to be.*

But for the moment it seemed there was nothing I could do to stop the road ahead buckling and twisting like a rope bridge. Cycling with my eyes closed wasn't as helpful as I thought it might be, and instead I fixed my gaze on the yellow lines, using them like rails, but found that I no longer had faith in the laws of physics or believed that continuing to pedal would be enough to keep me upright, and so, passing the recreation ground, I slowed until the bike pitched to the side and I allowed myself to fall and crawl from beneath it so that I could rest.

The grass was cool on my back, the stars circling the sky and leaving trails of light like a leap into hyperspace, and I spread my arms and attempted to dig my fingers into the baked earth to prevent myself flying off into the void. Closing my eyes, I searched for something else to cling to and found Fran Fisher, the way we'd said goodbye, the smile that seemed to play in the corner of her mouth when I tried and failed to speak, as if she really understood me. In a way that was not yet clear, she seemed to be the solution to a problem that was also unclear. But then nothing was clear to me. Best just to rest. I loosened my grip, rolled onto my side and lost consciousness.

At some time in the night, I had the strange sensation that Dad was there, his coat pulled over his pajamas, talking to me softly. That the car was behind him, door open, engine running, headlights illuminating the park. That he lifted me up like a fireman and staggered to the back seat and drove me home, with Chet Baker singing on the stereo. There was a snapshot, too, of me vomiting into the toilet, and another of me sitting in that tiny bath, knees up against my chest, warm water from the shower on my back. It all had the quality of a dream, but I do know that when I woke the next morning, badly bruised and with the poison still running through my veins, I was somehow in my own bed, in clean sheets, wearing pajamas I'd not worn since I was a kid.

Dad

FOR THE FIRST ELEVEN years of my life, my father raised me, though this makes the process sound a little too considered and wholesome.

He was a musician in those days, a saxophonist, at least in theory. With Mum's encouragement, and to my grandparents' fury, he had dropped his accountancy course and instead he'd play for three or four nights a week in a number of groups, sometimes jazz, sometimes cover bands, leaving the days free to "work on his music." The three of us lived in a rented flat above a butcher's in a Portsmouth shopping arcade. Mum worked shifts at the general hospital, and so my earliest memories are of endless, baggy hours, trying to get plastic soldiers to stand up on the carpet while Dad noodled along to records on his saxophone and a small electric piano that he sat behind like a child's tiny school desk. It was a sort of elevated karaoke, my father lifting the needle on the run he couldn't play or the chord he couldn't find and so lifting it often, listening again, nodding along with the sax across his chest, then trying again. Babies exposed to Bach and Mozart are said to develop more quickly, with sharp analytical minds, but no one knows what five or six hours of bebop can do. It certainly didn't make me prematurely cool or laid-back — quite the opposite — but there are still albums that are as familiar to me as nursery rhymes. *Blue Train, The Sidewinder, Go!,* and *Straight, No Chaser* provided the soundtrack to the time we spent, content in each other's company, in those three small rooms. My father was not the outdoor type. As a concession to parenting norms, we'd sometimes walk to the local recreation ground, as bleak and desolate as a military airfield. But the paddling pool was always empty, the slide was not slippery, and scary boys monopolized the swings, and with my encouragement we'd soon head back to the flat, the soporific glow of the paraffin heater, the TV on but muted, *Button Moon* soundtracked by Cannonball Adderley, *The Flumps* by Dexter Gordon.

And sometimes I'd just watch Dad play; a tall but not handsome, slightly stooped man, with a craning neck and a prominent Adam's apple that bobbed and flexed when he laughed or played, like a gannet swallowing a fish. Young only in theory, he seemed out of time, a product of the postwar years, of coffee bars and National Service rather than the sixties and seventies in which he'd grown up. Even in his twenties his face was crumpled like something long forgotten in a pocket, and his skin had an unnerving elastic quality — grab him by his cheeks and pull and his face would stretch alarmingly like a frilled lizard; the price, I imagined, of all that practice. But he had wonderful eyes, soft and brown, that would fix on us during his frequent bouts of sentimentality, and he was well liked and popular and kind — a talker to strangers, a helper of old ladies, and I loved him very much, and loved our life together in that flat.

Just before Mum returned from her shift, he'd join me on the gritty carpet to perform a little display of diligence in front of the fort, asking questions in the self-consciously earnest voice of a social worker or hurrying through an ABC, losing interest long before "M." My father liked to call himself an autodidact, frequent use of the term "autodidact" being the hallmark of an autodidact, though if he was self-taught, my mum would say, it was by a substitute teacher. Still, he retained a great belief in the educational value of natural curiosity, and so I learned about electricity by poking the toaster with a fork, about the digestive system by eating Legos, about water displacement by running my own bath. He wasn't the kind of father to build a kite, but if he had, then I'd have trotted off to play beneath the pylons. Occasionally there'd be bouts of plagiarized clowning: chopped-off thumbs, objects pulled from behind my ear, noses snapped off then reattached—I was easily satisfied—and then he'd drift back to his music. He was not neglectful, but he was . . . relaxed, easily distracted.

Later, at school, I would discover that most dads were terrifying drill sergeants, remote and frightening, storming in to inspect kit and quarters at the end of each day, their presence unnerving. As far as I can remember, my dad was always there, and for the most part we got on with our own small projects side by side, fueled by tea and juice, cheap biscuits and sweet desserts in chemical pink made with water from the kettle, and early childhood was scrappy and grubby and disorganized and also a kind of bliss.

They married in 1984. I'm in their wedding photo, three years old, dressed in a comical corduroy three-piece suit, Dad in a skinny tie standing unnaturally straight. My mother, in ironic white, stands in profile to emphasize the immense bump that contains my sister, and waves her fist at Dad in jokey rage. At least we took it as a joke. My friends now are careful to set the stage before starting a family, establishing career, the mortgage, spare bedrooms. Still in their early twenties, my parents chose to improvise. I remember wild parties, the flat crammed with musicians and nurses, nitro meeting glycerin. I remember lighting strangers' cigarettes.

Billie—after Holiday—arrived and for a while there would be four of us, stepping on the toys, waking each other at all hours. A comfortable sort of chaos became fraught and fractious, so that it was almost a relief to start school. Almost; my father cried at the gates as if I were an evacuee. "What I'd like to do," he said, holding my head in his long fingers as if it were a prize, "what I'd like to do, if you don't mind, is take your head right off and carry it around with me. Is that all right?"

These were the memories my mother had called on when she'd claimed that Dad and I were close, that we'd be fine living together, and, in fairness, there were flashes of that bond on days like this particular Saturday. On a tray by my bed, there was warm tea, a cold can of Coke, aspirin displayed on a paper doily. The window had been opened and a panel of blue sky suggested a lovely day, but I was unable to face the challenge of a staircase until the afternoon. Dad was crouched by the stereo, head close to the speakers just as he used to do, his fingers tapping the air where his saxophone used to be, as Ornette Coleman played a jazz rendition of the violent disorder in my own head.

"Could you turn it down a little, please?"

He twisted round, with an indulgent half-smile. "Have fun, did you?"

"Yes, thanks, Dad."

"I don't know, Charlie, you stay up all night, then come home *reeking* of cinnamon . . ."

The mystery of my return was not discussed and never would be, for which I was grateful. At some point I would need to phone Harper. Violence was fine as long as it looked like fun, but to lose control like that . . . I'd need to apologize. Through the haze, the image of the dent in the plasterboard returned, and I could recall, too, the snap of pleasure I'd felt as the pool ball had left my hand. I'd have to phone Lloyd too, to reassure him, and myself, that I'd meant to miss. For the moment, I could only curl into the corner of the sofa and try not to move my head. Weren't young people meant to be impervious to hangovers? Contact with the sofa cushions, even the air, bruised me.

"It's possible to drink in moderation, you know. You don't have to do yourself harm."

"I know!"

I would never drink again, or only in the urbane, sophisticated manner of people who drink wine, people like Fran; wine without a screw top, out of proper glasses. Another pang of guilt; I'd meant to spend the day reading *Romeo and Juliet*. I'd no hope of impressing her, but I didn't want to make a fool of myself, and the idea of opening that script . . .

Blissfully, brilliantly, the day had clouded over, which meant that it was possible for Dad to ask, "Want to watch films with me?"

We were at our ease in front of movies. With my friends, it was rare to watch a film that was not set in space, the jungle, the future or some combination of these. But on days like this I craved what I thought of as Dad films, long, grand and familiar. We'd been watching the same rota since my childhood, British films with Julie Christie and Alec Guinness, John Mills and Richard Burton, spaghetti Westerns and film noir, *Spartacus* and *The Vikings* and *The Third Man*. We couldn't afford to buy them but the library stocked a few, and working through the shelves was one of Dad's informal projects. "I've got *Once Upon a Time in the West, Where Eagles Dare* and *The Godfather Part II*."

That was nine hours at least, enough to get through the half-life of alcohol and take us into nighttime with tea on our laps. He joined me on the sofa, the remote within easy reach.

"We're going in," he said, and we sat in companionable silence, lulled by the familiar confrontations, the gunfire and explosions, as the alcohol sputtered out and dissipated, and this was a good day with my dad.

Sampson

ON MONDAY, THE FINE weather broke and I lay in bed, listening to the clamor of a whole summer's rain falling. The first rehearsal of *Romeo and Juliet* was at nine thirty, and at eight forty-five it was still roaring down, the light as dim as a December afternoon. Perhaps it was a sign. When I was sixteen, the sole purpose of weather was to send me personal messages, and the rain pelting the window was a hand on my chest saying, nothing good can come of this. You'll look like a fool. Forget her. Stay in bed.

I'd spent the previous afternoon trying to understand the play, revising for a test, the test of Fran's approval. In the rectangle of cement that counted as our garden, I sat as straight and scholarly as the deck chair allowed, took the script from my bag and began to read the prologue.

Two households, both alike in dignity, in fair Verona where we lay our scene . . .

I'd resolved that I would take it slowly, understand each line before I moved on to the next, and to begin with, this was fine, easy, practically normal English, the words following one another like handholds until I felt my grip loosen.

. . . where civil blood makes civil hands unclean . . .

Because how could blood be "civil," and what were civil hands anyway? Whose hands? Civil as in "civilian" or as in "polite" or as in "civil war"? There were two "civils" in the line, and perhaps both

"civils" had all three meanings, perhaps that was the point, perhaps
it was a "play on words." I remembered Miss Rice, our old English
teacher, telling us not to think of Shakespeare, of any poetry, as something that needs translating: "It's not a foreign language, it's *this* language, your language." But something would have to be done to make
this comprehensible; not translation exactly, more like the solving of
a riddle. Taking it one word at a time, I came up with: "the blood of
civilians dirties hands that should be friendly in the course of this civil
war."

There, that sounded right.

But *this was the fourth line of the play,* and now I remembered the
long, sleepy afternoon spent staring at *Tomorrow and tomorrow and
tomorrow,* the instinctive pleasure at the sound of the word turning to
frustration as every phrase demanded to be explained, paraphrased,
referred to in footnotes, those maddening Yoda-like inversions re-
paired. "Don't worry if your head hurts sometimes," Miss Rice had
said. "That's normal. It's like when you exercise and your muscles
ache." Perhaps I was trying too hard. Perhaps Shakespeare was like
one of those "magic eye" paintings that were popular at the time:
find the right balance between focus and relaxation and the picture
will emerge. "Oh, I get it!" someone would shout from the front of
the class, but I didn't get it, and sat feeling increasingly stupid and
frustrated. Did Fran Fisher struggle like this? Did any of those kids?

. . . *misadventured piteous overthrows*

Three random words that might as well have been "pig umbrella
satellite." I checked the number of pages—one hundred and twenty-four. A lifetime wasn't long enough to unpick all of this stuff, and
like generations of actors before me, I decided that I'd concentrate on
my own part. Perhaps there'd be something there to make Fran smile.

Sampson: *Gregory, on my word, we'll not carry coals.*

Gregory: *No, for then we should be colliers.*

Sampson: *I mean, an we be in choler, we'll draw.*

I slapped the script down onto cement. *I mean, an we be in choler, we'll draw*; even in Elizabethan England, I imagined black-toothed serfs turning to each other and asking, "What did he just say? Something about choler?" I'd been told that there were jokes. Choler, collar, collier. These were the jokes. And why was there no "d" on the "and"? Why?

I closed my eyes and reminded myself that, after the read-through, I would not actually be playing this part. It would just be a means to an end. "Ay, 'tis but a means to an end," I said out loud, picked the play up from the patio and read on. There was some stuff I recognized as "bawdy," about maidenheads and maids and the line *My naked weapon is out*, which made me wince, because I knew that I'd have to point to my groin. *'Tis well thou art not fish. If thou hadst, thou hadst been poor-John.* I had to say this. In front of Fran, in front of Lucy Tran and Colin Smart and Helen Beavis.

Sampson: *I will bite my thumb at them, which is a disgrace to them if they bear it.*

Abram: *Do you bite your thumb at us, sir?*

Sampson: *I do bite my thumb, sir.*

Abram: *But do you bite your thumb at us, sir?*

All in all, this was too much about thumbs. I bit my own at Shakespeare, hooked my fingernail behind my teeth and made a clicking noise. Perhaps Sampson came back later with better material. I skimmed a few more pages, words, words, words, and found myself back in the classroom, my brain skittering over the surface like a pebble thrown onto thick ice.

I closed the script again and closed my eyes. As a kid, I'd once dismantled a broken old watch, determined to repair it for Dad, the initial satisfaction at the intricacy of the workings turning to boredom, then frustration, until I'd simply crammed the cogs and springs back in, taped the whole thing shut and secretly dropped it down a drain.

Monday morning, nine o'clock, and still it poured.

If I didn't go now, I could never go, and if the rain was a sign to stay away, it might just as easily be a test of my determination, divine and supernatural forces presenting me with a knight's errand, a quest! Through the wall, I heard Dad in the bathroom. Thought of the two of us, watching morning TV, talking about the rain . . .

Quickly, I dressed, pulled on my old school anorak, stood at the front door with my bike and launched myself into the downpour like a boat down a slipway. Before I reached the end of the close it was as if I'd been pulled from a lake. The wax from my carefully molded hair stung my eyes, the jeans that I'd selected scoured the inside of my thighs with every turn of the pedal. Rain on summer tarmac created a gray chemical broth, and each passing car threw more of this oily sump into my face, burning my eyes and blurring my vision, so that even before I faced the steep lane up to the Manor, I was ready to turn back. Quests were bullshit. Still, I cycled uphill against the current, then on through the gates, pushed my bike over wet gravel, hurled it onto the lawn, went looking for the orangery, which I remembered as a massive greenhouse with nothing in it. I skirted the Manor, found it, pressed my face up to the glass to see movement through the condensation, found the greenhouse door and threw myself through it.

"*. . . both alike in dignity, in fair Verona where we lay our*—"

They were sitting on bentwood chairs in a large circle, and all turned to face me now as I stood, arms out to my sides, clothes plastered to my body, dripping onto the terra-cotta tiles.

"He made it!" said Ivor. "Big round of applause!" A few claps against the drumming of the rain. "No rush, Charlie. Let's regroup and start again. Take a few minutes, everyone just stay in your seats." I kicked my way through a field of overturned umbrellas towards a spare seat between Lucy and the bespectacled boy called George, reached into the rucksack at my feet and tore the cover free from the wad of papier-mâché that had once been my script. Somewhere in the circle, someone laughed.

"Here—take this," said Alina, and a fresh copy was passed around the circle. I glimpsed Fran, her wet hair slicked back brilliantly like the synth player in an eighties band. I'd have loved to take in the spectacle of this, but now Helen was touching Fran's elbow and holding out her hand as if expecting payment. Fran leaned back, squeezed her fingers into her pocket, passed her a coin . . .

"Charlie, a word?" Ivor and Alina were kneeling at my side, Ivor's hand on my wet knee. "Listen, we've got a problem," said Ivor in a low voice.

"Okay."

"The girl we cast as Benvolio? She's dropped out."

"Okay."

"We wondered, Charlie," said Alina, "if you would step into the breach and cover for her."

"Okay?"

"At the read-through at least," said Ivor, "then we'll see."

"Okay."

"You're up for it?"

"Yes. No. I mean, I can't really . . ."

"You know the play, yes?"

"Yeah! Yeah, yeah, course, yeah!"

"Don't worry about showing off," said Alina. "We have zero expectations of you, really."

"By which we mean, Simon—"

"Charlie."

"—Charlie, that we're expecting a very great deal of you, but not today. No Oscar bids today, okay? Just . . . get through it."

"You still want me to read—?"

"Sampson, yes. Do a different voice or—my God!"

"What?"

"Charlie, stand up!"

"Um—why?"

"Look, everyone, look." Ivor took both my hands and pulled me to my feet, holding me at arm's length as if we might start to waltz. "Look! You're *steaming!*"

And sure enough, a swampy mist was rising along the length of my arms, from all over me, as the rain-drenched clothes warmed against my body, and while everyone laughed and cooed and clapped, I stood and steamed like a vampire in sunlight.

"You know what this is, everyone?" bellowed Ivor. "This is *commitment.*"

Performance Anxiety

"I AM MILES, AND I am playing Romeo!"

"And I'm Polly, and I'll be the Nurse!"

"I'm Bernard. I'll be reading the prologue and the Prince."

"Hello, I'm Ivor. I'm the director and I'll be playing Lord Capulet."

"I'm Alina, I'm the codirector and choreographer, and I will be Lady Capulet."

"Fran, Juliet."

"Alex, Mercutio."

"I'm Helen, designing and playing Gregory until we find an actor."

"Morning all! I'm Keith, and I will be giving my Friar Laurence and various others."

"My name is Colin, and I'll be playing Peter and the Apothecary!"

"I'm George. I'm playing Paris."

"Hello, I'm Charlie. I'll be reading, um, Sampson and just for today Benvolio."

"I'm Lucy. I'll be playing Tybalt."

And now all eyes turned to two new arrivals, a dark, sleek, middle-aged couple, rather suave, like a husband-and-wife team of spies.

"Hello, everyone! We're John—"

"—and Lesley."

"We're friends of Keith," said John, "from the world-famous Lakeside Players!"

"And we've been drafted in to take on the more *mature* roles of Lord and Lady Montague."

"I'm Lady Montague!" said John, to great gales of laughter. "I'm kidding! Not really! Not really!"

"Great! Terrific. Okay, let's start again, and remember—I can't emphasize this enough—just reading, no acting allowed!"

"Yeah, they always say that," said George. "Watch, everyone's going to act their arses off."

"Bernard, when you're ready?" said Ivor. Bernard cleared his throat, settled his reading glasses on the very tip of his nose as if reading a shopping list, and we began.

"*Two households, both alike in dignity / In fair Verona where we lay our scene . . .*"

The prologue, which had once seemed so slow and dense, was now hurtling past, my own lines ahead like a brick wall, and all the while my one thought was who the hell is Benvolio? Flicking quickly through the pages, I saw that his first speech began at exactly the point where I'd stopped reading. Benvolio was the reason I'd given up. His first exchange was with Sampson, played by me, and I wondered, should I put on a voice to distinguish between the two, an accent, show my range?

What *range?* I turned another page and saw Benvolio's name above a great slab of text, and why had Helen been asking Fran for money, why was she grinning? Why were they all looking at me now? Because it was my line.

"*Gregory, on my word, we'll not carry coals.*"

The role of Gregory was read by Helen, and it helped somehow to exchange lines with someone who, if not worse, was certainly no better. "*No, for then we should be colliers,*" she mumbled, and we trudged on until it was time for this Benvolio character to speak.

I'd adopted a strategy of saying each word as simply as possible, one by one, like steppingstones across a river, with no variation in speed or emphasis: *"Part. Fools. Put. Up. Your. Swords. You. Know. Not. What. You. Do."*

But someone was shouting at me: Lucy Tran, playing a character called Tybalt, who also didn't like me very much, judging from the way she hissed each line, jabbing at my elbow with her pen.

"What? Drawn and talk of peace? I HATE the word as I hate HELL, all Montagues and THEE! Have at thee, COWARD!"

Clearly Lucy had decided to discard Ivor's "no acting" guidance, but I continued to dole out the words as if feeding change into a vending machine.

"Madam. An. Hour. Before. The. Worshipped. Sun. Peered. Forth. The. Golden. Window. Of. The. East . . ."

Then straight into another scene with Romeo, a seemingly endless dialogue in which Miles sighed and scoffed and laughed, the kind of unreal laughter that is spelled out "ha-ha, ho-ho." The rain had stopped drumming on the glass, and there really was no need to shout like that, but on he went, taking loyal Benvolio with him into the next scene and the next, more and more lines for me, and I started to think, *my God, this part is practically the lead. Why can't I have fewer lines? Please, let me do less.*

Polly, the nice lady who owned the house, was next, taking us on a road trip of the British Isles, from the East End to the Midlands, Newcastle and beyond, and I realized that the Nurse was "comic relief." Then another sticky patch as I described Tybalt's death, distributing the words like a child dealing a pack of cards, and after that, thank God, Benvolio finally shut up and I could allow myself to watch and listen until, finally, many hours after we'd set off:

". . . for never was a story of more woe / Than this of Juliet and her Romeo."

Some silence, an awkward shifting. Pages closed. Ivor, in a somber

voice, said, "Well—that was a *lot* of acting. Clearly there's work to
do. We're . . . we're going to have to pick the bones out of that one.
Okay, everyone. Fifteen minutes, everyone. Take fifteen."

The company stood and stretched, and for the first time, I caught
Fran's eye as she gave a closed-mouth smile: well done, you! I was too
embarrassed to cross to her, and besides, here was Romeo barring my
way.

"So, Benvolio—what did you think?"

"Great. You're very good."

He waved the praise away. "First read-through, so I'm still digging,
you know? I'll get even better. But look . . ." He placed a large hand on
my shoulder. "We've got a lot of scenes together, yeah? I mean, a *lot*."

"Yeah, I noticed that."

"So, can I just check—you're not actually going to *do* it like that,
are you?"

I wasn't going to *do* it at all. In the intervals between stamping out
the words, I'd taken in the performances, and even a non-expert like
me could see that this thing was doomed, with or without my involve-
ment.

First, there were the non-actors, the anti-actors, the ones who had
nothing on our side—myself, Helen and Bernard. Then, the largest
group, actor-impersonators, with their posh voices roller-coasting up
and down, strange pauses and stresses, their postures imperious even
when seated. It reminded me of the earnestness that small children
bring to playing at kings and queens in the playground. Perhaps this
was what acting was, playing at kings and queens, but what audience
would watch this of their own free will?

As to Fran Fisher, it's possible that I was not entirely objective. But
at that time, in that greenhouse, I thought she was easily the greatest
actor that I had ever seen, and her brilliance, it seemed to me, resided
in all the things she didn't do. She didn't pose or posture or strain,

she didn't put on a wildly different voice to the one that she spoke in. Unlike Miles, she didn't pause in . . . all the . . . wrong places then skitter forward in a fake version of natural speech, but neither did she mumble or throw things away. Somehow the words at which I'd stared, stared and stared, and which had seemed nonsensical to me, suddenly sounded eloquent, urgent and real. *Gallop apace, you fiery-footed steeds, towards Phoebus' lodging!* she'd said, and though I'd struggle to tell you where the horses came from, why their feet were on fire or where Phoebus lodged, in that moment I had somehow thought, *yes, I know just what you mean.*

Talent was not something I felt drawn towards—probably the opposite was true, and I was inclined to resent or jeer or run away from people who were good at things—but every time she spoke, the whole room leaned in closer. A character that in my head had been an illustration, a girl on a balcony, now seemed funny and passionate, smart and willful, rebellious and—a word that my sixteen-year-old self would writhe at—sensual. How could you act those qualities if they weren't at least a part of who you were? To perform them and not possess them would be like expressing a thought you'd never had. Next to Juliet, Romeo was a whiny lunk. What did she see in him?

A small crowd had gathered around her now, to Miles's clear resentment. "She'll be okay if she does the work," he said and stalked off. Too intimidated to speak to her, I decided to go outside.

"Hey, Charlie," she said as I passed, "well done!" I winced and hurried on.

The sun was out now, as emphatic as the rain it had replaced, and outside the door, Alina and Ivor were standing, heads close together, wrestling with a problem, the problem of me.

"Hello, Charlie," said Alina, her hair pulled back to its full extent, hoisting her eyebrows into exasperation.

"So—what did you think? About the new role?"

"Um, well, I was a bit unsure . . ."

"Yes, it felt like you were feeling your way!" said Ivor.

"It was as if you understood perhaps one word in nine," said Alina.

"Alina!" said Ivor.

"Have you thought about stage management?"

I was about to be fired, and I felt the most wonderful relief. "If you want to give it to someone else—"

"No! No, we'd love you to take a crack at it," said Ivor.

"Besides, at this moment there *is* no one else," said Alina. "Though that's not the reason!"

"Well . . ."

"We'd like you to persevere, for a week maybe."

"Okay," I said, keen to get away.

"But can I ask," said Ivor, lowering his voice, "have you ever actually been in a play before?"

I laughed. "What do you think?"

"So," said Alina, "what brings you here, Charlie?"

"Um. To meet new people?" I began to look around for an alibi. A little way off, Alex, Mercutio, was sitting on a bench, rolling a cigarette, a trilby tipped back on his head. New people. I raised a hand to Alex.

"Well, you're going to be great," said Ivor. "In time."

"And if not," said Alina, "trust me—stage management!"

I raised my hand again. At school I'd learned that it was not appropriate for a boy to comment favorably on another boy's looks or even to think such a thing, but Alex was extremely beautiful, long and languorous like a dancer. In the role, in life, he had the same amused look, a single bracket on one side of his mouth, amusement that I now felt must be directed at me. But he swept the rainwater from the bench with the edge of his hand.

"Come. Join me." Approaching, I felt, as I always would with Alex, that I should ask for his autograph.

Alex Asante—he was the other one with talent. We'd felt it the moment he'd started to speak. In one of our early lessons, our French teacher had promised that if we worked hard enough we'd eventually enter a kind of trance state in which the foreignness would fall away and we'd speak, think and even dream in a beautiful new language. I'd never found myself remotely near this state—I'd walked out of the exam after half an hour—but there'd been something appealing about the idea, and, as with Fran, there was the same kind of immediacy when Alex spoke. I had no idea who Queen Mab was, or why she didn't turn up onstage, but I knew what he was getting at, and I felt I ought to let him know.

"You're very good at this."

He waved a hand dismissively. "Only by comparison."

"No, really, I mean it."

He lifted his shoulders high, then dropped them. "It's my standard-issue gay-outsider performance," he said. "You did very well."

"I was shit."

He laughed. "Just think of yourself as . . . unformed clay."

"I think they're going to sack me."

He tapped the words out on my knee. "You. Did. Just. Fine. Besides, they can't *sack* you—the Arts Council won't let them. It's about the experience! Transforming young lives through Shakespeare! For as long as you turn up, you're in. As long as you're keen."

"Oh, he's keen, aren't you, Charlie?" said Helen, arriving now. "He's *very* keen—Fran and I even had a bet on it." She held the pound coin out between finger and thumb. "Fran said you wouldn't come back and I said you would, and I bet her a quid, and so I won." She ruffled my hair. "Bless!"

"What's going on?" said Alex.

"Charlie's in love."

Fran was approaching. "Helen, pack it in," I pleaded.

"He's in love with *theatre*, isn't that right, Charlie? That's why he's here. Oh, hi, Fran! I was just saying what a complete theatre nut Charlie is."

"Really?" said Fran.

"It's a recent thing." I shrugged. "More as, you know, a watcher."

Helen grinned. "I can't tell you how often, at school, Charlie and his mates will be, I don't know, setting fire to someone's homework, and one of the boys will say, hey, this is just like that scene in *Hedda Gabler*."

"Helen . . ."

"We have to tell him: Charlie, for just one minute, stop talking about *plays*. But no, it's Pinter this, Stoppard that, Chekhov, Chekhov, Chekhov . . ."

"Oh, really?" said Alex, head to one side, amused. "What's your favorite?"

Some time passed.

"So hard to choose."

"*Cherry Orchard*, isn't it?" said Helen.

"*Orchard*'s good."

"Ha! *Orchard*," barked Helen. "Yeah, that's what they call it, Charlie and the boys: *Orchard*. Who wants to come to London with me Saturday? I've got matinee tickets for *Orchard*—"

"Maybe we should go and eat," I said, and walked quickly away.

Beginnings

THIS WAS THE FIRST occasion the four of us spent time together —Alex, Helen, Fran and me—and given what we became, it's strange that I don't remember more. I know that rather than eat the chickpea casserole, we played a formless game of badminton, with no teams or net and with discarded, molting shuttlecocks and half-strung rackets —hoops, really—that we found on the lawn. And I remember, too, my surprise at taking part rather than watching with the others. It's with these small moments of inclusion that immense friendships start, which is not to say that there was anything spontaneous or relaxed about it. If I'd failed to speak Shakespeare, then it seemed doubly important that I excel at badminton. "Charlie, you look so *serious,*" Fran said as I cursed myself, swiping at air with a stringless racket.

In the afternoon, we returned to our circle of bentwood chairs to turn our attention to the text—always "the text" rather than "the play."

"Before we start, remember," said Ivor, "that although the text is called *Romeo and Juliet,* it's really about everyone in this world. For Romeo, sure, of course it's Romeo's story, and for Juliet, it's her story, but for Paris—well, it's a play about Paris! We've all got these great passions, these *amazing* private stories, secret loves and hates. So for the Nurse, it's about the Nurse; for the Servant, it's the Servant's story. And for Benvolio?"

Ivor looked to me expectantly.

"It's a play about . . . Benvolio?"

"Yes! That's right! Because just as in life, there is no such thing as a minor character!"

At my side, Miles made a skeptical sound. This socialistic ensemble-talk was all well and good, but everyone knew it was a play about Romeo. Who'd give up an August night to see a play called *Benvolio and the Apothecary*? I wasn't sure I would, and I was Benvolio. As a character, he seemed entirely blank. With no good jokes, no family, no love life, he seemed to bore or irritate everyone he spoke to. Everything he said concerned the actions of others, and when he wasn't informing, he was pleading with people to stop fighting or giving information that the audience already knew. He was Romeo's best friend, but you could tell that Romeo preferred Mercutio, and when Benvolio abruptly stopped talking halfway through the play, it was hard to believe that anyone would mind. At least Sampson had the stuff about thumbs. Benvolio was a sidekick, a conformist and observer; characters confided in him but felt no need to listen in return. Amazing, really, that people I barely knew had cast me so well.

The afternoon wore on with a classroom air, the same overwhelming torpor at two forty-five. In Verona they'd have had a siesta, but we forged on, and when my head lolled, I'd snap straight and rack my brains for something smart and incisive that would impress Fran and show an insight I didn't possess. But I didn't have the knack of talking about characters as if they were real, as if we were the same person. "The thing about *me*," insisted Lucy, "is that I live to fight," and I tried to square this with the silent girl I'd sat behind in double Biology, while all the time the glass roof warmed the still air, and the conversation turned in circles, and perhaps if I just closed my eyes . . .

I snapped awake again. I'd resolved that I would not look at Fran unless she was speaking, but it was those with the least to say who spoke the most, and so she sat with her chin on her raised knee and listened.

Eventually the conversation turned to the themes of prejudice and division, and Ivor adopted a hushed and sincere manner, leaning forward, hands clasped like a young cleric.

"So—what keeps us apart? As communities? Not in the play, but in general, in real life, now. What are the grievances and prejudices that divide us, not just as lovers, but as friends? And remember, there are no wrong answers."

"No wrong answers" was another thing people said without meaning it. We all knew that there were wrong answers, except perhaps for Miles, who took on Ivor's concerned tone and leaned forward in his chair.

"Yeah, well, there's racism," said Miles, and, by way of clarification, "judging someone by the color of their skin."

"Ha!" Alex laughed. "I think it's a little late for that, casting-wise. Look around."

"Not in *this* production—there's you, there's Lucy . . ."

"So all the white people versus two non-white people," said Lucy.

"White versus *all* the other races," said Alex.

"With white as the default—" said Lucy.

"I'm just saying, it's there as a theme."

"—unless some of you black up," said Alex.

"No one's blacking up!" said Ivor.

"I know!" said Miles. "But a different production with a different cast."

"In a town with more than one Asian person," said Lucy.

"Fine, forget it!" said Miles, holding both hands in front of him. "Christ, I thought there were no wrong answers!"

"Okay, move on, what else divides people? Remember, we're talking in general, not necessarily in the play."

"Can I just say—age," said Polly. "I think there's a terrific gap between the generations, both in the play and in life."

"Good, good, good," said Ivor, and while the older cast members nodded vigorously, the younger ones seemed keen to move on.

"Class," said George, his hand over his mouth.

"In life perhaps," said Alina, "but in the play, Shakespeare is careful to point out that they're 'both alike in dignity.'"

"Or, sort of connected—culture," said George. "Taste, music. Cultural tribes."

"Blur versus Oasis."

"North and south."

"No!" Alina winced. "No more regional accents, I beg you."

"East Sussex versus West Sussex."

"Besides, they're both from Verona, so—"

"Football!" said Keith, our Friar Laurence. "So it's like a United/City, Arsenal/Tottenham thing."

"Come on, you Spurs!" chanted Colin Smart.

"Oh, please," said Lucy.

"Education," said Helen. "It's like when we were at school, and the Merton Grange boys would always duff up the Chatsborne kids down the precinct."

"They didn't *always* duff them up," said Fran.

"Well, no, we did," said Helen, laughing. "Always."

"Hey!" said Fran and kicked Helen's chair.

"Mer-ton Grange, Mer-ton Grange," chanted Colin Smart.

"Just grow up!" said Lucy.

"No, that's good," said Ivor, "we can use that aggression, we can use that feeling."

"But isn't the problem," said a voice that I was surprised to find was my own. "Sorry—isn't the problem that there *is* no reason? In the play, I mean. All the stuff people fight about in life, it might be irrational but it's something you can give a name to. In the play, it's not 'cause one side's posh or black or white or whatever, it's just what they're used to. Fighting, lashing out, smashing things up. The boys mainly. They're just confused, angry boys."

Ivor took this in and nodded, and I looked back to the floor. The discussion moved on, and in the end it was decided that the Montagues could maybe wear red T-shirts and the Capulets perhaps blue, and that this would probably be enough to make the point.

Hobbies and Interests: Socializing

"HELLO THERE," SHE SAID.

"Hi."

"I thought I'd walk with you."

"Okay."

"Unless you want to rush off."

"No, let's walk. I'd like that."

And so this became our routine, like walking to school with someone, self-conscious and formal to begin with, then eventually a habit. Along the drive, left at the gatehouse, down the long, tree-shaded lane, taking care to walk a little way behind the rest of the crowd, in no hurry to reach the bottom of the hill.

The ground had dried out but the air under the canopy of trees retained the freshness of the rain, the scent of bruised leaves and warm, damp earth. We began with certain biographical information, the kind of questions you might find on a form. I'd read in some men's magazine that a subtle way of making girls like you was to get them to talk about themselves. "Ask questions," it advised, "make them think you're interested," and so I soon discovered that her parents were Graham and Claire, and she liked them about as much as you could like parents. "I mean I don't call them by their first names or anything, we're not weird." Graham Fisher was something administrative in the railways, was pragmatic and serious and worked long hours—"but at least he makes the trains run on time. That's his joke, his one joke. He's a real *dad,* if you know what I mean." Claire was a librarian in the next town over; she was the arty, bookish one and also her best friend, "which sounds weird, I know. Maybe I should get more friends. My own age, who haven't given birth to me. Anyway, she's a laugh, Mum; I'm lucky, there's nothing I can't tell her. There's loads I *don't* tell her, but in theory. No complaints, not yet anyway. I'm sure I will. One day." As with people who had good teeth and confident smiles, I was instinctively suspicious of people who got on with their parents, imagining that they must have some secret binding them together. Cannibalism perhaps. She even seemed to like her brother, who was older and very smart and studying Maths at Sheffield University. "He's the clever one. That's what they call him, Clever One, as a joke, which I love, as you can imagine."

At intervals, she'd leave a gap for me to fill in my part of the form, but I would leap in with my pre-prepared questions, slapping them down like cards in a game of Snap, priming the next question while she answered. This gave our chat an edgy, interrogatory air, as if I was hoping she might accidentally confess to a series of local burglaries, and the effort involved meant that I couldn't always listen as carefully as I wanted to.

"So Charlie, what about—"

"So d'you want to be an actress, d'you think?" It's also possible that she'd noticed what I was doing.

"Me? God, no. Or rather, I don't know. I mean I *like* acting, it's why I'm here. Same reason you're here—"

"Of course."

"But that's because I like the people and rehearsals and the words. I like all the corny melodrama of it. Putting on a show, right here in the barn! Three weeks and nothing's ready! I love all of that, but the actual showing-off bit, I'd be lying if I said I *hate* it, I'm *shy,* but it's a bit . . . egotistical, isn't it? A bit daft and vain, all that 'look at me, look at me!'"

"You are really good at it."

"No, I'm not."

"You are. I mean I understood every word and I'm thick."

"I don't think any part of that is true. But anyway, what about—?"

"So what *do* you want to do?"

"When I grow up?"

"When you grow up."

"You sound like a careers officer."

"Am I boring?"

"No, I just . . . I quite like French, but that's not a job, is it, far as I know. Wish it was—getting paid for just, I don't know, smoking and having affairs. Bit of a stereotype there. I had this idea I might do Law, because you get to wear wigs and make speeches, but if that's the reason, then I might as well act, which I don't want to do because, well, anyway." She waved the subject away. "It's a long way off. Except suddenly it isn't, is it? Now it's all 'choose your options,' which is just another way of saying 'narrow the possibilities.' Every time you make a choice, you can hear doors slamming in the distance. They tell you, you can be anything you want, oh, except the following . . ."

No one had ever told me that I could be anything I wanted. Computer Science, Art, Graphic Design—these were my theoretical fields, and I'd sometimes entertained fantasies of myself at a drawing board in an office full of drawing boards, sleeves rolled up, and though I had no idea what was on the board, I liked the idea of doing something creative but technical, all clutch pencils and shading. But that idea had been abandoned in June. Now, when I tried to imagine anything past September, I felt once again that fear of drifting, an infinity of me and Dad on the sofa, looking for jobs on Ceefax with Pasta Madras on our laps. As far as talent was concerned, I could crosshatch, I could play Doom, and I was working on my tan. Best to change the subject.

"So why not just do what you're brilliant at, and be an actress?"

"That's very nice of you." She shrugged and tucked her hair behind her ear. "The thing is, here I get to play Juliet, out there it'd just be, I don't know, *wenches* and milkmaids. I had this English teacher once, he used to really encourage me; you know, a real mentor, a Mr. Chips or whatever. We used to enter these school competitions, reciting Shakespeare and poetry, and he said, exact words, I had a nice, pretty face but no one could see it through all that puppy fat."

"But you're not even fat."

"Too fat to make a living as an actress, apparently."

"That's not true."

"Because there are loads of fat actresses?"

"No, because I think you look . . ." In the microsecond between words, I'd skimmed my thesaurus, discarded "beautiful" as too strong, "nice" as too bland, "great" as too groovy. "Pretty"? Too twee. "Attractive"? Too frank.

". . . lovely," I said, doubting the word as it left my mouth. It sounded like luv-er-ly, three syllables.

"Oh," she said. "Well, all right then."

And shouldn't it be luv-ly? Just two?

"So what about you?"

Too late now. In my distraction, I'd allowed a question through.

"Are you going to take up acting professionally, or—?" and she almost made it to the end of the question before a blurt of laughter stopped her.

"Bit rude," I said.

"I know. I'm sorry."

"I thought I was pretty good."

"You were, you really were! I'm sorry."

"And that was just the first time reading it."

"Really? Then you were amazing."

"Not amazing, I was just trying out something different."

"It was a choice."

"Yeah, I want to play him as someone who leaves a gap between each word. Like he's had a bad accident."

"Blow to the head."

"That's his—what d'you call it?"

"His backstory?"

"His backstory. He's been, I don't know, kicked in the head by Tybalt's horse."

"It's a bold and fresh approach."

"I think so." We walked on, grinning. "After the read-through, Miles came up to me and said, 'You're not going to do it like *that*, are you?'"

She laughed. "I saw that. I watched him when you were reading and he looked really *angry*. Like 'I can't be expected to work with *this!*'"

"I think it's 'cause he's jealous."

"In the face of fresh talent."

"In the face of fresh, unspoiled talent."

"Yeah, it's like when people saw Brando for the first time."

"Exactly. It's not *bad*, it's just *new*, and he can't handle it."

"You're raw."

"That's it. I'm too raw."

"Dangerous."

"Too dangerous."

Ahead of us, the crowd had stopped and turned to look, and we slowed so as not to catch up.

"So," I said, "given how raw I am . . ."

"Go on."

"Can I stop now?"

She punched me hard on the shoulder. "No! You've got to keep coming!"

"There's no point!"

"Why not?"

"Because I can't do it!"

"You can learn, you'll get better, you're just reading for the first time."

"It's not that. I don't understand what I'm saying. To be honest, I don't even like plays."

She laughed. "Oh, really. So why did you come back?"

"You know why! You bribed me!"

We walked on in silence, eyes fixed forward. After a while she nudged me and then, when I turned to her, looked away, though not so quickly that I couldn't see her smile.

"Not a bribe, an incentive."

"Whatever."

"And also I didn't say I would."

"You did."

"I said I'd think about it. And I will do so, during the course of this week's rehearsals." I threw my head back and groaned. "Okay, how about this—every lunchtime for an hour, we'll find somewhere quiet, the two of us, and we'll go through the play together, line by line."

"You're going to *teach* me?" I said.

"Yep. It's going to be *really* uncomfortable."

I groaned again. I didn't want to be taught anymore, least of all by someone my own age, someone I liked, but . . .

"Trust me, I'm an excellent teacher. Strict but fair. Come on. It'll be fun. Besides, who else can play the part the way you do?"

"Well, that is true."

"We need you. Which is a mark of how truly desperate we are." We'd reached the bottom of the lane now. At the bus stop the rest of the company waited and watched. "Sorry, I feel like I've just talked about myself. Tomorrow it's your turn."

"Well, we'll see."

"Tomorrow, then," she said.

"See you tomorrow," shouted Helen.

"Tomorrow!" said Alex.

"See you, Charlie," said George.

"Tomorrow," said Keith and Colin and Lucy, and I cycled away with their eyes on my back and thought, *well, no choice now.*

I'll give it to the end of the week.

Swords

AT THIS POINT IN my life, I had seen exactly one half of a play.

Miss Rice, our fresh-faced English teacher, had arranged a coach trip to the National Theatre to see a matinee of *The Way of the World*. With its witty wordplay and sly, satirical jabs at the social mores of Restoration society, it was a bold choice for a coachload of fifteen-year-olds, but we loved the concrete staircases and runways of the South Bank, whooping through tunnels and cheering the skateboarders. It was a great venue for a game of Laser Tag, and by the time we took our seats in the auditorium, hopped up on Lucozade and wine gums, we were in full-on *Lord of the Flies* mode. Irresponsibly, the box office had placed us in the first row of the stalls, and it didn't take long for war to break out, Class 4F on one side, actors and audience on the other. We were outnumbered, but with the actors constrained by their lines and professionalism, it was a desperately uneven match and soon a number of malted milk balls had found their way through the fourth wall, so that the cast were unwittingly engaged in a football match with hissed cheers whenever the chocolate was kicked off stage right. As Congreve's jokes sailed high over our heads, we laughed at the fop, not with glee but derision, so that the actor began to visibly doubt his performance, fixing his eyes elsewhere like someone trying to avoid a fight in a pub. Other actors were not so easily intimidated, delivering their lines with barely suppressed fury, even in the love scenes.

And oh, the battle was long, so long, the interval like one of those desert mirages that move further away the closer you get, the actors getting louder as their frustration grew, our running commentary losing its humor. There were complaints, and in the interval Miss Rice, close to tears, called us all together and told us how embarrassed she was, what a disgrace we were, and the fun had stopped abruptly. Most of us did not return for the second half—Miss Rice no longer *cared* what we did, couldn't *bear* the sight of us—and instead we wandered the South Bank and threw gravel into the Thames. On the way home, the back of the coach felt like the rear seat of a police car, and we never found out what happened to the witty young lovers.

If there was such a thing as a theatre bug, then I was immune. The problem wasn't acting. I was happy to watch people pretending to be other people in the films and TV that I sucked up indiscriminately. But all the elements that were supposed to make theatre unique and special—the proximity, the high emotion, the potential for disaster —made it seem mortifying to me. It was too much, too bare and artificial.

Then there was the whiff of pretension, superiority and self-satisfaction that clung to all forms of "the arts." To perform in a play or a band, to put your picture on display in the corridor, to publish your story or, God forbid, your poem in the school magazine, was to proclaim your uniqueness and self-belief and so to make yourself a target. Anything placed on a pedestal was likely to get knocked off, and it was simply common sense to stay quiet and keep any creative ambitions private.

Especially for a boy. The only acceptable talent was in sport, in which case it was fine to strut and boast, but my talents lay elsewhere, very possibly nowhere. The only thing that I was good at, drawing —doodling, really—was acceptable as long as it remained technical and free of self-expression. There was nothing of me in the still life of a half-peeled orange, the close-up of an eye with a window reflected in it, the planet-size spaceship; no beauty, emotion or self-revelation, just draftsmanship. All other forms of expression—singing, dancing, writing, even reading or speaking a foreign language—were considered not just gay but also posh, and few things carried more stigma at Merton Grange than this combination. This was why our school productions were populated almost entirely by girls in trousers with stick-on mustaches, speaking in low voices. Like the Elizabethan theatre in reverse, there was something disreputable about boys who did plays, and Shakespeare plays in particular. Shakespeare was play-acting in poetry, and all the beat-boxes and knife fights in the world could do nothing to change that fact.

So I had joined a cult. We even looked like a cult, all of us standing in a circle in loose garments in the morning light, barefoot on the lawn of a large secluded mansion.

"... and now I want you all to roll back up from the base of your spine, one vertebra at a time, into a standing position ... and now reach up, up, up high towards the sun ..."

No one could ever know that I was reaching for the sun. I reminded myself of the reason I was here, standing just a little to my right ...

"Charlie!" shouted Alina. "Eyes, please! Focus!"

Alina had none of Ivor's spaniel-like bounce. She carried with her an air of furious disappointment, like a cabaret chanteuse who has unaccountably found herself booked for a children's party, and we would stiffen as she walked amongst us, prodding at locked knees, pushing heads down closer to the ground as vertebrae popped, digging her fingers under rib cages to check the engagement of the diaphragm. I didn't even know I had a diaphragm.

"Deep breaths! Really feel the air. Don't forget to breathe ... and roll forward once again. Charlie—how can you be expected to move freely like this?"

In one last puny and self-defeating act of rebellion, I was still wearing jeans rather than the vests and jogging bottoms that the rest of the company wore, everything either too baggy or too tight. Alex was practically in a body stocking, but dancewear was a line I would not cross. What if I was knocked off my bike?

"You can't move like this, and if you can't move, you can't act. Tomorrow, please come prepared for the work in hand."

This would be the routine from now on, early starts and a company warm-up, after which we'd consult the schedule. Rehearsals took place in various spaces around the Manor, so while the Nurse and Juliet were with Ivor in the orangery, the Capulet and Montague gangs would be with Alina in the orchard, prowling like panthers, lunging like cobras. The end of each session was marked by the ringing of a giant triangle hanging from a tree. No other indication of time was permitted—no watches, no phones for those who had them, in this case Alex and Miles, the sixth-formers. In "free periods" when not required to rehearse, we were asked to go and find Helen and her production team in the stables, to help build scenery, dye costumes or work on publicity.

Next Friday afternoon, the whole company would come together on the Great Lawn for a workshop on the making and wearing of masks. There seemed no way that this could turn out well, and the prospect hovered over me throughout the week, like an appointment for some dental procedure. In the meantime . . .

"Montagues, Capulets, please—choose your weapons!"

In the orchard, we were invited to pull items from a tub of broom handles and bamboo canes. "Try out your weapon," said Alina with a Jedi's solemnity. "See how each of them feels in your hand. Let your weapon choose you. I want you to keep it in sight at all times, whether you're here or at home—wherever you are. I want you to carve it with your initials, keep it by your bed at night, decorate the handle if you wish. I want you to give it a name!" I looked at the sawn-off broom handle in my hand and searched the orchard for someone to laugh with. But there was Lucy testing the weight of her stick and Colin balancing his on the tip on his finger. Alex was testing the imaginary edge of his bamboo pole with his thumb, while Miles seemed to be whispering to the mop handle. Even George, usually watchful and reserved, was gleefully whipping a long, narrow bough of hazel back and forth, trying to make the air hiss and whistle.

And there was no denying that there was something satisfying about strutting around with a sword, even one made out of an old broom, the same primal pleasure I felt raising Harper's air rifle to my shoulder or playing with his dad's sharpened ax or flicking a penknife into the trunk of a tree. Better yet, we were each given a broad leather belt to be worn low on the hip like gunslingers. The idea, said Alina, was that carrying a weapon changed the way you walked and stood and sat and held yourself, and though a great deal of the morning was spent tripping over the thing, I finally gave myself up to it, posturing with my hand on the imaginary hilt while waiting for a cup of squash and a biscuit. Maybe if I wound it round with thick rope, I thought, and glued it for a better grip, or shaved a little off the blade and rounded the other end, varnished it perhaps, and *this is how they get to you, the cult. This is how they wear you down* . . .

Later in rehearsals there'd be proper fight training with realistic-looking swords, but for now we swaggered towards the outdoor buffet like the lusty young Italian noblemen that we'd become, and chose from an array of vegetarian dishes courtesy of Polly and her mysterious staff: loamy whole-meal pasta bakes surfaced with greasy cheese, chickpeas like a pile of goat droppings, salads of gritty grains and mulched beans, warmed and fermented by the sun. At a separate table, George stood hunched over a loaf of dense, mahogany-colored homemade bread, sawing away as if it was the joist of a barn. It was very generous of Polly, but this was a kitchen where flavor played second fiddle to the necessity of a healthy, regular bowel, and the communal flatulence gave an edge to all our warm-downs.

"It's certainly a lot of roughage," said George, sawing away.

"I swear," said Alex, grouting the grooves of a celery stick with hummus, "one day we're going to roll forward one vertebra at a time and all simultaneously shit ourselves."

I found a banana as green as a lime and a scrawny bunch of grapes, and there was Fran beside me, script in hand.

"So what have you named it?"

"I'm sorry?"

"Your sword, what's it called?"

"Stick," I said. "I'm going to call it Stick."

"Good choice."

"I didn't choose Stick, Stick chose me."

"So how do you and Stick feel about finding somewhere private?" With one hand on the hilt and the other holding the bowl of grapes, I followed Fran down to the meadow.

Pygmalion

WE SETTLED IN THE shade of a low-boughed tree, near the spot where she'd first seen me. At that time, I'd been reading with a cigarette in my hand and no top on, and perhaps she'd thought I was an intellectual. If so, it wouldn't take long to reveal the truth.

"I think we should just read it through, line by line, just to see how it sounds. Is that all right?" Though we strained for informality, there was something unavoidably teacherly in her manner. I'd not expected to be a student again, and I felt the old anxieties. "When you're ready." She put her hands behind her head and closed her eyes. "I'm listening."

I licked my lips and ran at it. *"Here were the servants of your adversary close fighting ere I did approach—"*

"Don't ignore the comma. Punctuation is your friend. Not your only friend, but it will help. And what does 'ere' mean?"

"'When'? When I approached—"

"Or 'before.'"

"So 'when' is wrong?"

"Both work, but 'before' is better than 'when.'"

"Before I approached—"

"As in '*even* before.' So he's saying it because . . . ?"

"It's an excuse? He doesn't want the blame?"

"And what are they doing?"

"Fighting."

"No."

"*Close* fighting."

"So it's . . ."

"Close combat."

"So it's . . ."

"Stabby?"

"Really stabby. So . . ."

"Here were your enemies, stabbing each other before I'd even got here."

"Not just enemies."

"Servants of your enemies."

"So he's a . . ."

"Snob?"

"Maybe. Maybe he's—"

"Posh. Posher than them."

"Now say it again, bit more acting."

"*Here were the servants of your*—"

"But not with a funny voice. Just talk normally."

"Aren't I meant to, what's it called . . . project?"

"Yes, but I'm right here," she said, and without opening her eyes, she reached above her head and, for a moment, laid her arm across my leg. "Just tell me what happened."

"*Here were the servants of your adversary, close fighting ere I did approach.*"

"Getting there. Again."

"*Here were the*—you do know there's pages of this stuff?"

"It'll get easier."

"You say it."

"No!"

"Just say it and I'll copy you."

"I can't do your part for you."

"No, but you do it and I'll copy you but it will be me. Say it!"

"No!"

I nudged her with my foot. "Go on! Say it."

"Just this once," she sighed. "*Here were the servants of your adversary, close fighting ere I did approach.*"

I copied her, the intonation and emphasis. "Okay. Let's go on, shall we?"

And so we did, tiptoeing through it until along came Fiery Tybalt, who "*cut the winds who nothing hurt withal hissed him in scorn.* O-kay."

"It's fine, take it bit by bit."

"What's 'withal'?"

"I don't know exactly, but don't worry."

"Is it 'as well'? 'Also'?"

"Or 'nevertheless.'"

"But which one?"

"It doesn't matter, I understand it."

"So the wind was not hurt."

"Because . . ."

I thought of George and his hazel stick back in the orchard, his helpless grin as he whipped it through the air, trying to make it whistle. Did boys do that four hundred years ago?

"He's swishing it about and missing, and the air sounds like it's sort of taking the piss."

"Exactly. So . . ."

"So?"

"So say *this* but mean *that*. That's all acting is, really. Knowing what you want to say but with the words you're given."

I nodded, then, "Can you repeat that?"

"Okay." She flipped onto her front to face me. "Okay, what I mean is, imagine I say, 'I hate you.' Not *you*-you, but you. I can say it like, God, I really *hate* you, or I can say it like I secretly love you, or I find you disgusting, or beautiful, or, hm, you *intrigue* me. I've got to say 'I hate you' because that's what's written down, but I can say those other things too. If I say 'I hate you' but I mean 'I really want to kiss you,' then you—not *you*-you, but you—will know what I really mean. Not in an obvious way but it will come across, in thousands of tiny little signs that we're not even aware of or able to control—the way we sit or an eye movement or whether we blush or whatever and . . . you will know what I really mean. Not *you*-you. The audience. Does that make sense?"

I reached for a word I'd heard but never used. "So, like . . . subtext?"

"Not just subtext. Irony and metaphor, all that stuff, they're all ways of not saying what you mean, but still saying it."

"I think it'd be easier if everyone said exactly what they meant in as few words as possible."

"It might be. But where's the poetry in that?" She lay back down, dropping the last of the grapes into her mouth. "And when does anyone say what they really mean? Seventy, eighty percent of what people say is—not a lie exactly, but . . . off to the side. Just coming out with feelings, complete honesty, I think it'd send people crazy. Besides, much more entertaining to work out what's really going on."

A moment passed in which I wondered if this was the most profound conversation I'd ever had. Not only had I used the word "subtext," but the notion that a conversation about subtext might itself have a subtext, the complexity of this, was as dizzying as standing between two mirrors in a lift. She nudged my leg. "Read it to me again."

"*He swung about his head and cut the winds / Who nothing hurt withal hissed him in scorn.*"

"There you go, that makes sense. It's quite . . . witty, isn't it?"

"Well, not laugh-out-loud."

"I mean 'wit' in the other sense."

"Okay."

I didn't know that there was another sense, and perhaps she knew this too, because she went on, "Not a ha-ha joke, but playing with an idea, improvising. So he's clever or he thinks he's clever or he wants the Montagues to think he's clever. That's something you could use. If you wanted to."

"I could wear glasses."

"Like clever people do?"

"You think that's too obvious?"

"No. I like it. Look at you, with your bold character choices." She stopped abruptly and spat something into her palm. "Sorry. These grapes are really manky. Carry on."

Jamming

IN THE AFTERNOON, FRAN rehearsed with her Romeo and we clattered with our swords back to the orchard to rehearse the opening. The thumb-biting business had been handed over to John and Lesley, the new arrivals from the Lakeside Players and, according to Keith, "practically semiprofessional, leading lights of the local scene." They certainly had a youthful lustiness, hanging off each other's necks in breaks, tucking their hands into the other's pockets.

"I think they might be swingers," said George.

"Semiprofessionals," said Colin.

"Leading lights in the local scene," said Alex.

"They're certainly very touchy-feely," said Lucy, "considering how ancient they are." They were perhaps in their mid-thirties, but were tireless and keen, and I was happy to sit in the shade and watch them bite their thumbs, and the afternoon wore on, as sticky and soporific as any in old Verona, until it was time to go. We gathered on the driveway, Lucy balancing her bamboo on the tip of her finger, Colin leaning on his and swaying from side to side like Fred Astaire, George writing his name on a broom handle with the fountain pen he kept in his top pocket; street toughs.

Wait for me, Fran had said, but she was trapped with Romeo. Exhausted from the work, he'd contrived to take his top off and now leaned against his car, a battered white VW Golf, sword at his hip, pausing only to drink deeply from the large bottle of water he carried everywhere; like a dolphin in transit, he could not be allowed to dry out. Miles had a *torso*—that was the only word for it, the musculature apparently crosshatched and shaded like one of my drawings, and he'd learned that trick, beloved of topless teenage boys, of grasping his left biceps with his right arm to bunch up his meaty cleavage. As he drank, the water ran down his neck and chest, and I heard a clatter as Lucy dropped her stick.

"Pop your eyes back in, Luce," said Colin, and Lucy jabbed him with her sword.

Bored, Fran glanced my way. "One minute!" she mouthed, and raised one finger. I saw Miles grasp Fran's arm and my hand went to my broom handle, but now Fran suddenly twisted Miles's nipple hard as if turning off a radio. He yelped and, laughing, Fran walked over.

"God, I thought he'd never . . . thanks for waiting. Let's go."

I braced the sword across my handlebars. "Did you know him before?"

"No, and yet it's like I've known him all my life, if you know what I mean. He's harmless, I suppose, he's just so hard to listen to. Have you noticed, whenever anyone else speaks, he gulps at his water? So he doesn't have to waste time listening, I suppose."

"What were you talking about?"

"The *demands of the role*. He's insecure apparently. 'I just don't know if I'm right for it.' That's what he *says*. He just wants to be contradicted."

"He's very good-looking."

"And I don't think that news would necess*a*rily come as a surprise to him."

There was a rumble of gravel behind us and we made way for Miles's car, his bare arm lolling from the open window, waving lazily as Bob Marley played on the stereo.

"Some reggae there," said Fran. "Little taste of downtown Kingston. Kingston-upon-Thames."

"He's jammin'."

"It's 'jamm*ing*,' Bob, you have to sound the 'g.' Who drives a car with their top off anyway? Those hot leather seats. When he gets out it's going to be like the skin off a roast chicken. Hey, don't say anything, but I think he's waxed his chest. His first big acting choice: 'Note to self. Make Romeo as smooth as an eel.' I mean he's *buff* and all, but believe me, girls don't like that stuff as much as boys think they do. Body like a wall chart in a butcher's shop. Sirloin, tenderloin, top rump, silverside . . ."

"I think Lucy likes it. I think she's a bit in love."

"Oh, I'm *sure*, he's a hunk. Hunk of cheddar, hunk of wood. Not wood — limestone."

"And you?"

"Me?"

"Do you . . . find him attractive?"

She glanced at me, half smiling, then away. "For the play I can. Real life?" She gave a little shiver. "Boys like that, they're just . . . all laid out. Walking CVs. Rugby in winter, cricket in summer, debating team, Oxbridge application on the go. What's left to find out? I'd much rather — ow!"

I had accidentally jabbed her in the ribs with the broom handle. "This is ridiculous," I said, ready to hurl it like a javelin. "I'm getting rid of it."

"You can't do that! You've got to bond with it!"

"I'm not going to *bond* with it, I'm going to chuck it in the woods."

"What if Alina finds out? Here, let's do this instead . . ."

We were at the gatehouse, the flint-covered cottage where the driveway met the lane. She tucked the stick out of sight in the doorframe, then hesitated a moment.

"What are you doing?"

She looked around to check no one was in sight, then rattled the door handle, barely held in place with loose screws. The paint was flaking, the wood decaying, and one good shoulder shove would have opened it. Instead she reached up and felt along the lintel—"Bingo" —pulling down a heavy key, red with rust like something from a fairy tale. "Shall we?"

The key jammed but she rattled the door and it suddenly opened onto a small, dim single room. Ancient faded rugs covered the floor, dingy yellow curtains hung over small, high windows. The room was as cool as a refrigerator, the only furniture an immense, ancient brown chesterfield, its leather cracked, leaking horsehair.

"It's where Polly keeps her hostages," I said.

"Cast of *Midsummer Night's Dream* from last year. 'Heeeelp us!'" She pulled the door closed. "Still," said Fran, "it's good to know," a remark that I'd come back to again over the next few weeks.

Brown Bottles

WHEN I RETURNED HOME, the house felt stuffy and silent, and I had to resist the desire to turn around and walk back out. Since the weekend, the sadness had rolled in like a fog, finding its way into every corner, and now here he was in the bedroom, curtains drawn, on top of the sheets with his back to the door.

"You asleep?"

"Just dozing. I had a bad night."

"So don't sleep in the day."

No reply.

"It's lovely out. You sure you don't want to—"

"I'm fine."

"You want something to—?"

"No. All good."

I loitered in the doorway. Someone smarter, kinder than me would have found the right tone, frank and easy and free of fear or anger or irritation. Perhaps crossed the room to see his face. But the air was stale, dust floating in the shafts of evening light, and I lacked both voice and language, and it was easier to pull the door closed and try to forget that he was there.

I went downstairs and turned on the computer to play games.

"A bit blue," that was one of the terms we'd used. Not himself, sad. Things on his mind. Concerned, anxious. A bit down, down in the dumps, in the mouth. Disappointed, suffering from a setback, under the weather, knocked back, confidence taken a bit of a knock, money worries. It was remarkable, really, our ability to devise coy phrases and euphemisms, like a parlor game in which you're not allowed to use a particular word.

And that word came bracketed with other terms — "clinically," "chronically" — which gave it an unnerving, medical edge, because if it was chronic enough for a clinic, then surely the psychiatric ward and the Bin couldn't be far behind. We took what comfort we could from linking his condition to his circumstances, the loss of his business, the bankruptcy, the breakup of his marriage. In the face of these bad breaks it was only natural to be a little grumpy, down in the mouth, blue. When circumstances got better, then the sadness would go away too.

But the malady had a deeper hold than this. His two great loves were music and my mother, and both had abandoned him. In giving up his own ambitions and taking up business, he had compromised for the sake of his family. Now he had failed even in that compromise, and this was not something that you shook off or got over, much as we'd have loved that.

Sometimes I wished that he'd cheer up just for my sake. Sadness and anxiety are contagious, and at sixteen, didn't I have enough to worry about? And it was boring, too; this torpor, the fussing, the hours spent behind closed doors, emerging with red eyes, the flashes of irrational and malicious fury and the embarrassment that followed. Boring to have Mad Dad sulking round the house, boring to listen to his pessimism and self-pity and negativity, boring to inspect the barometer of his mood when I came through the door.

Predicting that mood was made harder by two recent developments. My father had always been what was commonly called a social drinker, a little boozy but only in company, in a good-natured way. He drank at gigs, but only after he'd played and never more than three pints, and then he'd tell stories and jokes, flip beer mats and do tricks with matches.

Now he drank every day, spirits as well as beer, methodical and solitary as if it were a private hobby. It alarmed me more than I can say, and if he asked me to join him I would always decline, not because I didn't like alcohol—God knows that was not the case—but because I didn't want what he had. Whether accompaniment or catalyst, drinking meant self-pity, introspection, lethargy and now, more commonly, rage. When I was very small, he'd respond to spilled juice, to crayons on the wall or broken plates, with nervous laughter and an exasperated tug of his own hair. Now it was as if he'd discovered a new emotion and was embracing anger with the same passion other midlife men give to marathon training or rambling.

The most trivial infraction of the household rules, a coat on the floor, a mug in the sink, an unflushed loo, would bring on an awful, contorted fury, made all the more terrible when accompanied almost simultaneously by regret. You could see it in his red-rimmed eyes, his horror at this loss of control even as he snapped and bawled—*why am I doing this? This is not who I am.* And just as he discovered anger, I found out the pleasure of provoking it, and of feeling finally old enough to stand chest to chest and shout. We'd both discovered terrible new voices, and I confess I sometimes deliberately provoked him just for the satisfaction of reflecting the rage back into his face. It was a squalid, shabby kind of pleasure, like rousing an animal in the zoo by banging on the glass, and the only consolation I had was that in the aftermath we'd be excessively polite, lying head-to-toe on the sofa and watching old movies until he could sleep.

And here was the other development. On his bedside table there now stood a small cluster of brown bottles, the medications that he'd started to take to "even things out." Someone more well informed than myself might have seen the bottles and been pleased that he had a helping hand, some professional guidance. Like bankruptcy, prescription drugs might seem alarming but at least there was a process under way. Given time, we'd come out the other side. Perhaps he wouldn't need them anymore.

But no one said this, and under the influence of film and TV, I was incapable of seeing a brown bottle of pills without imagining the owner tipping his head back and guzzling the lot. Few things are more compelling than our parents' medications, and soon the bottles began to exert a terrible pull on me, and when he was out I'd go and look at them, press down and unscrew the lid, examine one of the pills in my palm, looking for . . . I don't know what, but I'd note the warning labels. "Take as prescribed. May cause drowsiness. Do not combine with alcohol." Really, he might as well have had a loaded pistol by his bed.

And now this possibility joined the roster of terrors and anxieties that accompanied me through the night and on until morning, and it occurred to me then, just as it does now, that the greatest lie that age tells about youth is that it's somehow free of care, worry or fear.

Good God, doesn't anyone remember?

Culture

"Madam, an hour before the worshipped sun peered forth the golden window of the east—"

"One more time."

We'd meet every day in the same spot beneath the tree, working methodically, the progress like crossing a jungle bridge, hopping happily from board to board, picking up momentum, then stumbling as my foot punched through rotten wood.

*"The worshipped sun peered forth the golden—*I can't do this."

"Yes, you can!"

"I feel silly!"

She scrambled up to lean against the tree. "But you understand it!"

"I'm not stupid."

"I didn't say you—"

"He means before dawn."

"Exactly!"

"So why can't I say 'before dawn'? Two words. Before dawn."

"Because this is what's written and it's better! Picture it—sun's little face peeking out the window . . ."

"Fine, you say it, then," I said and tossed the script into the long grass.

"But they're not my lines," she said, retrieving the script. "They're yours."

"Only till Friday."

"Rubbish. Come on. Who's he talking to in the scene?"

I took the script back. "Lady Montague."

"Exactly, the boss's wife, and all of a sudden he's changing the way he speaks and maybe it's because—"

"He's trying to impress her."

"Or maybe he's scared of her or he fancies her."

"Which is it?"

"I don't know! That's up to you."

So I tried to impress Fran. If I couldn't do it with talent or intelligence, then I'd be constant and persevere, and my reward would be to walk home with her each day.

I continued my policy of pelting her with questions, and soon I knew about her best friends at school: Sophie (hilarious, should meet), Jen (cool, I'd probably fancy her) and Neil (tells him everything, just friends). I knew her favorite music, which was either very old—her mum's LPs, Nick Drake and Patti Smith, Nina Simone and the Velvet Underground and obscure old disco—or so new that I'd not heard of it. She'd been listening a lot to the *Romeo + Juliet* soundtrack, not because of the film, which she "liked but didn't love," but because of the Radiohead track near the end, and I had what I thought of as the Radiohead reflex—a rounding of the shoulders, a concerned knitting of the brow. Her favorite movies, too, were what I thought of as "university films" by Jarmusch and Almodóvar, beautiful youths in large-framed spectacles, smoking in Tokyo or Paris, Madrid or the East Village. She had a favorite color Kieślowski film. Her taste in books was heavily influenced by the GCSE English syllabus, and she loved T. S. Eliot, Jane Austen and the Brontës. She liked Thomas Hardy too, but thought of him more as a poet than a novelist, to which I could only nod because I only knew him as a street name, and so thought of him more as an Avenue than a Crescent.

In short, she was as pretentious as to be expected at sixteen, and I rearranged my own tastes accordingly, shuffling *The Piano* up above

Total Recall, Thai green curry over deep-fried prawn balls, while the things she hated—Schwarzenegger, serial-killer movies, Tarantino —were quietly stowed out of sight. In all her cultural passions, her parents—her mother in particular—loomed large, and I found this strange because weren't we meant to form our personalities and passions in opposition to the older generation? I'd resisted jazz on principle, and countered with guitar music, great slabs of rudimentary chords in thumping 4/4 time, devoid of syncopation, modulation and improvisation. It was a puerile and predictable form of rebellion, but if ever I came close to liking any of Dad's music, it seemed important to keep it to myself. I wanted my discoveries to be my own, even if I secretly knew they were no good.

But perhaps this was one of the markers of the upbringing that had produced Fran. The Fishers weren't wealthy, but they knew things, they went on holiday so that they could walk great distances, had wine with meals and used fresh herbs, went to the theatre, and all of this weird, secret knowledge would be passed down along with the good furniture and expensive kitchenware. I wasn't intimidated, or I resolved not to be, but apart from jazz, I didn't have the same legacy to draw upon, and so listened instead until I knew her favorite places (Lisbon, Snowdonia, New York) and the places she'd like to go (Cambodia, Berlin), her musical accomplishments (grade-five piano, grade-three viola, thinking of giving up because "Who's ever going to say, 'Fran, play us something on your viola'?") and the band that she and her friends played in together, called either Savage Alice or Goths in Summer, depending on how seriously they were taking themselves. "We've played the Chatsborne Summer Fete, so it looks like things are going to take off for us soon."

"Well, if you're playing the fetes . . ."

"Next year it'll be school fetes all over the region."

"What kind of music?"

"We specialize in covers that no one recognizes. I shout out, 'Here's one you all know! Help us out with the chorus!' and everyone sort of looks at each other and shrugs."

I loved those walks home, our pace slowing as the days went by. I retained a sense that I was being taught—quietly instructed on what was cool—but I didn't mind. Music, books, films, even art, seemed to have a concentrated power at that age. Like a new friendship, they might change your life, and when I had time—I would have time—I would let some new things in. Over the days, the conversation became easier, so that every now and then I'd let a question slip through.

"What do *your* mum and dad do?"

"Hm?"

"You don't talk about them much."

"Well, Mum works at the golf club. She used to be a nurse, then she helped Dad, now she organizes weddings and events and all that stuff. But I don't live with her."

"You live with your dad?"

"Uh-huh. Mum moved out in April with my sister."

"You didn't say that."

"No."

"Christ, I'm such a cow."

"Why?"

"Banging on about, I don't know, my top three fruits, and you've not told me that."

"You asked before, I just changed the subject."

"Yes, why did you?"

"Change the subject? I don't know, living with my dad—bit weird, isn't it?"

"Well, it needn't be."

"No, but it is. It feels the wrong way round."

"And what does he do?"

"He's unemployed at the moment."

"He got made redundant?"

"Bankrupt. Lost everything. House, savings."

"But he used to . . ."

"Run the music shop on the high street."

She grabbed my arm. "Vinyl Visions! I loved that shop! I used to get everything there."

"Thank you. It didn't work out, though."

"I know, I saw that, just after Christmas. It's a real shame. Wait a minute, I know your dad — nice man, sort of tall, sort of . . . crumpled."

"That's him."

"Always playing far-out jazz in the shop, really wild stuff. When I was younger, he'd be playing this mad, brilliant afro-funk or old blues, nodding along with his eyes closed, and I'd go up to the counter with something by Boyzone or whatever, and he'd take it out of my hand and just sort of . . . smile really sadly. 'Oh, my child . . .'"

"Yep. That's my dad."

She peered at my face. "*That's* where I knew you from!"

"Well, I take after Mum, mainly."

"What happened?"

"Competition. Discounts in the big shops. I think he overestimated the local jazz scene."

"So what's he doing now?"

"This time of day?" I looked at my watch. "He's either asleep or watching *Countdown,*" I said and felt a shiver of self-disgust at that gesture, examining my watch like that, a shabby piece of theatrical business. In truth, I'd not seen his face for days now. For reasons I couldn't say out loud, I did not want to go home. But neither did I want to stay, not now that the conversation had been tainted with pity and mawkishness.

"Well. It's a shame," she said eventually. "I loved Vinyl Visions. Business is brutal, isn't it? Everything great gets stamped on in the end." She took my arm. "We could walk a little further. If you want to talk some more?"

The Jazz Section

IT HAD BEEN SOMETHING GREAT, our family enterprise, while it lasted.

My father's own musical ambitions had stalled. His only regular jazz gig was with Rule of Three, a trio that played the more open-minded local pubs, the kind of accomplished and committed outfit that is always being asked if they can play more quietly. For cash, he played the circuit in a famously slick wedding band, but he had grown to hate the kitschy eighties sax playing that this work demanded, the screwed-up eyes, the head thrown backwards, as posturing and silly as using two fingers to represent a gun. He had wanted to be part of a British jazz revival, not honk glumly though "House of Fun" at some anniversary, a surly "Careless Whisper" at the Rotary Club's Christmas do.

But neither did he want to inherit the family business. Vinyl Visions was a mini-chain, three branches on the high streets of small suburban towns, and my grandparents wanted rid of them. The term "independent record shop" suggests dedication and expertise, the kind of place that might be curated, but my grandparents' feeling for music was like an ironmonger's feeling for buckets. Music was a commodity, and each branch of Vinyl Visions was equally fusty, selling middle-of-the-road music to locals who couldn't face the "big shops." Before their mystifying left turn, my grandparents were stationers and remained stationers at heart, still stocking random items from that noble trade

—lewd and abusive birthday cards, a totem pole of crepe paper, random items that caught my grandfather's eye at the wholesaler's and that he felt belonged amongst the racks of popular classics, novelty records and easy listening on the Music for Pleasure label. Through disco and punk, metal and mod, post-punk and electro-pop and the early days of house, the shop's most consistent sellers remained Richard Clayderman and the soundtrack to *The Sound of Music*. If your heart demanded bagpipe music on cassette and some ancient tinsel, then Vinyl Visions was the only game in town, a music shop for people who didn't much care for the stuff.

The suburban high street was once the natural habitat of shops like this, ill conceived and inefficient, irrational and scrappy, with dusty, fading window displays, closed half-days on Wednesday. But in this new decade, the retail environment was less hospitable, and music retail in particular was changing at a dizzying rate. Should they drop cassettes and commit to CDs? Abandon singles? It was all too much, and so my grandparents called on Dad. It was, they said, irresponsible and immature to live with two kids in rented rooms. Bad enough that he'd dropped out of accountancy, but there must be, what, five, ten people in the country making a living from playing the saxophone, all of them trained at academies and conservatories, all with better contacts. Dad was an amateur. Silly to think he could be one of them. Besides, music retail was a stable business. People would always need music. In return for help with a mortgage on a proper house, why not come back and take over?

Respectability called. Five days a week, plus every other Saturday, serving and cashing up, meeting reps, sorting out the payroll—would it really be so bad? He could still pursue the thing he loved, but at weekends and in the evenings. And it wouldn't be forever; once the business was on its feet again, he could take a step back, employ managers and return to playing. Mum was more hesitant, wary of how easily the temporary becomes permanent. She'd never got along with her in-laws, felt that they bullied and smothered their only child, and to be under an obligation . . . the walls of our rented rooms were thin enough to hear both sides.

But Mum relented, and so we moved back to the town where my father had grown up, into the big house with the solid walls and the stained-glass sunrise. My grandparents retired to a holiday home on the South Wales coast, a bungalow with two reclining chairs and a sea-view picture window. Thirteen at the time, I was now cynical enough to picture Nan and Granddad Lewis cackling all the way down the M4, used-car salesmen who had finally unloaded some famous wreck. Or perhaps they had our best interests at heart. Either way, my father found himself, in his mid-thirties, the managing director of a business he was singularly ill equipped to run.

He took over with a reformer's zeal, pulling us along with him so that it became the Lewis family project. He'd always despaired of the shops' fusty, scrappy atmosphere, the desolate window displays, the aggressive strip lighting that illuminated the stained carpet tiles, the tacky promotional material. A life-size James Last had stood guard over the till for as long as anyone could remember, and he would be the first to go, along with the dull stock of middle-of-the-road croon-ers and ancient novelty records that no amount of discounting could ever hope to shift. Most urgently of all, he longed to take control of his parents' "Jazz Section," where brass bands and the soundtracks of forgotten movies were filed alongside music made by anyone who was not white: Ella Fitzgerald, Bob Marley, the soundtrack to Neil Diamond's *The Jazz Singer*.

Specialization, that was the future. Yes, there'd still be pop and rock and chart hits in the shops, but from now on the emphasis would be on the music that Dad loved. For one hair-raising month, all three branches were "closed for refurbishment." Flush with a large bank loan, the stock was refreshed with CDs and collectors' vinyl, all to be displayed in handsome bespoke pine racks. We took a Friday off

school and over the weekend traveled from shop to shop, alphabetiz-
ing against the clock. A credit card had paid for top-of-the-range stereo equipment—it was important that customers heard the music at
its best—and we cooed obediently at the dynamics and definition as
we played Miles and Monk, Mingus and Coltrane. "Listen to this one,
kids," he'd say, lowering the stylus with a watchmaker's precision, and
there'd be that familiar wash of cymbals and the squall of horns, as
incomprehensible in its appeal as coffee or olives. Like coffee, like olives, we'd grow into jazz, and in the meantime he'd intersperse hard
bebop with the Beatles for us, Bowie for Mum, and we unpacked the
boxes to this soundtrack as happily as if they were presents on Christmas morning, the sealed CDs as crisp and immaculate as surgical
supplies, the vinyl heavy, old-fashioned and luxurious—rare Japa-
nese 180g pressings and leather-bound box sets of studio outtakes. If
I suspected that Dad had bought these things for himself rather than
for the general public, then it was worth it to see how happy he was,
and Mum too. After all, the saxophone was a growling, disreputable,
sexual thing born of late nights and seedy clubs; it could never thrive
in the high streets and business parks of the Surrey/Sussex borders.
Instead he would evangelize, sell something with passion and fulfill a
need the customers didn't yet know they had. On Sunday we arrived at
our home branch and, fueled by fizzy drinks and takeaway, worked for
fourteen hours. When we were finally finished he made us lie on the
floor between the aisles, our heads touching in the center, and placed
one last record on the turntable.

"This is ridiculous," said Mum.

"Just listen!"

"I can hear just as well standing up, Brian."

"Shh. Close your eyes." He lowered the needle and joined us on the
carpet.

"In a Sentimental Mood," the John Coltrane/Duke Ellington version. I liked this one, the jangle of the old piano, the soft, warm sound

of the saxophone against the patter of the drums. It had a melody and
it didn't last too long, though still long enough for my sister to fall
asleep snuggled into Dad's arms. Without saying as much, the music
was intended as a blessing for our new endeavor, and when it was finished we stood silently, locked the shop door and walked into a new
era.

But it's hard to imagine a time less primed for a bebop revival
than the mid-nineties, when the only piano to be heard was in those
choppy house-music chords, the only saxophone a synthesized sam-
ple. Treacherously, I was listening to the chug of guitars when Fran
Fisher was buying that Boyzone CD and making my father's face fall.
But the economics of the independent retailer did not allow for snobbery, and so he'd bite his tongue and sell that too and edge the volume
up on the Modern Jazz Quartet.

And for a while it seemed to be working. People liked my father,
and I saw this and relished it. He had a swagger at that time, and a
work ethic that we'd not seen when he was still struggling to be a
musician. His optimism was contagious, and we were infected by his
confidence. This was the beginning of our family's golden years, and
if I could select a moment when my parents were most essentially
themselves, the parents I'd choose to remember, it would be about
this time.

The closure of the first shop was presented as a consolidation of
resources, a shrewd business move. The money they'd save from rent
and wages could be used to pay down the interest, and loyal customers would travel, especially now the shops were so much more appealing, so well stocked, so modern. This was the pitch I'd hear during
Dad's long, fraught phone calls to his parents in their bungalow exile;
he knew what he was doing, and wouldn't let anyone down. So keen
was he not to disappoint that he found it impossible to make staff redundant, and instead they were relocated to the remaining branches.
We'd see great crowds of them on our weekend rounds, chatting by

the tills, outnumbering customers three to one while *Kind of Blue* played over expensive speakers.

But the first closure also marked the start of the condition we refused to name. God knows, he'd never been an Olympian, but coffee and insomnia gave Dad a confused, exhausted air, as if perpetually struggling to snap out of something. Somewhere between his shoulder blades he seemed to carry a great knot of tension, an object, a ball of clenched muscle that he would press and probe throughout the day, rolling his shoulders, cracking his joints. In the mornings, getting ready for school, I'd sometimes catch sight of him through the bedroom door, bracing himself against the wardrobe as if pinned to the spot by some awful realization. I don't think anything frightened me more than those moments of baffled stillness, and I'd stand on the landing, holding my breath, waiting for him to shake it off. Outwardly at least, he remained affectionate and loving and funny, but it was the artificially bright good humor that precedes bad news.

Six months later, the second shop closed. My mother began to take a more active role, persuading my dad that diversification, rather than specialization, was the key. We began to stock batteries and cables, elaborate gift wrap and greeting cards. For my father, this was the curse of stationery, a terrible step backwards, and he felt heartsick. Wasn't music enough? Where was the love, the passion? Why couldn't they hear it in the music he played? Confidence shaded into plucky defiance, then sour resignation. "You know what I should have gone into, Charlie? Carbon paper. Crinoline petticoats, lace doilies, inkwells. There's more money in inkwells than this."

My mother was having none of this self-pity and defeatism. The answer, she said, was coffee. On days off, she would sometimes escape to London to meet up with old friends, and it was here, in a café near Berwick Street Market, that she'd hit upon her scheme. Soho was practically one big coffee bar. Why not shift the business sideways, invest in a secondhand espresso machine, bentwood chairs, some old school desks, and play music over the speakers. "What's this we're listening to?" the customers would ask, and we would sell them the CD. If not, the markup on a cup of coffee was *immense*. With only the fusty Cottage Loaf Tea Rooms and an Orwellian greasy spoon for competition, there was no way we could fail.

"You'd go, Charlie, wouldn't you? And your friends?"

"I don't drink coffee."

"Quite right too. But you will, and when you do—"

"I'm not doing it, Amy!"

"Why not?"

"Because it's catering! I'm not a caterer."

"You weren't a retailer either, but you learned, didn't you?"

"Well, apparently not."

"But you can make coffee. How hard can it be to stick a bun on a plate?"

"I don't want to sell *buns,* I want to sell records."

"And no one wants to buy them, not anymore, they're too expensive. Just try it. I'll help you, we all will. You'll see."

A meeting was arranged with the bank to approve a further loan. This was not the breeze that it had been the year before. It was no longer enough to simply stack high the piles of *Brothers in Arms,* and my father couldn't hope to compete with the three-for-two offers at the megastores. So instead they'd provide something new, a little slice of Berwick Street cool, tucked in between the Millets and the Spar. I remember them setting off to see the bank manager, my father in his wedding suit, my mother in a creamy ruffled blouse, like children in fancy dress. I remember them tumbling through the door, wide-eyed and hysterical with success like criminals after an audacious heist, and I remember the flurry of industry in the weeks that followed: stacks of secondhand chairs in the living room, multipacks of frozen croissants —dense, dusty pellets like agricultural feed—and the toaster oven to turn them into gold, and great catering sacks of oats, too, so that

Mum might manufacture flapjacks in factory quantities, the profit margin on a flapjack exceeding even that of coffee and wrapping paper, and once again there was a kind of industrious harmony in the household. I remember the secondhand coffee machine, the Santorini Deluxe, all pipes and dials and valves like a model steam engine. Most vividly, I remember coming home from school and stepping into a kitchen that smelled of warm sugar and melting chocolate, a buttery condensation on every surface.

They stormed through money, yet for all the fear my parents must have felt, we still thought of ourselves as stable. "Poor but happy, but not that happy"—this was my mother's joke, and the good humor we retained was down to her. I felt such love for Mum at that time, for her determination and resilience and ambition, the engine that kept us moving forward. Family life was unimaginable without her. She didn't care about money or status or what the front garden looked like, she only cared that we were all fine. My dad adored her of course, and relied on her, perhaps too much, but for all her teasing I never doubted that she still loved him. We groaned and looked away when they kissed or held each other, but secretly—what relief, what certainty.

The Blue Note Café opened in the same September week as my sixteenth birthday, and my father suggested that we combine celebrations and have an opening party for family and friends and our regular customers. There were fairy lights and candles, Dad played with his band, the last time he ever played in public, toning down his jazz stylings and playing the wedding party set instead. Mum sang, there was dancing and, as the pubs closed, curious faces pressed against the window. We felt famous in our town, successful, a little beacon on the dreary high street. I'd taken to drinking from discarded glasses, anything I could find, and so was too fuzzy-headed to recall the last part of the evening. But I do remember that my father took the microphone and gave a speech in which he talked about his fine young son—sixteen years! How did that happen!—his beautiful daughter

Billie, so smart, the inspiration Mum had provided, about his hopes for this amazing new venture after a rough couple of years. Cribbed from ceremonies seen on TV, the speech was sentimental, but I think, know, that I cried a little. Perhaps all families have these fleeting moments when, without ever saying as much, they take each other in and think, *we work and we fit together and we love each other, and if we can remain like this, all will be fine.*

But my father's optimism was misplaced, an acceptance speech for an award that had not been given. At Christmastime, the last shop closed, leaving nowhere to hide the ruinous debt that he had been moving from one failed enterprise to the next.

Stage Laughter

EACH DAY, THE COMPANY grew, bringing new faces to the circle on the Great Lawn.

"Hello, my name's Sam," said a handsome minstrel in a collarless cotton shirt and waistcoat. "I'll be providing the music and playing various small roles!"

"And I'm Grace," said the pale girl at his side, her long hair flowing down past the low waist of her dress, the kind of girl you'd see, said George, with her arms around a unicorn. Sam and Grace—Simon and Garfunkel, Alex called them—were Ivor's friends from the Oxford Medieval Society, though what happened at such a society, and why anyone would join, was another incomprehensible glimpse of the world of university. Perhaps it gave them access to the arsenal of tambours and recorders, stringed gourds and tiny bells that would provide the music for the show, backed, they told us, with cool, modern club beats.

"Fuck-ing hell," said Alex. Grizzled veterans of Theatre Sports week, we were cynical and wary of new recruits.

"Troubadours," sniffed Helen, who had been quietly assembling her own crack team.

"Hello, my name's Chris, and I'm going to be helping Helen on the design."

"Hello, my name is *also* Chris!" (gales of laughter—I swear, these people) "and I'm also going to be helping with design and stage man-

agement!" Chris and Chris had the same lank hair, the same mush-
roomy complexions, the same immense bunches of keys and jangling
penknives attached to the hip of the same black jeans with a prison
warden's silver chain. One of Polly's distant outhouses had been
transformed into the tech headquarters, commanded by Helen from
behind an immense architect's drawing board, and here they laughed
at private jokes, surrounded by squalor that in itself seemed like a set,
the den of a computer hacker or serial killer: Coke cans, scraps of
balsa wood, filthy, furred mugs and half-eaten pasties, squeezed-out
tubes of aircraft glue, empty crisp packets, scissors and scalpels and
rolls of chicken wire. Somewhere in the mess they'd concealed their
own toasted-sandwich maker and a supply of white bread, processed
cheese and brown sauce, and this became a source of great envy. But
"Actors—Keep Out!" said a handwritten sign in comic-book letter-
ing, and we were further discouraged from entering by the blare of
Goth (Chris's choice) and burbling trance (the choice of Chris), which
they played at volumes loud enough to end a siege.

The private coaching continued long after I'd expected Fran to lose
interest, returning to the meadow, turning the pages, scene by scene,
line by line. "We're working on my part!" I insisted as Helen slapped
the dried grass from my back, but it's true that an awareness of the
proximity of Fran's hip or head would sometimes cause my attention
to lapse, to wonder what might happen if I were to lean across and
kiss her while she explained the importance of iambics. "*You kiss by
the book*," says Juliet in the play. If it ever happened, I wanted very
much to kiss by the book.

Grandmothers aside, I had kissed, or been kissed, twice before,
though it might be more accurate to describe those events as facial
collisions. The first occasion was in a darkened audio-visual exhibit
on a History field trip to Roman remains. There's no reason why anyone should instinctively know how to kiss—like snowboarding or
tap-dancing, it can't be learned from watching—but Becky Boyne's

technique was to purse her lips into a tight, dry bud that she tapped around my face like a bird getting nuts from a feeder. Films had also taught us that a kiss was not a kiss unless it made a noise, and so each point of contact was accompanied by a little lip-smacking sound as artificial as the clip-clop that represents a horse. Eyes open or closed? I kept them open in case of discovery or attack, and read the wall display behind her. The Romans, I noted, had pioneered under-floor heating.

My second kiss was quite different, an angry, open-mouthed, frenzied shark attack by a girl called Sharon Findlay, jammed down the back of a sofa at one of Harper's den parties. I had never been more aware that the tongue was a muscle, a powerful skinless muscle like the arm of a starfish, and whenever I tried to raise my head it was ground back down onto the dusty underlay with the same kind of force and motion required to juice a grapefruit. I retain a certain memory that when Sharon Findlay belched, my cheeks puffed out, and when we finally pulled apart, she wiped her mouth along the entire length of her arm. The experience left me shaken and sore-jawed, but also strangely excited, as if after some harrowing fairground ride, so that I wasn't sure if I wanted to do it again immediately or never again in my life.

"Are you listening to me?" said Fran.

"I'm listening," I said and wondered, what did "by the book" mean? Which book? Could I still buy it?

As the days went by, the lines improved. Just as watching a foreign film with subtitles can lull you into believing you know the language, reading scenes with Fran provided the illusion of competence, and I found that I stumbled less, and sometimes got through great stretches with an eloquence that took me by surprise. Reading with Fran was like playing tennis with a competitor who wanted me to win, knocking the ball back courteously to my racket. Self-consciousness and embarrassment faded. I still didn't know what to do with my hands, but I no longer spoke as if reading from the bottom of an optician's chart.

Of course all this would be wasted if, as expected, I was replaced. It was one thing to hide in the crowd scenes, but to speak and be heard, this was a different matter, and I imagined Ivor and Alina engaged in frantic backstage negotiations with members of the Lakeside Players, the Cygnet Amateur Dramatic Guild, the Chalk Down Stagers, for any boy, girl, man or woman who might take my place. On Monday, I wouldn't have minded. By Thursday, I wasn't so sure.

This was to be the day of my first rehearsal with Romeo, nodding and listening mainly, and some laughter too, and so we practiced, lying on our backs in the long grass of the orchard.

"Ah ha ha ha! Something like that?"

"I like it. I like the little shake of the head," said Fran.

"Sort of 'Romeo, you crack me up!'"

"Yes. I got that. Let go of your chin, though."

"Ha-ha!"

"Oh, man, Charlie, you're bad at this."

"Okay, you do it."

"Fine, watch." Fran laughed, entirely naturally. "How was that?"

"Not great."

"Oh, because I didn't *hold my chin?* Well, fuck you, Daniel Day-Lewis. I don't know why you don't just go the whole hog and slap your thigh."

"Like this?"

"Exactly. Little Dick Whittington–type thing."

"Slap thigh. Okay, maybe I'll try that."

"Or you could just be natural. Be yourself."

"If I was being myself, I wouldn't be here."

"And yet here we are," she said. "Here we are." Up at the house, the triangle sounded. "And that marks the end of today's session."

"Thank you."

"What for?"

"For teaching me how to laugh again."

"Ha."

We walked back together. "How are you feeling?" she said.

"Bit nervous. I'm pretty sure they're going to replace me after this."

"Rubbish."

"Whenever I speak in the first scene, I keep seeing Alina pinch the bridge of her nose and shake her head very slowly. I say, '*Part, fools! Put up your swords!*' and I swear, she puts her fingers in her ears."

"Still, they're not going to replace you."

"But if they do?"

"Then I'll resign from the production. We all will. We'll down sticks."

"Would you do that for me?"

"No. No, probably not."

"Oh."

"Well, I've learned the lines now."

"That's very touching."

"But they're not going to replace you, so you're fine."

"But if they do . . ."

"What?"

We were at the house now, the large room Polly had cleared for rehearsals, French windows open to the air. "Do we still get to go out for coffee?"

"You're *obsessed* with this coffee."

"Or dinner or something?"

"Dinner. There's posh. Where?"

"I don't know. The Angler's?"

"Steak night or the Sunday carvery?"

"That would be completely up to you. Lady's choice."

"It is tempting."

"Or we could just . . . see each other."

"You don't think we see each other?"

"You know what I mean."

"Because I am literally looking right at you."

"I mean away from here, from all this . . ."

"Here he comes now"—Miles was approaching, gulping water as he walked—"Britain's most hydrated young actor. What's he wearing?" It was a basketball top, the neckline scooped well below his sternum, bare at the sides. "It's for netball. Well, good luck. Hey, what was the name of your best friend? In real life?"

"Harper."

"Just imagine that you're talking to Harper. Imagine you've both met girls that you really like and you've got to talk about it."

Was this subtext again? "Okay."

"You talk about that stuff, don't you?"

"Not really. Mainly we beat each other up."

"Well, pretend that you talk. That's all this scene is, two young men talking honestly and openly about their feelings. They managed it in 1594. Imagine if it still happened now. Imagine a world where you're not all quite so repressed."

Improvisation

I'D NOT HEARD FROM Harper since the fight with Lloyd. On Monday and Wednesday I'd worked my shift at the petrol station and stolen more cards in preparation for the handover, but he had not appeared. Phone messages, too, had gone unanswered and I wondered if perhaps some line had been crossed. In the great catalogue of physical and emotional violence that we'd visited upon each other over the years—the pushing off the pier, the fireworks thrown, the air-rifle scars—the pool-ball incident was surely minor. We'd once played a game in the field behind Harper's house, Agincourt we called it, taking it in turns to put on a blindfold and hurl three professional tungsten-tipped darts high, high in the air while the rest of us picked a spot and had to stand still, shoulders hunched, eyes closed, waiting for the darts to rain down. The game could only really end when someone received an injury, and sure enough, before too long there was an audible *thunk* and Fox stood with a single dart standing vertically from his skull while Lloyd, who had thrown the thing, curled up in a ball, unable to breathe for laughter. All of this was normal, "classic Lloyd," with no hard feelings. But throw one single pool ball at someone's head . . .

Now I was forced to imagine a life without Harper. In the chaos of our family's self-destruction he had quietly and unassumingly made himself present, and though I could hardly recall a conversation that might be considered personal or honest, in the strange, mute sema-

phore of teenage boys he'd communicated a sense of care and somehow passed on the message to the others, an unspoken command to
be, if not kind, then not actively cruel. At the time, I'd even gone so far
as to imagine I was a little in love with Harper. In a dog-eared library
book on the "facts of life" I'd read that "homosexual" crushes were
quite common amongst teenage boys. I knew that boarding schools
were rife with that stuff, and might there not be a Merton Grange version? Meeting Fran had rendered the theory obsolete, but I still found
that I missed Harper.

Would he ever know about Fran? *The thing is, Harper — Martin
— I've got tangled up in this, well, this Shakespeare thing, and, don't
laugh, there's this girl in it, not like the others, she's funny, really smart
and cool and we can talk and talk . . . you should meet her!* But the
scenario evaporated even as I tried to give it words, and I was forced to
accept that they really were better at this in the Renaissance.

"Tell me in sadness, who is that you love?"

"What, shall I groan and tell thee?"

"Groan! Why, no, but sadly tell me who."

"Okay, that's great, let's stop there. So — tell me, what do you two
know about these boys' relationship?"

Miles, it seemed, knew a great deal, and I sank into my classroom
silence as he filled in my backstory, the years we'd studied together
at Verona high school, how I looked up to him, how perhaps, Miles
speculated, I was a bit in love with him.

"This is great," said Ivor, "and now I want you both to imagine an
earlier conversation, the two of you, before the start of the play, where
you talk about love."

A pause.

"In your own time."

"Sorry, Ivor," I said, "you want us to . . ."

"Go off script, improvise."

"As . . . as these characters?"

"That's right."

"But using the language of the time?"

"I can do that," said Miles.

"Yes, but don't get hung up on it, Charlie. Keep it loose, it doesn't have to be historically accurate, it's more about how you relate to each other. Just . . . make it up."

"Okay, let's do it," said Miles, slapping his hands together. "Someone forgot their lines in *Twelfth Night* once and I improvised for, like, a page and a half, in iambics too, and I swear, if you wrote it down, no one would be able to tell the difference—"

"No," I said.

"No?"

"I can't do that, Ivor."

"Give it a go, nevertheless."

The doors to the patio were closed, but if I hurled myself through the glass—

No time. Miles was on me, embracing me in his big bare arms. "Benvolio, how dost thou? I have been looking for thee in all the squares and alleyways of this fair town."

"Ah, dear Romeo," I said, my cheek against his smooth bare chest, "I wast . . . at home. With my parents."

"Let us not talk of mum and dad but let us talk of love!"

"Ah, love," I said. "What dost *thou* think of love, fair Romeo?"

"Thou knowst that I scorn love, all poetry, all song. But thou, Benvolio, art a mystery. Dost thou not have a secret love? One that thou holdst dear? Pray tell, for am I not thy dear, true friend?"

"Great," whispered Ivor, "this is great!" and now they were both looking at me as I searched the ceiling, then the carpet, then the ceiling for something to say.

"Ah, love. With love, my experience hath been . . . both hit and miss . . . for love is like something . . . that I can . . . take or leave. And that, dear friend, is all I have to say."

"Okay," sighed Ivor, "let's remember what we've learned."

What I'd learned was that I was at my best when listening and nodding. Thankfully it was a listening, nodding sort of scene and as the afternoon went on, I began to understand it. Romeo claims to be in love with someone, and my response—Benvolio's response—is to point out that there are plenty more fish in the sea.

"Forget to think of her!"

"O, teach me how I should forget to think!"

And I had to hand it to Miles, he could really handle the "O"s, the "Ah, me"s and "Alas"es, could really sing them out, as he bounced around the room, squatting, sitting astride a chair, improvising business with the curtains or a lampshade. I did my best to keep up. "Try moving *on* the line, Charlie," said Ivor, "rather than before or after," but walking while talking was beyond me, especially holding the script. The other hand, which I was unable to squeeze into the pocket of my jeans, dangled limply from the belt loop like a flirtatious cowboy. Miles, meanwhile, found poses that he would hold for a suspended moment, like a model in a photo shoot. He didn't act *with* me but around me, as if I was a coffee table.

But along with vanity and self-absorption came a conviction that was catching, and once we'd "got it on its feet" and "kicked it around a little" I found that I no longer recoiled from his arm around my neck, the punch on the shoulder. Imagine you're talking to your best friend, Fran had said, and so I did, and soon Ivor was sitting hunched forward in his chair, earnest and engaged, gnawing on a knuckle. Alina joined us too, serious behind crossed arms but not scowling or pinching the bridge of her nose or shaking her head.

"Nice work, guys," said Ivor at the end of the day. "Great process," and I felt an entirely unexpected bloom of pride. Stepping outside, Miles squeezed my shoulder and offered me the magic water. "I think we're on to something." I felt another hand on my other shoulder, lightly touching as she passed by. "Someone has been doing their homework!" said Alina, with the bare ghost of a smile, and I knew that I was safe and could stay on, if I chose to.

And waiting for me on the wall of the rockery garden, kicking at the stones with her heel and grinning, was Fran Fisher, ready to walk home.

Forget to think of her? O, teach me how I should forget to think!

At the petrol station, I sat behind the till and muttered Shakespeare.

"*Madam, an hour before the worshipped sun peered forth the golden window of —*"

A horn sounded on the forecourt, and here was Harper stepping out of his brother's car, with two other figures in the back seat, slumped low. I stashed the script away and made sure my sword was out of sight. Harper entered and we went into our act.

"My brother has won some money on the scratch cards. Can I please cash them in here please?"

"Certainly! May I see the cards?

"Yes. Here are the cards."

I took the cash from the till. "Congratulations!" I said, but he was already walking away. I watched him cross the forecourt, and this was where I finally broke character and sprinted round the counter and outside.

"Excuse me! Quick word?" We stood stiffly by the bags of barbecue charcoal, Harper uncomfortably eyeing the getaway car.

"What is it?"

"Just wondered—how've you been?"

"I've been all right. I thought you said we were on video."

"We are, it's fine, no one watches. It's just if people drive off without paying. I haven't seen you since—"

"I came by your house. Your dad said you were out. He said he'd not seen you either."

"No, I've been . . . was he all right?"

Harper laughed. "I don't know, he's your dad. Same as always. We'd better go." I heard the rev of the engine, saw his brother tapping his watch, saw it was Lloyd and Fox low in the back seat. I raised my hand but no response.

"So, is Lloyd still pissed off with me?"

"A bit."

"Okay. Well, I'll come and get the money later."

"No, don't do that, it's late."

"Oh. Okay." It was not yet nine.

"I'll give it to you now, but I don't want to do this again."

"Okay."

"I'm earning good money with Dad; I don't need it. In fact, you can have the lot."

"No, you take half."

"No. You need it more than I do."

"Here? Now?"

"I've got it in my hand. I'll slip it to you, save the bother."

I thought for a moment. "Okay, be careful." We shook hands and I felt my fingers curl around the notes, which I tucked straight into my pocket. The handover felt smooth enough, underplayed and discreet, and it was only later, when it became evidence against me, that I thought of the furtive look each way, the glance I gave into the lens of the security camera, the stiff and twisted handshake that had no motivation. Why would the clerk be standing on the forecourt in the first place, shaking hands with a customer he'd not met before?

When performing on camera, it's always important to do less.

Prospects

THE CAPULETS WERE PLAYING rounders against the Montagues, Polly for the Capulets, crouching low, the bat held over her shoulder with two hands like an ax murderer.

"You're holding it too high, Polly," said Miles, about to bowl.

"Miles, I'm sixty-eight years old, don't tell me how to play rounders, please."

"But it's too high, it needs to be down here."

"Miles, I will send this ball directly at your face."

"No, not the face!" shouted Alex.

"Fine. Do it your way." The ball left his hand and with a satisfying *pok,* Polly sent it high into the blue sky as Fran and Colin and Keith left their bases and ran, followed by Polly, sliding home to whoops and cheers.

George was last in, picking up the bat with clear distaste. "Team sports. Fascism in action. The only reason I'm here is to avoid team sports."

He didn't last long, then it was my turn. Having failed at badminton, it now seemed vital to me that Fran think I was extraordinary at rounders, but I could only knock the ball a few meters into the hands of Lucy. The rest of the Montagues fell soon after, and then both houses lay sprawled across the lawn in the morning sun.

I'd promised Fran a week of my time. A week, I felt, was long enough to give up without misleading anyone, but—she must have known—the idea of leaving had faded day by day, and it wasn't just Fran that kept me coming back. As the individual faces of the company had come into focus, I'd grown to like these people and even to imagine a time when I no longer thought of them as "these people." In the same way that accents are contagious, I'd found myself adopting the company manner of irony, archness, deadpan. They made jokes *and their faces didn't move at all*. They spoke as if they hoped that someone was writing it down, conversation that aspired to dialogue, stuffed with inverted commas and in-jokes. They teased each other too, but without malice. Accustomed to the blunter tools of sarcasm and abuse, I wasn't sure that I could pull this off, but every now and then I'd say something and the company would laugh and I'd have that sensation, *pok,* of sending a ball into the sky. Yet just as often the conversation would take a turn that I couldn't follow and I'd find myself swiping at the air.

They were talking about college. Exam results were due in the last week of rehearsals, and if all went to plan—everyone knew that it would—then Fran, Lucy, Colin, Helen and George would all be joining Alex at sixth-form college. Though they liked to pretend differently, I knew that Harper and Fox would be going too, friends old and new at a party I was not invited to. Now conversation was spiraling off further into futures that they pretended were treacherous and uncertain but that we all knew were gilded and assured, because these were the book-token kids, smart and diligent and talented. In two more years they'd leave this town and migrate to cities famous for their nightlife and music and culture, their lively political scene and cafés. In candlelit bedrooms they'd have meaningful talks, making friends who'd introduce them to more friends, then more and more, loosening the old ties to make way for the new in a branching tree of friendship, of connections and opportunities. The contrived sense of

jeopardy was too much to bear. It wasn't an issue of class and education—or not *just* of class and education—but of that other, more
precious commodity, not unconnected: confidence.

I'd fouled up any chance I might have had to take part in this conversation, and now I could hear the voice in my head grow sarcastic
and resentful. Was university a safer choice than drama school? wondered Alex. Was a medical degree too much of a commitment? asked
Lucy. Envy is corrosive but at least there's a vigor in envying those you
hate, only something sour and lonely in envying those you like, you
love. Rather than making the sourness apparent, I stood and walked
away, not theatrically but not invisibly. It's hard to do anything invisibly with a broom handle dangling at your hip.

In the orchard, I lay down beneath the farthest apple tree and closed
my eyes, and soon I heard the swish of the long grass.

"If you don't come back, your beetroot will go cold," said Fran.

"You can have it all. I mean it."

A number of hard apples had dropped prematurely from the tree,
uncomfortable beneath my back, but I remained where I was, listening
as Fran settled cross-legged at my side.

"I don't blame you, ducking out of that one," she said, tugging at
the grass. "It's quite boring, isn't it? Exam results. Hopes and dreams."

"No, it's fine. I just don't have anything to say, s'all."

"I think everyone just presumes that you're going to be a professional actor," she said and waited. "Does this help, Charlie, or . . . ?"

"Sort of. I like you here."

"I heard you had a bad time."

"Who told you that?"

"Lucy, Colin . . ."

"Oh, God." At that time there was nothing worse, and nothing
better, than being talked about.

"They were nice about it, they weren't gloating or anything. They
just said . . . People were concerned, that's all."

"Well, I did fuck up."

"Maybe you did better than you—"

"Yeah, people always say that, like I'm just being modest. But no, I mean I really fucked up. Walked out, left whole pages blank. I drew pictures in my History exam. By the end I wasn't even turning up, so unless, you know, someone sat the Comprehension paper disguised as me . . ."

She was silent for a while, for which I was grateful.

"Exams are bullshit, though, aren't they? I mean it's just a knack, like learning a card trick. Someone like Miles, I tell you now, it'll be A's all down the page, A-A-A, like a fucking . . . *scream,* but he's still . . . well, he's not thick, but certainly not any smarter. He's just been taught the trick. What I mean is, it's the system that's fucked up, not you. Besides, it's good to kick against things. I wish I could. There are definitely times I want to wipe everything off the desk and walk out, but I'm way too conventional."

I took this in politely, gratified by the rebellious spin that she'd managed to give to failure. The truth was, I'd not deliberately kicked against anything, had no quarrel with formal education and no clear motive. I'd have been delighted to thrive in that system, and there were definitely circumstances in which I might have done better, might even have done quite well.

"So what happened?" she said eventually.

"I think I was making a point. It's just now I've got no idea what it was. Aren't we meant to be going through lines?"

"Not today. So what happened? Tell me."

"I think . . . I think I went a bit mad."

Examination

WE'D ALL GONE A little mad, each in our different way.

For me, it showed up most markedly at school. The promise I'd once shown had been leaching away for some time, but now, with exams looming, that process seemed to accelerate. "We're worried," said Mr. Hepburn at Mum and Dad's last joint parents' evening, "that Charlie is on course to fail." Dad slumped a little further in his chair. Mum reached for my hand, but I pulled it away and returned to rolling my school tie up into a tight little scroll, letting it unroll, then rolling it up once again.

"We don't understand," said my mother. "He was doing perfectly well."

"He was, and now he's not, and we've tried, we've really tried. Haven't we tried, Charlie? Don't you think that's fair?"

That night, Mum came into our room while my sister slept, knelt by my bed as I lay facing the wall, cupping the back of my head with her hand. "Want to talk?"

"No. Just sleep."

But each night I'd lie awake, the only sixteen-year-old insomniac in the world, and in the day suffer a bone-weary nausea like jet lag, or what I imagined jet lag to be. A clouding-over in my head, like steam forming on a mirror. Foggy, stupid I suppose, though the word was never used by anyone except me as I gave another fumbled answer, a sentence that petered out into nonsense; *stupid boy, stupid, stupid,*

stupid. I'd fall asleep with my head on my desk, then, half awake, stare at textbooks as impenetrable as Sanskrit, and my gaze would drift to the margin, then on to the grain of my wooden desk, and I'd lapse into that same dumb, frozen state in which I'd sometimes catch my father and think, *oh God, not me too*.

For my sister, the madness manifested itself as withdrawal into near muteness: evenings in the public library, lunchtimes in the school library or, on the rare occasions when I saw her outside, alone at the far reaches of the playing field. She had always been the clever one, but now books were something that she used to conceal her face. She might as well have been holding them upside down. In less turbulent times we'd argued over the TV remote or the injustice of bedtimes, disputes that now seemed trivial and irrelevant, yet we'd not worked out how to replace them, and passed in the corridor without speaking. Once or twice, I saw her duck around a corner to avoid me. Once or twice, I did the same.

Mum's madness was a kind of mania, frantic attempts to make amends. Three, sometimes four times a week after she'd moved out, I'd find her waiting in the car at the school gates, where she'd wind down the window, beckon me over and offer me tea and cake at the Cottage Loaf. I'd climb in, abducted by my mother while my sister, presumably, walked home alone.

In the café, no sooner did the cake arrive than the tea things would be pushed to one side and out would come the revision guides, fresh from the local stationers. "So what shall we do today?"

"Mum, I can do this by myself."

"How's French? How's your Biology?"

"I'm not doing Biology."

"You are!"

"I'm not."

"Well that was a waste of money," she said and dropped the guide onto the floor.

'Okay, English. *Lord of the Flies*, yes?" She took the York Notes and opened it at random. "Talk to me about . . . the character of Piggy in *Lord of the Flies*."

As an educator, Mum's great gift was her ability to instill a mutual sense of panic and futility. She had always been content to leave teaching to the teachers. Now she was like someone waking late for the airport, cramming clothes into the suitcase, unwilling to accept that the flight has already departed.

"The verb *voir* . . ."

"To want."

"Not 'to want.' To want is *vouloir,* as in *voulezvous.* Charlie, that's not even French, that's just Abba. *Voir.* Come on, you know this."

"Okay, to see."

"Yes! *Voir,* past tense. Go!"

". . ."

"Go!"

"*J'ai* . . ."

"Come on, *j'ai* . . ."

"I don't know."

"You do!"

"Shhh. Keep your voice down!"

"But you *do* know!"

"Mum, you saying I know won't make it true!"

"But you used to be so, so good at this!"

"Mum . . ."

"We were always led to believe you were doing really well."

"That's not true!"

"Or better than this, at least. Come on, you must know French. What have you been doing for five years! Put your tea down. Here, look at the answers for thirty seconds and we'll try again."

And so she would panic at my lack of knowledge, and I would blank because of her panic, and she would panic because I was blanking, and voices would be raised and one of us would storm out in scenes unheard of in the Cottage Loaf. We'd drive past the remains of our old shop in a crackling silence, back to the new house, where I'd leap from the car. The weeks passed, five until the exams, then four, then three, two, like the countdown timer on a bomb. With one week to go, she parked at the end of the crescent, well out of sight, and asked, "How's Dad?"

"The same."

She nodded, chewed on a knuckle. "Well. He just needs to get enthusiastic about something again."

"What, like a hobby, you mean?"

"No! Is he thinking about work?"

"Sometimes. I don't think he can at the moment."

"Why not?"

"Well, he's nuts, Mum!"

"Don't say that."

"All right, he is *mentally unwell*."

"He's having a hard time."

"Yes, getting out of bed, brushing his teeth . . ."

"All right, I know! But what can I do, Charlie? Tell me what I can do and I'll do it."

I didn't like being asked what to do by my parents. Even if I'd had an answer, she was no longer listening but sat curled around the steering wheel, pressing the heels of her hands against her eyes. "I know the timing's all wrong, I know I should be there, and I hate leaving things to you, *hate* it, but I wouldn't help if I was here, I can't, it's impossible, it would be total war. I make things *worse*, Charlie! What do you think that feels like? Knowing that you make someone so unhappy." She started to cry, and only then did I relent, reaching to embrace her but being jolted back by my seat belt. I twisted more slowly, trying to fool the braking mechanism, was halted again, tugged at the belt—

"Just unclip it!"

"All right!"

"Down there, just unfasten it and take it off! The red button! For Christ's sake, Charlie! Come here . . ."

I contorted myself over the gear stick and felt her face wet against my neck.

"Am I a terrible parent?"

"No."

"But have I been?"

"No."

"But I'm a terrible teacher, yes?"

"Yes, you are a terrible teacher."

She snuffled into my neck. "I do love you. And you're going to be fine," she said, "you're such a bright boy."

But she was a lousy actor too, and the blatancy of the lie, the hesitancy with which she told it, sent me clambering out of the car. I arranged my schoolbag over my shoulder, raised one hand and walked the short distance home, taking out my keys in anticipation of the part of the day that I dreaded most of all.

Because my father's madness was the most spectacular of all, the idea had fixed itself in my head, possibility shading into probability then certainty, that my father would kill himself and I would be the one to find him. I used to speculate on the circumstances of this at night, then during the school day, anxiety growing as I neared home. Would he be in the bedroom or in the hallway, in the bathroom or lying on the sofa? It didn't even matter if this was one of his good days, smiling when I left for school, hugging me sentimentally at the door. If anything, this made disaster more likely, because — another cliché from TV — acts of self-destruction were always preceded by just those displays of affection, delivered with glazed, numb serenity. "I love you, son, never forget that," and then you come home and — one more cliché — the envelope is on the table, propped between the salt and pepper. No, nothing signaled disaster quite as clearly as a parent saying "I love you."

My adolescent mind had a limitless capacity for this kind of melodrama, and I wish I could have directed my mental energy in some other direction. Instead these grim scenarios became so fixed and plausible that often my hand would be shaking as I turned the key, already shouting, "Dad, I'm home!" Sometimes he'd be on the sofa watching a black-and-white movie, at other times he'd be asleep, downstairs or up, and I would check that this was the right kind of sleep, that the brown bottles were in place, caps tight, no alcohol in sight. If he wasn't home, I'd be incapable of calming myself until he returned, and only then could I slip into our banal domestic natter: what to eat that night, what to watch.

"Shouldn't you be revising?" he'd say.

"I revised at school," I'd say.

"Important times," he'd say, and we'd leave it at that. I'd try to make him laugh if I could, providing an ironic commentary on whatever was on TV. If that failed, if he seemed not to be hearing me, if he lay down on his side or poured himself another whisky, then I would endeavor to lure him upstairs.

"Don't fall asleep here, Dad. Come to bed."

"I want to watch the end."

"You've seen it before. Come to bed, don't fall asleep on the sofa."

"You go on up, son."

And so I'd stalk off to bed to dwell on what I'd read about combining alcohol and pills, and the worry would start again.

And through all this, I don't think I ever said the word "depression" out loud. It was taboo, and I would no more have shared my fear and confusion with a teacher or friend than confided my sexual fantasies. Honesty was dangerous, and even if Harper would not have used it against me, I had no doubt that Lloyd would.

When, many years later, I finally told Niamh some, not all, of this, she told me that I sounded like my father's carer. Immediately, I recoiled from the word. "Care" suggested compassion, integrity, selflessness and devotion, and I had none of these virtues, not one. I'd certainly not told her the story to elicit the admiration that's due to those who truly *care*. The more my father required sympathy and compassion, the more I offered up pity and contempt; the more he required my presence, the more I disappeared. He frightened me, and when I wasn't frightened I was simply furious; furious to be robbed of my peace of mind and power of concentration when I needed them most, furious at being scared of something as banal as opening the front door. Bored too, bored of his zombified state, of the perpetual air of distraction that surrounded him like a cloud of flies around his head, of the impossibility of change. I didn't want anything as corny as a role model, I just wanted someone who got up every morning, someone capable of smiling in a way that was neither creepy nor contrived.

Everything good that I wished for my father, I wished for my own sake. More than anything, I wanted him to be how he used to be. For the best part of my childhood, he'd been funny and cheerful and affectionate. Now even his good moods seemed unnatural — what did he have to be happy about? I blamed him for our poverty, for driving Mum away, for my failing at school. I worried about him when he should have been worrying about me. Couldn't he see that things were going wrong? Not a carer, then. Was "resenter" a word? "Live-in resenter?"

That's only natural, Niamh assured me; it would be weird to feel otherwise. But in one final flourish of care-lessness, I couldn't bear the physical change: the sag of his flesh, pale and damp like the skin beneath a sticking plaster, the stooped shoulders, the dabs of unnamable whiteness in the corners of his mouth, the toenails like shavings from the horn of an animal. Just as a smile is said to light up a face, unhappiness had made him ugly, to me at least, and at some point, I no longer bothered to disguise the distaste, wrinkling my nose, shrugging his arm away. With youthful priggishness, I wondered, why can't the old man look after himself? I was sixteen years old; people wrote *anthems* about this time of life, and wasn't I entitled to joy and fun and irresponsibility, rather than fear and fury and boredom?

In one other sense, "care" was almost the opposite word because sometimes—and this was something that I would never say out loud—sometimes a part of me wanted the catastrophe. All children, I'm reassured, fantasize about the death of their parents, but rarely in such plausible circumstances. At least if something happened to him, I'd get the attention and sympathy I felt I deserved; at least I could get on with things, whatever those things were. These thoughts seem shocking and shameful to me now, and the only defense I'm able to come up with is that I both hated and loved my father more than anyone in my world, the strength of the first emotion proportional to the second. I could only hate him like that because I'd once loved him to the same degree.

I should recount one other incident, at the climax of the conflict that had preceded Mum's departure in the spring. The row that night had been apocalyptic: accusations, recriminations, brutal character assessments dripping with contempt, things that could never be unsaid and which would make any future life together quite impossible. I'd retreated to my room to revise, or rather to stare blindly and uncomprehendingly at my textbooks, fingertips drilling at my temples. My sister, in the bunk bed behind me, had taken to wearing Dad's large, expensive headphones in order to muddy the worst of the words, but tonight the flimsy membrane of our bedroom floor was vibrating like a speaker. The effect must have been the same for our neighbors too, because for the first time someone actually called the police.

Billie saw the blue light first. We stepped out onto the landing and watched from the top of the stairs as my father, astonished and humiliated, opened the door and showed the police into the living room. My parents stood next to each other like children caught in some act of vandalism. Had it really come to this? Were we really that family, the one the neighbors complained about? The voices downstairs were placating now, *No, Officer, we quite understand, we're all right now,* and I wanted to scream down the stairs, No, they're *not* all right, they're like this *all the time!* Instead I stomped into the bathroom, loud enough for the officers to hear, clattered through the cabinet to find the aspirin, slammed the cupboard door shut, pressed two into my hand, then a third, then paused. I opened the cupboard door once more, sorting through the tubes of lotions, the sticky bottles of ancient syrup, and found a brown bottle of liquid acetaminophen. I tossed the pills into my mouth with a swig of filthy liquid, craned my head under the tap to wash it all down and then, for good effect, unscrewed the lid of the same nighttime cough medicine I'd taken as a toddler, several years past its sell-by date and so presumably all the more concentrated and toxic. Hearing the door close on the police downstairs, I swigged at this too, wincing at the chemical sweetness, then arranged the packaging on the toilet cistern, the brown bottle left on its side for effect, a little diorama of despairing protest. Below us, my parents were speaking in sharp, urgent whispers. My sister lay on the top bunk, feigning sleep. I lay down beneath her, my hands clasped on my chest in anticipation, like a figure on a tomb.

This scene took place just before my father was prescribed his own medications, and I wonder if I'd have had the nerve to unscrew the lids of those particular brown bottles. I doubt it. I contemplated suicide in the same way that I contemplated murder, as a kind of thought experiment, and if I ever pressed the dull edge of the butter knife against the blue vein in my wrist, then it was in the same spirit as imagining where I'd bury Chris Lloyd's body. Even as I gulped down the ancient cough syrup I knew that expectorants were rarely fatal. The concern and remorse of my parents, this was the main aim. To pull themselves together, to remain together.

But in the morning I woke with embarrassment and regret, and rushed to the bathroom to find Mum waiting, the blister pack of pills in one hand, the sticky bottle held by the fingertips of the other.

"Charlie, is this you?"

"Yes?"

"So, Charlie, can I ask you not to leave stuff lying around like this?" She tossed the syrup in the bin. "*This* is out of date. And if you've got a headache, take aspirin or acetaminophen, not both. They're not free. And put. Things. Away!"

If such a blatant performance could go unnoticed, then something even more theatrical would be required. Fortunately, the perfect opportunity loomed just a few months away in the exam hall.

Some, not all of this, I told Fran over the rest of the summer, but in the orchard I just confirmed the facts of my academic catastrophe.

"F for fucked up. I just thought you ought to know."

She was silent for a moment. "What do you think I ought to know?"

"I don't want you to think I'm something I'm not. That I'm going places that I can't go."

"Okay. So you're warning me off."

I shrugged. "I suppose so."

"Well, it's true that I do usually like to know grades before I get to know someone. It's a simple points-based system, really, but if you do well in the practical and the interview—"

"No, but if someone's a screw-up—"

"It's continuous assessment, really."

"—or just dim—"

"The only time that you sound dim," she said, "is when you say that you sound dim. Does that make sense?"

"I think so."

"Well, there you go."

I'd closed my eyes again, draped my arm across my face, but still I felt the shadow fall and heard the movement in the leaves as she settled next to me.

"Come out tonight," she said, taking my hand. "Just me and you?"

"Nope, everyone. We're all going out together."

"It's not ideal."

"No. But don't go away." From the house, the triangle sounded. "At the end of the night, don't go anywhere without me, Charlie. It's very important that you understand. Nowhere without me."

Masks

THE PLYWOOD BOX WAS shrouded with a cloth and carried into place by Chris and Chris with solemn reverence, as if it might be the Ark of the Covenant.

"Okay, so this is a work in progress . . ." said Helen.

"I love this bit," said George. "It's when it feels real."

"There's still lots of work to do . . ."

"Just show the model, Helen dear," said Alina.

The cloth was tugged away to oohs and wows. I joined in. Chris and Chris were the kind of boys who haunted the aisles of Hobby Lobby, addicted to that particular pleasure of making tiny versions of very large things, and the model was exquisite, a miniature street corner in dusty white, skewed and twisted so that the buildings leaned forward drunkenly. It was a masterpiece of balsa wood, moss and ooo-brush work, and we all leaned forward while Helen stood over the scene like a puppeteer.

"It's kind of a modern Italian town but after the earthquake, the one in the play."

"'*Tis since the earthquake now eleven years,*" said Polly.

"Exactly, so the buildings are all twisted, like it could all collapse at any moment. Too busy fighting to fix anything. It's a metaphor — get it? There are balconies and walkways, but they're sort of precarious. I mean they'll be safe, we're not going to kill any of you, but there'll be stuff going on vertically. It'll look solid, but it's scaffolding and dust sheets mainly. We're playing with the idea of laundry—cliché, I know—and for the interiors, we'll pull the sheets tight like the sail of a yacht. See . . ."

Helen pulled a string, and we applauded.

"We've got these bulbs, bare bulbs, and we'll string them from roof to roof like fairy lights for the party scene. And for the big fight in act three, we were thinking about football in Italy, how the kids play in the town square and how when there's a big international match they set up all these chairs at night and watch it as a community, and that's how we want the fight to be, folding chairs flying around like you see on the news, and flares and fireworks being thrown—we're still working on that—and for the Friar Laurence scenes, we'll bring on this tree, dusty and white except for the leaves, and it'll be the only green you see on set because he's sort of nature and herbs and gardens, and anyway, that's where Romeo and Juliet get married. And this is what you'll all look like . . ."

She produced a stack of outsize playing cards.

"The thing is, we want everyone to look cool."

"Thank *God,*" said Alex.

"And we thought red and blue was too obvious, because we want to make Charlie's point that the differences are just in their head, and so Montagues are going to be this gray-white, Capulets this kind of light blue. So—I'm really shit at drawing. You ready? Be nice to me, you bastards."

She turned the first card. It was Fran, recognizably so, her shoulders bare in a pale gray shift, a nightdress or a shroud. The cards were passed round, revealing Miles as Romeo, chin in the air, his pale jacket slung over his shoulder, then the elder Capulets and Montagues in stiff, sharp suits and cocktail dresses, and on and on through each company member, faces suggested with just a few lines. Each drawing made that particular cast member grin and laugh in recognition, in anticipation of striking that pose. "We're mixing modern and a sort of vague sense of period, so you might have a nice suit jacket but sort of Elizabethan boots or jeans with a ruff, because we want it to be *relevant, man,* but also because that's what everyone does now. Basically I've just ripped off every RSC production for the last twenty years."

Miles, who had barely registered Helen's existence until now, held his own portrait at arm's length as if appraising an Old Master. "Can I keep mine afterwards?" he said, and Helen fought to hide her smile.

Years later, going through old things, I found the picture that Helen had drawn of Benvolio, in little round glasses, listening. I'd not seen the portrait for many years, and for the first time that day I laughed to myself. It was the kind of thing you see on the walls of every school's art room, in amongst the massive eyes, the pencil-shaded old shoes and self-portraits from reflections in a spoon. Even at the time I could see the nose was weird, the arms bent awkwardly, and she really couldn't "do" hands, just trowels. But it was the first time that anyone had drawn me without a penis sprouting from my forehead, and rediscovering the card, I laughed because I remembered how much I'd loved it at the time, how proud my friend had been, and how we'd shared her pride.

"This is going to be amazing!" said Lucy, thrilled with all the red leather she'd be wearing.

"Helen," I said, "you're brilliant. I'd no idea."

"Piss off, Charlie," she said and blushed, another thing I didn't know that she was capable of.

"Big round of applause for the design team, please!" said Ivor.

Then, in case we were getting too comfortable, "Mask workshop, everyone!" Alina called.

The orchard had been transformed into a sort of harem, with rugs and pillows arranged beneath the trees, sheets of plain brown paper and pots of some sort of porridgey paste set beside each pillow. The masks were needed for the Capulet party scene.

"This is also a relaxation exercise," said Alina, "so we are going to take our time. We are going to listen to the birds, to the insects, to the sounds the trees make. But more than that, it is about close forensic scrutiny of the face, and what we express even when we think we express nothing. Now — get into pairs."

"Get into pairs!" shouted Ivor, three words that always caused a wave of panic, heightened by the necessity of showing no panic. Etiquette demanded that we refrain from simply hurling ourselves at people we fancied. Besides, a whole afternoon sticking little bits of damp paper to Fran's face; it would have been too much. She had already joined arms with Alex, talent clinging to talent, leaving the rest of us looking around needily, each moment of glancing eye contact heavy with meaning. Like the lunge for a seat in musical chairs, the scuffle lasted for seconds. Polly the Nurse adopted Colin Smart; Helen latched on to Alina and seemed very pleased with this. Lucy clung to Miles's arm, and John and Lesley, our Burton and Taylor, stuck to what they knew. Keith, our Friar Laurence, always keen to associate with the younger members of the cast, was obliged to make do with Bernard, the ex-Guardsman now facing the prospect of his first mask workshop with grim forbearance.

Only George and I remained.

"I think this is called drawing the short straw."

"Don't be stupid, it's fine. Do you want to go first?"

He removed his spectacles, the glass as thick as his finger. Without them, he seemed dazed and vulnerable, and he blinked and placed them in his top pocket as if preparing to be blindfolded and shot.

He sighed. "I suppose so."

Perhaps I'd imagined it, but I felt a certain affinity with George. He was reserved and watchful, and though he rarely spoke, everyone listened when he did. In a rare moment of praise for someone else, Miles had revealed that George was "practically a genius," a great writer, an invincible debater, a violinist that it was possible to listen to. Perhaps this was why we hadn't spoken much, because what would I say to someone like that? Yet he rarely put these talents on display or used his intelligence as a stick to swipe at people. Instead he'd sit quietly and watch, one hand clamped to his chin or mouth, his forehead, the side of his nose, whichever part of his raw face caused him the most pain on that particular day. Watching his scenes in rehearsal, it seemed the role of Paris was to be a kind of anti-Romeo; the last person in the world that Juliet would want to be with—she would rather "*see a toad, a very toad, than him,*" says the Nurse, and marriage would be a fate literally worse than death. "O, *bid me leap, rather than marry Paris, from off the battlements of any tower!*" says Juliet, and I thought how harsh casting could be, to look at a teenage boy and think, *yes, we have our toad.*

Elsewhere, an air of meditative concentration had fallen on the orchard, an atmosphere that Ivor was keen to enforce by playing his CD of chill-out music. With his head on the pillow, his fingers linked, his eyes, his every muscle clenched, it required clear effort for George not to place his hands over his face. "Christ's sake." George exhaled through his nose. "Mask-making aside, I don't think there's anything in the world that makes me more tense than chill-out music."

"My dad calls it music for people who don't like music."

"He's a very smart man. What does your father do?"

"He used to have a record shop. Now he's unemployed, so—yours?"

"Civil servant. Works in the Foreign Office."

"Okay. Shall we start?"

"Please. Be my guest."

I began to conceal his face in glue-soaked paper, the technique familiar from primary school, covering balloons in papier-mâché then popping them with a pin. Now George's forehead was the balloon. "No need to apply grease," he said.

"Let's hope it comes off. I don't want you going home like this!"

I'd taken on a strained, jaunty tone, like a plucky nurse at a dressing station.

"Of course the best thing for all concerned would be to get a bag. Just a brown paper bag, put my whole head in that."

I carried on silently.

"Or bandages. Wrap the whole thing up like a mummy."

I applied the paper to the bridge of his nose.

"Maybe when you take it off my skin'll be miraculously clear. Maybe wallpaper paste is the cure I've been looking for—"

"George, you're meant to be silent."

"Am I? All right. Not a word."

"You're meant to listen to the trees."

"Fine. I'll listen to the trees."

I built up the layers of paper. We'd had boys like this at Merton Grange, their faces raw and scalded from scrubs and bleaches, hot flannels and astringents, boys who wore their school shirts at the weekend and too many clothes in summer, boys who were clumsy and fearful, huddled together at lunchtime like Christians in the Colosseum. Were the torments at private school any more genteel? It seemed unlikely that he'd made it through unscathed.

"How are you getting on with Fran?"

The question startled me, and while I tried to contrive a reply, I glanced in her direction. Alex was sitting astride her chest, fitting his thumbs into the hollows of her eye sockets.

"Not bad."

"You seem quite close."

"We're getting that way."

"And you like her?"

Perhaps it was the insidious effect of chill-out music, but the conversation was getting far too personal. "Yeah, of course," I murmured. "Everyone does."

"Charlie, I'm using the word 'like' euphemistically here."

I stayed silent.

George licked his lips. "What I mean is—"

"I know what you mean. We're not meant to be talking, George."

"But you do."

"Like her? Yeah, I really like her."

"Yes," he said. "Me too."

"Oh. Right." It was true, I'd noticed how he spoke to Fran, quietly and intently, his fingers masking different parts of his face in turn. I'd noticed, too, the little puff of pride when he made her laugh, which was often, more often than I could manage.

"I don't mind, by the way. It's not a competition. I think she likes you a lot."

"But is that 'like' as a euphemism?"

"You'll find out, I suppose. Eventually."

We were silent again until half his face had disappeared. There was a pearl of white in the curve of his nostril and, to the side of his eye, a pimple so large that it changed the shape of his face. It seemed that it might be hot to the touch, but I was determined not to hesitate, feeling, I suppose, very brave.

"I'm sorry that you have to do this," he said. "I don't mind."

"It's quite repulsive, I know."

"It's not so bad."

"The whole thing, you shouldn't have to touch it."

"Not true."

"I can feel it actually *fizzing*. You know, I sometimes think if I had a knife I'd cut my whole fucking face off," and here he grimaced so much that the drying paper crackled. I realized that I'd really need to find something else to say.

"You have nice eyes."

"Yeah, that's what people say when they can't think of anything—"

"Look, George, I don't know what to say. This is weird for me too,

but I think you've got a really nice face, all right? It's . . . expressive."
This was, I think, the strangest thing I'd said to another human being
at that time. A moment passed.

"You're right," said George, "we really ought to do this in silence."
Another moment.

"Thank you," he said, and then we stopped speaking altogether,
until it was done. When the mask was dry enough, I eased my fingers beneath the paper and it came away with a satisfying sucking
sound. George rubbed at his eyes with the heels of his hands and took
a cursory look. "Relief map of the Andes," he said. "Get it out of my
sight." I placed the mask with the others and took my turn.

The whole process took two plays of the chill-out compilation,
and afterwards, we all stood blurry-eyed, rubbing at the gum that still
lurked in corners and creases, and inspected the gallery of faces bak-
ing in the sun like some bizarre crop.

"Well, that was kinky," said Helen.

"Don't you all look splendid," said Polly.

"What a bunch of freaks," said Alex.

"Mine's amazing," said Miles.

"The one you made, or the one of you?" I asked.

"Both."

"Miles!" said Fran.

"What an interesting collection of personalities," said Polly.

"I think we're all beautiful," said Colin.

"Oh, Colin, please," said Alex.

"Death masks," said George.

"It's like a serial killer's basement," said Fran. I sought out her
mask from the others. It seemed to me like some rare and wonderful
artifact from a museum, one that I very much wanted to steal.

"Charlie," whispered Helen, "we must not tell anyone, ever, *ever*,
what we just did."

"Okay, well done everyone," said Ivor. "A good week's work. But

Monday—that's when we take things up a gear! Two and a half weeks until dress rehearsal. Long days, and I need everyone off-book and on the ball. Be here on time, people! See you on Monday. Now go. Disperse! Disperse!"

But something had changed. No one wanted to leave, and we loitered idly on the driveway, waiting for a plan to materialize, some way to stretch the day.

"That's it. We're going to The Angler's," said Fran, taking my arm. "Remember—nowhere without me."

The Angler's

OF THE LOCAL PUBS that catered for the underage drinker, The Angler's was the smartest. You were more likely to get served in The Hammer and Tongs, a speakeasy where it was not uncommon to see customers in school uniform, ties loosened, satchels tucked under the table. But The Hammer was the fightiest of the town's pubs, and drinking there was a nerve-jangling experience.

The Angler's was an altogether classier proposition, a new-build Tudor farmhouse at the edge of town, whitewashed and freshly thatched; a destination pub with a large car park. The ceilings were authentically low, the artificial timbers exposed and, on Sundays, families would cram into inglenooks and cubbyholes to gorge on the famous all-you-can-eat carvery, a festival of bottomless meat with two different kinds of gravy, dark and light. In happier times, Mum and Dad would take us and we'd sit and dehydrate on crisps and pink stringy ham, Britvic 55 and great mounds of fat chips. Now its great selling point for the younger drinker was the beer garden, a paddock of scuffed lawn that sloped down to an artificial lake—a large pond really—around which foul-tempered anglers—the epon-ymous anglers, I suppose—hunched late into the evening, drinking pints and glaring at any youth who dared come near and "scare the fish." That spring, on weekday evenings when we should have been revising, I would sometimes come here with Harper, shivering against the evening chill, topping up our innocent Cokes with the bottle of

rum concealed in his jacket pocket. At no point did we think any of
this was wrong or foolish. Laws were guidelines, and the age-eighteen
rule was only there to keep the fourteen-year-olds out. An informal
understanding had been reached: as long as we stuck to the holding
pen at the back, we were fine.

And that's where we found ourselves on that Friday, every single
member, young and old, of the Full Fathom Five Theatre Cooperative, ranged around two wooden picnic tables that we hauled together
across the dusty lawn. In the spirit of responsibility, Ivor refused to
buy anything stronger than a half of shandy for the younger members, and so we were obliged to drink them twice as quickly, and with
nothing to eat but two baskets of undercooked chips, the volume of
conversation soon began to creep up. It was that time of our lives, and
an era too, when all conversation aspired to stand-up comedy, and so
I told Helen, Fran and Alex the story of my Shakespearean improv
session—*with love, my experience hath been both hit and miss*—
and felt gratified at their laughter. The more we drank, the easier the
laughter came until, at a certain point of drunkenness, a switch was
flicked and the conversation turned confessional.

So—Keith, it seemed, was in the throes of a miserable separa-
tion, his own fault, after a fling with a fellow cast member from last
year's rival production, a girl playing his daughter, would you believe
("Tradition!" shouted Alex), but he still loved his wife, still wanted
her to take him back, and Lucy was telling Miles about the pressure
she felt to achieve top marks, and Miles was saying, yes, I know what
that's like, because if he wasn't the best at something, he had to have
a bloody good reason why not, and Colin Smart, who we'd always
dismissed as a dull and feeble swot, had revealed his brother was in a
young offenders' unit for dealing drugs, and before I could even take
this in, Polly, some way through a bottle of white wine, was saying
how lonely she and Bernard felt without their kids and grandkids, in
New Zealand now, and how much they loved being around us young

people, how youth kept them young. In a quiet, intent voice to my
right, Alina was telling Fran about her faithless ballet-dancer boyfriend back in Vienna, while Alex, on my left, worried about telling
his Ghanaian parents that he was gay. "They're liberal," he said, "but
they're not *that* liberal."

For the most part, I sat and listened, tuning in and out as if sitting
in front of a bank of TVs. There was something contagious about
all this confiding, and I wondered, should I join in, offer something
up? That I no longer saw my sister, was drifting away from my best
friends? That I hated my mother but wanted her back? That I worried
my father was suicidal, that I was a thief of cash and garage glassware, had flunked my exams and lay awake at night, fearful of a future
I could not imagine?

It was too much. There were few parts of my inner life that
wouldn't cause the listener to toy with their beer mat, and the only
unsullied secret that I felt compelled to share was my great, bursting
passion for the girl who sat alongside me now, our hips touching, her
bare arm brushing against mine, hand on her cheek — *oh, that I were
a glove upon that hand and somethingsomethingsomething* — leaning
forward, listening to drunk Polly as she held her other hand and told
her how beautiful she was as Juliet, how talented. Fran batted the
praise away but it was true. By my side was the smartest, brightest,
most brilliant girl I'd ever meet, the antidote to all the other shabby
dross in my life. I'd never wanted anything more than to be with Fran
Fisher, whatever "be with" meant, but which of these people could I
tell? Certainly not Fran Fisher.

Miles returned with a tray of drinks. "Chips!" said Helen. "You
forgot the chips!"

"And cigarettes!" shouted Alex.

"No!" said Ivor. "Absolutely no cigarettes!"

"Oh, I would *so* love a cigarette," said Alina.

"Alina, we have a duty of care!"

"A little something to eat might be nice," slurred Polly, "to soak up some of this white wine. Here, I have the money . . ."

"No, I'll go," I said, extricating my legs from beneath the picnic table, stumbling and placing my hand on Fran's shoulder, noting how just for a moment she reached up and held it by the fingertips. My God, I wanted to shout it out!

And no wonder. As I walked to the bar, the baked ground was now a swamp beneath my feet. The sodium lights had been turned on, and I noted how the moths and midges drifted like burning embers in the warm electric air. That's how drunk I was—drunk enough to make observations. Inside, the still air smelled of vinegar and hot oil. I ducked under the timber eaves, straightened up and prepared my voice in anticipation of speaking to the landlady. "I would like chips, please. Two, no, four, no, six portions. And eight packets of nuts. Four salted, four dry-roasted." I sounded like a drunk elocution teacher. "And four packets of salt-and-vinegar crisps." It would be expensive, but I had cash and scratch cards in my wallet and the shandy had made me devil-may-care.

"How old are you, sonny?"

"Eighteen?" Mistake to phrase it as a question. Never mind. Concentrate. I pressed the money into her palm like a bribe. "We just want chips!"

She sighed and handed me a large wooden fish, a number nine painted on its side. "Here's your order number. Listen out, we won't call it twice."

"And can the chips be cooked this time? The last lot were raw inside."

"Don't push your luck, junior," she said and waved me away. I scooped up the packets. All these snacks—I'd be greeted like a hero. In the beer garden I saw a family of five on the bench by the door, three girls, two of them identical, laughing at something their dad had said, and even before I'd passed, I knew the third girl would be my sister, out with my mother and her new boyfriend.

They'd not seen me yet. Jonathan was basking in their laughter and using a half-eaten chip to scoop tartar sauce from his ramekin, and I thought for a moment of ducking back into the pub and skirting the perimeter, but—

"Charlie!" shouted Mum.

"Hello, Charlie," said Billie, straightening her face.

"Hello, young man!" said Jonathan, lean and fit ("He *works out*," Billie had told me) in his button-down Ted Baker shirt, crop-haired and stubbled like my old Action Man. In our sole encounter at the golf club, he had treated my disdain as if it were a customer complaint, and he slipped into this manner now, patient, humble, leaping to his feet and dusting his hands on his khaki cargo pants before offering a handshake. My hands were full, and so instead he indicated the girls. "Have you met the twins?"

The twins looked up. In a parallel life, the one where Mum had taken me with her, I'd imagined myself as a sulky but intriguing rebel, a cuckoo in the nest, and I wondered if there might have been a weird, dark tension to it all, forbidden romance in the face of their father's disapproval. Perhaps that's why Mum had thought it best to leave me; I was just too dangerous to have in the house. Now that fantasy disintegrated in the face of their scalding indifference. "Hiya!" said one. "Pleased to meet you," the other; Chatsborne girls, healthy and hearty, as rosy-faced as if they'd just zipped away their rackets. They returned to picking at the side salad.

"What are you doing here?" said Mum, bustling things along.

"Just out!" I said, petulant, embarrassed by my petulance. Billie lowered her eyes and sucked at her straw.

"You work Fridays."

"Changed my shift."

"So—who are you with?"

"Just with some mates."

"The boys? Tell them to come and say hello!"

I glanced across at the table. Sam and Grace the musicians had
arrived, Sam putting his penny whistle to his lips.

"No, some other friends."

"Do I know them?"

"You don't have to know everyone I know, do you?"

"No, but I can be curious about them. Can't I?"

From the benches, I could hear the wheedling peep of Sam's whistle, playing a jig. Mum followed my look. "Honestly, who brings their
recorder to the pub?"

"Dogs won't like it!" said Jonathan, and the girls laughed.

Honestly, who laughs at their parent's joke?

"It's not a recorder," I snapped. "It's a penny whistle."

"I stand corrected!" said Jonathan, holding up his hands, and I
wanted to rip the pockets from his cargo pants. Billie sucked noisily
at her straw.

"Billie, love," said Mum, "I think the glass is empty now." At our
table, Grace joined Sam on the tambour.

"I've got to go," I said, and rattled the peanuts.

Mum shook her head sadly. "Yes, you go. I've really enjoyed our
little interaction here."

"Bye, Billie." Billie gave a hostage's tight smile and I hurried away
from Mum's glare.

I should never have gone to the bar. I'd lost my place next to Fran
—*nowhere without me,* she'd said—and now she was at the far end
of the table with Helen and Alex, distancing themselves from the new
great joke, Grace and Sam performing pop hits in the style of medieval troubadours, in this case "Saturday Night" by Whigfield. I might
have had some tolerance for this kind of Cambridge Footlights lark-
iness on the lawn of Fawley Manor, but here we were already subject

to the kind of looks reserved for new arrivals on B-wing. I reached for my drink, any drink. Along with the peanuts, I'd returned with furious resentment, not just of Mum and her boyfriend but of Billie too, out on a Friday night, laughing away with—was he her *step*father now? Were we in step territory?

The song had ended. "Now do 'Stairway to Heaven'!"

"No, 'Firestarter'!"

"'When Doves Cry'!"

"Charlie?" It was Fran, reaching her arm along the length of the table, mouthing the words *you okay?*

"Charlie?" said Mum, behind me.

Everyone stopped speaking and turned to look.

"Hello, everyone, I'm Charlie's mum!"

"Hello, Charlie's mum!" they said.

"Hello there," said Ivor, "do you want to join us?" I looked to Fran, who was smiling, half standing. "Yes, come and sit down . . ."

"No, that's all right. Just wanted a word. Charlie?" She was already walking away. I followed her down to the edge of the pond.

"So—how are you?"

"Fine."

Swallows swooped through clouds of midges on the water's surface.

"Anything going on?"

"Nope. Nothing's going on."

"Because I don't know *any* of those people."

"Well, I do!"

"Charlie, you don't know anyone who plays the *penny whistle*."

I kicked some gravel loose, gathered up some little stones and skimmed one across the pond. "I know Lucy Tran, I know Helen Beavis and Colin Smart, they were all at my school."

"The twins say they know that girl from Chatsborne." She was nodding towards Fran.

"We're not at school anymore."

"But you've never mentioned any of them, Charlie. It's not . . ." She put her hand on my arm and lowered her voice. "It's not a *Christian* thing, is it?" I laughed at this and she pinched my arm.

"Ow! What makes you say that?"

"They just have a *look* to them, all happy-clappy. I don't mind, it's your eternal soul, I just want to know!"

I skimmed another stone. I could have just told her, I suppose. It wouldn't have been the strangest thing, at sixteen, to be trying something new.

"Or is it a cult? Because I don't want to have to deprogram you, Charlie, I've got too much on."

But I wasn't ready to confide in Mum again. I still craved the hurt look. "It's not a cult and it's none of your business!"

And there it was. "Isn't it?"

"No, not anymore."

I skimmed another stone. "Are you trying to hit those poor birds?" she said and, when I didn't answer, sighed. "How's your dad?"

I skimmed a stone. "I've not really seen him."

"Since when?"

"Since Monday." The next stone pattered far across the water and I glanced at her, for approval I suppose, but she looked anxious and distracted.

"Why not?" she said, one hand to her forehead. I was, after all, her eyes and ears, there to reassure her.

"I've just not been home much, that's all. He's fine, we've just not spoken."

"Why not?"

"He's asleep when I get back."

"Where have you been?"

"With the cult. It's quite a time commitment."

"Charlie, seriously —"

"What with all the rituals and everything—"

"I'm only asking where—"

"And like I said, where I've been, it's none of your busi—"

"Why isn't it?" she said, suddenly fierce. "What's your thinking there?" I went to skim another pebble but she knocked my hand from below, sending them raining onto the water. "I am trying with you, Charlie. Please, at least acknowledge that I'm doing my best," and she turned, arms folded, head down, and walked back to the pub.

I remained at the water's edge, watching the swallows, the thrill of righteousness fading into regret. Up at the table, Full Fathom Five had turned to the English folk repertoire, a lavishly harmonized round of "Rose, Rose, Rose Red" that might never end. I could not go back to that. Even if I somehow retrieved my place next to Fran, I was shaken by my own admission that I'd not seen Dad. He gave no sign of enjoying my company but he didn't like to be left alone either, and four days must have felt like solitary confinement. I felt the old fears returning. I would leave straight away, get my bike, go home. I heard and felt footsteps behind me, a hand on my back, pushing me towards the water then pulling me back.

"Gotcha!" It was Alex, with Helen and Fran following behind.

"Look at you, all moody and alone," said Helen. "What mystery do these dark waters hold?"

"'I'm in mourning for my life!'" said Fran, whatever that meant.

"Not anymore," said Alex. "He's coming with us."

"Alex has a plan," said Helen.

"One rule in this life," said Alex, "when the folk songs start, it's time to go. Here's what to do. Charlie, tell everyone you're going home: 'Night, everyone, work in the morning,' then go to this address." He handed me a scrap of paper, torn from the cover of his script. "We've got a taxi on its way. Wait for us outside."

"What is it?"

"A party," said Helen.

"But I mean a *real* party, very exclusive."

"I won't know anyone."

"You'll know *us,*" said Fran. "Shouldn't I change?"

"Ideally, yes, but there's no time for that," said Alex. "This is . . . fine."

"Is anyone else going?"

"Just us. We're initiating you into our clique. You should feel very honored."

"I don't know if I should—" *Three, four days he'd been alone now.*

"Stop talking!" said Helen. "I have to—"

"Stop talking, stop talking, stop talking!"

"*Come,*" said Alex, "*we burn daylight.*"

"We *will* see you there," said Fran. "You did promise. Remember?"

And now Alex was steering me back towards the others, his hands on my shoulders, his mouth to my ear.

"Oh, Charlie. Can't you see what this is? Go! Go quickly, say good night, before they start another song."

The Pines

THE HOUSE WAS ON The Avenue, or Millionaires' Row as it was known, at a time when that still meant something. A coniferous Beverly Hills, captains of industry lived here, presenters of local news programs, respectable gangsters, a handful of actors who'd made good in seventies detective shows. Door numbers were too déclassé for The Avenue. Instead the houses had fanciful, faux-rural names with a whiff of the National Trust: Marble House, Stone Cottage, The Mount, The Hollies. My scrap of paper told me to look for The Pines, and for some time I swooped from side to side on the wide, silent street, peering at the gateposts of mansions hidden behind high privet hedges, until I found a great, impenetrable slab of artfully rusted steel, like the air lock of a space freighter.

Time passed, twenty minutes, half an hour, creeping towards midnight, as I loitered like a burglar casing the joint. The police paid special attention to Millionaires' Row. In my wallet, stolen scratch cards and cash from the till. What if I cracked under interrogation? I sat on the curb, listened to the *click-click-click* of automatic sprinklers, watched the bats tumble against the purple sky, a fox trot blithely down the center of the avenue as if looking for the party. The minute hand clicked over to twelve and, sober now, I began to wheel my bike away.

A minicab approached, Alex's head already protruding from the window. "Noooo! Stay right where you are!" They pulled over and tumbled out onto the wide grass verge, transformed: first Alex in a gray satin shirt open to the sternum; Helen dressed in the day's dungarees but with her hair gelled into random stalagmites, two thick black lines drawn under her eyes with what might have been a fat felt-tip, more war paint than makeup; and finally Fran in a black shift dress, a nightdress almost, lace-trimmed at the top and bottom, the same Adidas trainers below.

"We stopped at mine to change," said Alex, paying the driver. "Hope you don't mind."

Fran tugged at the hem. "What d'you think?"

"It's lovely," I said.

"Doesn't she look amazing?" said Alex. "It's my mother's *negligee*. Paging Doctor Freud!"

"I feel a bit underdressed, Alex," said Fran.

"Nonsense. It's underwear as outerwear."

"I'm wearing outerwear as underwear," said Helen.

"I'm not sure if I should have this on," said Fran and touched the red bra strap on her shoulder.

"No, you shouldn't. Take it off!" said Alex. "You're with friends."

"I don't think so."

"Later, then. The night is young."

"This feels weird too . . ." She touched her lips, the lipstick butterfly-shaped, overlapping the edges as if applied with the edge of a thumb. "What do you think? Alex did it."

"Great" was all I could say.

"It feels a little . . . mime-y."

"It's meant to be like that," said Alex. "It's Kabuki-style. This is a serious do, people, not the last-night party for *Bugsy Malone*. You've got to make an effort. And with that in mind . . ." From a Tesco bag, he produced a neat white rectangle, holding it flat like a tray then, with a conjurer's flourish, taking one corner and flicking it into a shirt. "For you."

"I can't wear this."

"Charlie, you look like the paper boy. They won't have you in there like that. Put this on."

"Here?"

"You can go behind a car if you're bashful."

I took the shirt by my fingertips, walked a little distance and turned my back. It was a struggle to flex every muscle and take off the T-shirt simultaneously, and I realized, as it passed over my head, that this morning's underarm Aztec had long lost its power. I rubbed at my grimy neck and under my arms with my old T-shirt. It seemed almost sacrilegious to climb into this pristine thing, which smelled of the airing cupboard and felt expensive and heavy and cool against my skin. The white shirts I'd worn at school were scouring, non-iron polyester things that came in packs of three. This label said Dior. I went to tuck it in—

"No, leave it like that," said Helen. "Let's look at you." I turned, rolled my shoulders, tried to tuck my hands into air.

"It will have to do," said Alex. "Are we ready?" He beckoned us over to stand beneath the security camera. "Band photo! Smile. Say 'eighteen'!" We arranged ourselves, assumed our most mature faces and Alex pressed the intercom button. "Hello, Bruno! It's Alex. I've brought some friends. Is that all right?" Time passed but we held our pose until finally, with a low industrial rumble, the great air lock began to slide open.

At the end of a long wood-chip drive lit by burning flares, the house emerged from the ground, low and long, smoked glass and gunmetal like an expensive coffee table, and immediately I recognized this as the drug lord's house from the old action movies. Somewhere, guarding the perimeter, there'd be a security guard in sunglasses, pressing his finger to his ear, reaching into his jacket just as he's pulled into the privet and garroted.

"Fucking hell, Alex," said Helen.

On the patio—I'm sure it had a better name—stylish men and women arranged themselves in stylish clusters like the plastic figures on an architect's model, and dance music thunked from the speakers concealed somewhere in the trees, the eponymous pines that shielded the grounds from outside eyes. Off to one side of the house we could see a rectangle of phosphorescent light that cross-faded pink to blue to green to red; a swimming pool, empty now but waiting.

"Again, I say it. Fuck-ing hell."

"I know, right?" said Alex.

"Should we have brought something?" I said.

"Four cans of Stella and a mixtape?" Alex laughed. "It's not that kind of party."

"It's an orgy, yeah?" said Helen, eyes lit up. "You've brought us to an orgy."

"Not until *much* later. Until then it's just a nice party with someone I know from the local scene."

"I didn't know we had a local scene," I said.

"Charlie, you're not *meant* to know. If anyone asks you—they won't—then you're all at college and, by some statistical freak, you've all just turned eighteen."

"I can't pretend that I'm at college."

"Yes, you can! Imagine school with less violence and everyone drinking coffee." He looked at us intently one by one, a fortune-teller. "Fran, next year you hope to study . . . Psychology at Durham; Charlie —Geography, Sheffield; Helen—PE and Politics at Loughborough. You want to be a games teacher!"

"Ha."

"So Alex," I said, "are we gate-crashing?"

I had gate-crashed parties before, in houses all over town, Montagues sneaking into the Capulets' ball. "We're friends of Steve," we'd say, or "Stephanie said we could come." I'd been to parties that had been gate-crashed by hordes as merciless, crazed and destructive as any Vikings; CDs and purses stolen, locks pried from drinks cabinets, sinks wrenched from the wall, sausage rolls ground underfoot and brawls on the lawn as the parents returned home in fury and shock. I'd been at parties that had made the local news. Once a helicopter had hovered overhead. Didn't all house parties end like this? With blue flashing lights and molehills of pink salt on the carpet?

"Are we going to get chucked out?"

"No, because you're not gate-crashing, you're my dear friends from the show. I'll go say hi to Bruno. Mingle! Go! Go!" and as he disappeared into the house, we were left, the three of us, gawping at the edge of this entirely new world. I had never seen so many attractive men and women in one place, so varied and glamorous, and I wondered, were these really the neighbors I saw in the Cottage Loaf Tea Rooms, the Boots and the Spar, the Trawlerman Fish Bar and the Golden Calf Chinese? The men wore expensive T-shirts or open shirts under linen suits, the women stylish summer dresses or ironic retro jumpsuits, like the covers of the house-music CDs my dad had sold so reluctantly. Even the middle-aged guests looked cool as they stood, drinks held out to the side, in a minty, soft-focus mist that might have been steam from the heated pool or haze from all those Marlboro Menthols, or just the flattering light that comes from money. "This is *so* not the Methodist church disco," said Helen, and I found myself trying hard not to stare at a statuesque woman in a red PVC catsuit, while another man, handsome as a model, walked directly at us, a tray held at shoulder height.

"He's coming over!" said Helen, gripping my arm.

"Mushroom galette?" said the model, and obediently we all took one and dipped our heads.

"Fuck me," said Helen, canapé halfway to her lips, "*caterers!*"

"Where I come from," said Fran, "these are called vol-au-vents."

"Oh, that's *rank*," said Helen, spitting it into her hand. "That tastes like soil. What's wrong with sausage rolls or cheese and pineapple?" and she tipped the mulch into a pot of bamboo. "Bloody yuppies. I can't eat this. I'm going to see if they've got Pringles."

Another tray passed by, shallow glasses filled with mounds of green alien snow, and I snatched two and hoped that caterers did not ask for ID. Alone now, Fran and I touched glasses and pouted and craned our necks towards the rims. We sipped, and Fran clenched her jaw and opened her eyes wide. "Look—I'm trying to be cool and not wince. Don't wince, don't wince, don't wince . . ."

"It's basically a lime-flavored slushy. You can get it from the newsagent's."

"Do they put salt on the rim at the newsagent's?"

"If you ask them. Under the till, big catering tub of Saxa."

She sipped again. "Tequila. Have you noticed, when you've thrown up on a type of alcohol, then it always reminds you of vomit?"

"Well, I've thrown up on pretty much every kind of alcohol, so . . ."

"Hey, James Bond. And you still like it?"

"I'm not sure you're meant to *like* it."

She patted my arm. "You're so *jaded*."

"I am. I'm very experienced," I said, and removed the straw so that it wouldn't poke me in the cheek again. "This is classy, though."

"It is," she said, and we perched on the edge of a tub full of cacti and took in the scene. "I feel like Daisy Buchanan."

"Who's Daisy Buchanan?"

"She's Jay Gatsby's first love. He becomes a millionaire and throws these amazing wild parties, just so Daisy'll fall in love with him again and leave her husband. I won't tell you what happens, but it's very sad. And sort of annoying too."

"I'll read it next," I said. I would read every book, see every film, listen to every song that Fran had ever mentioned.

"Christ, I needed a party. I feel bad about the others, though. We mustn't let on. I hate cliques. Except, you know, when I'm invited to join a clique, in which case cliques are great. Did you have them at Merton Grange? Cliques."

"Course. We didn't use the word 'clique.'"

"Were you in one?"

"Sort of. Just a gang of boys really."

"Yeah, that's what Colin said. He said your lot sort of ruled the school."

"Did he?"

"And Lucy too. Except she said they used to call her stuff. Like —what was it? Number Forty-two. Like on a Chinese menu, which doesn't even make sense, given that she's Vietnamese. Or her parents are."

This much was true. She had been called Forty-two almost conversationally, more often than her real name. And then there was Boat Girl and Vietcong and, for reasons I'd never understood, Buddha, and while I couldn't recall ever using those names myself, I knew that I'd not objected.

"And what did Colin say?"

"He said he got the gay-wimp stuff."

"*I* didn't say those things—"

"They didn't say you did." Fran put her hand on mine. "You think I'm telling you off. I'm not telling you off."

"I never said any of that."

"I know. She just said some of the boys did."

"That was mainly Lloyd and Fox."

"And Harper too. I remember, because I'd heard you talk about him."

"He's my friend, that doesn't mean he can't be a dick."

"I know."

"And Lloyd's not really a friend, he's just a friend of a friend, he just hangs around with us. He's not even talking to me at the moment. I'm not sure if any of them are."

"Really? Why not?"

"I sort of threw a pool ball at his head. Really hard."

She laughed. "Did you miss?"

"Yeah. But I didn't mean to."

"Why?"

"Something he said to me." I shrugged. "He says stuff."

"Well, it's a shame you missed, because he sounds like a real prick." She laughed. "Sorry. Sorry."

"No, it's fair enough." A moment passed. "When did you and Lucy have this conversation?"

"Doesn't matter. And you mustn't get annoyed with Lucy, she wasn't telling tales. The only reason it came up was . . ."

"Go on."

"She said she liked you more now. She said when you turned up with me that first time, she really hated your guts, because of all the . . . stuff at school. But you weren't who she thought you were."

"It was another time. Different person," I said, feeling that this was true.

"I'm really not trying to be pious or preachy, I can be a bitch too —trust me, I really can." She sipped the drink, winced and laughed. "I just wanted to be sure that if we were going to do this thing, that I hadn't got you wrong. That's all. Let's forget about it."

Do this thing, she'd said and continued talking. I wasn't able to take it in. *Do this—*

". . . should really mingle . . ."

Thing, this thing . . .

". . . and get a different drink. Tequila's never a good idea."

What "thing"?

". . . even in Mexico, I bet they're all, have you got something soft?"

"What 'thing'?" I said.

"'Thing'?"

"You said 'if we're going to do this thing,' this 'thing,' but what thing?"

I felt her press her arm against mine. "You know what thing."

"But *say* it."

She laughed, stretched her legs and pointed her toes. "It's not something you say, it's something you *do*," and I knew then that we would kiss later that night, and that it was only a question of getting it right —that small matter—and kissing by the book. "Come on . . ."

"You haven't got me wrong," I said.

"No. I didn't think I had. Let's go inside. See what else they've got to drink."

She took my arm and we passed through the other guests, who smiled and nodded, amused and indulgent, as if we were children who'd come down in pajamas to join the party, to light the grown-ups' cigarettes and sip their drinks. I practiced my alibi: Geography, Geography at Sheffield. Yes, it's a great uni! I am excited, very, thank you very much. Through sliding glass doors, into a kitchen, glass on every side like an aquarium, with the sink and surfaces *in the middle of the room,* a mystifying thing, and all the pots and pans and implements dangling artfully from hooks like elaborate percussion. On polished black marble, the bartender was lining up more cocktails, red and orange and green like pastel traffic lights, and we took two of the red ones while his back was turned and, a safe distance away, brought our faces down to meet the rims. They tasted of rocket lollies from the ice-cream van, and we carried them carefully down glass steps into a living room, sunken like an excavation and once again glass-walled, and I wondered what Mr. Harper, the Conservatory King, would make of it. "It's just one big bloody great conservatory!"

The sides of the living area were terraced like the Roman senate in gladiator films, the steps scattered with cushions and rugs on which the senators reclined, and here was Helen, arms clasped around a bowl of crisps as if protecting her child, and Alex telling a story, the crowd leaning in, smiling, laughing. Confidence and talent weren't entirely the same thing—Miles was the most brash boy I'd ever met, and pure ham—but there seemed to be some connection and I wondered, what must that be like, to have the full attention of the crowd rather than wadding your words into the gaps in other people's speech? The music was softer in here, an Ibizan bossa nova, and we were happy to stand a little way off and sip our drinks, sophisticates, and listen—

"My friends!" said Alex suddenly. "Come down here, don't be shy." The audience turned to look at us. "This is our Juliet, the very talented Frances Fisher. This is our Benvolio, played by Mr. Charles Lewis. Helen and I are trying to engineer a summer romance, isn't that right, Helen?"

Fran rolled her eyes. "Alex, pack it in."

"But where's Romeo?" said a shaven-headed man, elegant, Chinese, in thick black spectacle frames and a black shirt. "Why aren't you with your Romeo?"

"Romeo's not Juliet's type," said Fran, taking a seat, and the man offered her his hand.

"I'm Bruno," said the man.

"Bruno, your house is beautiful."

"Thank you, I've been very lucky. You're very welcome here. You're . . . ?"

"Benvolio."

"Ah, the Method approach! But in real life you're . . . ?"

"Charlie."

"Charlie, Frances, are you both at college with this one?"

"That's right," said Fran.

"Not me," I said, balking at the lie.

"Although we don't know that yet," said Fran.

"So what do you do now, Charlie?"

"I work. Part time."

"Where do you work, Charlie?"

"Well, in a petrol station."

"Oh. Which one?"

"The one on the bypass."

"I go there often. I was delighted the other day to win some very nice free tumblers."

At least I'd not stolen his scratch cards. "Well, don't put ice in them, they explode in your face."

"That's wise counsel; I'll bear it in mind. And next time I buy petrol—"

I thought I ought to move things on, try my interrogation technique and use his name. This was something older people liked.

"So, what do you do, Bruno?"

"I manufacture and distribute home computers," said Bruno, and I wasn't sure where to go after that.

"We've got a home computer" was the best I could do.

"Oh? Which one?"

I named the model and brand. "Dad got it off the back of a newspaper."

"Yes, they're our main rivals. We're Wang Computers."

"It's not very good. Yours are much better."

"The right thing to say. You'll go far, Charlie. I'm delighted you could make it. You seem like a lovely couple."

"Oh, we're not really a couple," said Fran.

"We haven't known each other very long," I said.

"I don't see what *that's* got to do with anything. Look at you both. Get to it! No time to waste! Now—why is no one in the swimming pool?"

"We weren't sure if it was allowed," said Fran.

"Of course it's allowed. That's what it's *for.*"

"And I don't have a costume," said Helen.

"Good God! Why are the young so prudish?" said Bruno, and drained his glass. "Now, I'm going to go and push someone in," and he bounded up the terraced steps and out into the garden. Alex and Helen, grinning widely, clambered towards us.

"Alex," said Fran, laughing, "are you sure he's okay with us?"

"Of course. Just don't let on about this . . ."

He held out his fist and beckoned us closer, then opened his fingers as if he'd caught some rare bug. In his palm, a small pill, mottled and fat. "I'm prepared to split it four ways. It'll hardly do anything, but who's in?"

We looked at each other for one moment like musketeers, then Alex nipped the pill between his teeth and we each took a tiny fragment, like the loose grouting from bathroom tiles, chalky and damp with spit. We each washed it down with our cocktail. It was hard to believe something so small could taste so foul, like a blast of hairspray directly on the tongue, and so we drank more of the cocktail that tasted of lollies and went to find the heart of the party.

Queen Mab

THE PILL HAD NO EFFECT, and we confirmed this to each other every ten minutes or so.

Except that now the music seemed to sound amazing. With a dreary fustiness that we passed off as integrity, my friends and I had always been hostile to dance music, because anything without guitars had no craft, was boring and repetitive, just *bang-bang-bang*. Harper's den was not a place to dance, it was somewhere to nod and bite our lower lips.

But then we had never been anywhere remotely like this. Outside, lights on the terrace marked out a dance floor, densely packed to its edges like a life raft, a speaker stand on each corner focusing the sound the way a magnifying glass focuses light. Alex whooped, took Helen's hand and bundled into the center of the crowd, and Fran and I shared a look and followed. Helen was one of those surprisingly brilliant dancers, very serious and intense, angry almost, eyes closed, fists clenched, muttering to herself as if daring anyone to interrupt. For Alex dance was a form of self-seduction, constantly slipping his hand into his own shirt, undoing his own buttons, squeezing his own pectoral or buttock or groin, so that I half expected Alex to slap Alex's hand away. I took my stance—feet planted, elbows tight in, hands pumping alternately in a milking motion, the kind of dance that would disturb no one in a crowded train carriage, while Fran went wild, grinning madly, her arms above her head, her hands dug into her own hair so that I could see the dark stubble in her armpits, and she caught my eye and laughed with her mouth wide, put her hands on my shoulders and said something.

"What?"

"I said this is *mad*."

"It is mad."

She spoke again. "Pardon?"

She pulled me close and put her mouth to my ear. "I said I'm really glad you're here," and we danced for a while like this, drifting away from the others to the edge of the raft, pulling each other close. It's hard to mention someone's smell without sounding like a psychopath, but I'd noticed her scent before, something warm and green like summer. Some years later, on a terrible, sad date, I caught this scent again, so vivid and precise that I thought Fran must be hiding in the room. "My God, what is that?" I asked. "Grass, by the Gap," she said, and I felt slightly disappointed that such a natural smell was in fact a body mist, and that Fran no more smelled naturally of grass than I smelled of Aztecs. Still, in that moment on the dance floor, I thought it was quite the greatest, most sophisticated scent, and I resisted the temptation to snuffle at it like a badger and instead rested my forehead against hers, her arms on either side of my neck, locked at the elbow, something I'd seen in movies.

But the music was too fast, and our foreheads kept rapping painfully against each other, and so we broke apart and pushed back through the crowd to its center. Now Alex and Fran fell into each other's arms, dancing closely, their legs intertwined in a corny Latin style, and I felt a little stab of envy that we hadn't danced like that. Helen tapped me on the shoulder and rolled her eyes, and we laughed and danced together for a bit, joke-dancing until it stopped being a joke and we also put our arms around each other. The *thump-thump-thump* felt like a soft mallet tapping on my chest and soon I even dared to raise my hands above shoulder height, to let my feet leave the floor.

Helen said something in my ear.

"What?"

"I said are you feeling anything?"

"Nothing at all," I said.

The pill had no effect, though it was true that time had taken on a strange quality, so that I couldn't tell if we'd been dancing for twenty minutes or two hours, and I decided that I should step out for a moment and get another drink. The dancing had made me light-headed and light-hearted, so at the bar I found that I could talk to complete strangers, something I had never done before. I talked to a nice woman in her twenties who was training to be a nurse, and I said my mum used to be a nurse, and we talked about nursing for a while and mothers too and then I spoke to her boyfriend, really nice, who worked for Bruno and we talked some more about computers and for some reason I mentioned that I'd screwed up all my exams except maybe Computer Science and Art and he said, hey, well, do that then, do Computer Science and Art, why not, if that's what you're good at, if that's where your talent lies, everyone's got a talent, you've just got to find out what it is and go for it and use it, and this seemed incredibly wise to me, the idea that you should do what you're good at and enjoy, as opposed to what you're bad at and hate, and although it hadn't worked out for Dad, had been a catastrophe, it might for me, because it was computers, not jazz after all, and I resolved to do exactly what he said, and I thought how strange it was to be having all these very frank and easygoing conversations with people when I wasn't usually very good at these kinds of things, so that when this wise man left to find his girlfriend, the nice nurse, I found that I was even able to talk to the woman in the red PVC catsuit who looked amazing, I said, and she said thank you in a thick, low Italian voice, and we talked about the difference between north Italy and south Italy and, more interestingly, the difficulties of getting in and out of a PVC catsuit, which wasn't PVC in fact but latex, and then the differences between latex and PVC and what happens when you want to go to the loo, which she said hardly ever happened, it's so strange, she said, you become like an *eskimo*, if you *can't* go, you *don't* go, and besides, you sweat so much inside, you see, and she unzipped the suit a little and invited me to run my finger along the neckline, which was silky with sweat and talcum powder so that it was both wet and dry at the same time, and this, I thought, was by some way the greatest conversation I had ever had in my life, accompanied as it was by the squeak of latex, like little yelps, until it took another turn when she said have you ever been tied up? and I said no, only with my best friend Harper's dressing-gown cord so he could fart on my head but it wasn't sexual, and she said, no, my friend, you just *think* it wasn't sexual, and while I was wrestling with *that* one, Helen was behind me, with her arms around my neck, saying is this man bothering you? Charlie, where the fuck have you been, remember why you're here, this is your chance, Charles Lewis, but we were talking about the difference between PVC and latex, I said, and Helen said I bet you were, you dirty sod, but come on now, you're wasting time, and when I turned to say goodbye the woman had disappeared but that was fine because Helen dragged me back to the dance floor where Fran had been all this time and she screamed and laughed when she saw me as if I'd been gone for years and held her hands out and we danced together just like she'd danced with Alex, her fingers linked behind my head, my hands on her waist, the slip of the fabric, the fabric of the slip, legs intertwined, her breasts pressing against my chest, the soft mallet thumping beneath my ribs, and over her shoulder I could see Alex talking to a guy and then kissing him and leading him from the dance floor towards the pool and when I stepped back to look at Fran her eyes closed, her damp hair sticking to her forehead, laughing and I said are you feeling anything? and she opened her eyes and said no, not from the pill and I said what do you mean? and she said oh, Charlie, I don't think I can stand this any longer, come, and she took my hand and pulled me out through the crowd and across the lawn towards the trees until we were at the edge of the light—

—and then she stopped and turned and even over the music I could hear our breathing and the blood pumping in my head as she took it between her hands and said kiss me and so we kissed, gently at first, her mouth very soft and tasting of alcohol and lemon, and then more intently, her mouth opening just a little but with no teeth grinding together this time, no sense of anything being wrong at all, here or anywhere else in the world, and oh, that, that was by the book.

After a while she pulled away and looked at me, breathless, her hand still on my neck. "Is there somewhere we can go?" We found a wall to lean against, an unlit, unglazed part of the house near a door where the caterers sometimes stepped out to smoke. I heard someone point us out in the darkness and laugh. "Don't stop," she said, and I placed my hands higher, on either side of her rib cage where the silk of Mrs. Asante's nightdress came to an end and Fran's skin began, and she took my hand and placed it on her breast and here I thought my heart might stop. All this time we kissed, more passionately now until Fran laughed and pulled away and rubbed her lips with the heel of her hand.

"I think they call this 'hungry kissing.'"

"Is it all right?"

"What do you think?" My hand was still on her breast, which seemed strange while we were having a conversation. What was the etiquette? Should I take my hand away and put it back later when we stopped talking? Would she notice? Instead she placed her own hand over mine and held it there.

"Has my lipstick gone?"

"A long time ago."

"You're wearing it now," she said, and we kissed some more, my thumb slipping inside the nightdress and then, with some contortion, into her bra. Again, I waited for her to move my hand away and instead she pressed herself harder against my leg, but I couldn't quite lose the awareness of the contortion of my arm, my elbow sticking out to one side as if leaning on a mantelpiece, and when one more waiter saw us, laughing and shouting "Go on, my son!" she stepped away.

"We should . . ."

"I know."

"I don't want to, though."

"One more minute," I said, and while we kissed, I wondered — should I tell her that I loved her? I'd not said this before, or rather I'd spoken it to Harper, dead drunk, and to inanimate objects, a pizza or a birthday present, but never in a situation where I might actually mean it. I'd come nowhere near. Now, suddenly, as if remembering a forgotten word, one that's been in your mind but just out of reach, I wanted to say it out loud.

Still I hesitated. Partly this was shyness; even in all this passion, I couldn't quite shake off the cheap familiarity of the phrase. Embarrassment aside, I had an old-fashioned, almost chivalric sense that those words should not be scattered around. Like a wish or a runic spell that summons up demons, the phrase had to be used with absolute care, and though I might then say it a thousand times, I could say it for the first time only once. Not yet, though. Instead I leaned back to look at her. Her face had changed somehow, her features differently proportioned, sharper even in the soft light, like in an eye test when the optician drops a lens into the frame. Nothing I'd ever seen came close to this and I said the other thing that I felt strongly.

"You're *so* beautiful."

She didn't laugh or jeer. She looked quite serious. "You're drunk," she said.

"I'm really not," I said. "Or if I am, then I still mean it. I've never known anyone remotely like you, not anyone. You are . . . the greatest thing."

She kissed me again, lightly this time as if to calm me down. "Let's go and find the others," she said, then she took my hand, and we walked back into the light.

The drug had no effect, but it is true that the rest of the night had the feel of a montage even while it was taking place. We could see the question in our friends' eyes as we approached the dance floor, and so we answered it, Fran pulling me towards her, holding my face and kissing me. "There—*happy* now?!" she shouted, and they laughed with Helen rolling her eyes, and we fell into a foursquare huddle before breaking apart and dancing until our clothes stuck to our skin with sweat. "Pool!" shouted Alex, somehow pulling the shoes from his feet as he ran, and tripping straight into a splashy dive. Helen went in fully clothed, lowering herself in down the steps, and for the second time that day I pulled my shirt over my head, less self-conscious this time, and laid it reverently out on the damp grass. "You can't swim in those," said Fran, and so I turned my back and took off my jeans and found myself grateful that I'd put on my best and plainest underpants, the pair I thought of as somehow classic. We held hands, took a run-up, whooped and landed in water that felt crisp and delicious, with a silver-blue, viscous quality like gin. For a moment we stood together soberly in the center of the pool, unsure what to do next. I was a pretty strong swimmer at that time and, wanting to advertise even the smallest of my talents, displayed a few strokes. But it didn't seem right, pounding lengths in front crawl and backstroke.

"Of course, it's basically all these people's bathwater," said Helen. "All these sweaty old people."

"Helen, don't be gross," said Alex.

"So we just stand here, shivering?" said Helen. "Is that it?" She slapped the water and, as if this was a signal, Fran rolled and twisted away towards the deepest part of the pool, where I followed, diving and forcing open my stinging eyes to see her somersaulting in slow motion once, twice, three times, the black of the nightdress spooling around her like squid ink. I took another breath, pushed off and swam closer, affecting a kind of merman grace but scraping myself on the pool's bottom. We surfaced, took another breath, submerged again and kissed underwater, closed-lipped then opening our mouths and laughing at the fizz of bubbles. We surfaced and I went to kiss her again, but there are limits to all passion—

"You need to wipe your nose," I said.

"What?"

"You've got something—" and I indicated the green emerald of snot that had found its way onto her upper lip.

"Okay. Sorry about that. Pretty sexy." She swiped at her face with the back of her hand. "Did you notice it?" she said. "Underwater?"

"Notice what?"

"Okay. Listen to this music!" Unfamiliar disco played, orchestral and lush. "Now go under!" she said, and as we sank below—nothing changed. Some finely tuned speaker system had made the water disappear, the music as loud and crisp as before. Amazed, we tried to dance, spoofy disco moves, grabbing at each other so that we might remain in the deepest part of the pool for as long as our lungs could bear, her nightdress black and slippery, her skin cool and dimpled with goose bumps. I placed my hand at the top of her thigh and, just for a moment, felt hers cupped between my legs before she laughed and pushed herself off to the surface. I grabbed at her ankles, but she was gone, and now I was faced with the new problem of getting out of the pool without drawing attention to myself. "No petting, no running, no bombing," called Alex, and so I stood, cool and pensive, and pressed my erection hard against the pool tiles, hoping to cut off the circulation like a finger trapped in a door. Somehow the four of us found ourselves back in the house, shoes in hand, clothes still damp,

hair clinging, finding drinks and padding from room to room. The
other guests continued to regard us with tolerant amusement as we
arranged ourselves on low modular seating, as if this was just another
Friday night, Fran's head on my shoulder, her hair scented deliciously
with chlorine. The pill had no effect, but I had a fantastic sense of
benevolence and open-mindedness, so that I felt no embarrassment at
all when Alex recited the Queen Mab speech to a small silent crowd,
quietly and plainly, and was surprised to find that I understood every
word.

For what might have been an hour or perhaps ten minutes, we lay
with our eyes closed, listening to the music, tuning in and out of conversations. The party was entering its final stage and, hoping to find
some life, Fran and I went back outside. The famous pines were silhouetted against the brightening sky now. On the abandoned dance
floor, she slipped her hand onto my back; I held her hip, her shoulder
blade, but the music was now too quiet to drown out the sound of
the blackbirds, the best and worst of sounds, and so we just clung to
each other.

"Today is tomorrow," said Fran, and I remembered a scene from
the play, the lovers complaining about the break of day, making excuses—the lark is just a nightingale, the dawn light a meteor—and I
thought it might be clever to slip into that dialogue. But my brain was
too fuzzy to recall a single line with any accuracy, and paraphrasing
something about larks and comets might make me sound mad.

Besides, a thought that I'd been suppressing all night had finally
gate-crashed its way in and, close behind, another, darker thought,
and I suddenly felt as sober as I'd ever been. The anxiety was physical,
as if realizing that I'd left a bath running for the whole week, and Fran
felt the snap of tension.

"What's up?"

"I've not seen my dad for five days now."

"Where's he been?"

"Nowhere. That's the point."

"I'm sorry, I shouldn't have made you come."

"Are you kidding? Of course I was going to come."

"But, go now! I have to get home anyway, before they wake up."

"Should we say goodbye to the others?"

She kissed me. "No, let's just leave. They'll know."

Shoes in hand, we crossed the cool, damp lawn, scattered with cocktail glasses, champagne flutes and empty bottles. Outside, I unlocked my bike. The village where Fran lived was four miles from here and I had an idea that she might sit on the saddle while I pedaled but, like the underwater kiss, this is one of those things that works better on-screen than in real life. Besides, the tires were soft and our combined weight made the wheel rims grind into the tarmac, and so we walked and every now and then Fran would climb on the bike and sit there, queenly, while I pushed.

We crossed the motorway, silent for the first time, as if we were the only people left on earth, and as the streets gave way to countryside, we would break off at intervals to fall upon each other, in fields and verges, prickly and dew-damp, the bicycle wheel spinning as if we'd been thrown into the cow parsley in some terrible accident. At one point we both urgently needed to pee, Fran squatting blithely across an irrigation ditch, me standing a short way off, the process taking longer than seemed possible. "Christ, I'm like a horse," said Fran, and I laughed and thought, *wow, look at us, weeing next to each other, filthy and sophisticated.* Certainly Alex's exquisite shirt was now a rag, grass-stained and rank, and later, when I smuggled it into our machine for a hot wash, I discovered that one rare and pearly button was missing, lost to the verge of a B-road, wrenched off while making love.

"Making love" is silly. The most precise term that I can come up with for what we did is dry-humping, which goes some way to illustrating the gulf between language and experience. "Groping" is gross, "fooling around" makes it sound frivolous, but whatever it was called, it meant that a journey of an hour or so took nearly three, and the village was stirring and stretching as we approached, stockbrokers walking the dog to fetch the weekend *Telegraph*. Here was Fran's house, detached, white-painted, sash-windowed, with roses in the garden.

"So. D'you want to come in, meet Graham and Claire?"

"Oh. It's half seven . . ."

"Come on, we'll wake them up, tell them the news!"

"Oh. Okay, so if you think it's—"

"I'm kidding, Charlie."

"Okay. That's really funny."

"I mean you'll meet them one day, but . . ."

"What will you tell them now?"

"I'll say I've been at Sarah's. They half know it's not true, but they're cool about it. Or they pretend to be. 'Been at Sarah's' is a kind of code for 'I'm sorry but don't worry.'" She took my hand and, between kisses, "Wish I could take you up to my room. Smuggle you in, keep you there."

"I wouldn't mind."

"We could wait till they were out, then I'd *fall* on you—we could stay in bed all day, listen for the car and then I'd put you back in the wardrobe."

"What would I eat?"

"I'd sneak food off my plate like in a novel, slide it under the door." We elaborated on the plan and kissed, but my jaw was aching now and Fran had the beginnings of a scoured rash around her mouth, a red ring like a clown's makeup. "You should go," I said.

"I know," she said, then, more earnestly, "but let's be clever about this."

"So—you want to keep it secret?" I'd expected this—most of the kisses I'd shared had come with stern vows of non-disclosure—but Fran just laughed.

"No! Bollocks to that. No, I want to tell everyone! I mean we're not going to put an advert in the *Advertiser*, but we're not going to hide it. We're going to be . . . cool about it." She kissed me. "We'll be cool with everyone except each other."

"So—what will you tell people?"

"I met this boy. I like him, I really do, and . . . we're going to see what happens. Does that sound about right?"

"Okay. I've got to work until nine tonight, but . . . could I see you after?" It was a joke, but not entirely a joke.

She laughed. "Nope."

"Tomorrow, then."

"No! Monday, after rehearsals."

It was essential, I knew, to betray no disappointment at this, but something must have passed across my face, because she held on to both my shoulders. "Don't worry. We will find a way." We kissed and stood holding each other as if I'd been banished to Mantua, and I thought that I might risk something.

"Sweet sorrow."

"What?"

"Sweet sorrow?"

"Oh."

"You know. Parting is such—"

"Yes, I got the reference, it's my line. I just didn't hear you." She mumbled something.

"What?"

"I said, 'It's important to enunciate.'"

"It is important."

"It is." We kissed again. "Okay, that's enough. Monday."

"Monday."

"Bye."

"Goodbye. Bye."

By now the tires on my bicycle were too flat to ride it home, and so I walked through the summer morning with a new conviction, one that didn't come from an entirely rational mind, and it was this:

That if I could be with Fran Fisher, if she could somehow accept me and all my past faults, all the squalor and weirdness and worry, then in turn I would become a better version of myself, a version so excellent and exemplary that it was practically new. I had not been the person I wanted to be, but there was no reason why this couldn't change. A new phase of life had begun, as precisely as if at the click of a stopwatch, and from now on I would no longer be defined by absences, the things that I was not. In the play, the Nurse lists Romeo's qualities: honest and courteous, handsome, kind and virtuous, and while "handsome" was not for me to say, there was no reason not to take the others on and to supplement them. I would be wise too, brave and loyal, a champion against injustice. I would be funny — was this something you could decide to be? — but not foolish, not a clown. I'd be reckless but not irresponsible, popular but not ingratiating. I'd read more and better books, wash more thoroughly, I'd brush my teeth with flair and zeal, devise a daily fitness regime and stick to it, carry myself differently, confident and straight, and get up earlier so that the days were as full as they could possibly be. I'd buy new clothes, get a smarter look, cut my hair, stop stealing, be more tolerant of Dad, more forgiving of Mum, a better older brother to Billie. I'd eat salad. Fish. Water — I'd drink a lot more water, two liters a day; no one, not even Miles, would drink more water than me.

On this warm, bright summer's morning, a lifetime's worth of New Year's resolutions were being made at once. An entirely new way of being — it was not something to take on lightly, an overwhelming project really, but one I couldn't wait to start, and I began to wish I had my headphones in my pocket and my portable CD player so I could give this all a soundtrack, an anthem of self-improvement. I'd write the resolutions down if necessary, pin them to the wall like a proclamation and stick to them, because being in love — no other word—was like being pushed out into a spotlight on a stage, and under that kind of scrutiny it was important that I get everything absolutely right. From now on I would live beyond reproach and I would move differently through this world. "A Good Town" said the road sign, *Bonum Oppidum,* and I thought, *yes, perhaps it is, perhaps it can be.*

At home, Dad was sleeping on the sofa, curtains drawn, a small flotilla of mugs and plates surrounding him, the TV playing Saturday-morning pop videos. I tugged the curtain to one side until the sunlight met his eyes, and he blinked and raised his hand, mouth opening with a sticky pop.

"Charlie?"

"Sleeping beauty." I began opening windows.

"There you are! I waited up for you."

"I've just got in. I went to a party. Sorry, I should have let you know." I would be more considerate from now on. This man had quite enough to worry about.

"Who with? Your mates?"

"Some other friends. I had to walk them home. I'll tell you later." Why "them," not "her"? I would be more honest and open, and I would change my voice and talk to my father like a friend. "I stopped and got us some bread and eggs." Brown bread, brown eggs, free-range. "I'll make you breakfast. I got these too." A plastic bag of exquisite oranges, warm and scented, six little suns that I'd got from the Spar. I'd get the sticky juicer out from the back of the cupboard. From now on we'd have oranges every weekend, like they do in the Mediterranean . . .

"Are you all right?" said Dad.

"What?"

"Are you still drunk?"

"Nope. Just . . . happy. That's allowed, isn't it?" And I wondered, and hoped, that if misery could be contagious, perhaps happiness could be too.

My father hauled himself upright and dragged his hands down his face. "It's unusual."

"It is."

"Not sure if I like it."

"Don't worry," I said. "It won't last."

PART THREE

August

What did he when thou saw'st him? What said he? How looked he? Wherein went he? What makes he here? Did he ask for me? Where remains he? How parted he with thee? And when shalt thou see him again? Answer me in one word.

—Shakespeare, *As You Like It*

Love

BUT LOVE IS BORING. Love is familiar and commonplace for any-one not taking part, and first love is just a gangling, glandular incarnation of the same. Shakespeare must have known this; take a copy of the world's most famous love story and pinch between finger and thumb the pages where the lovers are truly happy; not the buildup that precedes it, not the strife that follows, but the time when love is mutual and untroubled. It's a few pages, a pamphlet almost, the brief interlude between anticipation and despair. The confidences and intimacies of new lovers, the formation of private jokes, the confessions of doubt and insecurity, the reassurances and vows; there's only so much of that stuff that anyone can bear, and if Shakespeare ever did write the scenes where the lovers talk about their favorite food, or pick the fluff from their belly buttons, or earnestly explain the lyrics of their favorite songs, then he was right to exclude them from the second draft.

The beginning and the end, the anticipation and the despair, that's where the story lies, but the state of being in love, and in particular of being young and in love, is like listening to someone describe their parachute jump or their bizarre dream, the blurred photograph of a life-changing performance, taken from too far away. The more intense the experience, the less inclined we are to hear about it, and while we're happy that their life was changed and it must have been thrilling —can we move on?

So best to assume that when we were alone and we weren't talking, then we were kissing or fooling around, and that this was all amazing, so much so that I couldn't comprehend why grown-ups weren't doing it *all the time*—something, I suppose, that we all spend the rest of our lives discovering. Assume, too, that when we stopped long enough to talk, these conversations were all more open and insightful, free-flowing and intense, funny and serious and profound than any other conversation that has ever taken place; not just talking, but *really* talking. Assume that we were funnier than anyone we'd ever met and that the time when I made Fran laugh so hard that she wet herself, actually *wet herself* through her jeans, was one of the proudest moments of my life. Assume that nothing was felt in a halfhearted way, whether passion or anxiety, desire or fear. Assume that we made compilations and liked each other's music fiercely, and if not, pretended to; that we listened solemnly and silently to Nick Cave and Scott Walker singing about us, Nico and Nina Simone auditioning for the song that would be *our* song, the song that made us cry; and that other behavior previously thought to be silly or repulsive—holding hands, aggressive public kissing, the passing of chewing gum from mouth to mouth—lost its queasiness. Assume that we never wanted to be anywhere else or with anyone else, that time apart was time wasted, and that it was impossible to imagine the circumstances when we might not feel this way. There's some of this to come, not much more than a pamphlet, and it can't be helped. The greater part of it will go unmentioned, but also unforgotten.

First I would need to see her again, and in the forty-eight hours until our next meeting, I rediscovered that science-fictional awareness of time. The weekend crawled as if taking place on a distant planet. "*For in a minute there are many days,*" says Juliet, who, I'd come to realize, had all the best and truest lines. It was one of those moments in the play where I'd think, how does Shakespeare *know*?

Forty-eight hours, forty-six, forty-four. My God, imagine if I'd been banished to Mantua. How would I fill all this slow motion? I knew that this was in part a test, and I retained enough self-control to stay away from the phone or just-passing trips to her village. Instead I succumbed to a bone-deep tiredness and an ache in my jaw and an itchy, fidgety restlessness through the long, humid nights in the bottom bunk, in part a spiritual yearning, in part a sweaty, unpoetic horniness of the kind found in army barracks. "Agony": the word seemed to be thrown around a great deal in descriptions of parted lovers, but it certainly applied to the hours spent staring at the petrol station forecourt through the Saturday-night shift, my lover's paranoia relieved only by lurid and explicit memories of the things we'd done in the bus shelters and hedgerows on the way home. Forty-two hours, thirty-six, twenty-four; I might not have come up with the words, but I couldn't help thinking, *Gallop apace, you fiery-footed steeds* . . . On Sunday, in a regrettable fit of soulfulness, I thought that I might draw her from memory. Until now, most of the eyes I'd drawn had dangled from the sockets of skulls, and my attempts at her face, though not a bad likeness, had a generalized, conventional glamour that I knew Fran would have rejected, the eyes too large and wet, the lips too full. Be *true,* I told myself, but my attempts at sensuality resulted in the kind of homemade erotica that prison inmates pay for with cigarettes. The best attempt was a version of how she had looked somersaulting underwater, her toes pointed, the oily black nightdress floating up around her hips and clinging to her breasts. I could really go to town with the black in this one, was particularly proud of the rendition of her hardened nipple, viewed in profile, a single black mark with my Rotring 0.4 mm.

Four hours, three, two, one, and there she was at nine on Monday, pushing her bicycle for the first time. Some transformation seemed to have taken place, because she seemed even lovelier than I'd remembered—did a girl's face change once you'd kissed her?—and I was very taken with the way she let her bike, a beautiful old thin-framed racer, fall on top of mine in a way that I found fantastically *provocative*.

"Hey there," I said.

"Hello," she said and smiled.

We'd agreed to be cool with each other, but somehow word had spread before we could begin rehearsals.

"Nice weekend, you two?" said Lucy.

"Hello, lovebirds," said Keith.

"Well, Benvolio, you're a dark horse," said Miles, pinching the flesh above my collarbone as we made our way to the orangery.

"Well, I think it's lovely, two young people getting together," said Polly. "There's one every season."

Even Ivor and Alina seemed to know. "I think we should probably keep you two apart!" said Ivor with a bumptious wink, as we were divided into pairs for the Capulet ball, the first scene to involve the entire company.

Alina's concept was to begin with a traditional courtly dance, hands on hips and white handkerchiefs held aloft, then become increasingly crazed and wild and modern as the scene went on, before the whole company froze, holding their pose at the point where Romeo and Juliet finally see each other. Apart from the Macarena and the hokey-cokey, I'd never followed choreography, and now the concept of left and right, forward and back, seemed far harder as I wondered, did "hello" mean "it's over"? Might "let's talk later" mean "let's never talk again"? At one point in the formal dance, I had to take her hand for a moment and I wondered, what should I read into the interlaced fingers, the circular motion of her thumb in the palm of my hand? I found her palm with my own thumb and rubbed back frantically in a way that I hoped was erotic. "Wait for me later," she said over her shoulder. "Yes?"

At lunch, I walked with George. "So I hear congratulations are in order," he said.

"Christ, George, how does everyone know this stuff?"

"Word gets around. People say they do plays for the ideas and the art, but it's all about the sex. The last-night party, it's basically an orgy. That's the hope anyway."

"Well, it's nothing yet. It's probably a, just . . . you know . . ."

"A mere summer's fancy."

"I was going to say 'snog.' It's just a snog at a party. We'll see."

"Well, just so you know, I don't mind. Well, I do mind, but I'm not going to get weird about it and follow you both home. I'm . . . happy for you."

"Thanks, George."

"Furious too."

"Fair enough."

"But don't say anything, will you? To her, about me. I do have some pride."

I said that I understood.

We worked hard—no time for lunchtime meetings now—and at last, at the end of the long day, we found each other at the spot where the bikes lay on top of each other, pedals in spokes, brake cables around handlebars. "Look, we're all tangled up," she said, and I thought, *well, this is just too much.*

"I thought we could go somewhere, me and you. Run our lines," I said, and we began to push our bikes, but now Helen and Alex were running towards us.

"The gang's all here!" said Helen.

"How are you two feeling?" said Alex. "Any comedown, any crash?"

"No, I'm fine," said Fran.

"Bit sore," I said.

"I bet you are," said Alex.

"Alex . . ." said Fran.

"So where are we all going now?" said Helen. "The *four* of us."

"Actually," said Fran, "Charlie and me are going to run some lines," and their laughter rang out through the treetops.

"'Run some lines.' Well, I've never heard it called *that* before."

"Grow up, Alex."

"No, I think it's a great idea. Helen and I will come with you."

"Sorry, we've got bikes," I said.

"We'll jog alongside," said Alex. "Take us with you!"

"*So* childish. Charlie, get on your bike."

"But who's going to help *me* run *my* lines?" said Alex.

"We're coming with you!" said Helen.

"We're going now," shouted Fran. "Bye!"

"See you tomorrow!" I shouted, standing high on the pedals.

"But I want to run my lines!"

"Goodbye! Goodbye!"

Running the Lines

AND SO FOR THE next two weeks, we'd head off in the evenings and run our lines.

Nothing had ever looked cooler to me than Fran Fisher on a drop-handled Italian racing bike, and as much as we could we'd cycle side by side, the sun fluttering through the trees like light through an old projector, sometimes only making it a short distance before we'd pull over and, still kissing, stumble and stagger off our bikes. We ran our lines in woods and hedgerows and, in the absence of traditional haystacks, in the shadow of black-plastic-wrapped cylinders of straw, the new stubble digging into our backs like a bed of nails. One night Fran brought red wine stolen from her parents, pushing the cork into the bottle with a biro, the contents jammy and as warm as tea after a day in the sun. We took it in turns to swig the stuff, then, woozy and sticky-mouthed and struggling not to laugh, Fran took a mouthful and passed it into my mouth. "Sensual? Or was that just gross?" she said as a large part of it dribbled down my neck.

Memories of the previous evening and the prospect of the next sustained me through the long, increasingly urgent rehearsals. We'd watch scenes and what we saw was . . . not good, but better than the grandstanding and posturing of the early days, the weird vocal mannerisms fading away, the story and characters rising up through the murk. People looked at each other now, touched each other without flinching, urged each other on. I'd never played in an orchestra and never would, but imagined that this was what it was like to learn a long piece, to anticipate the bits you liked, find something to distract you through the dull stretches, to play your part with the intention of making the whole better, even if no one in the audience would notice. Embarrassment, I realized, was more embarrassing than making an effort, and so I did my best, without quite noticing the moment I became a member of the company, both in my own mind and in their eyes. Why would I not want to be part of something that Fran loved?

And though it's hard to imagine a less objective critic, I became more and more convinced that she was the greatest actor there had ever been. I loved the way her eyes and hands would track an idea as if following a bird that has flown into a room, and I loved her stillness, the absolute control and confidence that what she said mattered. I loved how she would make the words sound new, then make them new again the next time through, and I'd lean forward in my chair and watch, never once feeling jealous or unsure but only proud at what she could do, proud and a little amazed that we were together.

But during the day we never touched and only spoke in a pointedly platonic way, and there was further agony in sticking to this rule, like holding in a breath, released only in the moment we could wave goodbye to the others and hurtle away along empty lanes, searching for somewhere new and secret to "run the lines." Sometimes, in guilt or panic, we would even *actually* run the lines, with me as her slow-witted temporary Romeo, talking about saints and lips and prayers.

"*Have not saints lips, and holy palmers too?*" I said.

"*Ay, pilgrim, lips that they must use in prayer,*" said Fran.

"*O, then, dear saint, let lips do what hands do! They pray, grant thou, lest faith turn to despair.*"

"*Saints do not move, though grant for prayers' sake.*"

"*Then move not while my prayer's effect I take.*"

"Then the stage directions say he kisses her."

"Yes, but we don't have to do that. We're just running lines."

"I bet Miles does it."

"He does, but we have a contract. Strict no-tongues clause."

"Make sure he sticks to it."

"Oh, I will," she said and kissed me. "But do you get it?"

"He's trying to convince her that a kiss is the same as a prayer."

"That old line."

"And she's being all saintly."

"Or pretending to be. She wouldn't let him kiss her if she didn't want him to. I think she wants it more, if anything. That's the extent of my interpretation of the role."

"Juliet's up for it."

"*Really* up for it," she said, and we kissed again. "But do you get the shape of the thing?"

"Of what?"

"The lines. It's a sonnet. Fourteen lines, ending with a couplet."

I counted them up. "I didn't get that. So . . ."

"So it's like they meet and start talking in verse—not just finishing each other's sentences, but perfect rhyme and sonnet form. The final couplet is the kiss. It's brilliant, isn't it?"

I could see that it was, but was aware of being taught again. Miles, I knew, would recognize sonnet form, and these reminders of my ignorance troubled me more than the kiss. I didn't mind being taught if I could teach her something in return. But what? She even smoked better than me.

"Shall we go again? From the top."

Yet even in the rat-a-tat repetition of learning by rote I loved to listen to her, and though I'm not sure that I'd have admitted it, I also began to love the language, looking forward to passages in the same way that I looked forward to a key change or crescendo in a song: not always for the meaning—which still often escaped me—but for reasons that were in themselves musical, a change in pitch or pace or key, a rhythm. *My bounty is as boundless as the sea! The mask of night is on my face! Cut him out in little stars!* I'd listen all day and then again each night as we ran lines. My mind was more impressionable then, and even now I could recite great long passages. I can't imagine the circumstances in which that might happen, but they're there, like initials scratched into drying cement. She was also the first person to tell me I was funny, the greatest praise I'd ever had because it was the praise that I'd most wanted. Not in a stand-up-comedy way but with friends, small groups, which is where it mattered.

We'd try to get back to Fran's house before it got dark, but the lanes were unlit and too treacherous to cycle down, and so we'd walk. This was the second half of August, and I'd become aware of the accelerated shortening of the days, and fearful and resentful of it, as if our summer together was a coastline succumbing to the waves. The motion of the sun is but the thief of lovers' time and, like autumn waves, wears down the season's fragile shore; it was contagious, poetry. This kind of stuff occurred to me more often now, the words, ideas and feelings all tangled up, and though I had the good sense not to say it out loud, I wondered if I should write it down.

And perhaps the play was right in this respect too: that being in love might change not just how you felt, but the way you thought and spoke. Not sonnet form exactly, but as darkness came on, we'd talk in a different way; small confessions, revelations, the formation of little private jokes. We already knew each other; now the project was to *really* know each other. Such transparency involved a fair amount of deception, at least by omission; she'd have run a mile from the *real* real me, and any darkness I confessed had to be the right kind of darkness. I did not, for instance, tell her I was a thief.

But I did tell her all that I was prepared to say about the breakup of my family, my father's breakdown and what it was like to live with this. For perhaps the first time, I trusted someone entirely. There was nothing relaxed about our conversation, but even so I was aware that this was a new way of talking, free of prepared questions and answers.

It was both adult and a plausible impersonation of "adult," self-consciously earnest, effortfully profound. In short, we were ridiculous, but a part of us knew we were ridiculous and didn't care, and I think now of an illustration I'd once seen in a children's book, Maurice Sendak I think, of children dressed in grown-up clothing, hats falling off the backs of their heads, long sleeves hanging empty.

At her house, we'd hear the television through the open window and kiss goodbye for some time in the shelter of the high hedge. She'd invite me in to meet her parents, but I'd always say no. The next day we'd rehearse again and occasionally I'd take a night off from running lines to work my resentful shift in the petrol station, still stealing scratch cards but in moderation. Perhaps I'd use the money for some kind of gift—jewelry from Argos in Woking, an eat-in dinner at the Taj Mahal.

Then, on Thursday evening of the second week of running lines, she asked if I minded going a little further. "I've consulted a map," she said.

River

"LOOK — ORDNANCE SURVEY. Duke of Edinburgh Award scheme, you see. I think we have time," and she took the edges of the blue cotton dress she wore that day, bunched and tucked them into the elastic of her underwear, and we set off, laboriously ascending the brow of the hill behind the Manor, then freewheeling into an unfamiliar valley, Fran leading the way, the map flapping and cracking on her handlebars, a dark patch of sweat spreading on her back. We coasted down a long, straight avenue of poplar trees like something from a French film and, at the far end, slowed to a halt and paused while she peered at the map again — "What happened to your Duke of Edinburgh Award?" "I gave up after bronze. This way!" — then struck off across a meadow, walking single file along an overgrown footpath at the edge of a field, pushing past brambles dotted with crimson unripened berries. There were scratches on our arms and legs, but "It'll be worth it, I promise you." Sure enough, a sound was growing, a long, husky sigh, until suddenly we stepped out onto a low bank, a beach with black sand at the edge of a bend in a great dark river. The air trapped beneath the canopy of trees was hazy with midges, hot and still with a metallic smell like the air before a storm, and wagtails strutted at the water's edge, swallows and martins dabbing at the surface.

"What do you think?"

"Beautiful," I said and wondered if I ought to kiss her. But already she had dropped her bicycle, plucked off her trainers and, still walking, grabbed the hem of her dress and peeled it from her damp back and over her head. Eyes fixed forward, she unhooked her bra and, at the water's edge, pulled down and stepped carefully out of her underwear. With a gasp, she took two, three long steps into the water and stood there for a moment, one hand at the small of her back, the other arm across her breasts. Then both arms were above her head and she fell forward, yelped at the cold and was gone, silently and entirely, just a white shape against the green, carried downstream with the current. In all of this, I'd not spoken and perhaps not breathed and now I could only say, "Oh, God," before she surfaced again, some way downstream, squinting and pinching her nose.

"Why aren't you in yet?"

"I'm really sorry, I don't have my trunks with me."

"*Trunks!*" She laughed. "Well, you can't ride a bike in wet underpants, you'll *chafe!* I'll count to ten." In a spirit of discretion, she turned her back and disappeared beneath the water and I took the moment to quickly pull off my clothes. The pebbles were agony underfoot as I ran bowlegged into the river, stumbling and spinning with a huge splash and gasping at the slap of the cold water that caused my genitals to contract like a snail into its shell. You'll warm up, I told myself and half swam, half stumbled to the deepest part, the riverbed, here peaty and black-brown with a half-pleasant vegetable smell. The current carried me through patches of warm, then cold, then warm water down to where Fran now stood, in a sunlit patch at the far bank, crouching so that her chin touched the water, her shoulders brown, her breasts white triangles beneath the surface. She caught me as I floated past, tangling together, and we kissed, tasting the river water on her lips and mouth, and I pulled her towards me so that our legs were interlocked, and we wriggled our toes into the silk of the mud for anchorage and stayed like this until the water felt warm between us and our fingers pruned, until Fran pulled her feet from the mud, lifted herself and locked her legs around my hips.

But this was too much and, gasping, she pushed herself away suddenly, laughing then turning and swimming back upstream. I watched her leave the water, crouching, clutching her clothes to her body and disappearing up the bank and into the field above. I stood for a moment, then, like a drunk trying to sober up, submerged myself completely. I clambered out, untangled my clothes, dressed and followed.

I found her lying in the long grass, her arms out to the side, her underwear bunched in her left hand, her dress still wet and clinging to her like seaweed on a rock. She didn't look at me as I approached, and I had a notion that I'd offended her—she was still breathing deeply, as if she'd been crying—but she patted the spot at her side and I joined her, holding hands, drying out as best we could in the low, tired sun.

After some time had passed, she turned on her side and kissed me lightly. "That thing we almost did. The sex thing."

"Hm."

"I've been thinking about it and I want to wait."

"Okay. Until when?"

"Until you're twenty-one."

"Oh. Okay."

"Or the weekend."

"This weekend?"

"I thought so." She started to laugh. "Your face. Twenty-*one?!*"

"Yes, that was really funny."

"But the weekend, you can manage?"

"Me and you?"

"I think that was implied."

"This weekend?"

"Want to look at your diary?"

"No, no, I'm good."

"Good."

"I mean, I'll have to check the *Radio Times*."

"See what's on?"

"Exactly."

"That's if you *want* to do it with me," she said. "I don't want to take anything for granted."

"Well, I was saving it for someone I liked . . ."

"But in the meantime? As a stopgap?"

"It's more or less the only thing I think about."

She laughed. "I mean what we do now, the . . . fooling around, that's all right, isn't it?"

"I think so."

"We'd just be taking it to—"

"—the next stage."

"Well, then it's fixed," she said. "Think of it as the *ultimate* line-run."

"Good."

"Good. It's on." She kissed me and lay back down. "Anyway, sex underwater doesn't work. Don't ask me how I know, I just do. *You'd* be fine but I'm the one who'd get frog spawn and pondweed up there."

"Sticklebacks."

"Pond skaters. Fanny like a classroom aquarium. I don't want to miss my period then find out I'm going to have a perch. Also, we'd have needed a condom."

I had one in my wallet, one of a set of three—a lifetime's supply, I'd thought—that I'd purchased, heart racing, in the toilets of the golf club where Mum worked. I'd selected "ribbed," a powerful word, like the walls of a log cabin or the tires of a monster truck. If they'd sold "corrugated," I'd have bought those. Instead, I was alarmed at the gossamer flimsiness of the thing. To reassure myself, the first had been squandered on what I thought of as a "dry run"; the second, the "spare tire," was stashed in the cardboard sleeve of the Stone

Roses' second LP, because I knew no one would ever look there. The third of the trilogy I'd take with me on evenings that had seemed ripe with promise—trips to the funfair, for some reason, or to parties in Harper's den. I carried it now, the ring showing through the burnished wrapper like a brass rubbing. We might have used that in the river, but it would have meant swimming to shore to get it, walking back across the pebbles and perhaps holding it in my mouth as I swam back like a dog with a tennis ball. No, it was not the right time. It would have made a good story, I suppose, to have done it for the first time in the middle of a moving river, but I was glad we'd stopped because—

"What I really want," she said, "is a bed."

"A bed is a good idea."

"Because a tent or a haystack or a bench, frankly . . ."

"No good."

"With a door you can close and no one around."

But where would we find such a thing? "My dad's always home." Impossible to conceive of having sex with Dad downstairs, and there was the issue of the bunk bed, which still embarrassed me.

"And my room, whenever I've had a boy there—the *very* few times I've had a boy there—they just walk up and down on the landing, coughing and making the floorboards creak."

"And I ought to meet them first."

"Meet them properly, rather than meet them then immediately have sex with their daughter."

We went into our act. "You have a lovely home, Mrs. Fisher," I said.

"Call me Claire."

"You have a lovely home, Claire, Graham, now if you'll excuse us . . ."

"And Graham, mate—stay off the landing."

"But if they go out?"

"That could be ages," she said. "Anyway, mine's a single. A double's better, and my parents' bed, it's not ideal. That's a lifetime of therapy, right there."

"A double would be good."

"Like a wrestling ring. Room to roam." She turned her head. "You all right?"

"I'm fine."

She leaned over me, her face close. "You look quite flushed."

"No. I'm okay. We're being practical, it's good."

"And you're sure?"

"Yes."

"And you don't think I'm some sort of . . . wench?"

"Temptress."

"Seductress, for suggesting it?"

"No."

"And you're not nervous."

"No. A bit. I mean I want to get it right."

"Yeah, I want you to get it right too." She laughed. "And me." A moment passed, and she flipped to her side. "Okay, there is one possibility."

"Go on."

"Can you tell your dad you're staying at Harper's?"

"When?"

"Friday."

"I never really stay over there."

"But you could this weekend, you could stay until Sunday night."

"Until Sunday?"

"Or say you've gone camping or something. Can you?"

"I suppose so."

"Okay. Then I've got a plan."

Starry Starry Night

I KNEW THAT FRAN was not a virgin. She'd told me her history and we'd laughed at the word, like it was a GCSE: "We're doing that, and the Tudors." I knew about her boyfriends and had worked up a mental image and conventional hatred for each of them. In turn, I'd told her about my near miss with Sharon Findlay down the back of the sofa. "It's just as well you didn't have sex," she said. Otherwise you'd have to tell everyone that you lost it down the back of the sofa."

"Literally."

"*Literally.*" "Literally" was one of our private jokes. You see, I told you.

This conversation had taken place a few nights earlier, in a sloping field with a view of the town. Fran and I had a tendency to seek out these beauty spots, scouting locations for our own scenes.

"I don't know why people talk about 'losing it' anyway," she said. "You lose a sock or your umbrella; it's sort of passive or accidental. Much better to, I don't know, *throw* your virginity. Something active. Not 'lost it with' but 'hurled it at.'"

"Or maybe 'given.'"

"'Given.' Like a precious *gift*. Is that what you're going to do with your virginity, Charlie?"

"Yeah, but with the receipt."

"In case they don't like it?"

"Tried it on, sorry, not for me."

"Wrong size."

"Not my color."

"Can I have the cash instead?"

"Actually," I said, "I think it's only a gift if it comes from a girl. Boys have to take it." She frowned at me, and I quickly clarified. "Usually, I mean, that's what people say."

"Bit sexist."

"It is. *Really* sexist."

"Well, I think you should *give* yours, Charlie. Gift it. Bestow it, like frankincense, or a nice fountain pen."

"When I meet the right girl."

"When you meet the right girl."

We were silent for a while.

"Did you lose yours or give it?" I said.

"No, I sort of . . . fumbled it. Oh, God." She clapped both hands to her face and exhaled, took them away, opened her eyes wide. "We were rehearsing Romeo and Juliet's morning-after scene the other day, and Ivor had Miles and me all sort of tangled up in each other's arms, like we'd had this magical mutual experience and woken up transformed with lovely hair and clean sheets. I said to Ivor, I wonder if it was really *bad*, the first time Romeo and Juliet did it — really awkward, clumsy sex. Maybe there was blood and Juliet saying it's uncomfortable and maybe it only lasted ten seconds, Romeo apologizing, and maybe the Nurse kept walking about outside the door, putting them off. I think I sort of went off on one about it, this idea, Romeo and Juliet having bad sex, how they could still be in love and it be awkward. Maybe it was better, more real, if it *was* awkward, because they'd be working it out together like you're meant to."

"Workshopping it."

She laughed. "Exactly! Workshopping it. Anyway, Ivor was looking at me like I was mad. "It's not that sort of play, Fran," he said, and I said I disagreed — if Shakespeare's right about what first love is, why wouldn't he be right about first sex too? Of course Miles just flatly refused to accept the existence of sex that wasn't transcendent and life-changing, because, you know, he's Miles, and I was so near, so *near* to telling them."

"About?"

"The first time."

"Go on."

"The first time—you really want to know this? The first time was with this guy a couple of years above me."

"How old were you?"

"Fifteen. It was Christmastime, the one before last. Anyway, we used to have this thing called Battle of the Bands at Chatsborne— yeah, I know—and when I'd been in the first year, this fifth-year— Patrick Durrell, his name was—had gone up and sung 'Roxanne,' you know, 'unplugged,' just a boy and his acoustic guitar, and we thought it was daring because red lights and all, in front of the teachers too. *So* cheesy, but at the time there was this amazing hush, like we were in the presence of this *teller of tales*. About prostitutes. So. Three years later, we're doing Battle of the Bands ourselves, playing our covers no one recognizes, everyone shrugging away in time with the beat, and word gets out that he's in the audience. So we finish our three songs —'Good night, Chatsborne Secondary, you've been amazing!'—and at the party afterwards, there he is, chatting away with the headmaster over a glass of mulled wine, because he's one of those weirdos who's always coming back to school at holidays, a success story, Chatsborne at its best. Anyway, he sort of tracks me down. 'Nice gig,' he says. 'Shame it was all covers, you should really write your own songs,' and a little bit of me thinks, *piss off, you didn't write 'Roxanne,'* but even so, I've been fantasizing about this boy for years and he looks at me and says, 'I think you'd write great songs,' so I say, 'What makes you think I'd write great songs?' and he says, 'You just look like you've got something to say.' And of course I should have barged out the fire

exit right away, but I was younger then and he's telling me all about
university—Manchester, of course—and how amazing it is, and how
wild and *mad,* and how he'll have to watch himself next term, what
with all the *clubbing* and *ecstasy* he's been doing, and he does look
a bit ragged, to be honest, a bit spotty, but still, it's Patrick Durrell!
I've written his name on my exercise books! In three dimensions! So
the party ends at nine thirty, which it just so happens is when Patrick
Durrell comes *alive.* He's got a hip flask—a hip flask at a school con-
cert, God, what a dick—and he makes a big deal of pouring vodka
into my orange San Pellegrino. 'Now it's called a screwdriver,' he says,
and I know that's not *strictly* accurate but I let it go. 'D'you want to
come home? My parents are in but we've got a granny annex.' Well,
I'm only human. 'Can I bring the rest of the band?' I say. 'No, I can't
bring too many people back.' 'You don't want to wake Granny?' I say.
'She just died,' he says, "that's why I've got access to the annex.' 'So
it's swings and roundabouts,' I say, and he looks all offended but he
says, 'Are you coming or not?' Anyway, I find my mum and dad and
say I'm going to stay at Sarah's, and we meet in the car park and go to
the granny annex, self-contained, very nice and . . . that's where I lost
my virginity. Seventeenth of December 1995."

"And how was it?"

"The granny annex?"

"The experience."

"Well, it was . . . an experience. There was this little living area,
which was really floral and frumpy and still had her knickknacks on
the TV, and he'd tried to sort of club it up with candles, like a chill-out
lounge but, you know, with doilies and short figurines of clowns and
photos of Granny Durrell staring me out. And we had more screw-
drivers and he yammered on about his mates in Manchester, people
I'd never met and never would meet, all in this slightly nasal mad-
for-it accent, which annoyed me because I knew for a fact that he
was born in Billingshurst. His guitar was in the corner, and without

stopping talking, he reached for it and just started picking out little melodies, like he was accompanying his own monologue, and then he started *singing*."

"Oh, God."

"That cheesy Van Gogh song, 'Starry, Starry Night' or 'Vincent' or whatever. And I thought, *well, this is a bit weird,* because he was really going for it, eyes screwed up tight. And you can't do anything, can't get up and have a wee or anything, you've just got to sit there, and it suddenly seemed like a very, very long song. I thought, at the end, *do I clap? What if he does 'American Pie'?* So I clapped but just a little, and he said, 'Did you know that song is about Vincent van Gogh?' And I said, 'Really? Is that why he cut his ear off?'

"And he laughed but he was a bit offended. He still kissed me, though, and I reminded myself, it's Patrick Durrell! So we kissed for a while and I kept telling myself, he's still that boy, isn't he? That one I used to really, really love, so I just sort of — went for it, and then our tops were off and then the rest and then we were on his dead granny's bed. He asked me, 'How old are you?,' which, generally speaking, should never be a part of foreplay — you know, establish that *way* beforehand — and I said fifteen, and I'm not sure what he thought about that because we still did it. So."

"And . . . how was it?"

"Oh, you know. Painful. In every sense. At least it was short."

"Did he know you were . . . ?"

"A virgin? Yeah, I told him, and he said, I'll never forget, 'That's okay, I'll put a towel down,' which, again, wasn't the ideal response, but still."

She went quiet for a moment. "Anyway. Everyone tells you it's disappointing, but he went very thoughtful afterwards and I thought, maybe this is that melancholy thing men are supposed to get, so I said, 'What's up?' and he said — it was quite beautiful, really — he said, 'You do realize that, technically, that was statutory rape?' And — idiot

—I told him that I wasn't going to go to the police, don't let it spoil your Christmas, and can you drive me home, or at least put me in a taxi, and he looked really put out by that but he called the cab and offered me five quid and I said, 'How dare you, I'm not your Roxanne,' and he looked confused and said, 'No, for the minicab,' and I said, 'Yes, I know, I was joking—never mind, I've got money,' and I waited outside till it came, and I thought, why am I making all these jokes? Why am I making him feel better? Anyway, I cried all the way home and I never saw him again."

She shuddered and flexed her fingers. "Sometimes I wish I had gone to the police, not 'cause I was fifteen but just to report him for being a selfish shit or his singing or something. I mean he's *ruined* Van Gogh for me now. Not to mention Don McLean."

We were quiet for a while, the hurt radiating off her, a kind of vibration. I'd had no conversations like this and wanted very much to be a certain kind of boy—"man" would be the term—who knew what to say, a living antidote to the boy in the story. I was still in the grip of my resolution, to be exemplary at all times in her company, but the practical demands of this often escaped me, the right thing to say only occurring to me on the journey home. I felt a desire to track this boy down and seek vengeance that was almost Tybalt-like in its fury. I wanted, too, to comfort her, but a hug, an embrace, felt wrong and all I could think to do was take her hand. She lifted our interlaced fingers and examined them, curiously, as if she'd not seen them before.

"I'm sorry."

"No need to get all somber, it just wasn't ideal. I don't think it ever is, but I wish it had been with someone—stupid word—kind. I don't mean soppy and scared and all *sensitive,* that's the worst. Just . . . careful of your feelings. Anyway. Thankfully, soon after there was this Swiss boy on a ski trip, Pascal, we had a *much* better time. I mean, *that* was more like it. It wasn't a meeting of souls but it was very . . . slick and professional."

"That's your review."

"'Highly recommended. Would come here again.' But you don't want to hear about that one, do you?"

"Not really. But maybe you could count that as your first time."

"I don't think it works like that. But you, my virgin friend, you need to wait for someone special, someone you can work it out with and have a laugh."

"Workshop it."

"Exactly. Workshop it."

"If only there was someone like that."

"I know," she said and laughed. "If only."

Press and Publicity

BUT NOW WE HAD a plan. I returned from the river, dizzy with it, head full of preparations. It was a good plan, a great plan, and the thought of it carried me home in darkness, grinning all the way.

More often than not my father would be in bed when I returned, and I'd check the glass in the sink, sniffing to see if it was whisky or water. The words "do not combine with alcohol" haunted me, and I'd rehearsed a conversation in my head, matter-of-fact, non-preachy, in which I'd point them out. We'd yet to even acknowledge the existence of the medications, but when the time was right, we'd have that conversation in real life too. Now I was with Fran, surely there was nothing I couldn't say.

But on this particular night, the night we made the plan, the music was loud enough to hear from the lawn, John Coltrane's *Giant Steps,* every second of it known to me. When I entered, he was standing at the turntable, the album's sleeve in his hand, his head bopping at tremendous speed as if bouncing over cobbles.

"You having a party?" I shouted, to let him know I was there. He turned, his shirt unbuttoned, his hair crazed. On the lid of the turntable, a garage tumbler of Scotch. "There you are! You just missed them."

"Who?"

"Your friends. Whatshisname . . ."

"Harper?"

My father didn't like Harper, thought him glib and shallow. "And the others." He liked the others even less, and in turn Dad was a source of curiosity and, I suspected, derision for my friends. It still caused me physical discomfort to recall his attempt at hospitality as he played them the whole second side of *Bird and Diz*, the beers warming in the boys' hands, desperate glances shooting between them like passengers about to disarm a hijacker. They even had a nickname for him. He was The Jazzer, and the thought of them together, unsupervised, made my heart race.

"Did you tell them where I was?"

"I said you were out rehearsing."

"*Rehearsing?*"

"They seemed to know all about it."

"Because you told them!"

"No. Look . . ."

On the phone table where we kept the takeaway menus was a large, glossy piece of paper folded into quarters, a dot of Blu-Tack in the corner. In Harper's handwriting: "We missed you, stranger! So many secrets!" Without unfolding the paper, I knew what it would be.

We'd taken the photographs the week before, Alina summoning us one at a time to pose in front of a white sheet. In the quest for relevance, the intention was to pastiche the *Trainspotting* poster, with the same font and color scheme, individual black-and-white character portraits lined up like a police ID parade. "I need some charisma," Alina had demanded, "some bravado, like a movie star." The result had all the dead-eyed awkwardness of my school photos but with the added unhappiness of a sword pointing at the lens. Still, no one will ever see it, I'd thought, misunderstanding the purpose of publicity.

"I think you look very cool," said Dad, "with your sword and everything."

I'd already told him about the play, in the high-minded elation that had followed the all-night party. We'd been standing at the sink, me washing, Dad drying; it was always easier to communicate when we couldn't see each other's faces, which made me wonder if ideally we'd be in different rooms, shouting through the door.

"Benvolio."

"Who?"

"A guy called Benvolio. He's Romeo's friend." I glanced to my side, saw him tilt his head, confused, amused.

"Where did that come from?"

"I don't know. Just thought it might be, you know, a laugh."

"And is it?"

"Yeah. I like the people."

"And who are you playing again?"

"Benvolio!"

He muttered the name, as if Benvolio might be someone he knew from school. "Is it a *big* part?"

"Well it's not the eponymous role."

"What?"

"Quite big."

"So—you've got lines?"

"Lots of lines. Couple of big speeches."

"And . . . do I have to come and see it?"

I laughed. "Not if you don't want to, Dad."

He thought about it. "Is it long?"

"Quite long. Like I said, you don't have to—"

"No, let's see. Let's see," he said, picking at the egg on a frying pan. "I wondered where you'd been going. I thought you were just roaming the streets, waiting for me to go to bed." This was exactly what I had been doing. He slid the pan back into the water, and we said no more about it.

Now, cycling to Harper's, I told myself that it was not a big deal. I even practiced the words out loud. "Not a big deal," accompanied by a little shrug. It was, after all, Shakespeare, not ballet. The big house stood in its field, lights in all the windows. I leaned my bike against the cement mixer and ran to the door, adopting the wry, self-assured half-smile that said "not a big deal."

Lloyd opened it. "By my troth, 'tis thee!"

"Hello, Lloyd."

"Why dost thou call here so late in the even-time, arrant knave?"

"Look, is Harper there?"

"Aye, aye, he is, he is. Step forth." Lloyd bowed and beckoned me in. "But leavest thou thy sword outside."

I stepped inside. Earlier that day, we'd rehearsed the scene in which Romeo, returning from Juliet, is teased and goaded by Tybalt but, suddenly wise, floats serenely through the mockery and aggression with a hippie-ish, almost religious serenity, preaching peace and reconciliation. "*Thou knowest me not,*" he tells his enemy. "*I loved thee better than thou canst devise,*" as if being in love made him invulnerable and endlessly forgiving. That was what I aspired to, that act 3, scene 1 attitude.

Harper stood at the end of the hall, Fox grinning behind him, eyes bright in anticipation. "Lewis! You're full of surprises."

"Indeed, sir," said Lloyd. "Quite the dark horse, he is."

"Are you going to keep that up, Chris?" I said. First names. Keep calm. Stay in control.

"What of it, sir?"

"They're just leaving," said Harper.

"Aye, aye, we tarry not!"

"Because the joke's quite old now," I said.

"Of what dost thou speak, thou saucy knave?"

"Yes, I get it. I got it the first time."

"'Tis not a joke."

"You're not even doing it very well."

"All right, keep it down!" said Harper. Behind him, Fox started to laugh.

"Do not lose thy rag with me," said Lloyd.

"You are so tiresome."

A high-pitched, goading laugh . . .

"You too, Fox."

"Thy words have no sting, fancy lad."

"Pack it in, Lloyd," said Harper. "Fox, go home."

Fox stepped outside, but Lloyd was incapable of leaving without some final flourish. "We saw your dad, Lewis." He clicked his fingers quickly, crooner-style. "The Jazzer, jazzing out. Ba-da-ba ba-ba ba-ba-pow!"

Visions of terrible malice, of smashing his head into the door-frame, or running him through just as Romeo murders Tybalt.

"Lloyd!" said Harper. "Go!"

"Good night, sweet prince! Good night!" A moment, while the door closed, the laughter faded away.

"Is it too late?"

"No," said Harper. "Come on. Let's play pool."

"You break. I met this girl by accident. She's just left Chatsborne, Fran Fisher, do you know a Fran Fisher? You're stripes, I'm spots. And she was doing this play thing, the Shakespeare thing, the one they told us about in school. Nice shot. And the only way to see her was to join, so that's what I've been doing. A play. Bad luck, my go. And it's not bad, you know, it's fine, I quite like the people—yes!—bit pretentious but they're not taking the piss all of the time, and it's a nice venue. Shit! Your go. I even think it might be quite a good production. Of the play. Helen Beavis is doing the design."

"The Bricky?"

"Yeah, but no one calls her that. They call her Helen. It's refreshing. Also, she's really good at art and design and stuff—and it's open-air, site-specific, in this massive house—"

"It's *what?*"

"What?"

"You just said it's something . . ."

"'Site-specific.' I just mean that it's not in an ordinary theatre, it's specific to this house. Is it my go?"

"Why are you talking like this?"

"I'm just explaining why I'm doing this Shakespeare play. Your go."

"But you've never done a play before. You're on."

"No, and I never will again. It's just . . . the summer's so *long,* and I've got nothing else to do, and I don't know, don't you ever want to try something . . . new?"

"Yeah, but, I don't know, bungee jumping. Not a *play.* Fluke."

"Not fluke, skill."

"And aren't you just a really shit actor?"

"Me? Yes, I'm really terrible. My go, two shots. Well, not terrible. Fran worked on the lines."

"Fran's the—"

"The girl, Juliet. You should come and—"

"Come and *see* it?"

"Yes! Why not! You know a couple of people in it."

"Your go."

"Helen Beavis, Colin Smart—"

"Fucking hell, you're hanging out with Little Colin Smart now?"

"He's all right. Lucy Tran, she's really good in it."

"Number Forty-two?"

"Yes, except no one calls her that because it's racist—"

"It's not *racist.*"

"Of course it's racist, it is *literally* racist, it was always racist, and always stupid, too, because she's Vietnamese. Not even Vietnamese, she's British, she was born here, and even if she *was* Chinese, it would still be fucking racist and fucking stupid."

"All right!"

"Actually, no, don't come and see it. Just . . . forget it. Whose go is it?"

"You all right?"

"Yes, I just asked whose go?"

"Yours."

"All right, top right pocket. I don't know, Martin, it just makes a change from hanging around down here and taking the piss and being shitty to each other all the time."

"You think I'm shitty to you?"

"Not *you*, all of us together, the way we are. Don't you think it's *weird*? All the name-calling and jokes and stuff? I mean, when it's someone's birthday, shouldn't you, I don't know, buy them a present rather than nick their trousers and set fire to them? Isn't that deeply, deeply weird?"

"I think this conversation is weird."

"Is it? Probably. I don't care."

"I mean, yes, I think it gets out of hand sometimes."

"Yeah, you could say that . . ."

"But I don't think we're bad mates."

"No, and I didn't say that."

"When your mum was moving out—"

"No, I know, I know."

"When you were fucking up all your exams—"

"I realize that."

"When you were being all weird and moody—"

"Was I? Probably I was. I was a bit depressed, I think."

"You were nuts."

"I was. Your go."

"But we didn't go anywhere, did we? I mean we were there."

"Well *you* were. And I appreciate it. But if someone calls me Council or Bunkie or Nobody again, or talks about Dad like that, I'm going to . . . walk away."

"Your go. It's just banter."

"Is it?"

"Between mates."

"I know, but I don't need that anymore."

"Now you've got new friends? Unlucky, my go."

"A few."

"And this girl."

"Fran. Yes."

"Is she nice?"

"She's amazing."

"Attractive?"

"I think she's beautiful."

"So have you done it yet?"

"No. Everything but."

"Everything but, eh?"

"We've got a plan."

"Well, if you've got a plan. And you like her?"

"Yeah, I really, you know. I love her."

". . ."

". . ."

". . ."

". . ."

"Well, you'd better get your beauty sleep, Charlie."

"Let's finish this first."

"Top right pocket."

"Off you go."

". . ."

". . ."

". . ."

"Well done," I said. "You win."

Workshopping

". . . AND ROLL BACK up, one vertebra at a time, into a standing position," said Alina. "And now, before you go, here's one final word from your director."

"Here we go," said Alex.

"It's the D-day speech," said George.

"It's going to be *very* emotional," said Helen.

"Sh!" said Miles.

And sure enough, Ivor came to stand in the center of the circle. "Well, what an experience. Three weeks ago, I thought—there's no show. There's nothing here, no one's listening, no communication, it's all a waste of time. But you've worked so hard, *so,* so hard, and I don't mind telling you, this has got the potential to be, well, something pretty great, something Shakespeare might watch and think, yep, that's *exactly* what I meant. Now next week is going to be very technical, quite slow, boring in places and very hard work. I know, too, that it's a big week for some of you, with your exam results coming out, and so we're going to take a few hours off on Monday, to let the excitement die down."

I wouldn't look. I would stay in bed, pull the pillow down over my head.

"But the scaffolding will go up while we rehearse, we'll dress it. Tech on Tuesday and possibly Wednesday, Thursday dress rehearsal, then that night . . . we're on! There are still tickets, so please, get your aunts, your uncles, your cousins, your school friends along. Because I think they're going to see something really . . ." Ivor touched his knuckle to his lip, to contain the emotion. "Really. Special. Now. Go home!"

We were not going home.

"Pub?" said Helen.

"Or are you *running lines?*" said Alex.

"No, we can go to the pub," said Fran. The pub was part of the plan. "But we're on our bikes."

"Your bikes. You're so *wholesome.*"

"Aren't we?" said Fran.

"Well, give us doublers," said Helen.

"Doublers?" said Alex. "I'm sorry, is this the *Beano?* No one calls them doublers. They're croggies."

"Croggies is just made up."

"No, it is a croggy," said Fran. "It's the standard term."

"Must be a *Chatsborne* thing," said Helen.

"If anything, it's a backie," I said.

"Literally a backie," said Fran.

"Doublers don't work anyway. We're too big."

"Yeah, thanks, Charlie," said Helen.

"No, we're all too big."

"It works downhill," said Fran.

And so at the top of the lane the four of us clambered onto two bikes like a circus troupe, Fran and I taking the seats, Helen and Alex standing on the pedals. In passing, Alex noticed my rucksack —"Good Lord, what have you got in there? Are you running away from home?" and I wondered if I should tell him, *I'm spending the weekend with Fran, the whole weekend, just the two of us. We're going to have sex*—but already we were off, hurtling down the lane at terrifying speed; dead, surely, if we hit a fallen branch or met a car coming towards us. Dead and so close to having intercourse. "I don't want to die!" I said out loud. "Not now."

"Faster!" shouted Alex, and so we picked up speed, whooping and hollering, causing the rest of the company to split and scatter. "See you at The Angler's!" shouted Helen as we passed. "If we live!"

We walked the rest of the way, the others joining us later in the pub garden. Conspirators, Fran and I were careful to avoid each other's company. Instead she talked to Polly, subtly drawing out the intelligence we'd need while I sat and listened to George and Miles bicker.

And still I couldn't help looking at my watch, the aching slowness of the minute hand. *So tedious is this day, as is the night before some festival,* says Juliet, *to an impatient child that hath new robes, and may not wear them.* The play was stuffed with anticipation, talk of tomorrows, of sunrises and sunsets, hours and minutes, and if the characters had wristwatches, they'd not just check them but tap the glass, longing for them to run faster. If I'd been going to college, it might have made an essay — "Time and Horniness in *Romeo and Juliet:* An Exploration." I checked my watch again. Full sex. Of course it would be silly to think that there was nothing sexual about all the things we'd done so far, but this was *full* sex, like full volume, a full house, a full English breakfast; it contained *everything,* and after this there'd be nothing left to do except to do it again. I checked my watch repeatedly until eight p.m., when, as agreed, we said our goodbyes.

By one minute past, we were gone, smiling secretly. At the rival petrol station near the pub, I stopped to buy a bag of ice — I'd never bought ice before, associating an abundance of ice with millionaires — and I stuffed the bag into the top of my rucksack and felt it cooling and melting against my neck as we struggled to cycle back up the hill towards Fawley Manor. Close to the entrance, we stopped, checked both ways like spies behind enemy lines, stashed our bikes behind the high stone wall that bounded the estate.

The sun was low as we cut through the woods, so that Bernard and Polly would not spot us when returning from the pub. "They're seeing friends in London tomorrow," said Fran, "and going to the theatre. Back late and out all day Sunday." Approaching the drive, we heard the sound of their car and crouched in the undergrowth like kids playing soldiers. We saw Bernard step out of the old Mercedes to open the wooden gate, sober and straight like the old family chauffeur, while Polly's head lolled backwards on the passenger seat.

"We could have just asked her," I whispered.

"This is more *exciting*," said Fran and kissed me, not ten feet from Bernard, and once the car had moved on, we climbed the wall and made for the gatehouse. The key was still there on the lintel and Fran placed it in the lock and slowly opened the door. It creaked like a sound effect.

I think we'd both hoped for some miraculous transformation, a low-lit hotel room, but the cottage looked even duller in the fading evening light, a long-abandoned holiday rental, musty and scrappy. There'd be mice here, rats even, and fat spiders lurking in corners. "The honeymoon suite," said Fran, and I pulled her towards me and kissed her clumsily. "Let's get things ready first," she said, and we both slipped silently into our chores, moving furniture and sweeping the floor, pausing when we passed each other to kiss or touch, trying not to betray a sense of urgency or nervousness.

The first thing Fran arranged was the music: a Sony Discman, two miraculous mini-speakers and a small stack of CDs in a manila envelope. "Music to clean up by," she said and pressed play on the *Trainspotting* soundtrack. In the kitchenette, taps coughed and choked, the water a murky brown, but we wiped the dust off the red Formica kitchen table and unpacked our supplies.

A Swiss Army knife. Bananas, a tube of Pringles, the largest commercially available bag of peanuts, wine gums and own-brand digestives, a torch, four bread rolls, a cucumber and some thin-sliced Yorkshire ham, sachets of instant coffee from some holiday hotel, greasy pats of butter stolen from the pub, favorite T-shirts and underwear and a pot of hummus, tea bags, two oranges, plasters, roll-on deodorant, candles, night-lights, matches and some basic cosmetics. We'd shared the alcohol provision: I had vodka, a two-liter bottle of Coke and the bag of ice, Fran had cava and some Portuguese red wine. We plugged in the ancient fridge, which shuddered like a generator, and crammed the slushy ice into the tiny freezer compartment. The plan was to spend our daytime reading in the meadow, and I unpacked my chosen books with some pride: *Captain Corelli's Mandolin* and the six-hundred-page film tie-in edition of *The Name of the Rose*. Fran had *The Rainbow* by D. H. Lawrence and a school library edition of *Playing Shakespeare* by John Barton. I did not unpack the condoms — I'd amassed six of them now, an even more ambitious project than *The Name of the Rose* — but even so, the provisions laid out on the table were a strange combination of decadence and practicality. "We're sexy explorers," said Fran, shining the torch on the Pringles. "There's a party, but it's in Nepal."

Fran had also managed to pack two clean sheets. On a hunch, we felt along the bottom edge of the sofa and tugged and tugged again, half expecting it to shear off in our hands until, like a piece of ancient farm machinery, the mechanism gave and the sofa turned into a bed of sorts. We stretched the fitted sheet across and looked at it in silence.

"Lighting!" said Fran.

We'd resolved to use a minimum of electric light on the off chance that Polly or Bernard might drive by. Instead we lit candles around the edge of the room, so that it began to feel a little like a ritual, as if a chalk pentagram might be next; the great deflowering.

Nerves.

"I'm just going to . . ."

The bathroom was airless, dim and smelled of old flannels. Despite our preparations, we'd forgotten soap, but I found a shard, pink and cracked with an edge like a flint arrowhead, doused myself with cold, brown water and scraped at my armpits. Next door, the music stopped. "Charlie! Where are you?"

"One minute." My heart seemed to be pounding at an improbable rate, I could hear it in my ears, and I placed the heel of my hand on my sternum. A shame, now, to have to call an ambulance. I splashed my face with the rusty water, dried it with the edge of my T-shirt and went next door.

The night-lights meant that the room was lit from below like a Victorian music hall, casting high shadows on the wall. Champagne —cava—lay under ice in a green plastic washing-up bowl, along with two chipped mugs. Fran knelt, changing the disc. "Marvin Gaye or Elliott Smith? Or are they both too obvious? Marvin, I think." She pressed play and stood. In the minutes I'd been next door, regulating my heart, Fran had somehow contrived to change into a dress that I'd not seen before, black with large red roses and thin straps. There was a smear of lipstick too, hastily and unhappily applied because she was already sucking her lips to remove it.

"You look beautiful."

"Thank you."

"I didn't bring anything nice to wear."

"Well, go home and change! Sorry. Shouting. Um . . ." She tucked her hair behind her ear and looked round the room. "By the way, I've, um, found something for us to do. Board games!" She crossed to the shelves. "They've got Scrabble, Boggle, Pictionary. Operation's the sexiest. I mean it's practically foreplay, but the batteries are probably flat. Monopoly?"

"Maybe later."

"You don't want to start a game of Monopoly?"

"Not this second."

"You can be banker. I realize it's a time commitment. Or there's a jigsaw. View from Waterloo Bridge, five thousand pieces."

"Maybe if it rains tomorrow."

"Okay. So—what do you want to do now?"

"I just really want to kiss you."

"Do you?"

"I do."

"Good. Come on, then."

And so we kissed for some time. I knew from all of those songs about taking it slow, making the night last a long time and seeing the sun come up, that longevity was the key to success, and so we stopped to open the cava, and to make jokes and, once drunk enough, to slow-dance, stopping to move some of the night-lights that were dangerously near the curtains. "Imagine the headlines," said Fran, "'Virgin Dies in Blaze.'" We finished the wine, and I made two vodka and Cokes, and Fran put Portishead on the CD player, then took it off again—too doomy—and played Mazzy Star instead. But there was something a little awkward about it all, and the white sheet of the sofa bed glowed radioactively throughout until eventually we found ourselves there, undressing clumsily, then finally making love.

And again there's a problem of language, because there was scarcely time to *make* anything at all. It would be wonderful to boast of some great, modulated and sustained act, full of shifting moods and tempo changes like some epic symphony. But the mere fact of it, the responsibility to make things happen in a certain way, meant that the whole thing was quite overwhelming, threatening at all times to spin out of control. I'd been led to believe that in moments of passion, some ability would kick in, an erotic sixth sense, instinctive like dancing —not my dancing, someone else's dancing. Instead it was the most extreme version yet of not knowing what to do with my hands. Not just hands, but mouth and eyes and hips, and though I'd yet to learn to drive a manual car, I imagined the coordination required would be something like this. Why, in all the depictions of sexual intercourse I'd ever seen, did everyone move around so much and with so much vigor?

Surely that was a lie, and surely the only way to sustain the act for any length of time would be to treat it with steely, taut concentration, trying not to be distracted by the great cacophony of questions in my head. Should I maintain eye contact or is that creepy? If I look away, is that cold? Are we too near the edge of the bed? Does her head hurt, hanging off like that? Should we pause and budge up? "Budge up" — isn't that a funny phrase? That candle, is it still too near the bottom of the curtain, and now the sheet is untucked, should we stop and tuck in the sheet? If I close my eyes, will it last longer? She's smiling—is smiling good, or is she trying not to laugh? What's my face doing? Are we allowed to talk? Am I too heavy? Consequently, the moment of crisis was a little *too* much of a crisis, a thrilling panic, like that stretched moment when something irreplaceable, an ancient vase say, is knocked from a shelf, judders and then seems to hang suspended as you wonder, will it fall? Please don't fall, it's too precious, don't fall, before accepting regretfully that, yes, there's nothing you can do now, it's going to fall, so that the moment was literally breathtaking and something that I'd probably have to apologize for.

But despite all the anxieties, the overwhelming sensation was amazement; that I should be permitted to do such a thing and with such a person, that she should not just allow it but urge it on. Gratitude is too weak a word, humble and wheedling, but if it's possible to imagine an intense, active, passionate gratitude, then that is what I felt. Saying "thank you very much," as if I'd been handed my change in a shop, was out of the question. I'd also got the impression that saying "I love you" while making love was frowned upon, and that for those words to slip out in the throes of passion—especially the first time—would have been like passing wind: inappropriate and fatal to the mood. I'd resolved to do neither and had succeeded, but there was no doubt that I did love her and would never love or want anyone more as long as I lived, and that a sincere attempt had been made, not entirely successfully, to focus and communicate this in the act of love.

I wasn't sure I'd got this point across. Certainly, I wasn't able to put it into words. All I could manage was "Oh, God."

"You all right?" she said.

"Yes. Yes, just need to . . ."

"That's okay."

"Just a moment . . ."

"Okay. No rush."

"I need to . . ."

It was some time before I could speak again. "Bloody hell."

"Cramp?" she said.

"Not exactly. Was it . . . ?"

"'All right for you?'"

"I wasn't going to ask that," I said, though I was. "It was lovely."

"It was quite quick, I'm sorry."

"That's fine."

"I thought I'd get to move around a bit more."

"Next time."

"So you didn't have . . . ?"

"An orgasm. Oh, yes, about, what, nine?"

"Oh, God."

"Why, did you?"

"Ha."

"Shh. Just lie there. It was really lovely, like I said. And the first time is always a bit like that. It's just like, I don't know . . ."

"Clearing your throat?"

"No! That's gross. What I was going to say was, it's like . . . have you ever made pancakes? Well, when you make pancakes, the first one's always a bit of a tryout."

"Oh, Christ," I said, "I'm the bad pancake."

"It's not *bad,* it's still delicious, but the next one's better. What I mean is, everyone makes a fuss about the first time, but it's the second or the fourth or the twelfth that matters. And we've got all weekend.

The main thing is"—she took my hand and stared into my eyes—
"you came to me as but a boy, and now you are a man." We laughed
and she pulled up the second sheet. To be lying in a bed with the
whole length of our bodies pressed together was, in its own way, just
as intimate and startling as the sex itself, and I was newly grateful that
this had happened here rather than down the back of the sofa.

"Don't fall asleep, will you?" she said.

"Not for a bit. You look beautiful."

"Thank you. You too."

"Well, handsome."

"No, *beautiful*," and she laid her hand gently on my face and
slipped her little finger into my nostril.

"Can you not do that, please?"

"Is it not sexy?"

"No."

"Just trying something new. So. How does it feel? Manhood?"

"All right. Do I look different?"

"Worldly-wise. Also, this is new . . ."

"Oh, sorry." The condom still lay against my thigh like some
freshly shed skin. "Should I get rid of it?"

"No, keep it on. Wear it always, to remember me."

I removed the thing, tied a knot with a dexterity and deftness that
had escaped me earlier.

"Boys love to really *look* at it. Why is that?"

"Dunno. It's disgusting but sort of amazing too."

"Look at you, holding it up to the light. It's like you've won a goldfish. All proud. They should put markings up the side, in milliliters.
And at the top, write 'Kapow!'"

"What do I do with it?"

"Oh, keep it. You have to keep the first one."

"In my wallet."

"Yeah, like a lock of my hair. Take it out and look at it."

"But surely you should keep it."

"I'm okay, thanks. Put it down now."

We rearranged the sofa cushions into pillows of a sort and reached for our vodka and Cokes, syrupy and flat. Soon we were drunk enough to dance to old Prince songs, though Fran looked better doing this than I did, my nakedness providing one more reason not to lift my feet off the floor. We were also smudged with dust and grime. In the shower we squeezed beneath the feeble trickle, alternately scalding then freezing and barely wet enough to scrape the dirt from each other's bodies with the blade of pink soap. "It's like we're in a Bond movie," shouted Fran over the roar of the cheap plastic water heater. No towel, and so we dried each other on yesterday's T-shirts, and soon we were back on the sofa bed, less panicked and self-conscious this time, more at ease, and Fran was right, that was the time that mattered.

"I have bought the mansion of a love"

WE MUST HAVE DRIFTED off to sleep at three or four. We'd been listening to music as the night-lights puttered out one by one, and the last song I heard was "Lilac Wine," the Nina Simone version, the low thrum-thrum-thrum of it.

"I like how she sings 'lie-lark.'"

"Make wine from lilacs is terrible idea," she mumbled into my neck. We were very drunk now.

"'Sweet and heady,' she says."

"All right. Let's try it. Tomorrow."

"Have it as spritzer."

"Ha." I heard the crackle of her smile. "Ssh. Sleep." And so we slept.

But the novelty and thrill of having her there, the warmth of her in the heat of the night, her movement in sleep, the springs and struts of the sofa bed, meant that I was wide awake a few hours later, mouth dry, head booming. In the gray dawn light, the room had taken on a new type of squalor. We'd drunk the entirety of our weekend's supplies on the first night. The empty bottles now lay close to my face at the side of the bed, alongside a great many condom wrappers, a half-eaten packet of biscuits, a pint glass of cloudy water and the saucer we'd used as an ashtray. At any other time I might have groaned and clutched at my head, but this seemed to me like the bedside detritus of a new man, a man of experience, a lover's bedside. Looking at Fran, I actually began to laugh, a mad, gleeful laugh that I had to stifle with my hand.

She looked terrible, far, far worse than I had ever seen her before. Her mouth hung open gormlessly and I could feel her breath, hot and stale and boozy like the back room of a pub, and I loved this, loved the black smudges round her eyes and the grease on her forehead, the wine stains in her cracked lips and the spot on her chin that had formed in the night like a mushroom, and because I loved the stinking realness of her head on my shoulder and the damp warmth of her thigh across mine and the smell of bodies that seeped from beneath the sweat-damp tangled sheet, I wondered—if I stay very, very still, how long might this last?

But the bladder will have its say, and eventually I extricated myself. Standing in the bathroom, brushing my teeth and peeing at the same time, queasy and full of mysterious aches, I heard the sound of tires on the gravel. Thoughtlessly, I flushed the toilet, and now it seemed to roar like a dinosaur as, through the frosted glass, I watched the abstract shape of Bernard stepping out of the car. Crouching, I scuttled back to the living room where Fran sat with the sheet held across her. I pressed my finger to my lips and found a line of sight through the gap in the curtains. Bernard was a few feet away, fiddling with the latch on the gate to the estate while Polly strained to see her reflection in the wing mirror, wiping at the lipstick in the corner of her mouth. "Hurry, Bernard," she said, "we'll miss the train," and I was close enough to hear Bernard mutter under his breath and climb back into the car.

And then they were gone.

"Is it safe?"

"It's safe."

"We don't need to whisper anymore."

"We weren't whispering."

"We don't need to forget to whisper anymore," she shouted, and I leaped onto the bed and kissed her.

"You've brushed your teeth."

"Uh-huh."

"Cheat. I stink."

"You don't," I said, though she did, and we kissed until we both tasted the same.

We stood in T-shirts, frying eggs in butter and drinking instant coffee. We squeezed together under the pathetic shower, then went back to bed. Finally, late in the morning . . .

"Shall we take a walk around the garden?"

Like burglars, we had checked the grounds for alarms. The main house would be out of bounds, but the rest of the orchards, woods and meadows would be ours as long as we stayed out of sight of the road. *O, I have bought the mansion of a love,* says Juliet, *but not possessed it.* Here we were, the morning after, in full possession.

But the day was overcast, the light softer, the first leaves on the sycamores and oaks starting to curl and turn brown. It might have been the first day of autumn, and we pulled each other close as we walked through the woods that led to the main grounds, eerily quiet today, an empty stage.

"Imagine living somewhere like this."

"Must be weird, mustn't it?" said Fran. "It's not something I think about. Big houses, money. Maybe it's something that comes on when you're older. Love of *stuff.* I hope not."

"Harper thinks about it. He's got all these car magazines and he sort of paws and turns the corners of the ones he's going to buy. And hi-fis and all that stuff—cameras, big watches that tell you how far underwater you are. He's not showing off, he just likes it, like a hobby."

"But you don't want a big watch, do you?"

"No. Same time, I don't want to be poor." Spoken aloud, the word sounded so strange and old-fashioned that I wondered if I'd mispronounced it. Certainly I wished I hadn't said it.

"Do you worry about money now?"

"Not with the wages I'm pulling in at the petrol station."

"Big bucks."

"Loaded. But my dad worries, and I worry because he worries . . . so it's sort of infectious."

"I just want enough money not to worry about money."

"Me too."

"And a job I like doing."

"Famous?"

"God, no. I mean, famous as a byproduct of the work, not for its own sake. Fame's the big watch. Who wants that? I'd much rather be doing good work. With lots of friends, and in love and having lots of sex. There. Put it like that, it sounds really easy."

"I know."

"I mean, really, what's the problem? We're halfway there."

Abruptly, we lapsed into silence. We could talk with ease about anything except the future. September hung ahead of us like a heavy curtain. The subject made me sulky, but to not discuss what might lie on the other side was absurd and cowardly too. We were too young to have subjects that we couldn't talk about.

In a while, after taking a breath, she said, "I think you should go to college."

"Nah, I'm going to get a job."

"Sure, but even if you don't get the grades—"

"Which I won't."

"—you could work, then retake."

"It's not for me."

"Just Maths and English, so you could do other things."

"No, that's over now."

"But you're really smart, Charlie. I wouldn't be with you if you weren't."

"Let's talk about something else, yeah?"

"Okay."

She took my arm and we left the subject, but teetering, about to fall.

We'd brought books and an ancient Thermos flask we'd found and filled with instant coffee, and we walked down through our gardens towards our favorite spot at the top of the meadow, near the place where we'd first met.

"What did you think? The first time."

"I thought—who's this freak?"

"That's nice."

"Lurking about with his top off, scaring the shit out of people."

"I wasn't lurking, I was reading."

"I didn't think it for long. When I'd calmed down, I thought, he's all right. He seems safe."

"'Safe'?"

"Trust me, girls don't always think that with boys alone. It's a good thing. I thought you were funny, too, the way you looked at my ankle like you had this medical training. I watched your face while you did it. You looked handsome. You mustn't get bigheaded, but it's possible that I exaggerated the extent of my injuries—" and here she yelped with pain and slipped into a rolling, broken-hipped limp, one hand on my shoulder.

"Yes, I did wonder about that."

"You didn't believe me?"

"The limp, it kind of came and went."

"It did not! How dare you! Anyway, it worked. You came back, didn't you? When I saw you, on the second day, I just wanted to laugh, partly 'cause it was funny, you grinning and bearing it like that, me winning—"

"You didn't *win!*"

"Well, no, I did—and partly because I was *so* pleased to see you. I was surprised by it, how pleased I was. It felt like—I don't know—breathing out. Just . . ." And here she stopped walking, closed her eyes and exhaled slowly, and I recognized what I'd felt too. "And I loved walking home with you, and talking, I kept wishing it was further. I still do. The only thing you said that annoyed me . . ." She hesitated.

"Go on."

"The thing that annoyed me was you presuming I was going out with Miles, thinking 'cause he was that kind of boy, I must be that kind of girl. I mean, I like Miles, he's quite good-looking in a sort of action-figure kind of way. But you thinking I was that, I don't know . . . shallow."

"I was just jealous. I thought, Romeo, Juliet, aren't you meant to live the role?"

"Yeah, but the Method only goes so far. 'Specially if he's a bit of a dick."

"Bit older, he's got a car, money, posh education—"

"Stop it. You've got to stop it."

"What?"

"You've got to stop, the whole education, confidence thing. These people, they don't have special rights or powers."

"I think they do."

"They don't! I mean, they have *advantages* and privilege, and money's important, course it is. And even if the exams have gone wrong, I know you can still do something brilliant, something that will make you happy."

"Like what?"

She laughed. "I don't know! It's not for me to tell you, is it? You've got to work it out. But there's a . . . potential. Stupid word, school-report word, but it's what I mean."

We were silent after that. Her intentions were sincere, I knew, but it was undignified to be the subject of a pep talk, and I resented it. We found our spot in the meadow and settled in the long, dry grass, further apart than we might have. The silence continued.

And then her hand reached out and took mine.

"Sorry. I know you don't like talking about the future, but it is going to happen. That's what the future is, it's the thing that's going to happen. There. Isn't that profound?"

"It is."

"Literally."

"*Literally.*"

"You can't see it at the moment, 'cause all these things have just gone wrong, and you're nervous and angry about things you can't control and which aren't your fault. But if you . . . *hang on,* Charlie. I don't know. I just think there's something inside you and I love it. And you. I love you, Charlie."

And there it was. She'd said it and now I could say it back, that most banal and brilliant exchange of dialogue, which we'd repeat, over and over, for just as long as we meant it.

Back at the gatehouse, we tidied up and compiled a list of essential supplies for the rest of the weekend — vodka, ice and Coke, some Chinese takeaway. Though I'd made little headway with *The Name of the Rose,* I noted that we'd need more condoms too, and I felt a puff of pride at this. Despite my negotiations, I was still obliged to work three hours at the petrol station, but this would allow Fran to read and sleep. If I closed up promptly, I could be back by eight thirty, and we could start the party once again.

But something of the ease had been lost in contemplation of the future, and our future, and we were silent as we walked back through the woodland to where we'd stashed our bicycles.

"We could . . . go home," I said. "If you wanted? I mean, we don't have to stay two nights . . ."

"No! No, I want to. I'm just tired. Hurry back. Ride like the wind. We'll start again." And she kissed me and I lugged my bike gracelessly over the stone wall. "Don't forget the lilac wine," she said, and I set off towards town and the start of a series of catastrophes, each greater than the last, each following on immediately like the end of a Shakespeare play.

Mr. Howard

A PETROL STATION IS a forlorn place at the best of times, but on a long, dull, overcast Saturday afternoon at the end of summer, it has its own special melancholy. A deep ache had set in, an exhaustion that seemed quite overwhelming, and it would require something special to recover the mood of the previous night.

There were winning scratch cards in my wallet. Without an accomplice, the exchange was riskier, but not impossible if I used sleight of hand, and as a man of means I could try to buy champagne—cava—in the offie. As I was no longer a virgin, perhaps they'd hand it over without question, and perhaps I'd get something ritzy from the Golden Calf, the house special of fat pink king prawns, and three more condoms from the toilets. Cava, condoms, prawns, big bag of ice; it was the shopping list of a young lord, and contemplating these riches, I fell asleep, my head on the counter, trusting the beep of the pumps to wake me.

A large, blond, crop-haired man was standing over me, neck bulging in a shirt and tie, his knuckles rapping on the counter near my head.

"You all right there?"

"Sorry—dropped off. So sorry. Pump number . . . number . . ."

"Two."

"Two. That's thirty pound."

"Big night?" He grinned unpleasantly.

"Pardon?"

"You're asleep on your watch. Big night last night?"

It would not have been appropriate to tell him that I'd lost my virginity, and yet he seemed to want more, standing with his head cocked to one side, hands planted on the counter, meaty and pink like ham hocks.

"Big night, yes," I said and handed him his receipt. Still he didn't move.

"Anything else?"

"No. I'm good. You get some shut-eye." And with a roll of his shoulders, the big man turned and left.

And that was my last customer. A little before eight, I turned off the forecourt lights and set the till to chatter out its shift summary, took the tray from the till and, standing in the doorframe between the counter and the office, swapped the scratch cards for one twenty-, one ten-pound note. Cava, ice, prawns, condoms. In the back office, I loaded my rucksack with all the champagne flutes that I'd have to get rid of — I'd keep two back for the wine — and returned to the shop floor to turn off the lights.

The crop-haired man was there and, behind him —

"Mike! Hey there!"

Mike said nothing, just shook his head slowly and sorrowfully, and an awful, cold nausea rose up inside me.

"Charlie, do you recognize this gentleman here?"

"Yes! Hello, there! Pump two, thirty quid."

He smiled unpleasantly, arms crossed high on his thick chest, waiting for something. "Your scratch card! I accidentally forgot to give it to you! Is that why you're here? Hold on, I'll get one for you." As a performance, it was not my best, but what could they do about an honest accident?

"Charlie, Mr. Howard here works for a private security firm."

"Okay. Is this about me falling asleep?" Perhaps it was only that.

"I hired him, Charlie, because there have been some inconsistencies in the accounting."

Anything else he might have said was drowned out by a great roar of panic at what lay ahead, a deranged montage of both near and distant futures as I wondered what they knew, what my alibi might be and how I could hope to sustain it in the face of what was surely video evidence. I foresaw hours spent on plastic chairs in police stations and magistrates' courts. I imagined Mum's rage, my father's flailing shame and despair. I would be seventeen in three weeks' time—did that mean borstal or prison? And Fran, what would Fran think? The something inside that she'd spoken of, the potential she'd claimed to see in me, revealed as the deception of a shabby petty thief, a till-dipper, an incompetent scammer with a criminal record stapled to those terrible exam results.

". . . seems a large number of cards meant for customers have actually found their way into the pockets of staff . . ."

And how would she find out where I was? How long did they mean to keep me here? The light was fading now, and I thought of her alone in the gatehouse, lighting candles, eating the last of the food, anticipation turning to anger, anxiety to fear, like Juliet in the Capulets' tomb. Even before she found out, she'd hate me for abandoning her. I had to let her know and tell her the story in my own words . . .

". . . so we need to talk it through."

I forced myself to focus on Mike's words. At least he wasn't angry, more resigned, a sheriff who has been obliged to hire this gunslinger, now identified as a representative of a company called Croydon Investigations Agency, the CIA—how could I not have known? The big shoulders and small, sharp, judging eyes; the man was obviously a professional enforcer, and I cursed myself for succumbing to the cheap allure of Spanish sparkling wine and the house special at the Golden Calf.

"Perhaps if we could go through into the back office?" said Mr.

Howard, now stepping towards the counter. I lifted my bag and heard the chink of twelve champagne flutes, evidence, through the nylon of my rucksack. My God, they'd got me red-handed. A night in the cells, and Fran alone in the woods, the candles burning low, waiting for me . . .

I raised the bag carefully, so that the glasses would not chink. "If you could lift this, please," said Mr. Howard. The counter was separated from the office by a hinged panel, secured from below by a sliding bolt on the cashier's side.

"One moment, I just need to . . ." I slipped sideways into the office, and locked that door too.

"Come on, Mr. Lewis, stop fucking us about," said Mr. Howard.

"Hold on! Just need to—"

"Charlie, come on, mate," said Mike, siege negotiator. "It's just a chat."

I pulled the rucksack carefully onto my back as if it contained explosives, which in effect it did, and pushed sharply on the bar of the emergency exit.

And now I was out in the chill of the evening air. In this light, the bright shop interior looked like a cinema screen and I could see Mike's legs sticking out horizontally into air as he struggled with the hatch in the counter. Hands shaking, I locked the shop door too, sealing them inside. Catching the movement, Mr. Howard ran to the door, banging at the glass, but I was already on my bike and across the forecourt.

I powered out onto the long straight road that led back towards town, empty at this time. If I could just get to Murder Woods, dump the glasses, wait in the undergrowth for Mike and Mr. Howard to give up the search, then rush back to the gatehouse, kiss Fran and tell her everything, explain that I'd done something stupid but that I loved her . . . If Juliet could forgive Romeo for murdering her cousin, then surely, surely a scratch-card scam was redeemable too. There'd be tears but we'd make sad, poignant love as Romeo and Juliet do the night before his exile, and argue about larks and nightingales, and in the morning I'd find Mike and tell him I'm sorry, Mike, I panicked, and yes, I took a couple of glasses but no money. Or if there was evidence against me, then I'd pay it back; I still had most of the cash hidden in my room, and I'd work off the rest or borrow it from . . . I don't know, my sister's bank account or Harper or someone, but not my parents, my parents must not know. Mike would tell my mum, but my father couldn't know. It would kill him.

I pounded towards my hiding place, another future beckoning now, life in exile. If I could get my hands on my passport, there was nowhere I couldn't go. I'd buy a donkey jacket and a kit bag, join the merchant navy, whatever that was, and write beautiful, yearning letters to Fran from Singapore and Vladivostok and Mantua, and perhaps someday, on the jetty of some distant port beyond the reach of law—

I heard a car behind me and waited for it to overtake but instead saw it pull alongside. I'd presumed that I'd been traveling at extraordinary speed, but the big black Range Rover was barely in second gear, Mike close enough to lean out of the window and rest his hand on my forearm.

"Pull over, Charlie," he said.

"I can't talk to you now. I've got to be somewhere."

"Just stop pedaling, pal, we only want a chat." But beyond Mike, I could see Mr. Howard hunched over the steering wheel, laughing, and so I stood and powered down into the pedals. I would run into the woods and lose them there, I'd set out cross-country and in darkness to the gatehouse. Hadn't she said she loved me? I turned off the road but I'd misjudged the angle needed to mount the high curb and the bike juddered for a moment and then stopped entirely, sending me over the handlebars and onto the footpath.

And here it was again, the strange, elastic nature of time, allowing me to note the neatness and completeness of the somersault and how I'd stubbornly refused to let go of the bike, bringing it with me so that it might have made a fine circus trick. Most memorably—or did I imagine this?—time even allowed me to register the crunch of the champagne flutes that were, in their own way, breaking my fall, to feel them hold their shape for a split second and then collapse like an egg squeezed in a fist, the chain reaction, *pop, pop, pop,* the glass returning for the most part to sand, but also to diamonds.

Scars

"WHERE DID YOU GET these from?"

"Get what?"

"On your back. These marks."

"Those? Shark attack."

"Oh, is that right?"

"Garage glasses. I fell on a whole load of cheap champagne flutes when I was sixteen."

"Of *course* you did."

"The scars are where they picked out the little chunks of crystal."

We were on the beach when Niamh noticed them for the first time, the scattering of smooth, raised scars that were more likely to be felt than seen, except in the summer when they showed up white like invisible ink under a lamp.

"Okay. I know it should be obvious, but . . ."

"I'd stolen the glasses from the petrol station and they found out, and I did a runner and I came off my bike."

"Motorbike?"

"Bike-bike. Push-bike."

"Christ. Your dark past. Garage glasses and a push-bike. You're like Jason Bourne."

We were island-hopping in Greece, our first holiday together, at that stage in a relationship when an opportunity to show each scar is something to leap at. I'd seen the tear between her second and third finger from the edge of a catering-size can of chickpeas, the neat grid of stitches on her shoulder from the removal of a mole, and now it was my turn. The broken glass had peppered my back like buckshot, and I lay on the hot sand and let Niamh's fingertips trace the constellation.

"It's like Braille."

"What does it say, Niamh?"

"It says . . . hold on . . . it says, 'What . . . kind of dick . . . steals garage glasses?' Aren't they free anyway?"

"That's what made it the perfect crime."

"Stealing something no one wants?"

"Well, there was a certain amount of cash involved too."

"Ah. From the till?"

"Yes, though it was more complicated than that. I mean I was stealing scratch cards, not cash, so no one lost out. It was a victimless crime because the money didn't exist until you scratched the card. It was like that cat in a box. Philosophically speaking."

"And is that what you told them?"

"Yep."

"And how did that go down?"

"Not well."

"My God. A master criminal. I'm appalled."

"Oh, and you've never stolen anything?"

"Me? No!"

"All that time working in restaurants, not a bottle of wine? A steak from the freezer?"

"No!"

"A coffee you've not rung through the till?"

"Well. Maybe. Once or twice, but my upbringing means I've always felt shit about it."

"Well, I felt shit about it too. Especially getting caught. It was a *bad* time. And the stupid thing is, if I hadn't made a run for it, I'd have been fine."

"So why did you run?"

"Well—you'll like this."

"Go on . . ."

"It was for *love*."

Niamh lay back on the sand. "Oh, bloody hell. Not her again."

I think I was in shock for a while. Certainly, I couldn't stand or stop my hands from shaking, and so we just sat quietly on the curb in the fading light.

"We only wanted a word, silly boy," said Mike.

"We were just putting the frighteners on, that's all," said Mr. Howard. Already I could feel the blood on my back chilling and stiffening, so that when I rotated my shoulders, the skin seemed to stick unpleasantly to my T-shirt. Mr. Howard, who had, I was fairly sure, killed people, reassured me that it was nothing compared to some of the things he'd seen, but the blood had turned my fingertips to a dark brown that flaked like rust, turning black as night came on.

"We'll take you to hospital. See if there's any glass still in there."

I had already rehearsed the phrase "I want to speak to my solicitor!," though where I might find such a thing remained a mystery to me. Did a solicitor handle Dad's bankruptcy, or was that an accountant? "I want to speak to my accountant!" didn't sound right.

"But why did you try to get away? Silly, silly boy."

I allowed myself a few words now. "I had to be somewhere. That's all." And that was when the police turned up.

It was not in Mike's interest to involve the law, but a shaking, bloodied boy on a quiet road at night must have attracted the attention of a passerby, and now here was the patrol car, blue lights illuminating the plantation behind us. "Oh, fuck. We don't need this." Mr. Howard was already standing, hands outstretched, palms outward placatingly, and I felt an awful fear. Police stations. Magistrates' courts. Criminal record.

But before prison, the hospital. We drove for twenty minutes to the place where my mother had worked when we'd first moved to town, and I sat on the edge of a plastic chair while a weary policewoman asked me questions. Where had I been heading to? To see a friend. Had the driver run me off the road? No, it had been an accident. Had I been put in danger by the gentleman's driving? No, we'd been talking. Through the window of a moving car? Only for a second, then I'd lost control. What was I doing with all those glasses in my bag? Here I stumbled. I could see Mike, ashen-faced and fearful at the other end of the corridor, pressing down on his mustache as if it might come unstuck.

"I want to speak to my solicitor."

The policewoman laughed. Were they allowed to do that, laugh at us? "Do you *have* a solicitor?"

"No!" I said, indignant.

"Then how about we call your parents?"

"No. No, you can't do that."

"I'm sorry, son, you're sixteen and you're in shock. We've got to let them know."

"You can't. They don't live together."

"Well—who do you live with?"

"My dad."

"And his number?"

"We don't have a phone." Exhausted, the policewoman let her head drop forward. "We can't afford it," I said, halving the lie: we did have a phone and we couldn't afford it.

"Well, can your mother afford a phone?"

"Yes, she has a mobile phone."

"And . . . ?"

"I don't know her number." This much at least was true. The scrap of paper was kept in my bedroom and I'd not used it often enough to memorize it.

"Come on, son, don't waste my time. Her address?"

"I know what the house looks like."

"The landline, then."

"She lives with this guy. I never call her, she calls me."

"*Your* address, then. We'll send someone round to your dad's."

I thought for a moment. "Mike. That man there. He's got my mum's number." The policewoman stood. "I need to make my phone call now." I had it in my head that I would only be able to make one.

"Course. Just don't run away this time, okay?"

It was getting late, the corridor filling with town-center casualties, and I was no longer the only boy wearing clothes sticky with blood. I found the phone booth and, to my relief, local phone directories. I flicked through the grubby pages and found the number. In the scratched aluminum of the booth I could just about make out my reflection, face pale, hair gelled with sweat and the blood from my hands. I dialed the number and imagined the phone ringing in a long, wood-paneled corridor. I cleared my throat, ready for my nice-young-man voice. The phone rang and rang.

"Hello?"

"Hello, Polly?"

"Yes?"

"Polly, it's Charlie here. From the play?"

"Charlie?"

"Yes, Benvolio. From the play?"

"Yes, I know who you are."

"So — are you and Bernard in bed?"

She sighed. I seemed to be making everyone sigh. "Charlie, it's very late. Is something wrong?"

"No. No, I just need to tell you something. To ask you a favor really, to pass on a message."

"Can it wait until Monday?"

"No, no it needs to be now. The thing is, you know the little cottage at the start of your driveway? The gatehouse? The thing is—I'm sorry—but there's someone waiting for me there."

Forceps

I WISH THE NURSE had not shown me the forceps. Each cube of crystal made a clear tinkling sound as she dropped it in the kidney dish, and she seemed to be enjoying herself, digging and probing, humming and muttering. In a Western or an action movie, I'd have been given a stick to bite on as she doused the wounds with rough liquor. Here, I simply mashed my face into the paper towel that covered the trolley. "Ooh, nice big one," said the nurse, and there was the rattle in the dish.

Turning my head, I saw my mother standing in a gap in the screens. She was wearing her best black party dress, her makeup smudged, her face flickering between fury and concern and fury again, and I had the feeling, not for the first time, that I'd taken her away from something. She looked extremely beautiful to me, and painfully disappointed, and I was grateful to have the sting of the antiseptic spray as an excuse for my red eyes.

In the car, the discomfort meant that I was obliged to lean forward in the seat as if I might at any time open the door and pitch myself out onto the dual carriageway. This seemed a viable option. Mum, who had been obliged to leave her own dinner party—she had dinner parties now—had abandoned concern and settled comfortably into fury.

"Garage glasses! Honestly, who the hell steals garage glasses?"

"I wasn't stealing them."

"When they steal at the golf club, they steal bottles of vodka and gin. They steal joints of meat. They steal money."

"I wasn't stealing the glasses, I was getting rid of the glasses."

"Yes, Mike told me, so you could steal money!"

"I wasn't stealing *money*."

"So what was it, then?"

"It was just . . . scratch cards."

"Which you then exchanged for . . ."

"Money, but the money didn't exist unless someone—"

"What?"

"Scratched the card."

"Ah, so it was only stealing *conceptually*. Maybe they'll send you to some sort of *abstract, conceptual* magistrate, maybe there'll be some sort of theoretical, fourth-dimensional sentencing procedure. 'Yes, I've got a criminal record, but it's in a parallel universe.'"

"I'm not getting a criminal record. Am I?"

"If you're found guilty of a crime, yes! You were stealing prize money! It's the same as taking it out of Mike's pocket!"

"No it's not."

"In the eyes of the law!"

"What do you know about the *eyes of the law*?"

"I know that you're in trouble, Charlie, I know that." She indicated left, turned off the main road. "Mike said you had an accomplice."

"When did he say that?"

"In the hospital, he told me there was someone else coming in and taking the money, the same face every shift. He had it on video. Who was that? Was it one of your friends? Was it Harper?" I said nothing. "Honestly, Charlie, what happened? We didn't raise a thief."

"Except clearly you did. So."

This time she said nothing, and we drove in silence as I bunched the stiff, stinking T-shirt in my hands. As a further indignity, my clothes had been too shredded and gory to wear, so Mum had brought her lover's oldest tracksuit, a baggy gray thing like prison garb. We drove into The Library estate. "I'm sorry you had to leave your party."

"Yes, well. They were playing Trivial Pursuit, so I'd almost rather be in casualty. Almost."

"And how is it going with . . . Jonathan?"

Mum glanced at me with narrowed eyes, then back to the road. "It is what it is, Charlie. It is what it is."

We turned into Thackeray Crescent and parked a short distance away so that he wouldn't hear the car, but I could see the house lights on. "Does Dad know?"

Mum exhaled. "So. Apparently some girl phoned asking for you, and she was worried, and so *he* was worried, because apparently you *said* you were staying at Harper's."

"And . . . ?"

"So he phoned me—that's how desperate he was—and I told him."

"Everything?"

"Yes, because he's your father."

"Mum!"

"Well, what was I meant to say?"

"You could have just said I'd fallen off my bike."

"And landed on a nearby pile of champagne glasses? Come on, Charlie, he's bound to find out."

"Oh, God."

"D'you want me to come in with you?"

"Yeah, because *that* will make it better."

"No. Maybe not."

"I should go," I said, but neither of us moved.

"Who's the girl? New girlfriend?" Until then, she'd only ever said the word with a mocking leer, but not this time.

"I think so. She was. Before I stood her up."

"Is she in the play?" I looked at Mum. She knew. "Dad told me that you'd fallen in love with Shakespeare."

"She's in the play."

"Who is she?"

"Juliet."

"No, in real life, silly."

"Why do you need to know her name?"

"It's not an unusual question . . ."

"It's Fran. You saw her at the pub."

"Fran." She weighed the name. "Hm. And is she any good?"

"In real life or — ?"

"As Juliet."

"She's amazing."

"Are you good?"

"No."

"Do I have to come and see it?"

I laughed to myself. "That's what Dad said."

"No, I'd like to."

"No, you're excused." And now it really was time to go.

"Call me. If you need to, if he takes it badly."

"No, I think he'll be pleased."

"And call me Monday morning too." Monday was the exam results day.

"What for?"

"Well, because I'm your mother. Maybe you'll get a surpri —"

"I know I've failed."

She closed her eyes and exhaled. "Okay, let's not have this argument as well. Let's stick to one row at a time, shall we?"

I opened the car door and hesitated as if we were still speeding along the dual carriageway. Mum smiled stiffly and I twisted out of the car, wincing as the dressings tugged at the broken skin, and without turning around walked towards home.

Shame

HE WAS STANDING WITH his back to me, one arm bracing the stereo shelf as if holding it up. Perhaps it was holding *him* up. Big band music played, a great clattering blare like something falling downstairs. Buddy Rich, I thought, from the sound of the drums. A cigarette was pinched between his knuckles, the remains of others piled high in the ashtray next to the whisky bottle. I could see, as he raised the glass to his mouth, that his hand was shaking.

"Hi, Dad."

He swayed as he twisted to glance over his shoulder. "How much?"

I sighed. "You mean how much did I *steal?*" The best defense, I'd decided, was attack. If he thought I was a thug, I'd be a thug.

"Yes, how much money did you steal?"

"Not 'Hey, Charlie, how are you feeling? How's your back?'"

He turned quickly, stumbling, a moment of vertigo. "Mum told me you were fine, don't give me that."

"Try 'I was worried about you, Charlie.'"

"Oh, you think I don't worry about you?"

"Can we turn the music down?"

"You think I don't lie awake and worry about you?"

"Well, maybe if you didn't spend the whole day sleeping on the sofa, you'd sleep better at night."

"You don't know how I spend my days, you're never here."

"Why, what am I missing?"

"Don't change the subject. How much did you—?"

"I don't know. Couple of hundred."

"But you had a job!"

"Yeah, three quid an hour."

"Well, if you need more money, you work more hours, that's what work is."

I laughed and saw my father bridle.

"What's that supposed to mean?"

"I just don't know if you're in a position to lecture me about my work ethic. Or money."

"What?"

"Well, it's been awhile, hasn't it?"

"You know why I can't work!"

"Do I? Because you never actually talk about it."

"What's there to talk about? What do you think I'm going to tell you?"

"You've got pills by your bed! You think I can't read the labels?"

He looked dazed for a moment. "That is under control, that's not for you to worry about!"

"But I do worry! That's all I do! How could I not—Christ, I fucking hate it here!"

"Charlie!" He recoiled—I saw it—as if from a blow.

I kept going. "And I fucking hate living with you! Every day, it's like, 'Is he going to shout at me? Is he going to have another go?'"

Another blow. "That's not true."

"I come home and think, *it's five in the afternoon, is he going to be pissed? Has he been crying? Has he left the house today?* You're miserable, Dad, and you're miserable to be with."

"Charlie, I do know, I am aware."

"And I know there are reasons, but you don't talk about them, you don't talk about anything!"

"Why are we even on this now? It's you who's been stealing money. Why?"

"Because we haven't got any!"

Finally the music ended. Shaking, confused, Dad felt behind him for the sofa and let himself stumble backwards and fold over as if punched in the gut, and for an awful moment I had a terrible, spiteful sense of power. *This is me,* I thought, *I've done this, and I don't care.*

There was no sound except the soft click of the needle.

"Why didn't you stay together?"

"It wasn't my choice."

"But you could have waited. Kept a lid on things for a year or two, even a couple of months. Other parents do it, for the sake of the kids or whatever, just till we were older."

"I told you, it wasn't my choice!"

"But you drove her away! If you could have just . . . held it together!"

Time passed. Click, click. "Do I embarrass you?" he said.

"No."

"Are you ashamed of me?"

Click, click, click. "I don't know. Are you ashamed of me?"

"Of course not. You're my son, I love you."

"But are you *proud* of me, Dad? Actively, genuinely proud?"

He didn't speak. Instead he looked to the floor, frowning, then spoke quite clearly.

"No. Not right now. No."

Fete

I LEFT THE HOUSE, red-eyed and shaking, not even closing the door behind me. As far as I knew, my bicycle was still in the back of Mr. Howard's car, its front wheel buckled, another forfeit for my crime, and so I walked Forster, Kipling, Woolf, Gaskell and Mary Shelley. I walked round the town center, where the late-night drinkers still staggered towards the Golden Calf or Taj Mahal, or slumped on the steps of the market cross. I knew that I could not return home that night, but where to go? Harper's? Helen's? They'd all want to know the story, and I didn't have the words yet, so instead I found myself walking through the silent residential streets, heading out to the ring road, crossing the motorway bridge, alongside the wheat field, right at the bus shelter and up the wooded lane.

I arrived at the gatehouse at a little after three. It had been vacated in a hurry, the sofa bed still unfolded but stripped of bedding, and I imagined Fran, embarrassed and angry, sitting in the passenger seat, sheets bundled up against her chest, while Bernard drove her home, pajamas on beneath his hunting jacket. In the glare of the overhead bulb I noticed that the night-lights had been removed too, leaving a series of charred black dots around the edge of the room like holes punched in the wooden floor. Something else to be paid for.

Naively, I'd hoped that Polly would respond to our adventure like the Nurse, shifting her bosom and chuckling indulgently at the plan, pleased and proud to have played a part in the union of young lovers.

But on the phone she had been straightforwardly furious, a voice I'd not heard from her before. How dare we abuse her hospitality in this way? We were trespassers—no, burglars! She'd expected more of me. It seemed that everyone expected more of me, and I wondered what I'd done to raise their expectations.

Four thirty in the morning now. I lay carefully on the sofa bed, face-down to protect the wounds. With no bedding, there was only the filthy rug for warmth, and I pulled this up to my chin, pinched my eyes shut and surrendered to exhaustion and Romeo-like self-pity; ah me, such bliss and misery, both found in this same bed!

And such dread the next day. I would need to see Fran. What would be worse, the pain of seeing her or the agony of delay? In the night, stiffness had set in, some deep muscular strain from my passage over the handlebars, and I groaned as I stored the sofa bed away. I'd not brushed my teeth in twenty-four hours, still wore my mum's lover's awful tracksuit, required a speech for Fran but had none prepared. I drank the rusty water from the kitchen tap and swilled it in my mouth, rubbed my teeth and gums with my finger and set out.

Summer had returned, the air heavy and still like something to swim through, and the village, when I reached it, had turned into a small metropolis, cars lining the lane to the church where the village fete was under way, bunting overhead, a calliope playing, squeals from the bouncy castle. There was even a jolly vicar shaking hands, and no one would have been the least surprised if Spitfires had flown over- head. It was an English idyll, smelling of petrol mowers and freshly cut grass, and as I hurried on to Fran's house, I was more aware than ever of the heavy gray velour of my borrowed tracksuit, a sweaty, shifty convict on the run, ducking to peer through the privet of Fran's front hedge. The bedroom window was open, the bedroom that I'd not yet seen and probably never would. Perhaps she was lying on the bed, thinking about me.

Carefully, I lifted the latch on the gate and, looking both ways, stepped into the front garden. Transported to fifties America, I had an absolute compulsion to throw small stones at the window. From the rose bed, I selected a marble-size ball of soil and tossed it at the window, the local bad boy. Another, and one more—

"Can I help you?"

"Hello, Mrs. Fisher!"

Wholesome and healthy, Fran's mother wore gardening gloves and a green apron, a small pruning saw in one hand, branches in another.

"Hello, who are you?"

"I'm Charlie. I'm a friend of Fran's."

"Okay. Hello, Charlie." She blew at her hair, which was sticking to her forehead with sweat. "You can knock on the door, you know. It's pretty much the same thing."

"I didn't want to disturb you."

"I think this is more disturbing, if anything." Some time passed. "She came in very late last night."

"She did?"

"Yes. You don't know anything about that, do you?"

"No. No."

"Well, she's not here, Charlie."

"Okay."

"She's at the fete."

"Okay."

"I think she's hiding. She's not in our good books, you see."

"No?"

"No."

". . ."

"Well. Nice to meet you, Charlie."

"Yes, you too."

"Next time, just knock."

"I will," I said and hurried back along the lane to the church. "It's fifty pence to come in," said the lady at the entrance. In my pocket I felt the rattle of keys but no change.

"I'm sorry, I've got no cash."

The lady frowned. Sensing my bad-boy reputation, the man next to her leaned in. "It is for charity!"

"I know, I just left home without any cash."

The man shook his head slowly, but there was no security protocol for forced entry to a village fete. I walked on through.

"Hello? Hey, you," said the lady. Would they come after me? Tackle me to the ground?

"I'll pay you back! I just have to . . ."

I disappeared into the crowd—this was quite some fete—quickly checking the raffle tent, the house-plant sale, the cake stall, until I saw her, seated behind a trestle table of secondhand books, reading the back of an orange Penguin. She looked up, saw me, smiled, then removed the smile.

"Hello, Charlie."

"Hi there." We spoke across the table of books.

"What are you doing here?"

"I had to see you. I'm sorry."

"You look terrible."

"I have to explain."

"Yes, you do have to explain."

"I know, I'm sorry."

"Fucking hell, Charlie! Do you have any idea how embarrassing that was?"

"I know!" *I had a joke in my pocket . . .*

"Polly's furious, even Bernard's furious. My parents hit the roof."

"Did they?" *If I produced the joke at just the right time . . .*

"Why do you think I'm *here*? Anything's better than that."

I laid it down.

"Fete worse than death."

"*What?*"

"Fete worse than—can we go somewhere?"

"I said I'd watch the stall."

"Just for a minute."

Fran sighed, then stepped across to the neighboring stall, and after some bargaining, she was free to leave.

"So, tell me."

"What else could I do? I couldn't just abandon you, I thought you'd worry."

"And I did worry! I did, but I'm in such trouble, Charlie. You do look terrible."

"I've not slept. Or eaten."

"What are you wearing?"

"I borrowed it. My other stuff had too much blood on it."

"Blood! What? Charlie, what happened?"

"Let's find somewhere."

We sat between the tent pegs in the shadow of the refreshment marquee. I'd spent the night rehearsing an account that was both truthful and distorted, and she listened silently, hands in lap, eyes fixed on her feet until I leaned forward and unveiled the bandages. She gasped gratifyingly, but the sympathy was not enough to cancel out an uncomfortable truth.

"But . . . you were stealing the money?"

"Yeah."

"And now you're being prosecuted?"

"Maybe. Don't know yet."

"Wow. Okay. Okay." She took my hand again. "I'm sorry. That's tough."

"It was a mistake."

"To steal it? Or get caught?"

"Both, obviously," I said, then, as gently as possible, "Fucking hell, Fran. I don't need that from you too."

"No, I know. I'm sorry."

We sat, looking straight ahead. Through the canvas of the tent behind us, we could hear the raffle being called—"It's a blue ticket, number 443. Blue 443 for this beautiful doll's house"—to shouts and cheers. Silent, we sat through the bottle of champagne, the hamper, the selection of preserves, a leg of local lamb, a voucher for a cut and blow-dry at Scissors, and I felt a terrific sadness at how we'd come to this in the space of one day, unable to speak or to look at each other, the only contact between us the consolation of her head, cricked awkwardly against my shoulder.

"It's a green ticket, 225. Green 225."

Fran raised her hips, squeezed her fingertips into the pocket of her jeans and unfolded the green strip. "I'm a winner."

"You'd better go and get it."

"I'll pick it up later," she said, looking over her shoulder.

"Green 225 for this portable CD player," said the voice.

"I won't mind," I said.

"I've already got one."

"Last call, green 225."

"Go on," I said.

"Stay here," she said, stood and slipped through a gap in the canvas as if stepping onto a stage. I heard her shout "Here!" and there was applause and laughter and recognition at the arrival of the nice local girl. I stood and walked away.

She caught up with me by the cake stall, the prize tucked beneath her arm. "Don't slip away like that. Don't be all dramatic."

"I've got to."

"You can come back if you want. To the house. Meet Mum and Dad."

"Not now. Another time."

"Okay. So how will you get—"

"I'll walk."

"I can ask them to give you a lift?"

"No, it's fine. I've got time."

She glanced behind her, back to the stall. "I said I'd cover for my friend."

"Of course."

"I'll see you tomorrow."

"Yes," I said, though I already knew I'd not be going back.

Again, she glanced behind her, then walked up quickly and kissed me. "Love you?" she mumbled.

"You too."

Then she held out the box, the portable CD player. "Don't suppose you want this?"

"No, I'm okay. But can I borrow a quid? I need to pay the entrance fee on the way out."

"Course." She handed me the money. "Very thoughtful of you."

"Well, it's for charity, so . . ."

I passed the cake stall and spent fifty pence on two chocolate cornflake cakes. With my back turned, I crammed them into my mouth, then gave my last fifty pence to the lady.

Home

I WALKED ALL THE way back, just as I had on the morning after the party, that jubilant morning on which I'd made all those resolutions. But change, it seemed, was a myth. There were no new voices and no ways to move through the world except this one, defeated and heading home. Where else would I go?

I dreaded getting back, today more than ever, not because of what Dad and I had said but because of how it would be ignored as we slipped back into our old ways, the monosyllabic chat, the bickering and temporary truces, the air static with tension. And so I dawdled, and even paused to sleep at the edge of a field, the kind of sleep that serves no purpose except to pass time, like winding forward the hands of a watch.

It was early evening when I entered Thackeray Crescent and noted that all the curtains were still drawn despite the daylight. Even on his lowest days, this was not something I'd seen before, and I felt a sharp twist of panic so strong that I broke into a run, dropped my keys, retrieved them and crammed them into the lock, shouting all the time, "Dad! Dad!," tumbling into the house, taking in the mess downstairs, the ashtray, the TV on too loud, pounding up the stairs and into Dad's room, my father face-down and half naked on the bed, the whisky bottle on the floor. "Oh, Christ," I said out loud, threw myself at the bed, put my hand on his shoulder — warm, thank God, but feverish and clammy — and turned him over. The air from his lungs was hot and foul with alcohol, but he was breathing and I scrambled through the bedside mess, the bottles and glasses and foil packs, looking for clues. Should I call an ambulance? "Dad? Dad, wake up!" I brushed the hair back from his ear, as if this was the reason he wasn't responding. "Dad? Dad, please talk to me. Can you hear me, Dad?" But there was nothing, just the rattle of his breath catching the phlegm in his throat, and for a moment I recoiled, sat with my back to the wall, hot tears in my eyes. It wasn't right; it wasn't fair to have to deal with these things.

From films, I knew that sleep was the enemy, and so I scrambled back to the bedside and found the tumbler of water he used to wash down pills. I made a deal: if he didn't stir, I'd call an ambulance. I trickled a little on his cheek and into his ear, then more, then emptied the whole glass. He groaned and I saw the bulge of the cornea move beneath the eyelid as if sealed inside. Heartened, I braced myself, slid my arm beneath his damp armpit and tried to hoist him upright, succeeding only in dragging him down onto the floor with a thump. Downstairs the TV played, *Songs of Praise,* "Lord of the Dance." Panic rose inside me once again, but what use would panic be? Water was the key. I stepped over his body and into the bathroom and set both taps running in the bath, tossed the toothbrushes into the sink, filled the beaker with more cold water, returned to the room and once again trickled it onto his head, his cheek, a little into his mouth, which made him splutter and, with a lurch, shift his weight so that he was now half sitting against the bed's divan base, causing the whole thing to rumble across the room on its casters.

Now was the time. As he fell backwards, I slipped my arm around his back and into his armpit, pulled up through my knees with all my strength, and now we were both seated on the mattress, with me doing my best to prop him up, a ventriloquist crushed by his own dummy. I felt gravity pull him back and once again thought I might cry with frustration, but instead rolled him forward, rocking him onto his feet then carrying him, throwing him really, towards the bathroom, where he fell forward once again and came to a halt with his head against the toilet cistern, and here, thank God, he vomited, violently and wretchedly, for some time, watery stuff, peaty from the whisky. With one hand I rubbed his back, with the other reached into the bath and tested the water and turned off the taps, the water cool and uncomfortable enough to revive him without inducing a heart attack. Five, ten minutes passed while he spewed and spat and mumbled—"Oh no, oh, no no no"—and I helped him stand then, still in his underwear, sit on the edge of the bath and roll into the water like a scuba diver off a boat.

On the blaring TV downstairs, the hymns came to an end and the hunt for antiques began. This week they were in Staffordshire, and so were hoping to find some lovely examples of the famous local pottery, but I stayed squeezed between the bath and the door, keeping watch. Dad's boxer shorts had billowed up and floated on the surface, a Portuguese man-of-war in tartan. There was a tight, high, swollen belly, his chest thin and pale, and I felt that old repulsion, and so took in his face, digging for some old feeling. I saw the folds and creases deep enough to stand a pencil in, the sticky mouth, half open, the stubble peppered with white and as coarse as the bristles on a broom, the thinning hair slicked back with sweat, skin blue and papery beneath his eyes. He was thirty-eight years old.

I tried to find the traces of the younger man who'd played on the rug through those childhood afternoons. I couldn't see it, but I felt I ought to try. Of all the resolutions I'd made that summer morning, this one promise remained: to find a way to live together. I would not hide from him again.

After half an hour, it seemed safe to leave the bathroom. It would require some suppleness to drown in such a tiny bath, and so I left him soaking and tidied his bedroom, changed the sheets, laid out clean pajamas, cleared bottles and glasses and put the pills out of sight in a drawer. I went downstairs, washed up and opened all the windows, and all this time, without acknowledging the fact, I was looking for a note. Its absence heartened me, and there had been pills left in the bottles too, and surely if he'd meant to . . . never mind. I held tight to the idea that it was some solitary party that had got out of hand, a misjudgment, nothing that we would have to name or talk about, nothing to do with things I'd said or done. Returning to the bathroom, I found him in the same spot, the water cold now, and I cleaned and disinfected the toilet and floor while he lay there.

"Okay, time to get out," I said, holding out his dressing gown, a butler and his elderly charge. He stood and carefully stepped over the rim then, wrapped in the gown, stepped out of his sodden boxer shorts and walked towards the bedroom. I took his elbow — "No, you've got to stay awake a little longer" — and we walked slowly down the stairs. On the sofa, I constructed a nest of cushions to keep him upright, and fed him tea and toast and slices of orange. "Like a professional footballer," he said, sucking on the peel, his first clear words since I'd returned. We sank into the comfy sadism of the Sunday-night detective shows, and now and then I glanced at him, asking questions about the plot when I saw his eyelids grow heavy. D'you think the policeman did it? Do you think it was the wife? Eventually, when I felt that it was safe, I walked him upstairs, opened the window and put him to bed.

I changed my clothes and tossed the wretched tracksuit in the bin. In the mirror I saw myself, filthy and exhausted. If I felt any pride, then the ragged dressings on my back reminded me of my wrongs. I would need someone to help me change them, but that would have to wait. For the moment, I lay down next to Dad. I'd stay awake and keep an eye on him. But sleep overpowered me. I closed my eyes and was gone.

Results

IT WAS UNNERVING TO wake up with my father's head on the same pillow, but at least some color had returned to his face in the night. I decided that this was the right kind of sleep, and so sat and stretched and felt the sting of the scabs on my back, and it all came back. Fran's awkwardness, the impending prosecution, abandoning the show, the publication of exam results: a medley of disasters that I'd struggle to place in order.

The best thing I could do, I decided, was hide. The exam results would already be on display—the crowds of kids gathered round, the book-token set punching the air, others red-eyed and confused. I knew the scene already from TV news reports and felt no need to join in. Instead I'd focus all my attention on getting Dad back on his feet, but the day brought a parade of phone calls and visitors, each more urgent than the last.

"Where are you, Charlie?" It was Ivor on the phone. "We need you here now!"

"I'm sorry, Ivor. I can't do it."

"Don't be ridiculous, Charlie. We open on Thursday."

"I know, I'm sorry."

"Okay. Okay. Look, I've talked to Fran, I've talked to Polly. I know there was . . . an incident—"

"It's not that—"

"We're putting it behind us. While you're here, you're a member of the company, a very valued member. No judgment here."

"But it's not that. Not just that."

"What is it, then?"

I put my mouth close to the receiver. "It's a family matter."

"Christ, Charlie. This is hard, this is very, very hard."

"I know. I'm sorry." There was silence on the line. "I had a good time."

"So, come back!"

"I can't." More silence. "Look, what would you do if I'd been hit by a bus?"

"We'd . . . cancel the show?"

"No, but if you *had* to do the show without me."

"I don't know, we'd double one of the roles."

"I don't have any scenes with Paris. George could do it."

Ivor thought for a moment. "It's not ideal."

"I know." I saw a shadow pass the window. I didn't want Dad to wake just yet. "Good luck, Ivor. And thank you." I hung up and leaped for the front door.

"Where were you?!" Harper stood on the doorstep with the sheepishness that comes with great success.

"Just woke up. How did you do?"

"Good! Really good. I mean better than I thought, because I did, you know, absolutely fuck-all work!" Even at the moment of his triumph, Harper was determined not to admit to opening a book. "B's mostly, couple of A's. Enough for college."

"And me?"

"You're not going to go and see?"

"No, you can tell me."

He sucked air in through his teeth, a bad football result. "It's not good, mate."

I laughed. "I know. That's why I'm not going."

"There's two B's in there."

"Really?"

"I think so. You did better than Lloyd!"

"Well, that's something."

"Doesn't matter anyway, does it? In the long run."

"No. Exactly. Doesn't matter."

We'd been standing on the doorstep for too long. "I'd invite you in, but—"

"No, that's fine. We're going to try to get served in The Angler's if you want to . . ."

"No, that's fine."

"Okay." But he hesitated, and I sensed there was something more. "Your mum phoned me yesterday."

"She did?"

"Yes. She told me what had happened. With the police and everything."

"Christ, Mum."

"I think she wanted me to check you were all right. So . . ."

"I'm all right."

"Your back's okay? The cuts and everything."

"It's fine."

"Good. Good."

"You don't need to check up on me."

"Okay. Good."

But he wasn't done yet.

"Charlie, bit embarrassing, this whole stealing-money thing. If it does go to court, if it gets criminal—you won't mention my name, will you? I'd rather not be involved."

And then, and there, any hold that Harper had over me was broken and I could laugh at him too.

"What is this bullshit, Charlie, about you dropping out?"

It was Alina this time. "I'm sorry, Alina, I've explained this once to Ivor."

"It's very, very unprofessional."

"Well, I'm not a professional, so . . ."

"Hm." I heard her exhale down the phone. "George is no good."

"George is great!"

"You're right, he's technically a much better actor than you, but he's no good in this role. He's too distinctive. You, Charlie, you have a faceless, milk-and-water quality that is just perfect."

"Thank you, Alina."

"No offense, but the character needs someone neutral."

"Well, I'm sorry."

"The cast aren't happy, Charlie."

"Like I said—"

"None of us are happy. It can't be allowed. Not when you've worked so hard." There was a crackle on the line, a secret cigarette. "Charlie, many of the young people I work with, they know they're good, they're told they're good and they will continue to be good. Good, competent and able. Well, bravo to them, but really, what's the point in that? To be no good and then to get *so* much better—that's why we do it. *You* are why we do it. Without you—what's the point?"

Some time passed.

"I've got to go," I said. "Alina—I'm sorry."

I hung up the phone.

My father was awake now but still not ready to sit upright. I brought him tea and he groaned as I opened the curtains. I closed them again.

"Why does the phone keep ringing? And who was at the door?"

"Just friends."

"You're popular."

I laughed. "I am!"

Some time passed.

"I'm sorry, I can't get up yet."

"That's all right."

"My head."

"No, you sleep."

"Have you been to the school?"

"No. No point."

He went to speak, then hesitated. "Worth checking, though."

"Maybe."

And there was more silence, time that had the quality of a missed cue. I searched for the line, and . . .

"I don't think you should drink if you're taking antidepressants."

He frowned. "No, I know."

"They don't work if you do. There's side effects. And I worry. We all do. That's one of the side effects, us worrying. It's not fair."

"I know."

"What happened anyway?"

"It . . . got out of hand. That's all."

"Do we need to, do you want to . . . talk about it?"

"No."

"Because I can't be putting you in the bath again, Dad, it's really gross."

He smiled. "Well, you too. I can't be picking you up off the street."

"All right," I said. "Let's both stop that. Giving each other baths."

He laughed. "Okay."

"Good."

"But no need to tell your mother or sister. Or anyone really."

"I won't."

"I'm going back to sleep now, then I'm going to get up."

"Okay. I'll go to school. See you."

I went out and closed the door. It was a conversation of sorts, I suppose, and it meant that I could leave the house. I wouldn't be long.

For the sake of speed, I hauled Mum's rusting, turquoise shopping bike out from the backyard and set off, the basket rattling all the way. Out of term time, the school had the sad, abandoned air of a closed-down factory. All the kids who'd wanted to know their results had been and gone long before. Only Mr. Hepburn, Geography, remained, standing at reception, unshaven and tanned in civilian clothes, with the curious glamour of a teacher out of term time. "Mr. Charlie Lewis! Returning to the scene of the crime!"

"Hello, Mr. Hepburn."

"You're the last one! You know where to go. Have a look."

For months, I'd had a joke prepared. I'd look at my results and say, "F, F, F, F, U, U, U, U; it's like I've got a stammer!" It wasn't much of a joke, or consolation either, but it might see me through. The actual results didn't allow for such a neat line, and instead there was a mess of D's, E's and F's, and yes, a U or two. The work I'd submitted earlier in the year, before my flip-out, had saved me from utter humiliation, but it was still a jumbled, unimpressive haul. I made a quick note of some other marks: a string of A's for Lucy, the same for Helen. "A, A, A, A, A, A, A—like a scream"; that was Fran's line. In contrast, I had . . .

"A good hand at Scrabble." Mr. Hepburn was standing at my shoulder. "I've seen worse."

And in one vital respect, Harper had been wrong. The two B's he'd mentioned were in fact a B and an A, in Computer Science and Art. "You see that?" said Mr. Hepburn, tapping the A with his finger. "That's what makes it a good hand."

"Must be a typo."

"Pack it in, Lewis. These others"—he scratched at the D's and E's and F's with his thumbnail—"these either don't matter or we can fix them. I promise you, they can be remedied."

"I'm all right, thanks, Mr. Hepburn."

"Are you ever going to call me Adam?"

"No, never."

"Come back if you want to—"

"Maybe."

"Okay, Charlie. Off you go. Good luck. And you know where to find me."

"Yes, thanks, Mr. Hepburn," I said and left school for the last time, for the second time.

A deep sadness overtook me that day, like the first stage of an illness. Not only the sadness of failure confirmed, but the deeper ache of the loss of Fran. We'd not broken up, not yet, but surely that was imminent. The person she'd loved—she'd said the words just days ago —had gone, the mysterious qualities she'd talked about revealed as stupidity, dishonesty and mediocrity. The phone rang, the doorbell sounded, and each time I wondered—is this it? "Charlie, we need to talk . . ."

Instead came Mum and Billie, holding out a supermarket cake. "Yay!" they shouted. "Well Done!" insisted the writing on the cake, though even the icing seemed to lack conviction. Dad was up and dressed by then, and the four of us perched on stools at the breakfast bar and ate slices in an atmosphere of forced civility. "A for Art!" exclaimed Mum every few minutes, clinging to it like a tree trunk in a flood. "Imagine. An *A*."

"Yeah, think of all those jobs in the art section of the paper."

"That's not the point, Charlie."

"'Artist required, immediate start—'"

"Why aren't you at rehearsals?" said Billie, hoping to change the subject.

"I'm not doing that anymore."

"No!"

"What?"

"Oh, that's a shame."

"But we were coming to see it!" said Billie.

"You can still see it. I'm just not in it."

"You can't drop out now!"

"Mum, it was a boring part. I didn't do much."

"But we bought tickets!"

"Me too," said Dad.

"So go!"

"Don't be ridiculous," said Mum, "we're not going to go to a play if we don't have to."

"Fine! Leave it, then!" Some time passed. "But you should still go. It'll be good."

More time passed. "An A and a B. Also, a D is technically a pass."

"Mum, for Christ's sake . . ."

She reached across the bar, took my hand and rubbed at my wrist with her thumb. "Charlie, just take the praise, will you? Take the praise."

After they'd gone, Dad and I stood at the sink and washed up, eyes fixed on the backyard. "I don't think we did our job, did we?" he said. "Your mum and me."

I shrugged. "You had other things on your mind."

"Bad timing, though."

"It was a bit."

"Still. I am proud of you."

"For one 'A' and a 'B'?"

"Not for that. For other things." He placed one hand lightly on my shoulder for a moment and then we put away the dishes.

And still they came, on the Tuesday too, so many guests and visitors.

Next was Mike, my ex-boss. Dad opened the door and I saw him falter, torn between deference to the wronged party and loyalty to me. A conference was needed and, somewhat uneasily, we sat in a row on the sofa, too baggy and informal for such a solemn discussion.

"So there'll be no legal proceedings. That's a sledgehammer approach, and it was never our intention. As you know, Charlie here was employed on a, how shall we say, casual basis, as an apprentice."

"Illegally," said Dad, straining for lawyerly fire.

"Informally, Mr. Lewis, and it's in no one's interests to take it further. We could if we chose, there's plenty of evidence: video footage of accomplices, discrepancies in accounts, but—well, it's the principle really. We're just disappointed." The sofa was sucking him down, and he had to plant his knuckles firmly and hoist himself up from its depths. "We won't be expecting Charlie to return to work, and there'll be no employer's reference, either good or bad. There is the matter of financial recompense . . ."

"Oh. Really?" said Dad, the old fear returning. "How much?"

"Well, frankly, Mr. Lewis, it's hard to put a figure on it. It seems that all the staff were at it one way or another, and of course everyone's denying it . . ."

"I've got a hundred pounds," I said suddenly. "In my room."

I could see Dad wince. "You shouldn't have to do—"

"No, it's fine. I want to."

"One hundred should do it."

I clambered out and ran upstairs to retrieve my escape fund, the roll of notes hidden in the bunk-bed tubing. One hundred and five pounds—in one last criminal flourish, I'd lied about the amount, and though the fiver wouldn't get me far, I peeled this off and ran back down.

Even so, I hoped that Mike might tell me to keep the cash. He did not. Instead, he hauled himself from the sofa's maw, tucked the roll into his pocket, money to blow in the golf club bar, and held out his hand. "Well, Charlie, no hard feelings. You're a good lad."

"He is," said Dad.

One last caress of his mustache. "I wish you all the best. You too, Mr. Lewis," he said, and we stood on the front step and watched him go.

"I'd have offered him a drink," said Dad, "but all our glasses are nicked."

I laughed. "Doesn't matter now."

"A hundred quid, though . . ."

"It's worth it."

"Exactly. Clean slate."

"I'll start looking for a job tomorrow."

"Okay," said Dad. "Me too."

And we would be fine. We would find a way to fill the days, and the evenings would close in and wrap around us, and there was the TV, and films to watch from the library, and we'd settle back into our strange domesticity, Dad and me.

But first there would be one more visit, later that night.

Swings and Slides

I HEARD THE CAR horn before I saw them. Dad had just gone to bed, and so I rushed to the window and saw Miles's old VW Golf pulling up into the cul-de-sac, the doors opening and too many people tumbling out: Helen, then George, Alex, Colin, Lucy, Miles himself, then Fran, laughing and stretching out twisted shoulders and cramped legs, one — no, two — open bottles between them.

I stepped back from the window. If I pretended to be out, they'd ring the bell and keep ringing, but God, I was a mess, barefoot in a stained T-shirt, a souvenir from Portugal four years ago, the word "Algarve" across the chest, my deodorant far out of reach. I could see their shadows at the door.

"Is this the one?"

"Yep, this is it."

I could tell them to go away. Open the door on the chain, like some old hermit. Demand they leave me alone.

"Okay, everyone ready? One, two, three . . ."

"*God rest ye merry gentlemen, let nothing you dismay —*"

I threw the door open. "Shhhhh!"

"*For Jesus Christ our savior was born on —*"

"Be quiet! Dad's asleep."

"Sorry!" said George. "Sorry!"

"We know what you're thinking," said Helen. "You're thinking, *who is this ragtag bunch of gypsies?*"

"We need to see you, Charlie," said Miles.

"It's urgent," said Lucy.

"Why aren't you rehearsing?"

"We have been!" said Miles. "We've just done the technical run."

"It was a disaster!" said Alex, swigging from a bottle of wine.

"That's why we need to see you," said Miles.

"Are you all pissed?"

"I'm not," said Miles. "I'm driving."

"But yes," said George. "We've been drowning our sorrows to a certain degree."

"So are you going to let us in or what?" said Helen.

"No."

"Bit rude," she said.

"Okay, you've got to come out, then," said Colin.

"I can't."

"Why not?"

"There's no point."

"Charlie," said Alex, "we've gone to all this trouble to stage an intervention. It is extremely dramatic and emotional, and the least you can do is hear us out."

"Please?" said Fran. "Ten minutes." She stood at the back, just one of the group, and now I wondered, could I close the door on her?

"*Away in a manger,*" sang Alex, the others joining in, "*no crib for a bed . . .*"

"All right! All right, there's a park down the road. Give me a sec. I'll put some shoes on."

The sun was low, televisions babbling through open windows as we walked in the middle of the empty road towards the recreation ground.

"Is this the one that they call Dog Shit Park?" said Alex, his voice too loud.

"It is!" said Helen. "There's another Dog Shit Park on the east side —"

"The 'East Side'!"

"— but this is the original."

"The original," said George, "and still, I think, the best."

"Dog Shit Park West."

"The playground, yeah?" said Helen.

In the evenings, the tarmacked zone became a kind of shared conference room for local youths, and we checked it wasn't booked, moved the empty cans and bottles and arranged ourselves on seesaw, roundabout, slide and swings, where I found myself between Alex and Helen.

"The thing is," said Helen, "Charlie, we want you back."

"I can't. I'm sorry."

"No one else can do the part," said Alex.

"Oh, they can," I said.

"But not like you."

"It's not the same."

"Poor old George here is exhausted," said Alex. "Aren't you, George?"

George passed by on the roundabout. "The doubling doesn't work. I can learn the lines, but Miles here and I have zero chemistry . . ."

"It's true, Charlie," said Miles from the top of the slide. "He's terrible."

"Problem is," said George, "it's like trying to act with a gifted chimpanzee."

"George's not versatile," said Miles. "The audience will think he's the same character in a different hat."

"That's true," said George. "Like Miles, all my performances are essentially the same," and Miles ran down the slide to pull George from the roundabout.

"And Ivor's desperate for you," said Helen.

"He's not angry," said Alex.

"Alina is angry."

"Ivor's just desperate."

"I couldn't do it anyway," I said. "There's . . . too much going on."

"And we know about all of that," said Alex.

"The grades—who gives a fuck?"

"Only wankers care about GCSEs."

"Wankers and employers," I said.

"Fine, so retake or do something else," said Helen. "The play's not going to stop you."

"And as for the scam thing . . ." said Alex in a low voice.

"Big deal."

"I think it's cool if anything."

"Sticking it to the Man."

"We've all done worse."

"Believe me, *much* worse."

"There are other things," I said.

"Yeah," said Helen, "we know."

"We don't, though," said Fran from the swings. "Not all of it."

"Okay. No. Maybe not, but—"

"I've got to look after my dad."

"Fine," said Alex, "but you can leave the house."

"He'd want you to, surely."

"Four more days."

"I can't," I said. "He's not in a fit state to—"

"But if you tell him."

"Talk to him."

"I can't," I said. "I've got to be there."

Everyone was silent for a while. "Fine," said Alex. "Fine."

"But you'll think about it," said Helen.

"It's no fun without you, Charlie," shouted George from underneath Miles. "No fun at all."

We walked back to the car, in and out of the pools of street light, the rest of the group contriving to melt away until Fran and I were side by side, just like in the early days, except now we walked in silence.

"I'm sorry about the fete," she said eventually.

"That's fine."

"No, I wasn't very kind—I'd had Polly shouting at me, then Mum and Dad. Even Bernard gave me a harsh look. If I'd known what had happened—but I thought you'd just run off and left me."

"I wouldn't do that."

"I know! I should have listened—"

"It's fine."

"Charlie, you have to stop saying things are fine when they're not fine. It doesn't help anyone."

We walked on. After a while she took my hand.

"Nothing's changed. Not for me."

"No, me neither."

"So come back?"

"I'm sorry, I can't. I'm not fit for company."

"It's not a company, it's a cooperative!" A little further. "Can I ask, why not?"

I shrugged. "Bit blue, I suppose."

"And is staying home the answer?"

"No, but neither is coming back."

"Maybe not. Unless it is."

"Is it really a disaster?" I asked.

"Technical issues. Your going hasn't helped. Think about it, will you?" We were back at Miles's car now, the company jostling for the best seats. "I miss you. We all miss you."

"I don't," said Helen.

"Everyone except Helen misses you."

"The call's at nine tomorrow," said George. "Fight rehearsal. In case you change your mind."

"No pressure," said Lucy.

"Some pressure," said Alex.

"I'm in the front," said Helen. "You're dropping me home, yes?"

"Me too," said Colin.

"And me, please, Miles," said Lucy.

"I'm not a minicab," said Miles.

Finally, only Alex and Fran were left. "What a lousy intervention that was," he said, embracing me then folding himself into the car. "See you tomorrow, Mr. Algarve."

Miles turned the key in the ignition and Bob Marley's "Three Little Birds" began to play, and while they bickered and groaned and crammed themselves into every corner, Fran kissed me—"Tomorrow. Please?"—and then clambered across their laps.

I watched the laborious three-point turn, the car low on its axles, and waited for them to drive away. Turning back to the house, I saw Dad in the window. I went inside and closed the door.

Canada, Málaga, Rimini, Brindisi

MUM'S SHOPPING BIKE WAS not made for hills like this, with its pram wheels and its three gears, each the same, the rattling basket and mudguards threatening to fall off with each turn of the pedals. On the shaded lane that led up to Fawley Manor, it felt like a treadmill, all effort, no discernible forward movement. Arriving late, I dumped the thing behind a marquee that I'd not seen before—a refreshment tent—and followed the sound of shouts and cries, crossing the courtyard and coming out between two great scaffolding structures, raked seating straight out of a high school movie. I stopped in my tracks.

In the three days since I'd been here, a small town had appeared, baked to a dusty white by the Italian sun, twisted and tumbling down. The great green lawn had disappeared beneath some rough, pale, crumpled surface like the chalky fabric used to make a plaster cast, and on the street, a brawl was taking place with swords, real swords, flashing through the air as the combatants kicked up the dust, watched from above by the rest of the company, all in motion, shouting and stomping. On the walkway, Sam and Grace, our musicians, were thrashing away at snare drum and electrified mandolin. "*A plague a' both your houses!*" shouted Alex, laughing bitterly at the stage blood dripping from his hands. "*They have made worms' meat of me!*" and I could see the space onstage where I really ought to be.

"Charlie! Oi, Charlie, up here!" From the top row of the seating unit, Helen beamed down, then Chris and Chris, thumbs up.

"Shhhh!" said Alina, turning and seeing me. "Well, hello stranger!"

"Charlie!" shouted Ivor. "Charlie, my boy!" Onstage the action fell apart, and Alex started clapping with his bloody hands, then George, then the whole company, and then Polly was behind me—"I knew it, I knew you'd come back. Didn't I say?"—and Fran, laughing, and Ivor, bounding up. "The prodigal returns. Charlie Lewis," he said, pumping me by the hand, "we're all *very* pleased. Now, let's get you into costume."

I fell back into it, the corny, self-conscious melodrama of putting on a play, all tantrums and surmountable disasters: "I can't do this part" and "The costume's no good" and "We'll never be ready in time." We worked long, long hours, and each hour brought with it another crisis, another explosion. Miles dared to give Alex notes, and Alex gave notes back with added venom, and Lucy got carried away in the fight and poked Colin in the ear with her sword, and Polly kept forgetting her lines, and Keith kept sneaking off to phone his wife and coming back in tears. Pulleys jammed and props disappeared and a sudden summer wind blew up, tugging at the sheets like sails, causing the scaffolding to sway alarmingly, and George thought he might have flu until Alina forbade it, and the performances were alternately too quiet, too loud, too fast, too slow, too big, too small, and in the gaps between the crises and explosions we'd loll around, play cards or games of catch, work on our Italian tans, gossip and praise each other, sometimes sincerely, sometimes not. When she could, Fran would come and find me, and sometimes we'd find a private place to kiss and talk—really talk—until it was almost like before. Despite the melodrama playing out in rehearsals, things were calmer between us now, the relief that follows a confession, I suppose, and we felt so much older and wiser than the children we'd been five days before.

And on the Thursday night at seven p.m., after singing rounds and speaking tongue twisters, dressed in pale gray and powder blue like stylish ghosts, we all gathered on the lawn behind the stage for Ivor's final big speech, variations on the theme of pulling together, listening to each other, the necessity of going for it.

"This language, these words"—this in his religious-experience voice—"these are the greatest words you'll ever speak out loud, by the greatest poet the world has ever known. So relish them. And for goodness' sake"—contrived game-show chuckle—"enjoy your-selves!" There was a group hug. Break a leg! Not literally! We went to wait for our call, the boys and girls getting ready in separate tents, until, at half past seven . . .

"Beginners to the stage, please! Beginners' call."

I put on the spectacles that transformed me, magically, into Benvo-lio. On the way, I found Fran pacing, eyes screwed up tight, arms to the side, flicking out her fingers as she muttered to herself.

"Hey," I said.

"Hello."

"Can I talk to you or are you in the zone?"

"Yeah, the completely-shitting-myself zone."

"Don't shit yourself."

"You see! Suddenly everyone's got notes. Listen . . ." On the other side of the set, we could hear the murmur of voices, the bounce of planks on scaffolding.

"Your mum and dad here?"

"Uh-huh. Mum's coming every night."

"She's proud."

"Weird."

"Not weird. You're going to be incredible."

"Thank you. You too. What do you think of this makeup?" Her face had a powdery sheen, the tawny brown of old ladies' tights. "Polly did it. I look like a mannequin in Debenhams."

"But under the lights . . ."

"Yes, that's what she said, then she put these two red dots in the corners of my eyes. Makes them look bigger, she said, but it looks like I've got a sty, a pair of sties. Conjunctivitis!"

"Stay calm."

"Look!" She blotted at her damp forehead with the back of her hand. "It's coming off in clumps. It's like gravy granules."

"Okay, beginners please!" shouted Chris. "Beginners to the stage, now!"

"Can I kiss you? Will it spoil your makeup?"

"Sure. No tongue, I pray thee."

I kissed her lightly; she held my face and kissed me once again. "I'm so glad you came back," she said, then pushed me towards the curtained doorway where the others waited.

The lights dimmed, the audience fell silent, we heard the hum of the electricity surging through the wires and a burning smell like dust on a lightbulb. Onstage, Lesley and John lounged in the Italian sun, and went into their business, thumbs and fish and maidenheads. "We're off," whispered Alex at my side. *"Part, fools, put up your swords,"* I muttered. *"Part, fools, put up your swords."* There was a hand on my back: Lucy, grinning. "Let's do this thing!" she said, and I put my hand on my sword—a sword! I had a sword—and she pushed me out into the light.

Little Stars

FOR A LONG TIME, I owned a videocassette of the show. We all had one, a souvenir, handed out to us the day after the last performance, the day on which we all turned up, hung-over and sad, to dismantle the set, and even as we took possession of our VHS, we knew that we'd never watch it. Three hours of amateur dramatics shot from too far away: what torture that would be, as dull and uninvolving as watching the nativity play of a child you've never met. "An adequate production," proclaimed the local *Advertiser* the following week, "with some patchy verse speaking and wildly uneven acting. Frances Fisher makes a toothsome Juliet, and Alex Asante is a charismatic Mercutio, but Romeo lacks charm. Three stars out of five."

But to be part of it, that was thrilling, and all the tensions and rivalries were forgotten as we tumbled through this thing, watching each other's scenes, patting backs as actors returned to the wings like footballers who'd scored a goal — well done, nice work, amazing stuff, big laughs! When it was over, I threw myself into the sweaty hugging and overpraising along with everybody else. We were all *amazing,* and the audience overpraised us too, cheering and stomping their feet, so that we took far too many curtain calls, with people clattering down the steps and producing their car keys even before we'd left the stage.

Friday night, of course, was pure anticlimax. *"Fart, pools! Put up your swords!"* was Benvolio's first line, and things deteriorated from there. The Saturday matinee was disappointing too, and it seemed to me that being in a play was like hearing your favorite song, then hearing it again, and again, until the magic was completely gone. Without the romance of the fading light, the matinee was flat and inept, a walk-through in front of half-empty seats. There's no atmosphere in a flaming torch on a warm August afternoon, and to make up for the lack of enchantment we took to declaiming at each other, like tourists shouting "Echo!" into a canyon. "That," said George, watching Polly's first Nurse scene from the wings, "is some *big* acting."

"Acting you can see from space," said Alex.

But it was impossible not to succumb, and bellowing my way through my last big speech, I caught the eye of my sister in the second row, sticking two thumbs up, and saw Mum, eyes fixed on the floor, fingers pressed against her temples as if to dispel a migraine. "I hate matinees," said Miles, the seasoned pro. "It's like having sex with the big light on," said Alex, and even the virgins agreed that this was *exactly* what it was like. When it was over, finishing to polite applause, I trudged out to the refreshment tent and found Mum and Billie, frowns adjusting to smiles as I approached, Mum applauding with two fingers patted against the palm of her hand.

"Well, that was quite something," said Mum.

"Why did you come to the matinee? It's better at night."

"*Better?* Surely, no. It was lovely, Charlie. And weren't you good?"

"You can really sword-fight, brother," said Billie. "I don't think I've heard you speak so much in years."

"And didn't his voice sound nice?" said Mum. "I wish you talked that clearly all the time."

"Your girlfriend's good," said Billie.

"She was *very* good," said Mum, "and quite gorgeous. Talk about punching above your weight!"

"Mum . . ." said Billie.

"What is it, your personality?"

"Mum!"

"I'm teasing him, I'm allowed to tease him. She might want to tone the makeup down. That's my only criticism. Do we get to meet her?"

"No, not today," I said. "We've got to go and run our lines."

We'd arranged to meet in the long break between the shows, slipping away after the matinee, cutting through the woods to the gatehouse—where else could we go? It was better now, less ceremonial, a reunion, and afterwards we lay face-to-face in the cool, dim room.

"I don't ever want to do anything except this."

"I think," she said, "after a while it gets a bit sore."

"I wouldn't mind. I'd work through it."

"I know *you* would." We kissed. "Let's just stay here, then," she said. "Not bother going on tonight."

"I think they'd notice. You at least."

"Are you sad?"

"About what?"

"The last night. I always get a bit sad. All that work and it sort of . . . evaporates. You watch—at the party, it's all going to get *very* emotional." We curled closer together, like a knot pulled tight. Still, I felt a shudder of unease and longed for reassurance but knew that, just as in a horror film, to express a fear out loud risked bringing it to life. Instead we talked about the play, how she'd stumbled that afternoon in the scene where she thinks that Romeo, not Tybalt, has been killed.

"I'm meant to think he's *dead,* the great love of my life. When I get to that bit, I try to picture it, what I'd do if a person that I really loved was dead, and I'd be screaming, I'd be banging my head against the wall, and instead, in the play I've got to say, *Can heaven be so envious?* It's a terrible line. What does it even mean?"

But an idea had fixed in my head. "Who do you think of?"

"What?"

"In the scene, when you're doing your acting."

"'Doing my acting'?"

"Who do you imagine is dead?"

She glanced at me, glanced away. "You."

"Not Miles?"

"No, not *Miles!* You."

"So . . . you're thinking about me onstage?"

"Only sometimes."

"To upset yourself."

"It does sound weird, put like that."

"Me, but dead?"

"Not *just* dead. I think happy stuff about you too." Perhaps I smiled. "Don't get cocky," she said, "or I'll start thinking about someone different."

"When else?"

"Can we change the subject?"

"Okay. But when else do you think about me, when you're saying the lines?"

"I'm not going to tell you! You'll have to watch and see." We kissed, then, to move on, she added, "Monday, you can take me out for that famous coffee. I've got a while until college."

"I think we're a bit past the coffee stage now, don't you?"

"We can still do it. We've still got things to talk about, haven't we? More if anything. Nothing's changed, not changed in a bad way. Still love you."

"You too."

"Well, then we're fine." We kissed, and in a gesture out of a film, she reached for her watch, her arm far behind her, her neck elongated, her fingers patting on the floor, and in that moment, that gesture, I don't think I could have loved her more.

"Christ, the time—we've got to go. Are you ready? Last time ever?"

But back in the dressing rooms, all anyone talked about was the party. Ivor had insisted on soft drinks only, that it was perfectly possible to have fun with soft drinks, and so before curtain up we gathered in the boys' dressing room to itemize our stash, drawn from the dregs of the drinks cabinet—limoncello, cooking sherry, curdled advocaat, sparkling red wine—concealing the bottles and containers in shrubs and hedges around the gardens like squirrels hiding nuts for winter. At seven p.m. we warmed up, sang songs, group hugged. Ivor made another of his impassioned speeches—we were to go for it—and we began.

There were many parents there that night, the famous parents whose faults and failings we'd itemized in all those intense conversations, and during Friar Laurence's speech, we peered into the audience from the wings to point them out.

"There they are! Front row!" whispered Alex. "I told them not to go in the front row."

"They're proud!" said Fran.

"They're bored," said Alex. "Look at my father, trying to read his program." Beside him sat my father, leaning forward, chin cupped in his hands. I stood and watched him all the way through Fran's "fiery-footed steeds," his head bopping just a little—at the jazz of the words, I imagined—and I watched him as we waited for everyone's favorite line.

"Here it comes," said Helen.

Onstage, Fran stood in a cone of light.

"*Give me my Romeo,*" she said, "*and when he shall die / Take him and cut him out in little stars / And he will make the face of heaven so fine / That all the world will be in love with night.*"

I watched Dad grin at this, eyes widening at each twist on the idea —to be cut out in little stars, imagine—and I felt as if I was in possession of a great secret.

I did my thing too, trudging through it workmanlike, said my last line —"*This is the truth, or let Benvolio die!*"—and left the stage, with nothing left to do but fill an empty space in the final scene. In the meantime, we gathered in the wings and watched whatever scenes we could. "Aren't they *good?*" whispered Alex during Paris and Juliet's humiliating courtship, and I wondered who else could see the pain of George's kiss on Fran's cheek, the awful knowledge that he isn't loved but goes on loving just the same.

And then everything seemed to accelerate, and Paris and Romeo were fighting, and Paris was dead — *Oh, I am slain!* — and Romeo was drinking poison — *O true Apothecary, thy drugs are quick!* — a line that had always made us giggle, but not tonight, because, oh God, now Juliet was waking up and looking at his corpse with this terrible, blank stare. The dagger in her hand had a retractable blade. We'd all played with it, our favorite toy, and surely the audience could see the artifice of it, how ridiculous it was. *O happy dagger!* — you could hear the spring rattle in the hilt. But when I sought out my father in the front row I could see his hands clapped to his face, pulling down on his cheeks, eyes glinting at the awful bitter tragedy of it all.

Time for our last entrance, Chris handing us our flaming torches so that we could stand and soberly confront the repercussions of our feud. The long, prosaic scenes after Juliet's death had always seemed fantastically dull to me, but this was the last night and, following Ivor's instructions to "go for it," Polly's Nurse was practically hyperventilating with grief. We sang the minor-key madrigal we'd been taught, the Capulets embracing the Montagues, and Montagues, Capulets. The dead bodies were carried aloft, Miles's handsome, sweaty head dangling over my shoulder as we processed through the audience. Look them in the eye, Ivor had told us, because this play was still incredibly relevant to audiences today, even if we'd be hard pressed to explain exactly why.

"*For never was a story of more woe / Than this of Juliet and her Romeo.*"

We stood beneath the scaffolding, looking up at the audience's shins as the music faded and the last light disappeared. From here, the applause sounded immense, feet stomping on the wooden boards over our heads, and we were laughing, and then stepping back out for the curtain call with that perky little skipping run practiced by gymnasts, flopping forward to show just how emotionally exhausting the whole thing had been, holding out our hands to Miles and Fran, resurrected and strolling on arm in arm. And then all discipline broke down and we were pushing Ivor and Alina to the front of the stage, and supermarket bouquets were appearing, and the audience was perhaps getting a little tired of clapping, would quite like to head home now. Squinting against the light, I saw Alex's father clap and look at his watch at the same time. "Encore! Encore!" they shouted, while privately thinking, *please, don't do anything again.*

But Dad was on his feet, attempting to force an ovation through the sheer vigor of his clapping. When it became clear that he wouldn't stop, the rest of the audience caved, my father cheering louder than anyone, arms above his head, more, more, more, and not for the first time that summer, I wanted simultaneously to run away and to stay there forever.

Last Night

BACKSTAGE, BOYS AND GIRLS barged into each other's dressing rooms for glimpses of underwear, no one trying too hard to remove their makeup. Tumbling out in our party clothes, we found the streets of Verona lit in reds and greens, the audience clutching plastic cups of warm white wine. Entire families were there, school friends, teachers kissing and hugging. Everyone, it seemed, was the best thing in it. I stood on the corner for a while, smiling as if watching a stranger's wedding on the street, pleased to see the confetti but with no reason to join in.

And then I saw Dad approaching through the crowd, beaming but still red around the eyes as he threw his arms around me.

"Well done, my boy," he said. "I'm *very* proud of you."

Automatically, I replied, "Proud of you too, Dad."

"What for?" he said and laughed. "That doesn't make sense."

Dad left soon after, cadging a lift into town from Mr. and Mrs. Asante, and now it was time for the party to begin. Chris and Chris had fixed the lights to turn Verona into a dance floor, and we threw each other around until we were all soaked in sweat, breaking off now and then to poke through hedges for bottles. There were sentimental speeches that went on for too long, and my attention turned to the bats in the night sky, looping and wheeling overhead. Then Polly drank too much white wine and had to lie down on the grass, and Lucy and Miles were seen snogging in the grotto, and Keith was dancing all alone. Concerned that someone might get hurt, George — very drunk — was tidying away all the bottles and cups. House music turned to dark techno. "I had a bag. I can't find my bag," said Colin Smart over and over again. "Has anyone seen my bag? I can't leave without my bag!"

"High-level meeting," said Alex, drawing the four of us together. "This party is over. We are getting out of here."

"Shouldn't we say goodbye?" said Fran.

"I have these," said Alex, dangling car keys. "Mum's car. If anyone wants an adventure . . ."

"Yes!" said Helen.

"Let me just say goodbye to George," said Fran.

"No, we have to go *now*," said Helen.

"Alex, are you too drunk to drive?" I said.

"I swear, I'm sober as a lord," said Alex. "Come on. We're going to see the sun come up," and we slipped away into the night.

We drove south down silent, frightening lanes lit up by our headlights like the corridor of a haunted house. To hold our nerve, we shouted along to old Madonna and Prince songs, Fran and me in the back seat drinking vodka and lemonade from fragile plastic cups that sloshed onto our wrists at each bend.

"Where exactly are we going?" shouted Fran.

"I want to dance," shouted Alex. "Let's go to Brighton!"

This seemed like a fine idea, and we whooped and headed for the motorway, Helen lining up the songs and cranking up the volume until the speakers buzzed. We felt tireless, immortal, invincible. Entering Brighton, we found ourselves in traffic — a traffic jam at two in morning, what a town! — and peered, amazed, at the crowds of people still out on the streets. We parked in a grand square close to the beach, delirious at the sight of the actual, literal sea, and underneath the promenade, we put on our most sober faces and joined the queue outside the nightclub in the arches, attempting a kind of world-weary nonchalance at the bowel-shaking *dumpf-dumpf-dumpf* of the bass, the sweaty, shirtless, goggle-eyed insanity of the skinny boys stumbling out for Marlboro Lights and water. We looked and felt like children in comparison, even Alex, and soon we'd been turned away from every place he knew. "Doesn't matter," said Alex, "we'll have a private party," and we found a spot on the beach itself and stomped the shingle down. Alex and Helen went off on an expedition for booze and chewing gum, chips and music and cigarettes, and Fran and I passed the time by kissing, clumsy and drunk like all the other lovers there, dark shapes on the shingle like a colony of seals. Then we lay for a while, our faces close enough to be a blur, our hands on the other's cheek.

"I mean, your face . . ."

"And yours."

"Will we always know each other? Even if we're not—"

"Sh. Hope so. I don't see why not."

It was four in the morning now, and on Alex and Helen's return we summoned up enough energy to dance once more to house music on Alex's tinny CD player, retrieved from the car. Nearby, some other all-night revelers sat round a man with a guitar. "Could you turn it down, please?" shouted one of them. "Hippies," muttered Alex, but the sky was lightening, exhaustion and self-consciousness were setting in, and we surrendered, turned the music down and sat, huddling close for warmth.

Drunk and sentimental, we said out loud what we loved about each other and made declarations of lifelong friendship that would embarrass us when we recalled them the next day but which we hoped would hold true.

"Helen—are you crying?" said Alex. "My God, I didn't think you could."

"What's up, Hel?" said Fran, taking her hand and shaking it out, and Helen laughed.

"I don't know. I just suddenly thought—what if it doesn't get better than this?" and she wiped her face with the back of Fran's hand.

"Don't wipe your snot on me," said Fran, crying too. "It's disgusting."

"Look," said Alex. To our left, out beyond the Palace Pier, the sun was rising. "*Night's candles are burnt out and* something something something."

"*. . . jocund day stands tiptoe on the misty mountain tops*," said Fran.

"I don't feel very jocund," said Helen. "I feel sick."

"I suppose we ought to think about heading home," said Fran.

"Bit longer," I said. "Maybe we should try to sleep first."

And so we huddled close and closed our eyes, but something was happening behind us. The music in the clubs had stopped abruptly and now the crowds were spilling onto the beach all at once as if a fire drill was taking place. Steam rose from their bodies as they loitered, arms round each other, shaken and bedraggled and sucking on cigarettes, and now a crowd of clubbers was forming around a sea fisherman nearby to listen to his radio. A group of girls staggered past, high heels sinking in the shingle, some crying, others looking dazed, one girl laughing and crying at the same time and swearing to herself. "What's up?" asked Alex, but they didn't stop, marching unsteadily to the sea where the laughing, crying girl began to wade out into the waves.

The world was coming to an end, with no hope of salvation. Ballistic missiles were minutes away, an asteroid perhaps, or a solar flare, the one we'd been waiting for. The group with the guitar must have heard the news too, bundling up their stuff and trudging up the beach.

"What's up?" shouted Helen. "What's going on?"

"There's been an accident!" a girl shouted back, then something about Diana, a tunnel in Paris. "She's dead."

Of course we didn't quite believe it, not until we were back in Alex's car and listening to the news on the radio, driving cautiously along the early-morning roads, the sun shining bright on the last good day of the summer, the four of us quite silent all the way home.

PART FOUR

Winter

And summer's lease hath all too short a date.

—Shakespeare, Sonnet 18

1998

WE BROKE UP IN JANUARY. A love we thought would outlast all storms and struggles could not survive Fran's daily commute to Basingstoke.

Until that time, and for some time afterwards, I'd told myself that I would happily give my life for Fran Fisher. Well, not happily, but I would give it. "Take me, not her," I'd say, though it seemed an important part of the deal that she should know the sacrifice was being made. If I was going to drink the potion, I didn't want it to be a waste. I think, too, that she'd have sacrificed her life for me, to begin with at least, though a willingness to die seems a rather blunt measure of devotion. Was there some sort of sliding scale? Did a day come when she thought, *Well, I'm not sure I'd die, but I'd definitely give an arm,* then a hand, a kidney, then maybe a toe, a little toe? Some hair, until finally, *Take him, not me!* If Juliet had woken to find her Romeo dead and, instead of reaching for the happy dagger, had decided to carry on, to learn to live with grief and work towards reconciliation in the community, would we think less of her? What if she met someone else and lived happily into old age? No, self-destruction was the gold standard. In our case, the opportunity did not arise, and with a banality that no one would ever bother to dramatize, we came apart.

We did our best to prevent it. Fran's results—all excellent—meant that she'd go to a college that specialized in the performing arts, and while she began the daily commute, I started to look for a job. We both knew how things might go—envy and exclusion on my part, self-consciousness and awkwardness on hers as this new world opened up—and we'd laid down strategies to avoid these tensions. She would be free to do whatever she wanted, to go to parties, to study, to talk about the course if it excited her, and in turn I'd be free to come along and meet her friends or to stay away if I chose to. There'd be no jealous-boyfriend act, and we'd see each other three, or at least two, evenings a week.

I met her parents properly and grew to like them, though they never lost the question in their eyes: is this someone we really *need* to get to know? Is it worth the investment? But I was allowed to stay over in the same bed, holding our breath and waiting until they were asleep before cautious, silent lovemaking. We'd take the train to London at weekends, go to galleries or to see the arty movies—not movies, "cinema"—that never made it anywhere near our town. We went to restaurants—restaurants!—sometimes just the two of us, sometimes with her friends, and I did my best to get along with them as I had with Full Fathom Five. I was "taking some time out"—this was the line that we both chose to stick to. Really I was one of them, a student, just twelve months behind. We both learned to drive, and for my seventeenth birthday Mum bought me a battered old Citroën with wind-down windows and moss growing in the window seals. As autumn faded into winter, we'd drive out to the coast and walk on the cliffs or beaches, then go back to the car, find some hidden spot, collapse the back seat and make partially clothed love behind the steamed-up windows.

There was a tenderness to that time, a sense that we were taking care of each other, and for a while it seemed plausible that we might make it through. But through to what? Would I come to university open days with her? What would she say when she discovered that I'd not filled out the college forms? I had a new job, I had the house with Dad and friends in town, and what was this obsession with education anyway? I understood the arty films as well as she did, I was reading more, and not everyone wanted or needed A-levels or a degree; to expect it was just snobbery. I rehearsed this argument in my head, ready for the day when I'd have to use it out loud.

Then, in early November, we had the accident. We'd had sex in the back of the car, giggling and cracking shins and elbows, but this time I'd failed to fit the condom properly, and it was only after we'd collapsed and pulled apart that we discovered it had disappeared like some terrible magic trick, only to reappear soon after, sticky and alarming. We'd both been frightened, but it was Fran who'd insisted that we drive into Brighton first thing for a morning-after pill. "I just want to do it as soon as possible, for peace of mind," she'd said, and I'd sat in the driver's seat on a wet, gray Monday morning and watched as she pressed the pill from its packaging and washed it down with water as if it were an antidote to something.

Which, of course, it was, and we were both relieved. But if she had become pregnant, who would have had the most to lose? My father had become a parent at twenty-one, which wasn't so much older, though perhaps my parents weren't the best example. Still, an accident that was a disaster for Fran would, for me, have been—not ideal, not what I craved but something that I might have embraced. I wanted only to be with her, but she wanted very much more. An inequality had been illuminated, of achievement and potential, ambition and desire.

The breakup took place early in the new year—she had, I suppose, wanted to "get through Christmas"—so that it had the quality of a resolution: (1) drink more water, (2) end relationship. The scene itself was conventional and predictable, with the fraught and overwrought quality of a drama-class improvisation. Even the location, the beach at Cuckmere Haven, in drizzle on a desolate Sunday afternoon, gave the breakup that site-specific quality. I'd become angry, said Fran, and negative; we weren't natural or at ease with each other; and I, in turn, got to make my speech about her snobbery. "Charlie, when," she said, "when have I ever, ever said any of those things?" And though I couldn't point to examples, I think she was shocked and saddened by how viciously I turned on her student friends, the parents who clearly thought she could do better. It was an argument from which neither of us could recover, and as the light failed and the drizzle turned to rain, we were left with the practical problem of how we might escape this bleak and windswept beach. She would not get in the car with me, I would not leave without her, and even when we finally set off in silence, we had to pull over frequently, to shout or scream or cry a little more.

There were a few more encounters after that, late at night on the phone or in city-center pubs, then out onto the street. The couple that you sometimes see in tears at closing time, alternately clinging to each other then pushing each other away: that was us.

But though I fought for her, I knew these were the final skirmishes in a battle that was already lost. Fran Fisher walked away to get a minicab home. I wouldn't see her again for more than twenty years, but I would see her again.

2x 4x 8x 16x

IN THE ERA OF Dad's VHS machine, one of my smaller talents was an ability to fast-forward with great accuracy, watching the action spool past and pressing stop at precisely the right time to allow for the momentum of the whizzing spools. In the digital era things are easier, and instead of seeing every single moment speeding by, transformed into silent comedy, we skip and hop directly to the things we want to see. It's more efficient that way. So:

As soon as I could drive, I got a job at the airport, clearing the tables and trays of first-class passengers in the twenty-four-hour executive lounge. It was a job that might have been invented with the specific intention of filling me with loathing: loathing for the way the customers filled their glasses with free champagne they'd never finish, the rare roast beef scraped into the bin; loathing for the squalor of behind the scenes, the gray-faced staff sucking on cigarettes in doorways, the stinking lockers and vacuum-sealed packs of smoked salmon like great blocks of pink alien flesh. The gulf between customers and staff, us and them, was like something from the Soviet-era propaganda machine, and the only way to get through each shift was to engage in petty acts of spite and sabotage that led in turn to that other, most poisonous, form of loathing. A Sussex University Philosophy student, slumming it for the summer, told me about Sartre's waiter, fixing his smile and taking his orders and living his life of bad faith, and I thought two things: *Yep, that sounds about right*. Also: *Fucking students*.

Like the gold card members of the Executive Club, I made the most of all that bounty, but while they were only passing through, I was on a fifty-six-hour week, living on pretzels and Brie. I became the over-time king, working all the hours I could, and with my first pay packet I bought a bed to replace the bunks in my room, then methodically paid off our household debts. In December, Social Security sent Dad to work at the Royal Mail sorting office, and something about the early mornings, the routine and some old-English quality of the job struck a chord and he became a full-time postman. "Finished by two and the day's all your own!" he said as if he couldn't quite believe it. He stopped smoking, cut down on his drinking and his highs and lows became less extreme, so that for the most part we were calmer, more peaceable, more sedentary.

On the evenings when I didn't have to work, we watched the same films and TV shows, ate the same meals, read the same books one after another, washed and dried at the sink. "You and your father," my mother said, on one of her final visits before she moved away, "are like an old married couple," a weird and depressing vision of domestic life that underlined just why she'd left. She didn't say it warmly. It was a warning.

Though we'd sometimes bump into each other on the streets, I didn't see much of old friends who'd gone on to college, and all too soon that September came round when they all flew away to Manchester, to Birmingham and Hull and Leicester, to Glasgow and Exeter and Dublin. I'd heard that Fran Fisher was at Oxford ("at," not "in"), reading (not "studying") English and French, and I thought, *well, that sounds about right. That makes sense.*

Harper, who'd worked steadily when no one was looking, went to

study Civil Engineering in Newcastle, where he was rarely seen outside without a traffic cone on his head. Fox, who'd relentlessly jeered
anyone caught holding a pen, went off to train as a games teacher,
and at Christmas they'd meet me in the pub and tell me stories of
legendary piss-ups. Soon Harper had a serious girlfriend, a woman of
impossible glamour, studying tourism. They were going to go traveling together, perhaps drop in and see Lloyd, who now did something
shady in Thailand. "Unless he's in jail," said Fox, and we all agreed
that a Thai jail was probably an environment where Lloyd could really
thrive. We'd all softened a little, in our manner and around our waists,
and laughed in a different way. I felt fond of them and we'd even try
to revive the old nicknames and scuffles. But if we were a band, then
we were past our best, re-formed, a nostalgia act, still playing but a
member down and with only the old hits to perform. Harper skipped
one Christmas, Fox another, and after that we no longer met up.

In my first summer after school, I'd noticed posters start to appear
for Full Fathom Five's new production. His hair was slicked back,
and without glasses his eyes seemed puffy and small, but I recognized
George as a beetle-ish, hunchbacked King Richard III, in some ways a
promotion, in others not. The following summer it was *As You Like
It,* then, because enough time had passed, time for *A Midsummer
Night's Dream* again. I was no more likely to buy a ticket than I was
to gate-crash the school-leavers' disco, but I still felt a childish resentment that they were carrying on without me. Shakespeare, performing, books, music, poetry, art; the promise had been that these things
changed young lives, gave a sense of self-worth, of community, al-
tered the way in which we moved through the world. With missionary
zeal, this was what Ivor and Alina had strived for, and it had worked.
But the process was reversible, and now nostalgia turned to bitterness
whenever I recalled that summer. In 2001 it was *Macbeth,* and this,

appropriately, was the production that killed them off. I imagined Ivor and Alina selling off the Transit van, dumping the beanbags and the yoga mats, and felt an unpleasant relief when they didn't return.

I was in a rut, and knew that it was a rut, and took some pleasure in the shelter it provided. In the war movies and science-fiction films I loved, there was a stock character, the plucky corporal, wounded in the stomach or spine. I'll only slow you down, he says, go on without me, and surrounded by explosives, and with a grenade clutched to his chest, he sits and waits for the enemy and the most destructive time to pull the pin. I always admired that character, his masochistic nobility. I'm not sure who I thought of as the enemy, but I was happy, in my own way, to sit and wait while others made their escape, despite not having slowed them down at all.

Mum and Jonathan moved away to Exeter to be nearer his parents, both finding management jobs. "Boutique hotels, God help me," said Mum. I missed her, and I think Dad missed her too, but leaving no longer felt like a dereliction of duty, and she'd never really liked our town. Billie excelled in her GCSEs, then her A-levels, and went off to study Chemistry at Aberdeen, "because it's so far from Exeter."

And I did miss Billie. She'd left home at the point where we might have become friends, and I never told her about the worst of times with Dad. In turn, I'm sure she had her own struggles in that stranger's home, but though she remained my sister, we no longer felt like family. Our paths diverged too soon, and every choice she made took her further away. Perhaps some time in the future those paths will come back together.

I became very good at pool. And darts, and the slot machine. The Angler's became my local, the staff who once refused to serve me became my friends, and I graduated to a regular stool at the end of the bar. I had a few flings with girls I'd met there, consummated in cars or, in celebration of the spring, in the nearby churchyard. A love affair that begins up against a tomb is unlikely to flourish, and soon phone calls went unanswered. Once a drink was emptied over my head, just like in films, and I wondered, my God, is this who you're becoming—someone who has drinks emptied over their head? What would Fran say?

On Christmas Eve in 2002 I had taken up my spot at the bar, privately resenting the part-timers who packed the pub at this time of year. Like worshippers who turn up once a year at midnight Mass. I wondered, where was their commitment? The woman on my right had wedged her elbows onto the bar and now was slowly pushing them outwards, shouting to the barmaid, "Excuse me? Miss?"

A loop of Christmas pop hits was playing loudly but still I recognized her voice and, for reasons that I couldn't have explained, tilted my face away. A man had joined her now.

"I *need* my drink!"

"Fuck's sake, just wait a moment, will you?"

"Do you think I should ask for a vodka martini?"

"In The Angler's? Straight glass or tankard?"

If I swiveled to my left I might slide off my stool, take my pint and sit elsewhere . . .

Too late.

"Oh. My. God."

"Hello, Helen."

"Charlie! Charlie Lewis, come here!"

"Hi Alex!" I mumbled into his shoulder as they wrenched me from the stool.

We moved to a table. Despite the solemn vows on Brighton beach, we'd drifted apart in their college years. Now they'd both changed just as they were meant to, Helen with a smart military haircut and a small black stud in her nose, Alex looking skinny, poised and quite beautiful, a louche millionaire in a slim black jacket.

"Thierry Mugler, if you must know."

"Secondhand."

"Your donkey jacket is secondhand. *This* is vintage."

If I'd not known them, I'd have felt intimidated. Knowing them, I felt intimidated, but still cautiously pleased to see them. Predictably, they were both in London now, a Sociology degree for Helen, last year of drama school for Alex, sharing a big house in Brixton with playwrights and artists and musicians, just back for family duties at Christmas ("Boxing Day, seven a.m., we are *out* of here"). When it was my turn, I told them about my work, trying to make a dark joke out of it, the comedy sounding a little darker than I'd intended. They laughed but looked concerned. Perhaps I'd had too much to drink. Certainly, I'd finished my glass some time before they finished theirs. I escaped to the bar and realized, as I waited, that it was not nostalgia that had brought them here, but irony. The Angler's was a joke to them, and I wondered if I was too, and so I lingered at the bar through "Last Christmas" and "Mistletoe and Wine" and "Merry Christmas Everybody," in no hurry to be served, occasionally glancing over to the table to see their heads close together. I bought myself a beer and a chaser, and when I finally got back, Alex got up "to make a call," and Helen and I sat in silence.

"You all right?" I said.

"Yeah, just admiring the view." She nodded towards the bar and the row of three male backsides, the cleft of their buttocks visible over the backs of their jeans, heads down, no conversation.

"Don't wind up like that, will you?"

And now I could say it. "Snob!"

"Hey, I'm not a snob! No one in the world is less of a snob than me—"

"Because you sound like a snob, Hel."

"Coming back here, with your clever college ways—"

"Yeah, exactly that."

"Except I'm *not* a snob! I don't give a fuck what you do—live where you want, do what you want. I mean, I get it, it's your wilderness years and that's fine."

"Helen—"

"But what's this?" She tapped my shot glass.

"It's just a chaser."

"A *chaser*?"

"What's wrong with that?"

"You're too young to have a local. Honestly, Charlie, fuck that. You need to move away, just for a bit. You can come back, but you've got to do something else. Try at least. There's plenty of time to hate your life. Do it when you're middle-aged, like everyone else."

"I don't 'hate my life.'"

"But you don't *love* it, do you?"

"Why, do you?"

She laughed. "Yes! Yes, yes, finally, I fucking do! And you could too, if you weren't so scared."

"I'm not scared."

"Well, good. That's good to hear. Because it brings me to my next point . . ."

Mariah Carey was singing "All I Want for Christmas Is You," and now Alex was back, sitting on the other side of me, pinning me in. "Have you told him yet?" he asked.

"Told me what?"

Helen took a deep breath. "We've got a spare room."

"In the house in Brixton."

"It's a shithole really. In the basement; it's dark and damp."

"But it's free."

"Well, shared bills."

"But you could get a bar job, or temp or something."

"And in September—go back to college."

"I'm not going to do that."

"No, but you *are*."

"You know you are, so why fight it?"

"I can't. Dad—"

"You said he was better."

"He is for now, but—"

"Well, it's an hour and a half away, Charlie, it's not New Zealand."

"But I can't just walk away."

"You wouldn't walk. We'd give you a lift."

"We're taking you with us."

"On Boxing Day. We'll wait until seven."

"Charlie," said Alex, "all we want for Christmas is *you*."

In September 2003, at twenty-three years of age, I went back to school. Technically, I was a mature student, though there was very little maturity on display, just a great many false starts, wrong turns, hangovers and missed deadlines. First I had to fill in the gaps left by my bodged exams, then complete the equivalents of A-levels, then find a university that was open-minded enough to overlook the great blank expanses on my CV, all of this while working weekends and nights in bars and restaurants where the end of the shift marked the beginning of the party. Those years were a kind of second adolescence, the obligation to work hard rubbing up against the desire to do no work whatsoever, and my education began to resemble an immense, unfinished jigsaw that's been left out on the table for far too long. The temptation to abandon the project and sweep the whole thing back into the box was extremely strong. I would not have got through it at all without Helen and Alex, urging me on, checking the homework, ensuring that I filled in the forms on time, and it occurs to me that the good luck we have in school, in our work, is nothing compared to the great good luck of friendship.

Two qualifications, Computer Science and Art, provided the shaky foundations for all of this. At a party in August 1997, a stranger had told me that the trick in life was to find the thing you're good at and go for it, but computers and art were like onions and chocolate; there was no way to combine the two. At university, I learned that I was not academically bright and never would be. I was not a gifted programmer and had never felt like an artist, but my tutor suggested that I take a course in visual effects and animation, and I learned how to use software with imposing names like Premiere and Fusion and Nuke. I spent my bartending wages on the most powerful home computer I could afford, and taught myself compositing and rendering, wireframe modeling and matte painting, and while I assembled all these skills, something happened to the culture around me.

The zombies and vampires, spaceships and aliens that I'd loved to draw took over, and those years spent watching movies and playing Doom were revealed to have been part of an unwitting apprenticeship. I already knew how to draw an eyeball dangling from a skull socket, and now, with the right software, I knew how to make it glint and sway repulsively, and how to turn a crowd of twenty into two hundred thousand, and how to shave the years off the leading man. And so now that's what I do: visual effects. Computer Science and Art.

Chasing the work, Alex Asante went to Los Angeles. We still see him all the time but mainly on TV, playing cops or ambitious young lawyers who'll do anything to win the case, including break the law. He's quite well known, though never quite as well known as he'd like to be.

No longer students, we moved out of the student house. I met Niamh, exchanged restaurant work for full-time post-production and then, not so long ago, set up a company with colleagues. Occasionally, we'd be invited to the premieres of films that I worked on, finding our seats at the very rear of the auditorium, and peer down at the actors, distant and alien, taking their bows.

Helen met Freya, fell in love and moved to Brighton "like a complete stereotype." Walking on the beach there, she told me they were getting married and asked me to be her best man.

"Okay. Do I have to?"

"Of course you do! It's a great honor, you homophobic bastard. Also, Alex is filming, so—"

"Fine, but do I have to make a speech?"

"Uh, *yes.*"

"And does it have to be funny?"

"Of course it has to be fucking funny, it's the best man's speech."

"It's a lot of stress. I'm not a natural performer."

"Oh, I know that."

"I can't be funny."

"You can be funny, you just have to do it out loud. The main thing is to be *heartfelt.* Tell everyone I swear too much and you cherish our friendship. There you go—I've written it. Now you have to say yes."

And so I was Helen's best man, and when the time came, I asked her to be mine.

And then a month before the wedding, an email arrived, a screen grab of a Facebook page announcing a London reunion for the Full Fathom Five Theatre Cooperative, 1996–2001.

Got to be done, don't you think? See you there.

Digging Down

I PULLED ON THE jacket while Niamh watched from the doorway.

"That's not your wedding suit, is it?"

"No."

"I didn't realize it was that kind of party."

"Got to make an effort . . ."

"Of course. She'll be expecting it."

"*They*'ll be expecting it, all of the people there."

Was my behavior so unusual? It's true that I'd always resisted the tug of nostalgia. I skipped school reunions, rarely went home, had few photographs, did not chase down old girlfriends online. Life was a series of befores and afters, the dividing line shifting every seven years or so: before and after meeting Fran, before and after moving away, before and after Niamh, the divide between each era as distinct and precise as the stratification in geological layers of rock. As long as the after was better, why dwell on before?

Marriage would mark the next great divide, and yet here I was, three weeks before the ceremony, digging down through one, two, three layers. It was uncharacteristic, and Niamh saw this too, and the lightheartedness she'd put on when I'd first explained the expedition had faded as the date drew near.

"I've told you, you're very welcome to come."

"Someone else's am-dram reunion? That's desperate. No thanks, I'm not *deranged*."

"Helen'll be there."

"I can see Helen anytime. You'll both be wanting to talk to all your old friends anyway. Doing your vocal warm-ups, tossing your bean-bags, playing your *trust exercises* . . ."

I laughed. "If it's like that, I'm not staying either. I probably won't even know anyone."

"Oh, I think you'll know *some*one."

I sighed and slumped onto the bed. "I don't have to go, if you don't want me—"

"Oh, no, don't pin it on me. You're a grown-up, you can do what you want. Do you want to go?"

"Well, yes, I kind of do."

"Why?"

"I don't know. Nostalgia."

"Curiosity?"

"Bit of that."

"So go. I'll have a nice night in by myself. Google old boyfriends. Photoshop my face into their wedding photos."

"Goodbye."

"Don't get any lipstick on your collar."

"Like in the song."

"What song?" she said.

"That's where it comes from. *Lipstick on your collar / Told a tale on you.* You know that song."

"No, because I'm not one of the Andrews Sisters. I wasn't born *between the wars.*"

"Who gets lipstick on their collar anyway? How would it get there?"

"Lipstick on your dick, more like. That's what I'll be looking out for."

"You're filthy."

"I am. So hurry home."

Now that we'd laughed, I felt able to leave, but on the bus I found myself unaccountably nervous. I'd once seen a documentary about locusts or cicadas that hide as dormant adolescents in the sun-baked soil of Arizona, or Mexico, or the Sahara, then, after precisely seventeen years, rise up simultaneously in a great, destructive swarm. What if first love was like this? Dormant but gathering its strength, then laying waste to everything stable and good? These things happened.

It seemed unlikely. I loved Niamh like mad, and besides, Fran and I were entirely different people then, bizarre sixteen-year-old aliens, and first love wasn't real love anyway, just a fraught and feverish, juvenile imitation of it. These things don't happen if you don't want them to, and if I summoned up the thought of Frances Fisher, I felt a kind of fond embarrassment. Something else too, harder to name and hardly the stuff of great destructive passion, but still enough to make me change my clothes and brush my teeth and leave the house on a damp Sunday in November.

The venue was the top room of a pub in Stoke Newington, the start time an innocent six p.m. Family-friendly, the invite had said. I met Helen in a bar across the road so that we could revise. "Who was the guy who played Friar Laurence?" said Helen.

"Always crying."

"Keith something."

"And those musicians?"

"Sam and . . ."

"Go on."

"Grace!"

"How come you remember all this, Charlie?"

"I just do."

"You know who won't be there?" said Helen. "Polly and Bernard."

"They're not . . . ?"

"Yep. Both of them."

"When?"

"Bernard died years ago, Polly earlier this year."

"How do you know this?"

"Facebook."

"Oh, Christ. Polly and Bernard."

"She was nearly ninety, it's not a surprise."

"I know. Still, people get fixed, don't they, in your mind. Bernard I don't think I ever spoke to, but Polly—she was always nice to me. Nearly always. I lost my virginity in Polly's cottage."

"Yes. I know this."

"Oh, God. Poor Polly. Lousy actress, lovely woman."

"They could put that on her tombstone. Along with your virginity thing."

"Poor Polly." We touched our glasses together. "I feel sad now."

"We could stay here."

"No, come on. We've come this far."

And so we drained our drinks and crossed the road, trotted up the narrow stairs to the function room, made our big entrance and recognized no one. The cast of *Macbeth* was there, the *As You Like It* gang, the *Midsummer Night's Dream* crews (both of them), laughing and telling stories, but from *Romeo and Juliet,* not one familiar face.

"Okay, let's leave."

"Five minutes," I said. "Then we can go."

To look less lonely, we stood in front of a noticeboard of old black-and-white production photos.

"Maybe they forgot the camera our year."

"There's Miles," I said. "So I think that's the back of my head."

"A much-treasured company member."

"I was! I carried that show."

"And yet almost entirely absent," said Helen, laughing, and I wondered if this was the great peril of reunions: the discovery that we aren't as essential to other people's memories as they are to ours.

This could not be said of Polly, and another pinboard was given over to her old acting head-shots from the sixties, hair cropped, kohl-eyed, pure Carnaby Street, and photos of her varied roles and similar expressions, eyes and mouth always open to their full extent. After a while, we were joined by someone who looked like Colin Smart's dad and who turned out to be Colin Smart. "Look how much I've grown!" he said, though he had not grown. We chatted for a while, threw names around, and I tried hard to concentrate and not to scan the room over his shoulder. Had I expected something wilder, a last-night party? There were children here, eating crisps at the buffet table, and at the bar I found myself standing next to Lucy Tran, a pediatrician now, brisk and pleasant and funny until talk turned to our old school. Did I still see Lloyd or Harper or that lot?

"No, not for years. You know how it is. We grew apart."

"Good! Good news. They made my life a misery, those boys. Little shits."

"Yes, they could be mean."

"So could you, Charlie. You weren't as bad, but you never stood up to them."

"No, that's true. I think about that sometimes. I apologize."

"Yes. Well. You got better."

"Did I? Christ, I hope so."

Some time passed. "Anyway . . ."

"Have you seen her?"

"Seen who?"

"Well, you didn't come here to see me."

"No, I just presumed she wasn't coming."

"Oh, she's here. She's sitting down somewhere. Look — over there."

And through a gap in the crowd, I saw her on a chair by the window, one hand resting on the bulge of her pregnant stomach, talking intently to one of the children, a girl, ten years old, who could only be her daughter. As I watched, she reached over and tucked the girl's hair behind her ear.

"Aw, your face," laughed Lucy. "What was it? *O, she doth teach the torches to burn bright . . .*" She patted my arm. "Good luck!"

Fran Fisher laughed at something the girl had said, then sent her off and, in doing so, saw me. She laughed again and opened her eyes wide, clapping both hands to her face. Through gaps in the crowd we made a series of garbled gestures—*Look at you! Why are we here? Talk soon. Five minutes? Come find me*—and then Colin Smart was there, embracing her over her bump, and I stood alone for some time, strangely breathless and unsure of what to do.

"Hey there!" A hand was on my elbow. "You all right?"

"George!" I said, and we performed a little dance, half handshake, half hug.

"Seen a ghost?"

"Nothing but ghosts."

"It's weird, isn't it?" said George. "We thought about not coming."

"It *is* weird," I said.

And I thought, *we?*

"I saw Helen. Isn't Helen great?"

"She is great."

"Have you spoken to . . . ?"

"No."

"I know she'll want to speak to you."

And I thought, *how do you know?*

"You look good, Charlie."

"You too, George."

He did look better, healthy and assured, though even without glasses he still retained that blinking, surprised quality, as if woken by a bright light. "Contact lenses and no dairy." With the old gesture, he put his hand to his face. "Skin should clear up any day now."

"Your skin looks fine."

"Yes, people have been telling me that for twenty-five years."

"Sorry."

"It's fine. It's fine."

"So. What else, George?"

"What do you want to know?"

"Tell me everything that's happened in the last twenty years."

He didn't tell me everything, but enough.

Last Love Story

GEORGE PEARCE WENT TO CAMBRIDGE, as planned. One tangible legacy of Full Fathom Five was an interest in Shakespeare, the Elizabethans and Jacobeans, and after graduating with a first, he took his MA, then his PhD. He steered clear of acting—too many Mileses involved in that game—and Shakespeare too, because what was left to say? Instead he specialized in Jacobean playwrights, their grisly tragedies and confusing comedies, and when a London company put on a production of Webster's *The White Devil*, he was asked to talk to the cast about the play. There, in the back row, grinning broadly, playing the role of Lady-in-Waiting, was Fran Fisher.

It was all he could do to speak in proper sentences, and afterwards they embraced and went for coffee to catch up and talk about old times. Fran was married to another actor, a wild, impulsive move on a long world tour, because "you've got to fill the days somehow." That was five years ago, and now they had a daughter, Grace, two years old. Coffee turned to wine and Fran began to drop dark hints about the marriage—the husband was a drinker, a possible philanderer, irresponsible, stupidly handsome and handsomely stupid. But she loved him and loved being a parent, and thought they could stay together, thought they could survive, if he sorted himself out. She was going to give up acting, though. She was nearly thirty and was never going to make it, not in a way that would ever make her happy. Doing all those plays as a kid was one thing, but now it made her feel silly and powerless, and one actor in the family was enough.

"Our scene in *Romeo and Juliet,* d'you remember?"

"You were good in that."

"We both were, George. Frankly, it was all downhill after that."

They said goodbye on Waterloo Bridge, exchanged details and promised to keep in touch, and George Pearce walked away, furious and elated. His great first love was his great unrequited love and also his only love, a combination that can derail a life entirely, and it was maddening—in the sense that it might send him mad—to see her like this. He had her number but he would not call it. What was the point? He was no Paris, throwing his dignity, his life, away on someone who would not and could not love him back.

He changed jobs and moved, coincidentally, to London. Met a girl, moved in, broke up, moved out, and five years passed. One Friday he was invited to a dinner party; a woman would be there, a French translator, single mum. He didn't want to go, of course, thought he'd stay at home and read, but the friend insisted and . . .

God, I don't know, I listened, but I couldn't really take it in. What did I feel? Jealousy? Not precisely. Of course I knew that there'd be others, some mistakes and some that she'd cut out in little stars, and it would require a sourer heart than mine to resent George's obvious happiness, his glee, doting on the stepdaughter who had joined us now, hanging from his arm.

"Grace, this man here," he told the girl, "used to know your mum when she played Juliet." Grace looked indifferent and I felt the pompous indignation of the ex-boyfriend. *Has she not spoken about me? Do you have any idea who I AM?* "Charlie and your mum were very close," said George. "Of course, I was *furious* about it."

Was I furious in return? Hardly. There was a kind of sense to it; they'd always made each other laugh and I was pleased that George had shaken off that persecuted air, was happy and successful and in love. Someone who I liked very much was with someone who I'd loved. Good news!

Still, I was silent for a while, and perhaps it was envy, not of the fact of Fran and George, but of their story. It was a good story, a better story than mine; it made sense and ended in the right way, which is to say that it didn't end at all. Even after all these years without seeing them, I knew that they would be happy together, and once Grace had gone, I put my hand on his shoulder, squeezed it hard and tried to express this.

"George, you bastard."

He laughed, a little nervously. "It's weird, isn't it? I can see that it's weird."

"No, it's very . . . *romantic*."

"And what a truly terrible word that is. Well, if it's any consolation, it's pretty loveless. Isn't that right, Fran?"

"It's true," said Fran, appearing at his side. "It is grim."

"Hello, Fran." I leaned over the bulge, tapped her cheek with mine.

"Come with me," she said, taking my hand. "And I'll tell you all about the dark side."

Pleasure

THE PUB HAD A roof that overlooked the terraced gardens of Stoke Newington, the air misty with fog and Sunday-night stove fires. Crates of empty bottles, a rusting barbecue, tropical palms turning brown. "Are we even meant to be up here?" she said, looking for somewhere dry to sit.

"Doesn't look like it. Do you want to go back down?"

"If we go down, people will talk to us."

We sat on an old bench damp enough to soak through our overcoats and, just as when we'd first met, took it in turns to summarize great chunks of time. I was more inclined to answer questions now than at sixteen, and it seemed that she knew something of what I'd been doing, though I didn't ask how.

"You're doing well."

"Not bad, for the moment."

"Well, I'm pleased but not surprised. I knew you'd find something," she said and placed her hand on the bulge of her stomach.

"How long now?"

"Three weeks to go."

"Boy or girl?"

"A boy."

"Name?"

"We're calling him . . . well, the fact is we're calling him Charlie."

Not really, she said and laughed, said they'd not decided, though

Charlie was a nice name. I asked, how had she been? In general, she'd been quite unhappy, she said, which had surprised her. An accidental marriage, a thwarted career, worries over money. "My twenties —they were *brutal*. I thought that would be my time. I had all these hopes and expectations of how it was going to be, like a party that you think about and plan what you're going to wear, clothes all laid out, and how you're going to behave. Then you turn up and the people aren't nice, the music's terrible, you keep saying the wrong thing . . ."

"Mine was the same, except I was off my face for most of it."

"Well, there was a bit of that too, with this lunatic—I got married, did George tell you? Some couples, you know how they get drunk and go and get tattoos together? Well, we got married. Christ, what was I thinking? If we'd got tattoos, at least they'd have lasted. We argued once—this was when I knew I'd made a mistake—about whether seahorses were related to horses. You know, on a *genetic* level. 'Frances, I just refuse to accept that it's a coincidence!' That's a very good impression, by the way."

"Uncanny."

"All my best impressions are of people no one knows. I shouldn't be mean about him, he was charming and handsome and he's still Grace's dad, but basically he was an idiot. My parents, oh man, my parents *hated* him."

"More than me?"

"They never hated you! My mum *loved* you. She said she caught you throwing little stones up at my window once. She said it was the most romantic thing she'd ever seen."

"I remember that. At the time she looked pissed off."

"Well, now she thinks it was very charming."

"And how do they feel about George?"

"Oh, George is a doll. George can do no wrong."

"George Pearce, eh?"

"*Professor* George Pearce. Now, *he* knows the difference between a horse and a seahorse."

"No dark side, then."

"The worst thing he does—if he's in a restaurant and we've finished eating, he starts to clear the table. Scraping the leftovers, stacking the plates. He'd load the dishwasher if he could, it's really maddening."

"Well, if that's the worst thing . . ."

"Exactly. I'm much happier now. Found a job I wanted to do, found someone I wanted to be with. He was worried about you coming, you know."

"Was he?"

"He wondered how you might take it. He thought that you might lash out."

"Twenty years ago, I would have."

"Or some old spark would reignite and we'd elope."

"Well, that *is* why I'm here."

She laughed. "What does it say on the box? 'Don't return to the firework once lit.'"

"There's got to be a time limit, though, hasn't there?"

"I think twenty years is long enough."

"Twenty years is safe," I said, but a thought had occurred to me, paranoid I knew, but still I had to ask. "Hey, you didn't . . . like George back then, did you?"

"When we did the play? Course not." She took my hand. "I was in love with *you,* wasn't I?"

"Well, you too."

"I mean, you must have noticed?"

"I did."

"I loved you a lot, and I mean a *lot.*"

"Well, the same."

"Which doesn't happen often, believe me."

"No. I'm sorry it ended badly."

"Was it bad? It was painful, but not *bad*."

"All that shouting in shopping centers."

"I suppose so. But I think if it ends amicably, it probably should have stayed amicable in the first place. If you can give it up without a fight . . . Anyway, we were seventeen. Different people."

"Entirely."

Somehow we were holding hands now, sitting in silence, and I found myself wishing we could sit opposite each other so that I could look at her, rather than steal glances, take in the old laughter lines etched a little deeper around her eyes, new lines bracketing her mouth like the indentation of thumbnails in clay, the small raised seam in her lower lip, the chip in her tooth like the folded corner of a page. She tucked her hair behind her ear, turned and smiled.

"Your tooth!" I said, without thinking.

"What?"

"I remember you used to have this little chip on your front tooth."

"Oh, that!" She bit her thumb to display the tooth. "I had it filled. Not vanity—my agent said it was stopping me getting commercial work. Turned out that wasn't the problem after all."

"It's a shame. I liked it."

"I've had some fillings, if that's any consolation," she said, hooking her finger into her mouth.

"That's okay."

A moment, then: "At these things, when people say 'You haven't changed a bit,' even if it were true, are you meant to be pleased?"

"I think it means 'You don't look any worse.'"

"But you look much better," she said.

"In middle age?"

"Are we middle-aged?"

"The borders."

"Well, it suits you, Charlie, you look good."

"Please don't say I've 'filled out.'"

"Yes, what does that even *mean*?"

"It means fatter."

"It's not that. No, your face, you've grown into it, like you've . . . grown up to meet it."

"Well, you look great. Glowing, is that what people say?"

"Blood pressure and rage. Bigger hips too. That's babies for you. You don't have any?"

"Kids? No. We'd like them. I mean desperately. We're trying—I think that's the phrase. I mean really trying."

"Well . . . good luck!"

"Thank you. Thank you."

And I wanted to change the subject, but had nothing to change it to.

"So," I said.

"So."

"We should go down."

"Oh. Okay."

"It's good to see you."

"You too."

"Looking so well."

"Well, bit tired."

"No, I think you look beautiful. I can say that, can't I?"

"I don't know, George is a man of great violence. I think so."

And here we should have stood and left, but instead she lifted my hand and looked at our interlaced fingers. "This is weird."

"It is."

"Not terrible."

"No, but . . ."

"I thought about it, about what I felt, about this, and I don't want to get mawkish or anything," she said, "but first love, I think it's like a song, a stupid pop song that you hear and you think, well, that is *all* I will ever want to listen to, it's got everything, it's clearly the greatest piece of music ever written, I need nothing else. "Course we wouldn't put it on *now*. We're too hard and experienced and sophisticated. But when it comes on the radio, well, it's still a good song. It is. There, isn't that profound?"

"Very."

"And you are happy, aren't you?"

"I am."

"Well, so am I! So am I! There you go. We had a happy ending."

"So we're not eloping, then?"

"Well, normally I'd say yes, but I've got a cesarean booked and you're getting married, so . . ."

"We'll leave it, then."

"Yes. Let's leave it."

She tapped her head, just once, against my shoulder, and we looked back to the view, the drizzle in the air caught by the yellow light. Fran shifted on the bench. "The rain's soaking through now, so . . ."

"Let's go down," I said, and with a groan and a long exhalation, she stood. At the top of the stairs, we paused. "Hold on," I said. This would be goodbye, I knew, and so before I could think too much, I said the words that had been caught in my throat all night.

"So what I came for . . ."

"Go on."

"It's really corny. Don't throw up."

"I promise nothing."

"Well, that was quite a weird time. I wasn't very happy, I don't think, when we met. And then I was. I mean, delirious. So I think it's just—thank you."

She puffed out her cheeks satirically, but then she leaned back against the doorframe, looked at me a while and smiled and gave a nod of her head.

"Pleasure," she said.

Back at the party, George and I exchanged phone numbers with no expectation of using them. "We'll have you to dinner! With your wife!" I stood at the edge of a crowd and listened to a man in his late forties, long-haired and plump in a ruffled shirt: Ivor, our director. I'd hoped to see Alina too. I imagined that after twenty years she'd have aged into something grand, fierce and spectacular, and I liked to think she'd have remembered me as one of her successes. But she was not around, and instead Ivor caught my eye, tried to place me—a face in a photo that he couldn't recall—then continued with the anecdote. A member of the *As You Like It* company had uncovered the old pub piano, played a broken chord, and now they began to sing "It Was a Lover and His Lass," all harmonies and fruity vibrato, and before the verse had ended, Helen barreled across the room and grabbed my elbow.

"Let's get the *fuck* out of here!"

"All right, let me just say goodbye to—"

". . . *with a hey, and a ho, and a hey nonino* . . ."

"No, now, Charlie, NOW!"

I grabbed my coat and looked for Fran and her family, but it seemed that they'd already gone.

Curtain Call

LAST YEAR, MY FATHER DIED. The event that had preoccupied me for so much of my childhood and teenage years finally took place, though thankfully in different circumstances to those I'd once imagined so vividly. A heart attack, almost instant I was told, though I'm not sure that even a quick death is ever quick enough. Who knows?

He was not yet sixty, and although it would be comforting to tell a story of complete recovery, depression came and went through all of his last twenty years. But I like to think that the happier times were more frequent and that I—we—got better at anticipating and managing the lows. Largely this was down to his wife, his second wife, Maureen, whom he'd met at work. Serious, teetotal, churchgoing, Maureen was a kind of negative image of Mum, and I should confess that in my London twenties, I found the atmosphere in their bungalow—a bungalow!—almost unbearably dull and soporific, and so I rarely came to visit and never to stay. The role of surly stepson was custom made for me at that time. This was marriage as early retirement, and I could never bear more than an hour or two in the neat, overheated living room. Maureen was devoted to my father, and devotion is dull to be around, but I know they also laughed a great deal and went for walking holidays, ticking off the South Downs Way, Hadrian's Wall, the South West Coast Path like super-extended delivery rounds. Maureen even developed an interest in jazz, a taste that I could never acquire myself, though I still try from time to time, and as I got older I began to appreciate the relative happiness and stability she brought to Dad's later life. My father and I didn't have much in common except a tendency towards gloomy introspection and a sentimental and unspoken belief in love as a remedy, if not a comprehensive cure. The flip side of this for my father was a fear of being lonely, unloved or, worst of all, unlovable, but after his second marriage this fear faded away, and I like to think that in the years before his heart stopped, suddenly, halfway through his morning round, he was more content than he'd ever been. I like to think that.

Predictably, his death was the catalyst for an excavation of the past, often fraught and painful, results outlined above. But when I thought of my father, it was always that summer I returned to. He was the same age as I am now, and those months seemed to contain both the best and the worst of all that passed between us.

One scene is missing, though: the meeting of my father and Fran Fisher.

From the side of the stage I watched them speaking after the final performance, Fran laughing at something my father had said, her hand on his forearm, then dipping her head, ducking almost, at what I imagined was praise. I watched them for some time, pleased that they were getting on so well. I knew that he would love her and hoped that she would see something in him that had yet to rise to the surface in his son: an integrity perhaps, a kindness.

And so I watched. To have joined them would have risked spoiling things, and besides, I'd presumed, with all the hope I'd had in that moment, that there'd be endless opportunities to spend time with them, the two most important people in my life at that point. They spoke once or twice on the phone but never again in person, and I'm startled now to realize that I won't see either of them again.

Never mind.

Never mind.

This is a love story, though now that it's over it occurs to me that it's actually four or five, perhaps more: familial and paternal love; the slow-burning, reviving love of friends; the brief, blinding explosion of first love that can only be looked at directly once it has burned out. A single word can carry only so many meanings, and maybe there ought to be different words for something so varied and weighty. For the moment, this one word will have to bear all of the above, and married love too.

My wife. Will I ever get used to saying that? In the self-pity and melodrama of those immediate post-Fran years, I swore I'd never speak those words, and in the haze of my twenties it seemed unlikely that I'd need them anyway. Now, stepping out into the evening air, slammed back into the present, I felt an urgent need to get back home.

I ran for the bus and willed it onwards. I'd given in to nostalgia and curiosity when the present, the future were what really mattered. Long before my stop I pressed the bell once, twice to be sure, then stomped through the damp streets, feeling the fond embarrassment of a child who has run away from home and only made it to the corner before turning round with relief. Niamh would tease me, I knew it, and that would be fine and fair. I took our stairs two at a time, opened the door to find her asleep on the sofa.

Sentimentally, I might have sat and watched her for a while, allowing some time to contemplate how lucky I'd been to find her, this bright and brilliant woman, my greatest good luck. But the reading lamp had slipped and was so close to her head that the room smelled of singed hair. I twisted the light away and she started awake.

"What? Hello."

"It smells of burnt hair in here."

"Hm? Yes, that's my new scent. For the wedding. *Cheveux Brûlés.*"

"I like it."

She yawned and felt her scalp. "What time is it?"

"Nine forty-five."

"Wild man. Where is she, then?"

"She's waiting in the car downstairs."

"Is that right?"

"I just came up to throw a few things in a bag."

"*Our* car."

"Yes, we're taking the car."

"Seems harsh. Can I keep the TV?"

"Won't it remind you of me?"

"Not especially. Who's going to call the caterers?"

"Leave it till tomorrow." I kissed her. "Can I sit down?" Niamh shifted, and we sat with our heads resting against each other.

"It's great that we can laugh about these things, isn't it?" she said.

"The thing is, Niamh, you *can* laugh about these things."

"Can I?"

"Yes, you can."

"Good."

"Let's go to bed."

We didn't move. "But how was she?"

"Older."

"There's surprising."

"She was nice. Everyone was. She was happy."

"You too?"

"And me too."

"Well, there you go," she said. "That's all you can hope for, isn't it? That's what you want. And now you know."

And now I know.

Acknowledgments

Thanks are owed to my early readers, Damian Barr, Hannah Mac-Donald, Roanna Benn and Michael McCoy, for their support, encouragement and good judgment. I am endlessly grateful to Jonny Geller, Kate Cooper, Catherine Cho and all the team at Curtis Brown.

At Hodder and Stoughton, Nick Sayers continues to be the best possible editor, and I'd also like to thank Amber Burlinson, Cicely Aspinall, Lucy Hale, Carolyn Mays, Jamie Hodder-Williams, Alasdair Oliver, Susan Spratt, Jacqui Lewis, Alice Morley and that four-time veteran of author neuroses, Emma Knight.

Finally, I would like to thank Bruno Wang for his generosity, Emmanuel Kwesi Quayson, Karen Fishwick—a brilliant Juliet—for her insights and Ayse Tashkiran for putting us in touch. I'd also like to acknowledge a debt, in mood and tone, to the Pulp song "David's Last Summer."

Finally, as always, love and gratitude are due to Hannah Weaver for her humor, patience and support.

About the Author

David Nicholls is the best-selling author of *Us, One Day, The Understudy* and *Starter for Ten*. His novels have sold over eight million copies worldwide and are published in forty languages.

David trained as an actor before making the switch to writing. He is an award-winning screenwriter, with TV credits including the third series of *Cold Feet*, a much-praised modern version of *Much Ado About Nothing, The 7.39* and an adaptation of *Tess of the D'Urbervilles*. David wrote the screenplays for *Great Expectations* (2012) and *Far from the Madding Crowd* (2015, starring Carey Mulligan). He recently won a BAFTA for *Patrick Melrose*, his adaptation of the novels by Edward St. Aubyn, which also won him an Emmy nomination.

His best-selling first novel, *Starter for Ten*, was selected for the Richard and Judy Book Club in 2004, and in 2006 David went on to write the screenplay of the film version.

His third novel, *One Day*, was published in 2009 to extraordinary critical acclaim, and stayed on the *Sunday Times* top ten bestseller list for ten weeks on publication. *One Day* won the 2010 Galaxy Book of the Year Award.

David's fourth novel, *Us*, was long-listed for the 2014 Man Booker Prize in fiction and was another number one *Sunday Times* bestseller. In the same year he was named Author of the Year at the National Book Awards.